THE TWELVE SPIES OF MOSES

BRUCE R. HAMPSON

CONTENTS

The Twelve Spies Of Moses

Bruce R. Hampson

Bruce R. Hampson

The Twelve Spies of Moses

https://brucehampson.com

First Edition

PAPERBACK ISBN 978-1-7772460-0-6

EBOOK ISBN 978-1-7772460-1-3

Cover design and artwork by: Vilmas Narečionis

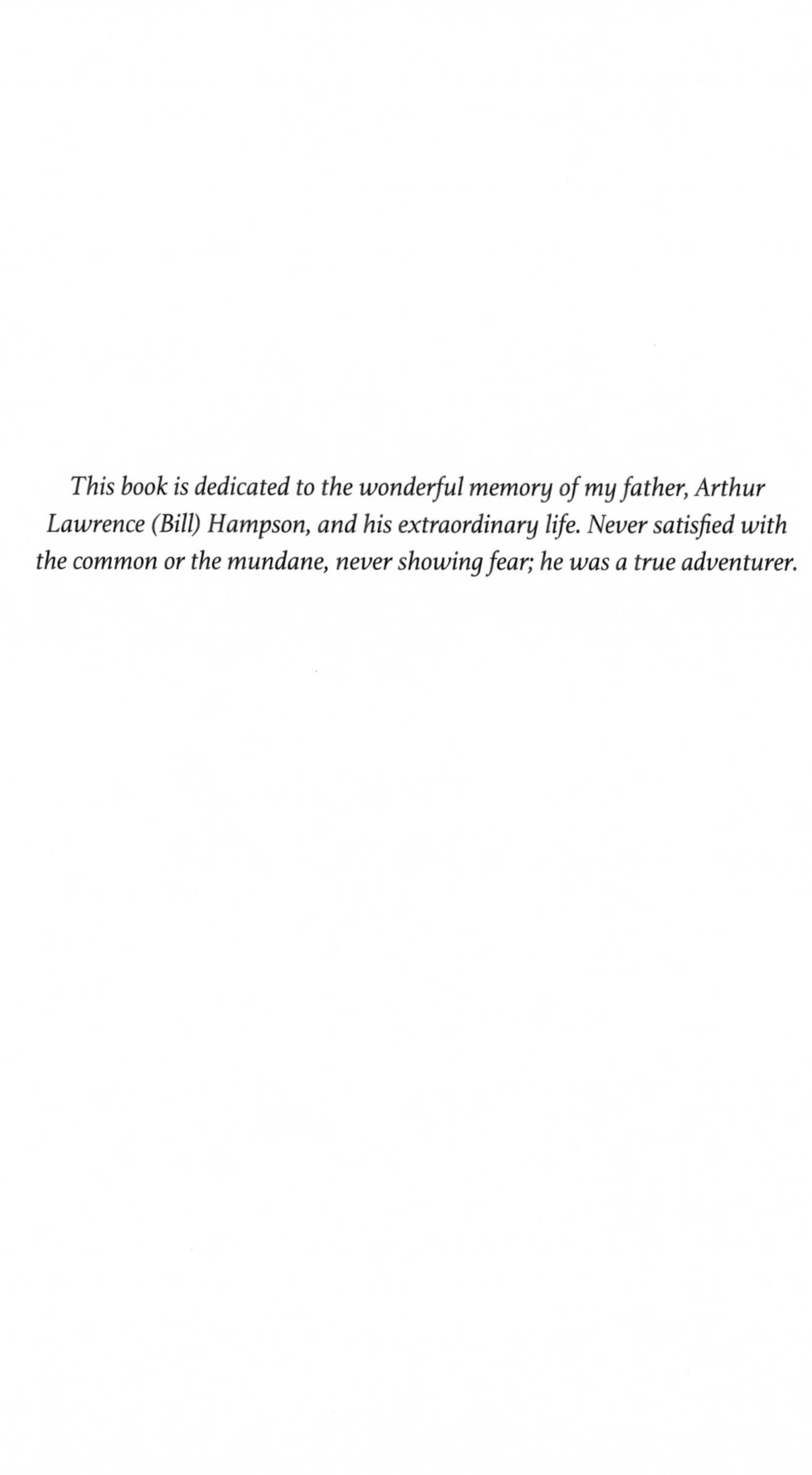

This book is dedicated to the wonderful memory of my father, Arthur Lawrence (Bill) Hampson, and his extraordinary life. Never satisfied with the common or the mundane, never showing fear; he was a true adventurer.

ACKNOWLEDGMENTS

My gratitude goes to Dr. Don Carmont for challenging me and giving me balance, Amanda Bidnall for her incredible attention to detail, Carol and Roger, for our exciting discussions at SFU writers' meetings, and to my wonderful wife, Alge, for her proddings, contributions, ideas, for never doubting me.

But you came to me and said, 'Let's send men ahead of us to spy out the land, so that they can tell us the best route to take and what kind of cities are there.'
That seemed like a good thing to do, so I selected twelve men, one from each tribe.

Deuteronomy 1:22–23

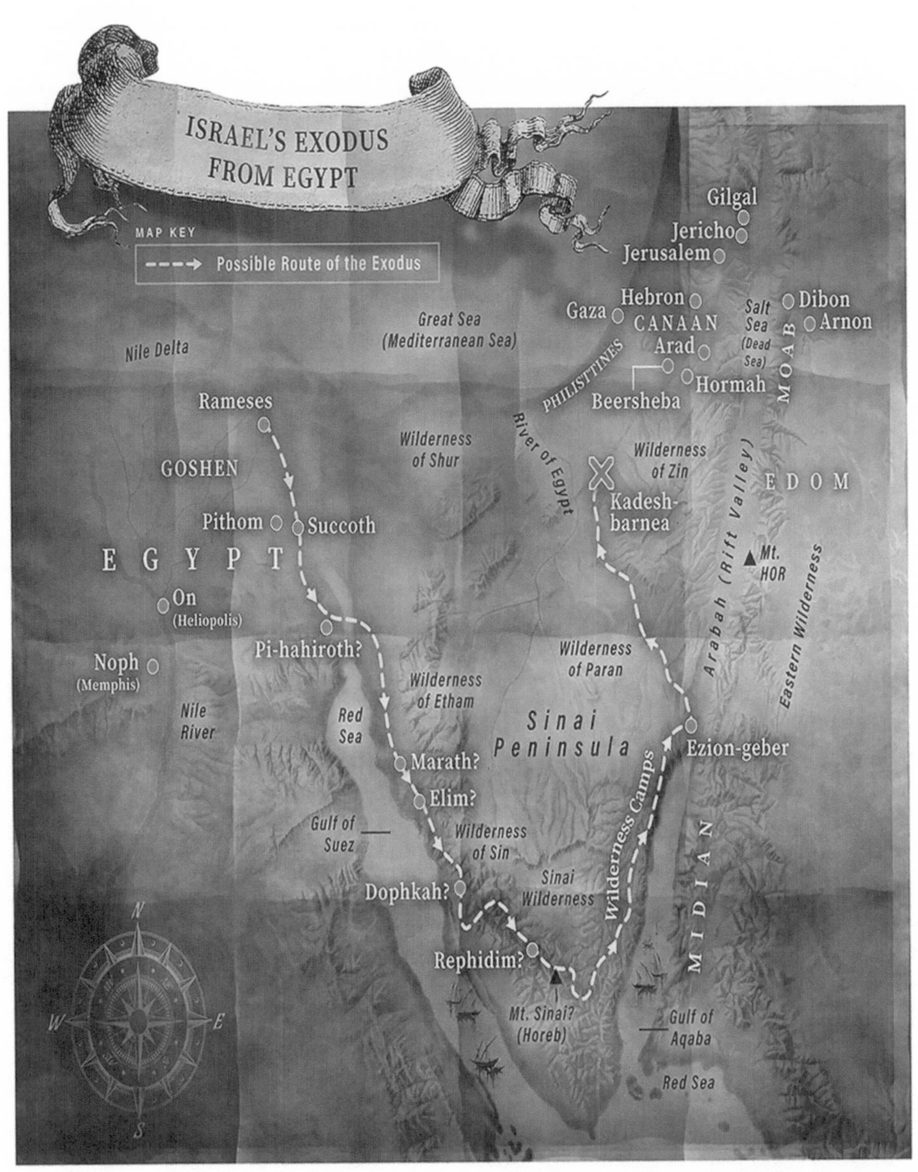
ISRAEL'S EXODUS FROM EGYPT
MAP KEY
Possible Route of the Exodus
Gilgal
Jericho
Jerusalem
Hebron
Gaza
CANAAN
Arad
Hormah
Beersheba
PHILISTINES
Salt Sea (Dead Sea)
Dibon
Arnon
MOAB
Great Sea (Mediterranean Sea)
Nile Delta
Rameses
GOSHEN
Wilderness of Shur
River of Egypt
Wilderness of Zin
Kadesh-barnea
EDOM
Pithom
Succoth
EGYPT
On (Heliopolis)
Arabah (Rift Valley)
Mt. HOR
Eastern Wilderness
Pi-hahiroth?
Noph (Memphis)
Wilderness of Paran
Wilderness of Etham
Nile River
Red Sea
Sinai Peninsula
Ezion-geber
Marath?
Elim?
Wilderness Camps
Gulf of Suez
Wilderness of Sin
MIDIAN
Dophkah?
Sinai Wilderness
Rephidim?
Mt. Sinai? (Horeb)
Gulf of Aqaba
Red Sea
N
W
E
S

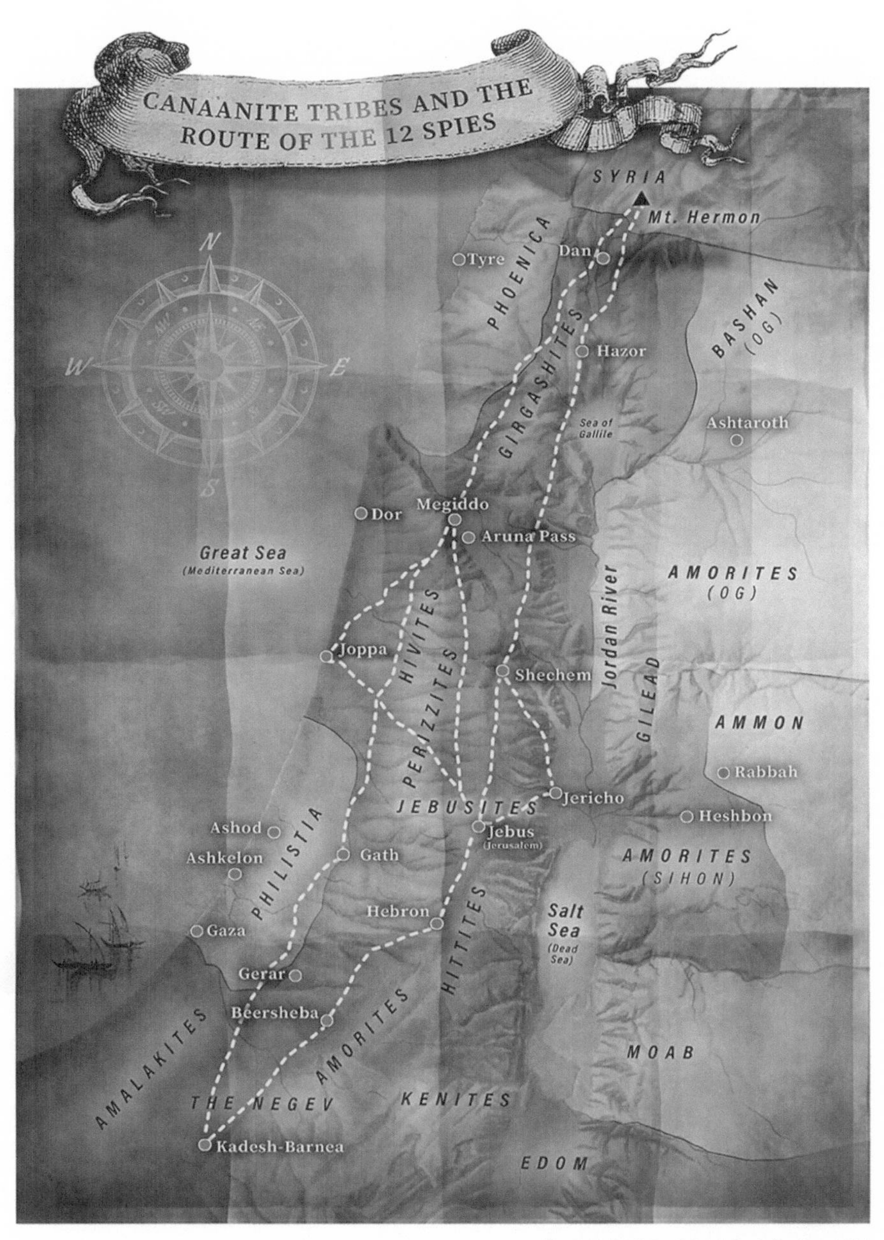
CANAANITE TRIBES AND THE
ROUTE OF THE 12 SPIES
SYRIA
Mt. Hermon
Tyre
Dan
PHOENICA
BASHAN
(OG)
Hazor
GIRGASHITES
Sea of
Gallile
Ashtaroth
Dor
Megiddo
Aruna Pass
Great Sea
(Mediterranean Sea)
AMORITES
(OG)
Jordan River
HIVITES
Joppa
PERIZZITES
Shechem
GILEAD
AMMON
Rabbah
Jericho
JEBUSITES
Heshbon
Ashod
Jebus
(Jerusalem)
Ashkelon
Gath
PHILISTIA
AMORITES
(SIHON)
Hebron
HITTITES
Salt
Sea
(Dead
Sea)
Gaza
Gerar
Beersheba
AMALAKITES
AMORITES
MOAB
THE NEGEV
KENITES
Kadesh-Barnea
EDOM
N
E
S
W

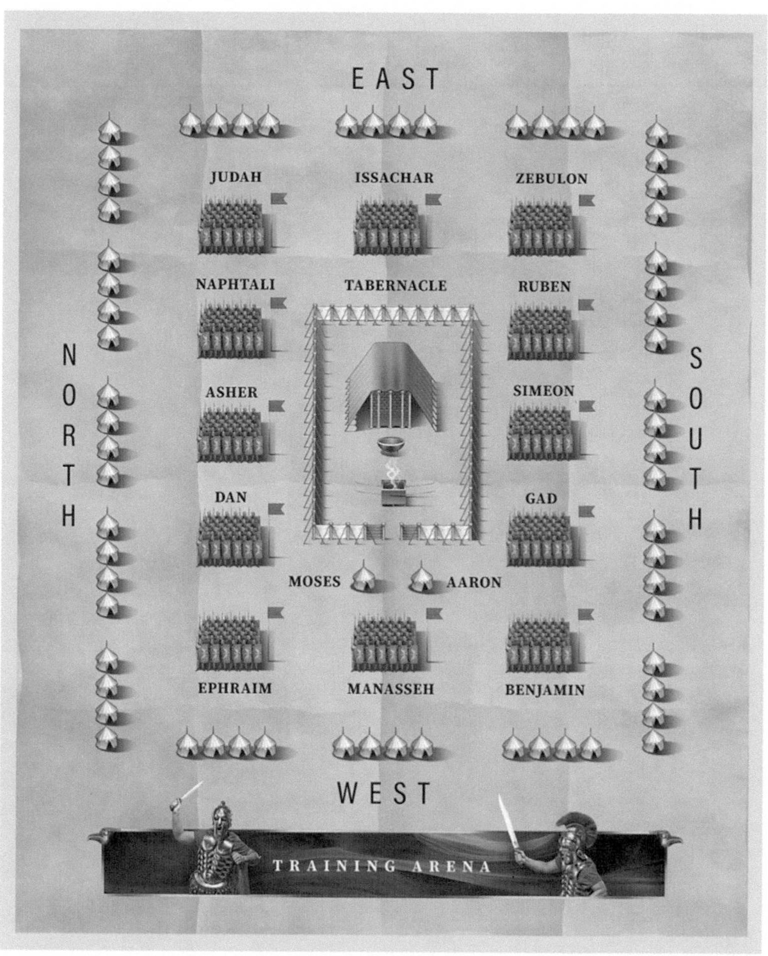

Units of Measurement

This story uses historical units of measurement common in ancient western Asia.

1 cubit = approx. 75 centimetres, 30 inches

1 dunam = approx. 0.1 hectares, 0.25 acres

PREFACE

The Bible is easily the best-selling book of all time. It is a collection of sixty-six books divided into two parts, the Old Testament and the New Testament, and it has been unchanged and unchallenged since the earliest days of the Christian church. The Bible predates even the start of the Christian faith. The Old Testament—specifically the first five books attributed to Moses and known as the Pentateuch or Torah—is the cornerstone of Judaism, Christianity, and the Islamic faith. However, it is even more than that. It is a book of history, a study of continuous chronological proceedings, and a record of important events, trends, miracles, and gaffes. It contains innumerable detailed incidents and episodes that captivate the reader.

On the other hand, some titillating occurrences it only briefly touches upon. One that captivated my imagination was when Moses, after leading the Jews out of slavery in Egypt, decided to send spies into the land of milk and honey to do a thorough reconnaissance of their destination. Only three Bible verses, in the thirteenth chapter of the book of Numbers, tell us what happened on that mission. But the consequences of the events they describe were mind-boggling, affecting more than six hundred fifty thousand people. Moses, the indisputable leader himself, was denied entry into the promised land.

My story is fictitious and not intended to be a scholarly treatise. I am mindful of the fact that the Bible is meant to teach us lessons. There will be those who will argue that the Bible was never meant to be a diary or a history book and that only the events that have a lesson relevant to us today are recorded. I am not trying to rewrite any section of the Bible; I just let my imagination flow. However, it is true to Scripture and based on my years of study on the subject. I have used real Bible characters but invented characters, myths, and legends to enhance my storyline. By no means do I attempt to proselytize, convert, or coax. I have never believed that going to a church makes you a Christian or going to a synagogue makes you a Jew, any more than I believe going to a garage makes you an automobile. This novel is just a fantastical narrative of what might have been.

Maybe there was a good reason the details of this forty-day secret assignment were not recorded in the Bible. Does what happens in Canaan stay in Canaan?

1

FRIDAY, JUNE 17 / SIVAN 29, 1439 BCE

Kadesh-Barnea

Trust in the Lord with all your heart, and do not lean on your own understanding. In all your ways acknowledge him, and he will make straight your paths. (Proverbs 3:5–6)

It was another sweltering day in the desert furnace. The wind blew from no particular direction, creating mini whirlwinds that danced through the training arena, picked dry leaves from the sand, and sent them upward into obscurity. The sun that one moment gave life to foliage and brought light to the darkest morning seemed obstinately angry today, cooking the warriors as they trained.

The clanging of swords and pounding of shields formed a rhythmic bass to the high tenor battle cries as the men thrust forward with shouts and deflected blows with baritone grunts.

Hoshea spun as the sword thrust barely missed his shoulder. He lifted his shield and deflected the weapon. He simultaneously lifted his right leg and kicked Shammua in the belly. Shammua, forced back a couple of steps, saw his opportunity and crashed his heavy sword down on Hoshea's exposed head. Hoshea raised his sword defensively, protecting himself against Shammua's attack. While Shammua was concentrating on another downward blow, Hoshea swept Shammua's leg off the ground and dropped him onto the soft sand. Hoshea put the point of his sword to Shammua's neck, declaring himself the victor, and they both broke out laughing.

Caleb, watching the scrimmage, jumped on Hoshea, and Hoshea's sword went flying from his hand. They rolled in the sand, using their fists and elbows. Caleb balanced himself on top until Hoshea flipped him and lay across Caleb's chest. Hoshea grabbed his arm, and used his legs to hold Caleb's body stationary. He twisted Caleb's muscular arm downward. Caleb shrieked in pain and acknowledged his defeat by tapping Hoshea three times in submission. Now all three—Caleb, Hoshea, and Shammua—roared in pleasure.

"The enemy will not be so kind," Hoshea declared, still smiling. "We must be vigilant and aware of all his strategies in battle. Even when you go for your kill strike, Shammua, remember your unprotected side and guard it with your life at all times. In hand-to-hand combat, as in life, if you are overconfident, you will make a mistake and fail. Pride always comes before the fall."

Rubbing his sand-coated arm, Caleb snickered. "You were just lucky this time, you big bear. I was moments away from putting you asleep."

"Yeah, sure, 'big dog.'" Hoshea could not hide his sarcasm. "Whatever you say." And tears of pleasure poured from his eyes.

As they lay supine on the desert sand, a young, breathless man hurried up to them. "Hoshea, the commander-in-chief has summoned you and Caleb. You are to go to his tent immediately."

"Shammua, I leave you in charge of the training. Teach them well. We will soon be in battle again." Hoshea did not like his men idling.

Shammua stood at attention, slapped his right hand on his heart, and bowed his head. "Aye, Commander." He turned toward the sixty warriors engaged in their tactical military practice and started shouting instructions.

Hoshea reached for his fur-trimmed, hardened leather helmet and placed it on his head. Over his white tunic, he wore a scaly, light-brown leather vest that had been boiled and hardened in herb-infused water, so it repelled arrows and spears. A one-half-cubit flap over each shoulder protected his biceps. The vest was tightly laced together with goat sinew, and the symmetrical design on the front was pleasing to the eye.

The training area, just west of the tribes of the Ox, was quite a distance from the central tent where Moses sat as the commander-in-chief. The camp, which now housed almost two and a half million people, looked more like a city. Thirteen tribes made up the Israelites, who were divided into five groups, each displaying their own vexilloid.[1] Hoshea, the son of Nun, came from the tribe of Ephraim, where the Ox flag waved defiantly. The tribes of Ephraim, Manasseh, and Benjamin all shared the northern part of the city. To the south, the flag of the Lion waved proudly. This is where the tribes of Judah, Issachar, and Zebulon pitched their tents and cooked their meals. To the east of the city, next to the flag of Man standing tall in the desert, Shammua's tribe of Reuben's descendants lived, along with the tribes of Simeon and Gad. To the west, the flag of the Eagle fluttered over the tribes of Dan, Naphtali, and Asher. The Levite priests, displaying no flag, occupied the centre of the tent city dedicated to the tabernacle. Moses's tent was the largest in the Levite section.

It was a military city cleverly designed to protect their religious artifacts and their sacred covenant box. On the outskirts of the military camp, small groups of non-Israelites huddled together in makeshift living quarters. These were men and their families who had witnessed the divine phenomena when the tribes marched through the city of Elim, won military victory in Rephidim, trekked through the land of Esau and Ammon, and finally arrived in Kadesh-Barnea.

Hoshea, at twenty-two, was an old soul. His steely green eyes, wide smile, and jet-black hair that fell to his muscular shoulders enchanted many young tribal women who dreamed that perhaps one day they might become his wife and live in his tent.

As Hoshea and Caleb approached the headquarters, their bodies still covered in sand, a little boy about seven years old, with a wooden sword and a warrior helmet, sprinted toward Caleb.

"Abba, Father... Attack!" He twirled his sword, turned three hundred and sixty degrees, and with a downward blow made a loud *kiap*. Caleb smiled at his son Hur, feigned an injury, and fell. Hur jumped on his belly and cried, "Surrender or die, heathen!" Caleb put his long arms around the little rascal and kissed him on the neck until Hur burst out laughing.

"My strong and fearless lion, you have defeated your enemy."

Ephrath, Caleb's beautiful wife, smiled proudly as she watched Hur and Caleb bond as father and son. A light grey robe with a carefully embroidered red design caressed her body and dropped to below her knees. Her head was covered by a white cotton cloth draping onto her shoulders and fastened by a bright-red headband. She wore no sandals on her sandy, calloused feet.

"Where are you going so determined, my husband?"

"Moses has summoned us to the big tent. Shamefully, we are dirty as we have just come from the training arena."

"Will you be home for dinner?" Ephrath loved having her husband close to her. "I am making your favourite quail recipe tonight. Hoshea, please come as well. You are always a pleasure to have in our tent."

Hoshea glanced at his friend and nodded.

They continued along their way, passing the makeshift corrals for the camels and warhorses, and then the sheep and goat enclosures. If they hurried, they would be there in ten minutes. It was always an honour to visit the commander-in-chief, and they didn't want to keep Moses waiting. Before entering Moses's pavilion, however, they stopped to dust off the sand that stuck to them like skin.

Moses's tent was the largest in the city, as appropriate to the commander-in-chief of two and a half million people. Like all the tents in the city, it was constructed of black panels of goat hair. The hair was carefully spun into strands and then woven together, forming two two-cubit panels that could be sewn together to make tents. The panels on Moses's tent were bleached after two years of the hot desert sun. Some of them had been removed and replaced by fresh strips. The woven goat hair was ideally suited the desert weather. When the sun was beating down on the encampment, the walls could be lifted to allow the breeze to pass through. In the bitter night, when the cold stung, the black panels absorbed the heat and, together with a fire built just inside the door, kept the Israelites warm. The fabric was not dense, and the moonlight found its way between the spaces on the black roof, giving an impression of brilliant stars sparkling in the night sky. But when it rained, the fibres expanded to form a watertight roof. Poles, secured by strong ropes and four-cubit pegs driven into the ground, made the tents unmovable in the strong gusts of desert storms. The entrance to the tent was the most crucial part for most nomads; it was here that the father of the family would sit, as on a throne, watching the commotion and goings-on of the tribe. A thick curtain, decorated with the four characters of the nation of Israel—Ox, Eagle, Man, and Lion—covered the entrance.

Four bulky guards stood stoically at attention at the entrance of the marquee, swords strapped to their sides and tasselled, lethal bronze spears in their hands. They wore helmets like Caleb and Hoshea's, and their armour, although a different colour, was similar in design to Hoshea and Caleb's own.

Five steps led up to the entrance. Seeing their approach, the guards stamped their feet and crossed their spears to block access.

"Caleb and Hoshea to see the commander-in-chief," Hoshea barked.

One of the guards went inside the tent while the others stood their ground.

A few seconds later the guard returned. "Let them pass." The soldiers stamped their feet one more time, withdrew the spears, and, with faces unmoving and eyes ahead, formed an opening for them to enter.

———

Moses, now eighty-two years old, sat high on sheep- and goat-skin pillows at the end of the marquee, deep in contemplation. He was a complex man, often tormented by his responsibility and his accountability to God. The burden of having become the prophet and commander-in-chief of this multitude of Hebrew slaves weighed heavy on his shoulders. Moses had led them out of Egypt to this place, now called Kadesh-Barnea, and they were so close to the promised land. God had always given him direct and explicit instructions; there was never any doubt of what He wanted Moses to say and do.

This vocation wasn't something Moses had sought. Whatever the reason, God had chosen him to be His messenger, His spokesman to the people of Israel. When God gave him his assignment to go to Egypt and lead the Hebrews to freedom, had Moses not asked God to send someone else?[2] He didn't want the job. He felt inadequate, insufficient, and incompetent. He had murdered an Egyptian soldier, deserted his people, and chosen a life of unsociable, solitary enjoyment.

Upon God's call, however, Moses had obediently, begrudgingly travelled to Rameses, Egypt, and brought great news to his brethren: those imprisoned and enslaved by the Egyptian overlords were to be set free and brought to a land flowing with blessings and prosperity. The Israelites, however, complained bitterly and didn't co-operate with Moses and the divine plan. They said his talk of freedom only encouraged Pharaoh to make things worse for the Hebrews. Many of them demanded Moses "let them alone." Even after their escape from Egypt, when God provided water for them to drink in the scorching heat of the desert, they complained that it was bitter.

Moses was radically different from the other prophets God had sent to the tumultuous tribes of Israel. The prophets of the past had received their prophecies in dreams and visions, while Moses received his when he was wide awake. God spoke to His other prophets in oblique and symbolic parables—but to Moses, He spoke directly and lucidly. All other prophets were terrified when God appeared before them, but God spoke to Moses face to face, as a friend. The prophets of the past needed to undergo time-consuming preparations to hear the divine word, while Moses spoke to God whenever and wherever he wanted or needed to.

Every step of the journey, God had always imparted specific directives to Moses. However, now at Kadesh-Barnea, the people were worried about what lay ahead of them in the promised land, so they came to Moses and asked if it was possible to send men ahead to assess and anticipate the next leg of their journey.[3]

Moses was appalled at their audacity. How could they show such rude and disrespectful behaviour toward the promise of God? Oh, how their impudence tortured him. Moses then consulted with God and let him know the people's request. He expected God to be angry. So imagine his surprise when, for the first time, God told him to do as he saw fit. "You want to send spies? Fine—send them as determined by your understanding. I will not tell you what to do in this case; you make the decision." And although Moses found the request of the people despicable, he felt if God didn't mind, he would give in to their will. He was tired of clashing and arguing with them. This was the route of least resistance, and he welcomed the prospect of less stress in his life.

Directly across from their encampment was the promised land, where Moses's people would settle and flourish. They were so close, Moses could almost taste it. He could smell it in his bones.

The front gate sentry approached Moses and snapped to attention, bringing his right arm to his heart. "Sir, Hoshea and Caleb are here to see you."

Waking up from his daydreams, Moses smiled. "Excellent. Send them in."

They stepped through the curtain into the tent and found themselves in the men's partition. It was refreshingly cool, and the smell of old leather and seared rosemary filled the air. On the sandy floor were some of the sun-damaged goat-hair panels from the outside tent.

Sheepskins and Egyptian rugs were sprawled and scattered along the path to where Moses sat. Tribal-made carpets embroidered with depictions of their long journey from Rameses decorated the walls. Behind and to the left of Moses's chair was an entrance to the woman's salon, where they could hear children playing and Zipporah, Moses's wife, scolding them lovingly.

Moses, tall and handsome, sat on his elevated seat, stroking his long, curly beard. If you could ignore the grey in his beard, his smooth skin, sparkling eyes, and alert movements would convince you he wasn't a day over forty. A white cotton cloth covered his head and fell to his shoulders. Bright red twine fastened it in place on his forehead. The buttonless tunic that covered his slight pot-belly was brown with vertical red stripes. It wrapped around his long white sarong, which brushed the floor. Moses was quite the antithesis of the armed warriors who stood before him.

"Please, s-s-sit," Moses stuttered.

As they lowered their bodies onto the cushions in front of Moses, two female domestics poured red wine into goblets. Vessels of honey and pomegranates were scattered in front of them.

After the servers finished their duties, Moses signalled for them to leave the tent.

"How are you, my treasured comrades? P-p-please, have some fruit, and drink some refreshing wine. How are the training activities?"

"The training is progressing well, sir. We now have approximately 603,500 willing and able fighting men, and we are training every day. We have created some short-range tactics, teaching our soldiers hand-to-hand combat with and without swords and daggers. This tactic is now essential preparation and compulsory for all our troops. We have also established numerous specialized squads adept in medium-range attacks, and they are developing elite skills in handling and throwing spears and javelins. Our long-range strategy has been and will continue to be slings and archery. We have an extraordinary unit of left-handed men from the tribe of Benjamin. They are so accurate with their slings that they can throw a stone from twenty cubits at a strand of hair. They are truly gifted."[4]

Moses nodded approvingly.

"We learned a lot in our battle at Rephidim against the Amalekites. We are ready for new battles. God willing, if He leads us into battle, we will be victorious. We blundered at Rephidim by exposing our weak flank to the open plain and lost many of our undertrained stragglers. It will not happen again."

"What you sh-sh-should have learned from this battle, my brothers, is that God and only God gives victory or allows defeat. Yes, it is important to be the best we can be, and to always be prepared to do God's will, but it is God who determines the outcome, not us. Without God's blessings, we will trip, fall, and f-f-fail."

"Amen," Hoshea and Caleb sang in unison.

"Surely our living God, who brought us out of Egypt, who opened the Red Sea for us to walk through, who fed us and gave us water in the scorching desert, and who defeated the Amalekites, would never forsake us or forget His promises to us," Caleb piped in.

"I never worry about God forgetting us, Caleb, but I do worry about our complaining and b-b-belligerent people. They constantly forget what God has already done, what He is doing now, and what He will do in the future. He brings water out of a stone one minute, and the next minute everyone is grumbling about the lack of variety on their table. He turns a desert bowl like Kadesh-Barnea into an oasis, and yet they say they were better off in captivity in Egypt. Here we are, ready to enter the promised land, and the people complain and want to know what is ahead of them. A starving man, when offered a loaf of bread, doesn't ask about the ingredients before he g-g-gobbles it down, does he? Instead of celebrating and remembering God's marvels, our people look out over the wilderness and grumble. It weighs so heavy on my heart. Our tribes complained about being hungry all the time as we marched through the wilderness, even though God was feeding them like a mother sparrow feeds her newborn chicks. They complained when I didn't come back quickly enough from the top of Mount Sinai, and they began to worship an unresponsive, lifeless image—a man-made golden calf. It is blatant idiocy to th-th-think a piece of lifeless metal could rescue them from anything. All through our pilgrimage to the promised land, they complained to me about the food. Even my flesh-and-blood brother and sister, who helped me execute the horrible plagues God sent to the Egyptians, criticized my leadership. Know this, Hoshea and Caleb: a man's heart is deceitful above all things and desperately wicked. No man can honestly know his own heart, and God alone can test the mind."

Caleb felt his heart beat quicker, took a deep breath and turned to look directly at Hoshea's steely eyes to see if he had sensed it as well. Something big was about to be announced and they were going to be part of it.

"I c-c-called you here to inform you that God has allowed me to select one leader from each of the tribes—except for the Levites, of course[5]—and to send them as spies into the land of Canaan. Ahead of us is the land He promised to our ancestors. It is ours in which to live and flourish. I want these spies to be multilingual, to be well trained in the martial arts. I want them to go through this land and find out what kind of country it is. I want to know how many people live there and how strong they are. They must let me know if the land is g-g-good or bad and whether the people dwelling there live in open towns or fortified cities. I want to know if the soil is fertile and whether the land is wooded or cleared. If it is indeed fertile, I want some of the fruit that grows there as proof. I want you to return in forty days."

Hoshea and Caleb reacted with open mouths and utter disbelief.

"But sir, we are ready to go as an army. No nation could withstand our power. We are not spies; we are soldiers. Why would we have to spy out the land that our God has said is overflowing with milk and honey?" Hoshea swallowed nervously. "I say we should give the order, march our people, and take our prize."

"You will do as you are t-t-told," Moses snapped. "If God is willing, we will take this land, but I think we must take the initiative and discover the best place to enter. We must construct a plan. We cannot just wander in blindfolded. We never plan to fail; however, if we fail to plan, we will not fulfill God's will. You both know God doesn't create miracles unless there is a reason. We could march our two and a half million people into an ambush. A proper battle p-p-plan needs intelligence to be successful. The more facts and information we have, the better equipped we will be to make our triumphant entry.

"Here is the list of men I have ch-chosen prayerfully and carefully. You are to read the list to our warriors tomorrow at training session, and you will leave after Shabbat, two days from now. Hoshea, you will exemplify your tribe of Ephraim, and you, Caleb, will be the representative of Judah. The papyrus lists the other ten men."

Hoshea looked at the list. "Sir, I know most of these men. They are young and strong. However, except for Caleb, they lack life experiences."

Moses felt his pulse ramping up, and the back of his neck prickled with a thousand little needles. "It is not your place to argue with me, Hoshea. You will d-d-d-do as I command you to do!" He slammed his fist on the table. He hated being questioned, especially by someone he loved as much as Hoshea.

Both Hoshea and Caleb jumped up, snapped their heels together, raised their right arms to their chest with a clap, and cried out in unison, "Yes, sir!"

"One more thing, Hoshea. Because of our military conquest of the Amalekites, your name has become well-known in the land of pagans and heathens. From this moment forward, I g-g-g-give you the name Joshua,[6] which should help your disguise. We do not want the enemy to recognize you."

"Yes, sir. With God's help, we will gladly accomplish our assignment, and we will report back to you in forty days."

"You will ride Arabian stallions, and a caravan of three camels will follow, upon which you shall load food and water. You will be p-p-provided with some gold and silver to purchase what you need along the way. You will also take rugs, carpets, and the pottery that our tribes have made. Disguise yourselves as harmless merchants looking for venues of trade. Now go with God's blessing, and accomplish His will."

The two soldiers departed and headed toward Caleb's tent, taciturn and deep in thought. Caleb broke the silence, shoving Joshua fondly. "Well, we have our mission, my friend." He smiled in a consolatory manner. "Let's go and see what Ephrath has prepared for us."

As they walked into his tent, which was a fraction of the size of the one they had just left, the smell of goat meat welcomed them.

"Good news. I changed the menu tonight, husband. We have been eating quail and manna too often, and I felt we needed a little bit of variety. I hope you will enjoy it."

To honour Hoshea's attendance, Ephrath had made a special effort to turn their modest supper into a feast. On the table a dish of butter and cheese stood next to a tall tower of flatbread. There was a bounty of figs, grapes, and dates spread out between the small pomegranates that she had procured at Hazeroth. There was a large jug of sheep milk, but more importantly, there was an enormous flagon of delicious red wine. As they wolfed down hind legs of goat meat and washed them down with their wine, Caleb told Ephrath in detail what had occurred in the tent of Moses.

Hur was mesmerized by the battle stories his father and Hoshea swapped back and forth and struggled to keep his big brown eyes open. He was like a cub at his father's feet, especially because Caleb looked more like a grizzly bear than a Hebrew. Finally, his long dark eyelashes signalled to Ephrath that it was time for his bed. As she reached over to pick him up, his puppy-dog eyes flashed open again.

"It is time for bed, my little warrior," she whispered in a soothing voice reserved for her child.

"No, not yet," Hur cried in panic, trying to buy a little more time. "Father, tell me a story. Tell me the story of Moses again, *please!*"

Caleb smiled. "Very well, but then straight to bed. Do you agree, my mighty soldier?"

"Yes, sir." Hur clapped his chest with his right arm, mimicking the soldiers in the training arena.

"It was in the year 2372 from the day of Creation,[7] on the seventh day of Adar,[8] that Moses was born in Egypt. It was a difficult time, as we Israelites were enslaved and imperilled to the harsh and cruel decrees of the pharaoh. Fearing the proliferation of Hebrew peoples and perhaps the birth of a leader who would take the Israelite slaves out of Egypt, the pharaoh proclaimed that all newborn Israelite boys should die by drowning."

"Father, what does proliferation mean?" Hur interrupted.

"It means the Israelites were growing in numbers, and our tribes were multiplying." Caleb looked at Joshua and grinned again, amazed at how well Hur had pronounced the word.

"Moses's mother and sister concealed him from the evil Egyptians. When he turned three months old, they put him into a waterproof basket and set him afloat on the mighty Nile River. From afar, his sister saw Moses being retrieved by the pharaoh's daughter, a woman named Bithiah. Bithiah then raised him in the palace, schooling Moses in all the learning Egyptian society had to offer.

"As he grew older, Moses observed the suffering of our Hebrew brothers. One day, he witnessed an Egyptian cruelly beating a Hebrew slave for no apparent reason. Moses killed the Egyptian and hid his body far off in the deep sand of the desert."

"How did he kill the Egyptian, Father? With his bare hands?" Hur's eyes were now wider than the dishes on the table.

"Hur, it is late. Do you want me to tell you the story? I cannot go on if you keep interrupting me."

"Sorry, Father. I will be quiet."

"The following day on his morning walk, Moses saw two Hebrews quarrelling. As one of them was about to strike the other, Moses stopped and chastised the would-be attacker. The man taunted Moses and asked him if he was going to kill him like he'd killed the Egyptian the day before. Moses realized he was losing respect and could no longer stay in Egypt, so he fled to the Midian wilderness. As the years went by, loneliness grew hard on Moses, so he married a beautiful princess named Zipporah and fathered two sons, Gershom and Eliezer.

"One day, while Moses while shepherding his father-in-law's

sheep—he was already eighty years old at this time—God revealed Himself in a burning bush and instructed him to return to Egypt and liberate the children of Israel from the cruelty of the Egyptians. Moses had many doubts and fears about doing this. He felt he was too old and unworthy, and he thought neither the pharaoh nor the people would listen to him, especially with his speech impediment.

"Upon his return to Egypt, Moses found his brother Aaron, and together they confronted Pharaoh, demanding him to let our people go. He reasoned that it was time for our Israelite nation to leave Egypt for the land that God had promised our ancestors. Pharaoh refused to listen.

"The fury of God and ten plagues then descended upon the Egyptians. It started with the Nile River turning to blood and ended with the death of every first-born Egyptian, including Pharaoh's son. Finally, terrified, the pharaoh agreed to let us all go. But after seven days of watching us take the treasures we had accumulated over four hundred years of captivity, the pharaoh greedily changed his mind. He decided to chase and to wipe us from the face of the earth. Running as fast as we could go, we reached the Red Sea twenty-five days after leaving Egypt. Just as we despaired of crossing the deep waters, God parted and opened up the Red Sea. We passed through the torrents of water on each side of us, while the Egyptians pursuers died in the churning sea behind us.

"Okay, time for bed, young man," Caleb ordered.

"But Father, you left the best part out," Hur said, looking to delay bedtime at all costs. "The part about the mountain and God giving us his laws. Please, Father, finish the story, and then I promise to go asleep right away."

"No more excuses after this... Where was I? Six weeks after our triumphant exit out of Egypt, we came to Mount Sinai. God's presence, in the form of a dense cloud, covered the mountain entirely. Then God spoke, giving His instruction directly to all of us in his loud, deep voice. Filled with trepidation, we all listened, but we only heard the first two commandments."

"Father, what does trepidation mean?"

"A kind of nervous fear," Ephrath said, jumping in. "Just listen to the story, Hur."

"Moses served as our translator. He heard all ten commandments clearly and repeated them to our people. He then ascended Mount Sinai while our brothers and sisters waited for him below. For forty days, Moses fasted and listened to God's words. At the end, God gave Moses two tablets of sapphire on which He inscribed His commandments. But in the meantime, some of our people panicked. When Moses did not return right away, they feared he had died and reverted to the idolatrous ways of our Egyptian captors. They melted some of our gold to fashion a repulsive calf, pleading with it for their safety. Upon his return to the camp, Moses was sickened to witness the revelry and debauchery of those people worshipping this idol. In anger, he took the tablets and smashed them over the head of the golden calf. He ordered the execution of those who had fashioned it and went back up the mountain to plead with God for his forgiveness. Another forty days later, he came down with God's complete mercy and a second set of tablets, which were inscribed with all of God's commandments.

"We departed Mount Sinai and travelled through the vast and fearful Paran wilderness, full of snakes and lizards. We passed through the hill country ruled by the Amorite warriors and finally arrived here, at this large dustbowl called Kadesh-Barnea. Exactly two years and sixty-three days after leaving Rameses, Egypt, we are now at the very portal of the long-awaited land we have all dreamed about: the land of Canaan."

"How old was I when we left Egypt, Father?"

"You were five years old. Now off to bed, so you can grow and become a strong warrior," Caleb said sternly. "No more stories."

"Okay, Father. I am filled with trepidation that I will anger you," Hur laughed as he stumbled toward his cot, holding Ephrath's hand tightly.

Caleb's heart melted as he watched, knowing he would be away from them for such a long time. Angelic Ephrath had winced when he'd told her about the mission, though she'd tried to hide it. She was so sweet and so innocent at times. But she was a good wife and knew the challenges the wife of an Israelite warrior had to bear. Caleb's job was to protect the family; however, in the unlikely event their tent was attacked while Caleb was on a mission somewhere, Ephrath had to be able to defend Hur and herself. Ephrath was strong, and Caleb had trained her to use a sword and shield proficiently. She was muscular and agile with a natural penchant for fighting. Ephrath fought and loved passionately. She could be tough when she had to be, but she was also an affectionate lover, his friend, and his trusted confidante. She was a saint and a sinner, just as she was a child and a mother, a sister and a wife.

Caleb thought how well they blended. He always focused on the singular obstacle that faced him directly—the rotten tree, for example, that had to be removed. Ephrath was able to look past the dead tree and see the forest behind it. It was not easy being the wife of an Israelite soldier. Caleb disappeared for days and weeks at a time, leaving her to manage their household on her own. As they were of moderate status, they had no servants to help with the laundry or cleaning up. Ephrath was in charge of all the homemaking activities, but she willingly submitted to Caleb's leadership and final direction. She cheerfully participated in the community, weaving blankets and rugs with the other women of the tribe, preparing food for festivals and celebrations, and enforcing religious laws and customs in her small family. Caleb knew she wanted her man around at all times, but she understood it was her duty, both to their tribal nation and God, to make personal sacrifices. Caleb prayed that God would look at the space and distance between them at all times and bring him back soon. He cried invisible tears as his heart pulled him in two different directions. At times like this, he was envious of Joshua's lack of worldly attachments. Joshua's focus in life was not divided between love of a family and Moses; all his energy and efforts were holy, religious, and sacred. What Joshua did not have, he did not miss or pine for.

2

DAY ONE: MONDAY, JUNE 20 / TAMMUZ 1

Southern Negev Desert
Shammua, Son of Zaccur

Iron sharpens iron, and one man sharpens another. (Proverbs 27:17)

Shammua was uncomfortable in the heat. His head hurt from the excessive wine he had drunk during the celebration the night before. The Levite priests blew the silver trumpets[1] to summon the troops, and his head throbbed. Standing in front of him underneath their tribal vexilloids were the twelve tribes. The men were divided into separate military corps, each of which comprised forty-five thousand soldiers. Each corps was made up of thirty-six divisions, and each division consisted of fifteen thousand troops. Nine divisions stood under the vexilloid of the Eagle, nine divisions were combat ready under the banner of the Ox, nine divisions lingered under the sign of the Man, and nine divisions proudly stood beneath the standard of the Lion. Corps were organized into three units, including twelve divisions specializing in close hand-to-hand combat; twelve trained in medium-range warfare with spears and javelins; and twelve trained in long-distance warfare with bows, arrows, and slings. Within each division, there were three brigades of five thousand men of varying skill levels. In each brigade were five battalions of one thousand fighters, hand-picked by Joshua and experienced in battle. Five hundred forty thousand Israelite legionnaires were standing rigidly at attention in full military regalia, with swords and shields by their side.[2]

It was an astounding sight. Shammua, his ginger hair fluttering in the wind, stood on the high rock just behind Joshua, with the ten other men Moses had chosen for this covert mission. As Joshua took three steps forward and raised his hand, the crowd in front of them hushed to complete silence. Only the crickets by the camp water source, chirping in the newly sprouted reeds, defied his command for attention.

"My brave warriors, children of Abraham, Isaac, and Jacob. You have come a long way from Egypt and the slavery we escaped. By inflicting plagues on the pharaoh, God freed us from chains of oppression. He carefully led us through the desert and to the Red Sea. The enemy thought we were trapped. With the Egyptian overlords behind us and the sea in front of us, it looked hopeless. But God opened up a path through the deep sea and delivered us onto dry ground, while the overconfident Egyptian army was destroyed and drowned behind us. He led us through the desert, using a cloud to protect us from the heat of the day and fire to light our path and keep us warm at night. He has finally brought us here, to the entrance of the land promised to Abraham. Ultimately, every one of us will cross the threshold and enter this land of milk and honey."

The troops beat their shields with their swords and roared with pleasure.

Shammua always respected his friend Joshua's leadership skills and military strategy. Joshua had earned the tribes' respect during the battle against the Amalekites in Rephidim. Shammua recalled Moses on the top of the hill, watching the battle. God had told Moses to observe the fight and raise his arms for his warriors to win. As soon as he did, Joshua prevailed against the heathen hordes. Whenever Moses tired and lowered his arms, the Amalekites began to dominate.

It was a struggle for Moses to raise his arms for such a long time, but with the help of Aaron, his brother, he kept them up until the sun went down. The Amalekites were obliterated.

Shammua sometimes found God's ways and methods strange. Divine power had won that battle. God had given the Amalekites into the hands of the Israelites. God had taught them to follow a plan of attack. If they had not, if Moses had dropped his hands, defeat would have been forthcoming. The plan given by God to Moses was simple enough—raise your arms, and you will win with divine intervention; lower your arms, and you will lose.[3] Joshua had said it succinctly the night before, after informing Shammua he was to be one of the spies to go into Canaan: "If we fail to plan, we plan to fail. We must develop a plan to conquer the promised land. The only way we can come up with an intelligent initiative is to discover what we are up against. This means reconnaissance and investigation. We must scout these land-dwelling inhabitants who occupy the territory we want to seize."

Shammua was excited to have been chosen as one of the twelve men to gather information. So excited that he had imbibed too much wine the night before. He took another deep breath, hoping to clear his groggy mind, and focused on what Joshua was saying.

"With God's protection and sheer determination, we will claim our promised land. We will defeat the insidious designs of the enemies of God and the people of Israel. We will continue to train here in Kadesh-Barnea, we will continue to drill, we will perfect our combat abilities until our hands bleed and our muscles no longer have the power to thrust a sword. When called to do battle, we will distinguish ourselves as the children of Israel and the children of the living God. This day we start our momentous task. The eleven men who stand before you, dressed as traders, represent each of our tribes. It is our honour to have been chosen for this secret task.

"We will travel through the land of Canaan, starting in the south at Beersheba and going as far north as Lebo Hamath, east-northeast of Damascus. God willing, we will return with a report that will help us plan our major assault. Pray for us that our eyes are not clouded, that our ears are not blocked, that the pagan gods of the heathen do not bewitch us, and that we return with the information we seek."

The whole army thumped their shields with their swords and cried in unison, "God is great; God is mighty; God is alive."

The task force, led by Joshua, descended from the rock and headed toward their prepared horses and cavalcade of camels. The cheering continued from the crowd: "God is great; God is mighty; God is alive." Moses smiled and nodded in approval as they marched up to where he was seated with his brother Aaron and his sister Miriam.

"Give us your blessing, Moses." Joshua was smiling from ear to ear.

Moses, his face shining like the sun, turned away from the other eleven warriors and looked directly into Joshua's face, which now reflected Moses's glow like the moon reflected the sun. Moses whispered to him, "May God bless you and d-d-deliver you from any conspiracy from the spies. Go with God, and return with the answers to the riddles."[4]

Shammua whirled around and looked at Caleb in disbelief. Why was Moses giving only Joshua his blessing? Caleb stared straight ahead and showed no emotion, nor did he acknowledge Shammua's reaction. Shammua was reminded of Joshua's unique relationship, and undying love and loyalty, to Moses.[5]

Two hours after sunrise and Joshua's stirring discourse, Shammua, with the eleven other saboteurs, mounted their horses and began their expedition through the wilderness of Zin toward Beersheba. Embankments and dunes of wind-blown sand stretched out in front of them. To the east were steep walls of porous limestone that dated from before Abraham and Isaac walked the land. To the west, sedimentary stones jutted out of the dunes. Soft white knolls, like danger flags, warned explorers and voyagers not to enter this forbidden land.

Shammua grabbed the hanging cloth of the merchant's turban he was wearing and pulled it over his nose and mouth. Only his red, curly beard blustered about in the gritty sand gusts. He rode third in the procession, behind Joshua and Caleb. But he disliked being second and hated being third. Impetuous as always, he broke formation and kicked his horse ahead to ride alongside Caleb.

"What was that all about when we were leaving? Why did Moses exclude us from the blessing?" Shammua whispered.

"Excluded, Shammua? Joshua is leading us, so he got the blessing," Caleb responded nonchalantly. "Do not make a giant dune out of a few grains of sand."

Shammua did not relent. "The rumour last night was that this mission was Moses's initiative and that God only allowed him to do it.[6] So Moses must be fully aware of the hazards. Why could he not bless us all? Why could he not impart his spiritual prowess to us as he did to Joshua?"

"Try to understand the uniqueness of the response that God gave Moses. God consented to Moses's petition to send spies. However, our mission is 'by our own understanding.' God has never uttered these words before. The success of Moses's decision, and our success in executing this mission, will be entirely up to us. We will be guided and empowered solely by our understanding and skills. Joshua is leading us, so I would assume that is why Moses gave his blessing to him."

Shammua pulled back on his reins and fell in line without responding further. He was proud to be of the tribe of Reuben, the first-born son of Jacob,[7] the father of the Israelites. He often felt that the other tribes snubbed his certified ancestral hierarchy. He was a Reuben first and foremost, and an Israelite second.

Zaccur, his father, often scolded him for being so impetuous, for making quick and impulsive decisions. When Shammua got something in his head, he rushed to accomplish it, blocking out everything else. Zaccur had warned him about his lack of control and urged him to take his time and reflect upon the possible implications of his decisions. Once, Shammua had quarrelled with the clan chief Elizur. Migrant foreigners were tagging along with his clans and families near the outskirts of the camp. Shammua didn't think it was sensible to take food from the mouths of his brother and sisters to feed these refugees.

He had spoken directly to Elizur. "Their hygiene is terrible. They are laden with disease. They cannot speak our language and make no effort to do so. We know nothing about them, not even where they have come from. They could be criminals running from the law of their land for all we know. They understand nothing of our laws, customs, or people. Within their faction, there is violence and brutality. It is a fraternity of broken families and poverty. And what do we do? We feed and provide for them!" Shammua could not hide his frustration.

Elizur, a wise governor of the two hundred thousand members of the tribe of Rueben, did not need many words to put this youngster in his place. "Shammua, know your place. Until God relinquishes His pledge to sustain all of us and puts you in charge of this awesome responsibility, you are to be silent and give thanks to the One who always provides. Take your men, go back to your tents, and ask God's forgiveness."

Later, Zaccur managed to talk Elizur into keeping this incident to himself instead of bringing it up with Moses—a silence that kept Shammua's standing high and without reproach. If Moses had found out, Shammua was sure he would not have selected him for the mission.

Shammua's horse trudged on, pushing hard with its hind legs. As the sand absorbed much of its forward force, the horse compensated by pulling with its front legs. After two years of trekking through the wasteland from Egypt, these horses had developed strong forearm and shoulder muscles and were well conditioned to move in the desert powder. Together with the swaying, rocking, baggage-carrying camels behind them, they made a picture-perfect convoy. At the end of the firm and muscular legs of the camels were thick pads linked together by two toes, which helped them float on the loose sand.

Shammua was excited to get away from the boredom of camp. For over two years, he had felt like a prisoner in his father's small tent. He wanted to see new things and meet new people—who knows, maybe even a woman or two. The thought made him smile mischievously, and he felt a pull in his groin. He gulped water from the goatskin tied to the saddle's horn and spat it out over his horse's head.

As the sun passed overhead, the group spotted a tamarisk tree by a small pool of water, standing out like a timeworn lion ostracized by his pride. They decided to rest the horses, stretch their legs, and take shelter in the shade it provided. Shammua studied the other eleven men and their horses and camels. It was an enigmatic company. Strong and muscular, with steely constitutions, they didn't look like traders. He had never seen a group of merchants that looked like they did. He smiled to himself. One certainly wouldn't want to argue about price with these men. He hoped they could prevent the heathens from discovering they were spies. The twelve warriors were already quite familiar with each other because they trained together daily in the community training arena. They were all proficient in combat encounters, as far as Shammua could remember, but each of them brought other talents to the group.

There were at least another five hours of sunlight before nightfall, and the men mounted their refreshed and hydrated horses and proceeded with their journey. The landscape was slowly changing from brown and uninteresting desert to undulating, green earth dunes and beautiful rock formations to the east. After five more hours of riding, they approached a large water basin fed by a single riverbed and surrounded by steep walls. The scorching heat had little effect on the pistachio trees, buckthorn, and globe daisies that grew unbridled around the pool.

A perfectly camouflaged family of gazelles grazed on the bright tulips near the edge of the water. Shammua impulsively kicked his horse into a full gallop toward the end of the cliff. The other horses spooked and careered in obedience after him. He jumped off his mount and started untying his tunic. "I am going in the water—who is coming with me?" he shouted. The outlandish band booed and jeered him between their fits of laughter and delight. Shammua was the first to hit the water, and the rest of them followed. Stark naked, they splashed and splattered in the crystal-clear, lukewarm water of the river, disrupting the stillness of the wilderness around them.

The pond became just another training arena as they wrestled with each other. The bacchanalia entertained a fat desert rat as it watched from a log. As the sun was seeking its well-deserved evening rest behind the horizon, the night sky revealed a plethora of glimmering stars. There was enough moonlight for them to get out of the water and find their clothes, but they were soon robbed of their leisurely exit.

"If you move, you will die," a voice called from the darkness. Four arrows whizzed above their heads. Shammua looked in the direction of the baritone voice and saw twelve soldiers with bows pointed directly at them. They had been bagged, without their weapons or their clothes, and they had no means to defend themselves.

"Who are you, and what are you doing in our land?" The deep voice echoed like thunder. "What is your business here?"

"We are lowly Egyptian merchants, kind sirs," bleated Joshua. "We are but passing through this land, looking for opportunities to trade our merchandise and goods. Do not waste your arrows or your time on simple traders such as we are. Let us dress and take our leave from this refreshing pool, which you have been so kind as to let us use. We mean you no harm."

"If you move a muscle, our arrows, which we never waste, will find their targets. I have seen many merchants in my time, but none that look like you. Did you build your muscles by lifting heavy barrels of wine or weaving baskets?" The other archers snickered. "Tell me now why you are here. You—the spokesman for these so-called merchants. Get out of the water and come here to me."

Joshua slowly stood up and headed toward the shore where his armed assailants stood.

"Why are you circumcised according to the ancient laws of Abraham?" the man exclaimed.

"Because we are indeed the children of Abraham, the descendants of Isaac and Jacob. Our God has freed us from slavery in Egypt, and we are travelling through this land to find trade and commerce that would be mutually beneficial for our two nations." It was a partial confession. "We mean you no harm or foul. If you allow us to dress, we will fetch our horses and continue on our way."

"And why would I allow you to leave when you serve under somebody related to us?" The man smiled as he waved his hand down, signalling his comrades to lower their weapons.

Now Joshua was perplexed. "I am sorry, kind sir; I do not understand."

"You serve the prophet Moses, correct? Well, Moses married Zipporah, the daughter of Jethro, one of our high priests when he was living in the Midian. That makes us family. We are the Kenites, cousins of the people of the Midian. We acknowledge and respect Moses as a man of God."

The tension on everyone's faces instantly turned to smiles.

"Does that mean we can get dressed now?" Joshua smirked. "It is embarrassing to stand naked before a firing squad, especially one that we are related to."

"Yes, of course. All of you can get out of the water and dry yourself off. Let us make some campfires and warm you up. I want to hear all the gossip."

The Kenites lived in the hilly regions where the spies now found themselves. They had been there since the time of Abraham[8] and were on friendly terms with the Israelites. When Moses fled Egypt after killing the Egyptian soldier, he had come to the land of the Midian and met Jethro, a Kenite priest.[9] Jethro had seven daughters, and Moses, being unmarried and lonely, married Zipporah, the most beautiful one. He thus married into the Kenite tribe. Moses lived as one of them for many years until he received his mandate to go back to Egypt and become God's spokesman. The Kenites and the Midian people knew enough about the one true God to maintain a priest. Jethro, when he heard Moses had left Egypt, joined him, bringing Zipporah and his two grandsons. Jethro travelled with Moses most of the way to Canaan.[10]

Hebo, the deep-voiced leader of the Kenite group, was in his early thirties. He was short but had a muscular frame. His complexion had a golden hue, and his eyes were not round like those of the Israelites, but angular and oval-shaped. His thin black hair was cut to the skin on the sides, then braided and tied into a topknot that hung to the middle of his back. Three scars etched on his face marked an enemy's attempt to blind him. Hebo and his men had been on a hunt when they had stumbled upon Joshua's gang in the pool. Having already shot four gazelles, they put two of them on the fires for the night's dinner.

Shammua assessed the Kenites warily and wondered who would win if they had to face each other in battle. He was sure it wouldn't be a difficult contest, all things being equal. Shammua's group had a secret weapon that the Kenites did not: the light-skinned, bloodthirsty Shaphat.

It was getting late, so they all stretched out and tried to get some desperately needed sleep. There was no need to set up a sentry. They were in Kenite territory tonight.

3

DAY TWO: TUESDAY, JUNE 21 / TAMMUZ 2

Negev Mountains
Shaphat, Son of Hori

Superstition is an unreasoning fear of God. – Cicero

The morning came quickly. *Everything moves quickly in this wilderness*, Shaphat thought. *It doesn't matter if you are a lion or a gazelle. When the sun comes up, you had better be running. You must run faster than your pursuer to survive. You never see gazelles lying calmly with lions.* Shaphat thought of himself as a lion, not a gazelle. Like Shammua, he shared his tent under the Man vexilloid at the south end of the Israelite camp. But in these wild hill countries, he felt like a lion. He didn't fear death. Death, in Shaphat's mind, was what life could never be: permanent, painless, and pointless. He had a lot of life ahead of him. Shaphat was audacious. He was always willing to take a risk, and the higher the risk, the greater the reward. He understood why Moses had chosen him for this mission. Whatever mystery or mayhem might be in this land, Shaphat would make sure he was ready.

After the soldiers fed on meat left over from the night before, they broke camp and packed up their mounts and camels. Hebo, before he left, looked at the spies and grinned warily. "Travelling through this country in such an auspicious group is probably not the smartest thing to do if you are trying to be anonymous. Even with your disguises, you do not look like merchants. You look like mercenaries. It is not my business, but I would suggest you break into perhaps four smaller groups, so you attract far less attention. Anyway, may God protect you, and may you fulfill your mission with success." Hebo saluted the Israelites and galloped off with his cavalcade of Kenites, leaving Shaphat and the scouts in a cloud of dust.

Shaphat rode forth. Unlike the Kenites, the Israelites moved slowly, allowing the camels behind them to meander at their slow but steady pace. There wasn't much chatter as they reflected on Hebo's parting remarks. His advice made sense, but they would have to figure things out as they journeyed.

The landscape had changed substantially since they'd left Kadesh-Barnea. They were trotting along paths surrounded by gentle slopes, and the grassy knolls were a test of obedience for the horses—the temptation to reach for the succulent prairie roots was overwhelming.

Shaphat was superstitious about almost everything. When they were choosing horses for the mission, he noticed only one white horse among the selection. He knew this was bad luck and insisted that at least two horses be white, or none at all. Shaphat took time to inspect all the horses' feet because too many white feet on a horse could bring misfortune. He would never say it out loud, but Shaphat still remembered the poem he'd learned when he was in Egypt:

If you have a horse with four white legs, keep him not a day,
If you have a horse with three white legs, send him far away,
If you have a horse with two white legs, send him to a friend,
If you have a horse with one white leg, keep him to the end.

Shaphat had insisted on his wife washing and rewashing the merchant clothing he had to wear on this mission. He'd dragged the tunic through the mud and then washed it again and again to make it look well-worn. It was bad luck to wear anything new while hunting or on a military mission.

Some people described Shaphat as aggressive, violent to the extreme, even bloodthirsty, like Simeon, the founder of his tribe.[1] A long time before, Simeon's beautiful sister Dinah decided to visit her Canaanite friends and left the Israelite camp for the day. When Shechem, son of the well-respected chief of the region, saw her walking alone along a lonely street in town, he pushed her into a back alley and brutally raped her. Her beauty and youth captivated him, and Shechem fell in love with her. He tried unsuccessfully to win her affection. Frustrated with rejection, Shechem pleaded with his powerful father to use his political authority to pressure the Hebrew tribe into giving Dinah as Shechem's bride.

Hamor loved his son and did what he could. He met with Jacob, Dinah and Simeon's father, and promised economic concessions, land giveaways, and free citizenship if the Israelites would allow the wedding. Shechem, obsessed with Dinah, was seemingly unable to exist without her.

One day he approached Simeon in town and pleaded, "If you agree to give me your sister in marriage, I, along with my people, will do anything you ask." Simeon, still profoundly shocked and furious that his beautiful sister had been disgraced, came up with a cunning plan to get revenge. He feigned empathy for Shechem's suffering and suggested it was impossible to allow his sister to marry a man who was not circumcised in the Israelite fashion. He asserted that they could allow Dinah and Shechem's union only if all the males in Hamor's city were circumcised as the Hebrews were.

If Shechem agreed, the Israelites would settle in their city and become one nation; if he did not agree, they would take Dinah and leave the area. Shechem could not bear the thought of being separated from Dinah. He discussed the proposed terms with his father, and they agreed it was a small price to pay for Shechem's happiness. He wasted no time. Shechem, along with all male inhabitants of the city, were begrudgingly circumcised that evening. Three days later, while the men were bedridden and in excruciating pain after the operations, Simeon led his brothers into the city with their swords high and killed all the men, starting with Shechem and his father, Hamor. In sweet vengeance, they took their flocks, cattle, donkeys, and anything else of value.

It was a great story of cunning and deception that was told time after time around the campfires as they travelled through the desert, and Shaphat was proud his heritage was part of it. He was a genuine member of Simeon's tribe. He felt real concern and loyalty to members of his clan. He would disregard convention to defend its honour.

Seven hours into their travels, the silence was interrupted by a multitude of vultures flying in circles about two thousand cubits ahead of them. Vultures feasted on the remains of any unfortunate animal that didn't run fast enough, and the birds' shrill complaints warned that blood or death was on the horizon. Joshua directed Shaphat to ride ahead and find out what was so interesting to them. The other eleven men continued their monotonous up-and-down trot until they heard the galloping of Shaphat's steed flying back in their direction.

"Sir, it's Hebo and the Kenites—they are in trouble," cried Shaphat. "They are surrounded by what looks like a war party of about twenty-four soldiers. They are not far from here, just over that hill in the valley beneath it. They are on open ground and have circled themselves away from their horses. Their shields have taken a lot of arrows, and it looks like a few of them are mortally wounded."

Joshua ordered his men to don their armour and tie up the camels. He commanded three of his soldiers to load their bows with as many arrows as they could carry on their horses. The rest of his platoon grabbed their swords and shields, hidden at the bottom of the camels' baskets, and spurred their horses toward the fight. Within minutes they arrived at the scene, and true to Shaphat's report, there in the middle of the grassland were their friends from last night, fighting for their lives.

Surrounding them were the Amorites, also called the Amurru or

Martu. With disgust and contempt, Shaphat remembered what he had learned about these barbarians. They were tribal nomads who warred with the Kenites and any other tribe that got in their way. They took what they wanted and spared nobody. The mountain Amorites were tall people with fair skin, blue eyes, curved noses, and pointed beards. Legends told that some of their rulers slept on beds five cubits long. Fierce and ruthless, they never showed mercy to their adversaries. Shaphat recalled the nursery rhyme the Israelite children used to sing around the campfire.

The Martu, who know no grain
The Martu, who only love pain
They know no house nor town, the boors of the mountains
They do not care about pretty fountains
The Martu, who dig up truffles, who do not bend their knees
to cultivate the land or any of the trees
Who eat raw meat
and like nothing sweet
With no house during their lifetime, they are never buried after death.

The Israelite platoon started their attack, their arrows flying toward the enormous Amorites. One well-directed arrow was not enough to mortally wound these brutes, but two, three, four arrows fired in succession at the same spot seemed to accomplish the task. The unexpected torrent of arrows made the Amorites turn away from their captive prey. It gave Hebo the opportunity to reorganize his defence.

Shaphat led the other eleven warriors, their swords drawn and shields high. The odds were now even: twenty-four beastly Amorites against ten Kenites and twelve Israelites. The Amorites, rethinking their offensive, charged directly toward their new assailants. Shaphat led his platoon, swinging his sword in fast circles. The Amorites, although much bigger than Shaphat, were more sluggish in their actions. One of them brought his shield up to deflect Shaphat's blow only to detect that Shaphat was now under his shield and sword. Shaphat moved quickly and sliced off his leg below the knee. The giant Amorite fell to the ground, howling in pain. Shaphat finished the kill with a strike to the jugular vein and smiled, relishing the smell of blood. *One down, twenty-three to go.* As swords and shields clashed on the grassland, Hebo and his men charged from the rear.

The Amorites, although bigger and stronger, were no match for the Israelites' speed, physical dexterity, and training. Martu after Martu fell to his death. They might have looked like merchants, but beneath their secular robes, the Israelites were genuinely skilled warriors. It was not long until the last remaining Amorite was fighting bravely. He had to be the commander of his group, and it seemed none of the Israelites were able to defeat him. He deflected, dodged, and blocked the lunges and thrusts thrown at him. Shaphat, although exhausted, decided that he would fight this beast.

"Back off, men. This animal is all mine," he commanded. Shaphat kissed his sword three times, touched it to his forehead, and lunged forward with the speed of a mountain lion. They fought furiously for about five minutes until Shaphat, using his leg, swept the Martu off his feet, landing him flat on his back.

Shaphat had raised his sword for the kill when Joshua called out. "Enough. Show mercy to this warrior. He has fought bravely, and we serve a merciful God."

Shaphat grimaced and slowly brought his sword down to the giant's neck. "The God of Israel will spare your life today, but if we meet again, I swear I will take your life."

The defeated enemy lay flat on his back, blood flowing from his nose and mouth, his eyes oozing with hate. "Kill me now, or I will kill you, your wife and children, your uncles and aunts, and anyone related to you pig Israelites," he cried.

Shaphat pressed the sword harder onto his throat. "Do not tempt me, you godless brute." He looked toward Joshua, hoping for a change of heart.

"Tie his legs and hands. We will make camp over by the creek where we left our camels," Joshua commanded.

Hebo had lost three men, but the Israelites hadn't suffered any losses. Neither did they have any wounds, mortal or otherwise. The Kenites dug shallow graves and buried their lost soldiers. They left the fallen Amorites for the vultures above.

"I need to thank you for saving us," Hebo confessed to Joshua. "If you had not come when you did, it would be us laid out for the vultures to feed upon."

Joshua smiled. "God is good and protects the people who fear him. I am sure you would have done the same for us." The two embraced.

They emerged into the clearing where Joshua had left the camels and gathered some dry wood for a campfire. The Kenites procured more leftovers from the gazelles they had killed the day before, and the soldiers devoured it greedily.

Ammiel, the Hebrew spy chosen from the large tribe of Dan, brought some venison to the shackled prisoner and offered him a vessel of water. "What is your name, mighty warrior?" he inquired.

"My name is Sihon. Remember that name, Israelite, as I will destroy you and your posterity. I swear this vow to our mighty god Molech. You are a weak, pathetic, and gutless people. No real soldier needs to put his meat over a fire before he eats it. You cannot make me suffer! You should have killed me today. If you knew what honour was, you would not permit me to wallow in the humiliation of my defeat. That makes you eviller than me."

Ammiel, who realized the conversation was going nowhere, said, "It is hard for me to imagine that a strong and mighty warrior such as yourself, a giant of a man on this earth, could be so small-minded. There is only one God, and that is the God we serve. He spared you today; you should be giving Him thanks. But to whom do you turn? Some lifeless stone named Molech? You 'mighty warriors' take your young children and defy common sense and sound reasoning by slaughtering them on Molech's altar to mollify and appease a lifeless hunk of rock.[2] Where is the logic in this? Is there any intelligence in your bird-sized brain at all? Now you covet and crave retaliation for the humiliating defeat you received at our hands today. These aspirations of revenge will cause you enormous suffering, more than any wound or injury we could inflict upon you. You are correct; you will suffer in shame as you remember this day."

Ammiel turned away and went to join the others at the fire. As the embers burned down, the men all fell asleep.

When they woke up in the morning, Sihon was gone. Beside the tree was a mound of ropes—and a sharp-edged flint stone that Sihon had clearly used to cut his way to freedom.

Shaphat stared at the tree and felt a surge of anger in his veins. Although rested from the night's sleep, his body tightened up, and scorching emotions ran wild through his brain. He had laid this monster on his back and held a sword to his throat. And now, in the name of compassion, the Martu had escaped.

Shaphat was careful not to show his rage to the others and rammed it deep into the pit of his soul. He had learned that anger only impaired his ability to make good decisions, clouding his judgments and terrifying those around him. Sihon's escape was Joshua's fault, but if Shaphat kept thinking about it, it would only make him angrier. He knew how to control his temper: slow down his breathing and focus on each breath instead of the ropes piled by the tree. Shaphat inhaled, counted to four, and exhaled to the count of six. He tensed the muscles in his abdomen and shoulders, then relaxed them.

There was something not right about this mission. Sihon's escape had been bad luck, and Shaphat hated terrible luck. He inhaled deeply through his nose, turned, and spit out the mucus, accidentally biting his tongue in the process. More bad luck. The taste of the warm, sweet blood from the laceration calmed him down. He would have to talk to Ammiel about this bad luck, for Ammiel knew most everything.

Hebo and the rest of the Kenites embraced their Israelite comrades, said their thanks and goodbyes, and galloped off toward the higher mountains in the north. At a much slower pace, the spies set off on their northern journey.

4

DAY THREE: WEDNESDAY, JUNE 22 / TAMMUZ 3

East Of The Dead Sea
Ammiel, Son Of Gamalli

A mind all logic is like a knife all blade. It makes the hand bleed that uses it.
– Rabindranath Tagore

"How many of each animal did Adam take onto the ark when God sent the flood?" Ammiel mused out loud, trying to break the boredom of the moment.

"That is easy," Shaphat responded with a twang. "According to our tradition, there was a male and a female of each species. So the answer is two."

Ammiel burst out laughing. "Wrong! Adam did not take any animals onto the ark; it was Noah."

Everyone snickered, but Shaphat's cheeks flushed with embarrassment.

"Okay, you want a hard one; here it comes," Ammiel continued. "Did or did not Adam have a belly button—you know, a navel?"

"How can anyone know the answer to that, Ammiel? There are no records of such trivial details. Anyway, who cares? It cannot be important," Caleb interjected.

"Oh, but you are wrong, Caleb; it is imperative to know this detail. If God created Adam from the dust of the earth and gave him a belly button—the scar left over from our connection to our mothers—then He created the world in a mature form. He created everything in an aged condition. It would be different if he created Adam without a belly button. If Adam did not have a belly button, then God created him—and the world—brand new. If the world were created in a mature form, that would explain the iron in the rocks, and the imprints of ferns and leaves in the limestone, which we have seen but cannot explain."

"Your questions and answers are hurting my brain, Ammiel. Can we just ride in peace, please?" Caleb said. "I honestly do not care if Adam had a belly button or not, and I do not think anyone else here cares either."

Ammiel prided himself on his curious, academic mind. While in Egypt, Gamalli, his father, compelled him daily to do his schooling and pressed him even harder to develop a love for learning. Gamalli, a mentor to many of the influential Israelite leaders, organized many scholastic activities during their captivity in Rameses. He understood that knowledge was the key to unlocking life's mysteries. During their travel through the desert, Gamalli insisted that Ammiel put as many hours into study as he did into military training. While Levites were the priests and experts in theological law,[1] Gamalli and Ammiel studied analytical reasoning: the ability to consider a group of facts and rules and use them to determine what must be true and false.

Ammiel remembered a session with his father just before the spies had left. His father had put a riddle to him: "On the second day of the week, you will perform six activities for me. You will bring food to our tent, you will sharpen your sword, you will train in the arena outside the camp, you will groom your horse, you will collect some firewood, and you will say your prayers. Here is the puzzle I wish you to consider. You will perform each activity once and one at a time, but the order in which you perform them must be subject to the following conditions. Bringing food to our tent must be done immediately after sharpening your sword. Your training session must be completed before bringing food to the tent. You must say your prayers before you bring the firewood. You must say your prayers immediately before or immediately after your training in the arena." Gamalli smiled slyly. "Now, having said all this, if collecting the firewood comes earlier than grooming your horse, and grooming the horse must happen after you bring food to the tent, then sharpening your sword must be what numeric order of activity?"

"That's an easy one, Father. The only answer it could be is third." Ammiel did not have to think twice about this.

"Hmm. You are right. This was too easy. If we changed the order of your schedule and made you groom the horse before collecting the firewood, what effect would it have on your schedule and activities? What would be the last of these six tasks?"

"It is a tougher question; however, my battle training would be completed immediately after my prayers were said. I would have brought the food to the tent as soon as I finished sharpening my sword. My horse would have been nicely groomed and the only task left for me to complete would be to bring the dry firewood for you to start a fire. Am I correct?"

His father smiled proudly. "Well done, son."

Ammiel's progenitor and founder of his tribe, Dan, was the fifth son of Jacob. Jacob, later known as Israel, when growing old, prophesied, "Dan will provide justice for his people as one of the tribes of Israel. Dan will be a poisonous snake at the side of the road that strikes at the horse's heel so that the rider is thrown off backward."[2] Ammiel's fighting skills were respectable, but his most deadly sting was his intellect. Like a serpent as it slithered and crawled, Ammiel would leave signs and waymarks showing where he had been. The battle at Rephidim was a perfect example. The tribe of Dan was always the last tribe that marched into battle because the Danites protected stragglers at the edges and rear of the procession of Israel.[3] Yes, Israel had a skilled and proficient army, but sometimes even the civilian population—mostly the weak, sick, and elderly—became intoxicated by their tribe's xenophobic euphoria. Amalek, the leader of the attacking enemy hordes, was well acquainted with Israel's battle methods. Seeing the enervated group at the rear of Joshua's army, armed with only wooden clubs, spades, and sickles, he split his central force and sent a brigade of five thousand regulars to decimate them.

Soldier's honour did not exist amongst the Amalekites. They believed the only good Israelite was a dead Israelite, no matter their age, health, or gender. As the Amalekites screamed toward what appeared to be a stooping, geriatric march, flailing and thrashing their weapons, Ammiel and his commandos removed their disguises, stood upright, raised their swords, and massacred their confused enemy. With his well-exercised analytical reasoning, Ammiel was that snake Jacob said he would be. There was no place for the fear of snakes in God's army.

As the spies bumped north along the trail, Ammiel reflected on the events of the past three days. He was stunned to have been chosen as one of the spies to go into the land of Canaan on this reconnaissance mission. He was a master of reason, and it did not seem logical for Moses to choose him to preview Canaan.

He considered Hebo and the Kenites they had encountered on the trail. They were fortunate the Amorites hadn't surprised them in the pool at the crater. Their mission would have been over immediately, for how could they defend themselves without their weapons or even their clothes? What ecstasy Sihon would have felt. Ammiel agreed with Hebo: they were too numerous to remain incognito. He would discuss it with Joshua when they reposed for the evening. They didn't look like merchants, and even if they fooled some, why would twelve merchants be travelling together? A couple of smaller groups would probably go unnoticed, or at least blend in better with the surroundings. It was logical.

The fight with the Amorites was still fresh in Ammiel's mind. It was a pleasure to watch Shaphat demonstrate his martial skills. He was indomitable, fighting two and three men almost twice his size at one time, never showing fear or trepidation. What Ammiel didn't understand was the blood lust that possessed Shaphat. Ammiel fought to win like the rest of them, but Shaphat fought to kill, and relished the process. Ammiel was happy that he would never have to face Shaphat in combat and even more delighted that Shaphat had his back covered yesterday.

They trotted up one more hill covered in green foliage and bushy pistachio trees. Joshua called for a break, to Ammiel's relief. The insides of his knees had become chafed from holding onto his horse, and he was thirsty. In the distance, they could see a settlement they were sure was Beersheba. The ground before it was mainly flat with a few undulating dunes. There was a haze rising from the sun-drenched sand that made the scene almost dreamlike. The light rays were bending and distorting reality. Ammiel had seen mirages before, and the heat does strange things. There appeared to be reflections from a small body of water in front of the walled city of Beersheba, but there was no water; it was an optical illusion. There was nothing but sand and more sand leading to the enclosed settlement of the city.

As the sun was quickly disappearing, they decided to make camp on the hill and enter the town the next day. They would be a spectacle arriving at this time of day, and the twelve of them would not easily find a place to stay. They still had plenty of provisions, so they made a fire and retired for the evening.

Ammiel sat with Joshua and poured out his thoughts. "Joshua, these are the facts: God is all-powerful and all-knowing. God has prepared an exceptional land in which we can live and thrive. Yes, this land is filled with pariahs that don't belong here, and they will no doubt fight to keep what they think is theirs. However, will not God watch over the words He speaks and complete everything He pledges?"

"What are you trying to say, Ammiel?" Joshua said respectfully, admiring Ammiel's ability to formulate an argument.

"What is a group of twelve spies going to find or discover that God doesn't already know?" Ammiel remembered that his father always told him that his strength was in arguing legal opinions—in interpreting the law rather than formulating it. "I have been thinking, and Hebo confirmed it earlier: it just is not logical to travel in such a large group. I understand there is safety in numbers. However, does it not make more sense to split up into groups of two or three? We would not be so conspicuous and could travel relatively unnoticed. It would probably be safer."

"I do not completely disagree with you, but my priority is the safety of our group, and we have no idea what lies ahead of us. A larger group offers more protection than smaller ones."

"But we could travel quicker and see much more territory if we split up," Ammiel countered. "We would be more efficient, blend more into the cities, and better achieve our objective."

"Look, Ammiel, by being part of a larger group, an individual is less likely to be a victim of a mishap, attack, or any other bad event. There is safety in this group."

"Respectfully, Joshua, putting aside the argument that twelve brawny men are more obvious than two or three, it is a fact that individuals become less productive as the size of the group increases. I have seen it myself. When one person pulls on a rope, he gives it one hundred percent of his effort. However, as you add more people, the individual effort goes down." Ammiel loved it when he was able to formulate an argument and back it up with likelihoods and probabilities. Sethur, Ammiel's best friend, once told him he never looked more alive than when he was arguing passionately.

"And now I am at the end of my rope with this discussion, Ammiel," Joshua aid sternly. "For the time being, we will travel as twelve. Each of us will pull on the rope, and the burden will lighten as more hands pull. That is my final decision." He threw another log on the fire.

5

DAY FOUR: THURSDAY, JUNE 23 / TAMMUZ 4

The City of Beersheba
Sethur, Son of Michael

I call him religious who understands the suffering of others. – Mahatma Gandhi

The crows fighting for their breakfast in the nearby trees woke the travellers. It was a beautiful morning. The sun was allowing some paltry respite before demanding the full attention of its victims.

At Kadesh-Barnea, Sethur and Ammiel had their tents under the same banner, the Eagle. Sethur, son of Michael, took a break from the push-ups he was doing, wiped the sweat from his face, and put on his tunic. The men were already getting on their horses, and Ammiel was holding Sethur's steed by its reins for him. Sethur mounted his horse and joined the procession toward Beersheba.

"How did your discussions with Joshua go last night? Sethur asked.

"We are still a group of twelve, so that should answer your question. I lost the argument."

"That does not happen very often." Sethur smiled widely but regretted it when he saw the disappointment on Ammiel's face. Sethur frowned and gave his friend a sympathetic nod. He admired Ammiel's intellect, but the two of them couldn't be any more different. He had been thrilled when Joshua told him he was selected to be one of the spies five days before.

"Ammiel, did Joshua say anything about me when you were talking to him last night? Do you think he approved of Moses selecting me to go on this mission?"

"Why would he talk about you? You know your greatest weakness, my friend, is your need for affirmation and approval."

"Do you not care if anyone likes you or not, then?" Sethur retorted.

"No, not really." Ammiel laughed. "I care if they like my arguments and logic, though."

It was true. Sethur knew that Ammiel didn't care if anyone liked him. "Do you think, my mighty reasoner, that there is something wrong with wanting to be liked? I certainly do not."

"Look, Sethur, Moses must have seen something in you to choose you for this mission, as he did for all the other men. Although what it was he saw in you, I will never know," he teased.

Beersheba was a heavily fortified city located at the crossroads of a significant trade route. And although it was built on the bank of a dry riverbed, the floodwaters during the winter months would do no significant damage. Its four-arch main gate on the east side was made of sun-baked bricks and stood about nine cubits high. The high fortified walls stood on strong stone foundations. The walls that surrounded the city gently sloped down from their pinnacle, exposing any would-be attackers to the defenders' arrows and spears. The large door on the gate was wide open, and crowds were coming into the city with carts of merchandise, sheep, and goats. It was a relatively peaceful time, so there was only a small military presence at the entrance. As the masquerading merchants proceeded through the entryway, chickens scattered beneath the horses' hooves, and the pungent smell of unclean sheep suffocated the spies like a filthy blanket. It was a chaotic scene clouded by dust and unsanitary debris. There was a wide corridor leading to what appeared to be the mayor's palace with its numerous rooms and separate reception hall. Lining the street on each side were merchant stalls, along with plenty of badly treated indigent mendicants.

"There are many low-life beggars here in Canaan," Ammiel shouted out to Sethur ahead of him.

"Ammiel, for the love of God, these are poor unfortunates who are only looking for charity. Show some compassion. I do not understand why people treat beggars so unkindly. If you treat a man as he is, wretched and worthless, you typically make him worse than he is. If you treat him with dignity, as if he already were what he potentially could be, then you make him what he should and could be."

"You are such a bleeding heart, Sethur. You suppose that imagination is more powerful than knowledge—that dreams are stronger than facts. You do realize that these Canaanites are descendants of Ham, the youngest son of three sons of Noah.[1] Ham was the naughty son who destroyed his relationship with his father. Quite a tragedy," Ammiel lectured.

"I remember my lessons, Ammiel." Noah had disowned Ham and his future descendants.[2] But can you explain to me why they have prospered so well since that time? Look at this place. It is amazing."

"That I cannot answer Sethur, at least at this time."

Sethur reached into his satchel, grabbed a piece of bread, and tossed it to an older lady sitting by herself. She devoured it in seconds.

"Ammiel, you see tragedy and failure as the logical result of actions of the past. I believe in looking ahead and believe hope always triumphs over experience. You trust in tears of grief, whereas I prescribe laughter instead."

"Are we not the eloquent philosopher today?" Ammiel said. "You are so easygoing—and an easy target for the deceitful. You should be thankful you have a friend like me to protect you from all the takers in the world."

Knowledge, to Sethur's mind, certainly could make you a deep and profound person—but too much knowledge, especially about trivial subjects, could be dangerous to your well-being. Sethur enjoyed life to the fullest. He liked luxury and good living and was generous when he could be.

Behind the main buildings were rock-hewn dwellings built closely together, climbing gently up the hill and forming an outer, circular defensive wall with only a narrow opening for a gate. All the dwelling doors opened inward, toward the central square, where all the domestic livestock meandered. To Sethur's right was a well-made, circular, stone well that must have supplied the freshwater to all the inhabitants.

"Do you remember the story about Abraham purchasing a well here in Beersheba? Do you think that is the one he bought so many generations ago?"[3] Sethur asked.

"Could be, but perhaps it was the well that Isaac dug,"[4] Ammiel replied.

The peripheral area inside the walled city was divided into four quarters, and tamarisk trees lined the dusty, circular streets. The trees had grey-green needles instead of leaves and were almost twelve cubits high. Sethur immediately recognized them as the trees Abraham had planted when he made a deal with the ruler of Philistine.[5] The nostalgic feeling caused his arms to bristle with excitement.

The main corridor cut through the centre of the city. All the streets met at the square, inside the gate, where the market was thriving. Men and women stood in front of their partitions, calling out their wares to whomsoever would listen. It looked like you could find anything you wanted here. There were fruits and vegetables, carpets and rugs, clothing and pottery.

Sethur, like his other companions, was smiling ear to ear. He hadn't seen anything like this since he'd left Rameses in Egypt. He could hardly wait to meander through the market and see what treasures he could find. He noticed that everyone looked different, and there were no similarities in their facial features. The city was an interracial, multi-ethnic mix of prosperous profiteers.

The men tied up their horses and camels and decided to examine the bazaar in more detail. After all, they'd come into this land to discover what grew and flourished here. It was funny, Sethur thought; they were called Israelites, descendants of Abraham, Isaac, and Jacob. The people of Beersheeba were called Canaanites because they lived in Canaan. But, listening to their banter, it didn't sound like they shared a common language. What they did share was a lust for gold. In the eastern part of the city stood three tall, pillared structures. Sethur guessed they were probably the city's storehouses.

They walked around in pairs, and Ammiel and Sethur strolled together. Sethur loved having Ammiel as his best friend, because he could explain all the things Sethur didn't know. Makeshift dividing walls served as the partitions for the booths. Amid the merchandise for sale in the stalls were images of numerous deities.

"What is that statue, Ammiel? Sethur pointed at a wood carving.

"It is supposed to depict El, the chief god of the Canaanites. Those smaller ones beside him are Ashera and her consort Baal. Baal and Ashera are considered fertility deities."

"Do you know about their religious rituals and ceremonies?"

"I do not know all the details, but they include human sacrifice. Believe it or not, there is some logic behind this act of brutality. They believe that if their gods give the best gifts to their worshipping people, then the people should reciprocate by offering their best treasures to the gods. Their 'best' often means their children."

"How awful and barbaric that is."

"Yes, horrific, but not so barbaric. They are amazingly progressive in many ways. Their women are often selected to serve as priestesses, and women can own land, enter into contracts, and initiate divorce."

"I am not sure under what conditions a community would resort to human sacrifice, especially of children, but I think perhaps they have absorbed the concept from the Amorites, Sihon's people."

Ammiel's complex and inquiring mind, Sethur noted, encompassed a fascination for the pagan religions. He was not sure if that was a healthy fascination. Ammiel always defended this interest by stating that it was driven by his desire to know why the people in these the lands would be so spellbound and drawn into the devotion of idols. However, Sethur thought it was more of a ghoulish obsession.

The city stood on its particular strength, and no king unified the Canaanites. Depending on the city's resources and the power of the city's ruler, the community would prosper or fail. Beersheba must have boasted a robust leader because it appeared to be quite affluent.

An older, bushy-bearded man and a young woman stood on a platform close to the mayor's palace, bound in chains. Their keeper called passersby to come closer and examine his unfortunate slaves.

The woman was first to go—to a lust-filled, dirty farmer and his son for a few pieces of silver. All that was left was the older man.

"He can cook, and he can work the ground like no other," the auctioneer cried. "Do not let his grey hair and wrinkled face discourage you; these only show the experience and wisdom he has gained over the years. He is stronger than he looks. Come and see. Look at his resilient teeth and powerful muscles."

Sethur stopped walking and threw a pitiful gaze upon the disheveled, bearded merchandise on the platform.

"Your price is too high," a man too well-dressed to be a simple merchant called out. "I will offer you half what you are asking."

"But, kind sir," the salesman pleaded, "it is but a tiny sum for such a great prize. Look at the size of his hands. Whatever you require of him would be efficiently done."

The potential buyer laughed loudly. "I will buy him for target practice, so the sum must be low." He threw a few pieces of silver at the feet of the vendor.

The older man on the podium turned ashen and began to shake, keeping his eyes downward. The vendor tried one more time to increase the selling price. "He has many good years ahead of him, with much to give to his master."

"It is my final offer. Take it or leave it!" The salesman picked up the pieces of coinage, smiled, and unlocked the chains.

As the older man shuffled off the podium, eyes still downcast, his new owner reached for his bow and loaded it with a long arrow. "Now run, old man," he ordered, grinning. "If you can escape my arrow, you are free."

Barefooted and awkward, the man scuttled away from his master, sheer panic on his face. He got ten paces, fifteen paces, and then twenty paces away from his soon-to-be executioner. The slave's new owner raised the bow and steadied his aim. Crowds of shoppers moved to the side, making way for passage of the poor slave. The arrow was released and propelled through the air with power toward its victim. The man was running hard down the corridor now, breathing heavily as he went, and the spectators stood as far away from the victim as possible. But just before the arrow found its target, Sethur reached for his dagger and sliced the wooden shaft of the arrow as it sped through the air, deflecting the deadly tip into the dirt. The old man fell to the ground by Sethur's feet, not sure if he was alive or dead.

A slow, breathtaking silence fell over the market. All gazes bounced between the slave hunter and Sethur as the other Israelites gathered behind.

"I wish to buy your slave," Sethur called out, reaching into his tunic for his silver. "Your slave managed to escape your arrow and is now free. However, so you are not out of pocket, I will pay you what you so foolishly spent." He held out his hand, offering the two pieces of silver.

The coiffed gentleman appeared annoyed and embarrassed that his game was interrupted. "You offer two pieces of silver for such a fine specimen of a man? You insult me, foreigner. You heard the slave trader: he is worth much more than this. I would not accept anything less than three shekels of gold for such a fine trophy! Pay me now, or the old man can run one more time, and I assure you the arrow will reach its target. The profit I make on this scumbag will ease my disappointment at your interference."

Sethur looked toward Joshua for approval. Joshua nodded and passed to Sethur the coins needed.

Stunned that these strangers were passing him such a large sum for such an old man, the man gave his bow to his aide and warned, "This is not the last you will hear of this." He stomped off in a huff.

"What is your name, Canaanite?" Sethur asked the runaway slave lying prostrate at his feet.

"Zidon, your excellency," he bellowed, still breathless from running the gauntlet. He was now kneeling and clutching Sethur's legs. Joshua and Ammiel were standing with Sethur and extending their arms to help him to his shoeless feet. "If you will allow me, over time, to give you back everything you paid for me, I will do it gladly. In the meantime, I will serve you loyally, even with my life if need be."

"Zidon, we do not need a slave," Joshua said. "We give you your freedom. Go your way and stay free."

"No, kind sir," Zidon said as he fell to his knees, bringing his clenched hands together in front of him prayerfully. "Where you go, I will follow. I will serve you until my debt is fully repaid, although I can never repay the kindness you have shown me today."

Igal, representing his tribe of Issachar, and always the opportunist, piped in. "You know, Joshua, we could use a guide for our journey, and he speaks the local language much better than we do. It is not a bad idea."

"He is correct, Your Highness," Zidon said. "I can help you with many things. Let me show you what I can do. I do not eat very much, and I can run alongside your horses if you do not go too fast. I will make sure the camels are groomed and fed. Please, kind sir, let me repay your kindness, however I may."

Igal smiled, and the spies turned to Joshua for his definitive word.

"Fine," Joshua finally said. "Igal, take him to the well and clean him up. Give him some fresh clothes from the basket on the camels. We will see how it goes. We could use a local guide."

With an acquiescing frown, Shaphat turned away and walked back to the market, thinking how much the old man Zidon would slow them down. He was angry at Sethur for interfering. It was not any of their business. Whoever had shot that arrow would now be their enemy as well. Considering Sihon's escape, that made two enemies they would eventually have to deal with. It would only interfere with their mission.

Sethur, on the other hand, was happy. He had saved a life. He fed a young dog a piece of meat he had stored away in his tunic. It looked like the dog hadn't eaten for days, and by the way it was scratching itself, it had never had a bath.

Igal didn't waste any time. He scooped up the malodorous Zidon by his armpits and hurried off to the well.

Joshua, after he sent Shammua to see if there was any room in the inn for the twelve of them, continued his walk, chatting with Caleb as he went.

Tonight, Zidon would sleep with their camels, not in his grave.

6

DAY FIVE: FRIDAY, JUNE 24 / TAMMUZ 5

The city of Beersheba
Igal, Son of Joseph

Rescue the weak and the needy; deliver them from the hand of the wicked.
(Psalms 82:3–4)

It was time to get up. The early bird always got the worm. Igal wanted to check on Zidon, firstly to make sure he had not run away, and secondly to make sure he was all right. Zidon was probably in his mid-forties, and although healthy for his age, he would be no match for a group of thieves looking to steal what their camels were transporting. As he entered the cowshed, he heard what he assumed were the camels and horses grunting, but the noise was coming from Zidon, flat on his back, snoring louder than a butchered sheep. Instead of waking him at that moment, Igal turned around and went for a walk through the deserted square.

Igal's sallow yet intelligent facial expression seemed always to have an air of despair. His delicate forehead and youthful, round jaw hinted at his easy upbringing and high status among the tribes. Back at the Kadesh-Barnea camp, his friends considered him precise, mathematical, and a hard worker, probably because of his common sense and his need for rational explanations.

But in fact, Igal believed that perfection was the enemy of progress; success was all about compromise. What most of his friends overlooked were his intuitive business abilities. Igal felt proud that he was able to camouflage this skill and preserve the upper hand in any negotiation he made. No one suspected him of being a financial mercenary. His father, Joseph, had owned a small shop back in Rameses, Egypt, buying products for a low price and then reselling them at a much higher rate. Igal, with his business acumen, was able to turn his father's stagnant retail shop into one of the most popular in the Hebrew quarter. He wasn't overly aggressive, but he never lacked initiative. His father Joseph worked at his business for the money and the lifestyle it would produce, but Igal did it for the excitement he felt. It intoxicated him. It was a game that he loved to win time and time again. He liked the money, of course, but it was only a reward for his cunning, not the fuel that fed him.

He reflected on the events of the day before. He loved the activity in the market, with some people winning, some losing. The Canaanites appeared to be good merchants. He was amazed at the variety of products available to purchase, the size of the fruit and vegetables. Then suddenly Zidon the slave had fallen into their lap. Zidon would be an essential connection for their mission. He spoke multiple local languages, he knew the surrounding areas, and he was indebted to them for life. He was a great opportunity, and Igal was happy Joshua had listened to his advice. Big things are almost always composed of small components, and the way Igal saw it, Zidon was now one of those essential components.

Slowly now, more and more people began to wake up and enter the streets. As Igal rounded the corner by a two-storey mud-brick building, he turned at the sound of barking dogs fighting with a cat. In the window, on the second level, he noticed a burly young man embracing a youthful and beautiful woman. It was Shammua with his shirt off, his long hair falling toward his face. Igal stopped and looked again to make sure the early morning light wasn't playing tricks on him. Then he ducked and hurried past the building so as not to be noticed. He smiled to himself. This might be something he could later use to his advantage. Igal was always thinking about how he could win. *The righteous Shammua is not so moral*, he snickered to himself.

Igal headed toward the cowshed where he'd left Zidon twenty minutes ago. When he arrived, Zidon was already up, brushing the horses and feeding the camels.

"Shalom," Igal chirped, taking a quick whiff of the barn air. "How did you sleep, my smelly friend?"

"Good morning. I am not so smelly after the bath yesterday, although sleeping with these camels has added to my manly fragrance," Zidon joked. What he lacked in physical attributes he made up for with his quick wit and sense of humour. "What will you have me do once I have finished grooming the animals?"

"Come now, let's find the men and have some breakfast. You didn't lose your appetite in that dirty bathwater yesterday, did you?" Igal joked.

"Sir, I could eat the blankets these animals are saddled in. Even that dirty bathwater would look like delicious soup to me this morning." Zidon brushed himself off, removed some straw from his heavy beard, and headed barefoot to the open door with Igal.

"Do not forget your sandals, old man," Igal reminded him.

"Thank you for reminding me. I have not worn shoes since I was sold into slavery almost three months ago." He scampered to recover them. Igal was surprised at his newfound energy now that he had rested.

As they walked to the eatery, Zidon started to tell him his tragic story, but stopped suddenly when they came face to face with the well-dressed man who had bought Zidon the day before.

"Look, Father, what the vultures dragged in from the desert. This is the slave I bought and sold yesterday. Can such a crumb be worth three pieces of gold?" he said mockingly.

Zidon put his head down and stared at his new shoes.

"Peace to you, sir. We wish you no harm," Igal countered.

"Who are you, stranger?" the older man asked quietly, ignoring the greeting.

"My name is Igal, a merchant of many wares from the land of Egypt. I am travelling with my comrades to find new business activities and opportunities here in the land of Canaan." Igal recited his spiel from memory.

"But my son tells me you are not selling but buying slaves," the hoary-headed Canaanite grumbled, "and embarrassing him at the same time in front of our good citizens of Beersheba."

"Because we are not well acquainted with the trade routes and somewhat limited in our language abilities, we needed a guide to help us navigate the best places to sell and perhaps buy. This old man will do this job for us."

"If it is a guide you are looking for, I can recommend many good and trustworthy ones for much less a price than what you paid for this old pile of bones."

"It is not necessary, kind sir. We are happy with our purchase. But I thank you for your concern and graciousness."

"Will you stay long in our city of Beersheba?" the man asked.

Zidon didn't lift his eyes.

"We leave today, kind sir, although the enticement to stay, with the amazing market and beauty of the city, is almost irresistible. May I ask to whom I am speaking?"

"I am Mizaim, the mayor of this city, and this is Jokian, my son, from whom you bought the slave. Did you and your fellow merchants pay your entry tax to our beautiful city yesterday?"

"Tax? No one told us anything about an entry tax," Igal stated defensively.

"The local people are taxed three times a year. Visitors, providing they purchase only from the stalls erected, are, for the most part, exempt. However, there is a tax on purchasing slaves. How else do you think we can afford to build and keep such a beautiful city for people like you to enjoy?" Mizaim and Jokian smirked.

"And what tax would you levy for such a 'pile of bones,' as you call him?" Igal inquired.

"The tax is calculated on the same figure you paid for the slave. You paid three pieces of gold, so you owe the city also three shekels of gold, or else we will confiscate your purchase."

Igal knew he was being duped. "I will inform my boss, kind sir. Where should we go to pay this tax?"

"You can pay my son." Mizaim pointed at the big palace at the end of the market. "His office is in there, and pay it by the end of the day." And they walked away, laughing to each other.

Igal was fuming. So this was Canaan, the land of cheats and thieves. Zidon was whimpering, following behind Igal in tears and wondering what his fate would be. They lumbered along to the eatery to find the men and tell them the news. He would have to wait to hear Zidon's story. Igal hated to lose, but he hated someone cheating him even worse.

"Three more pieces of gold?" Joshua complained, looking directly at Igal.

Shaphat and Shammua looked at each other in disgust.

"Let us just leave," Sethur blurted out. "What can they do to us? Kick us out of their precious town? We will come back with our army and flatten this city. We saved the life of this old man. No man has the right to kill another just for the sport of it."

"I am so sorry for the trouble I have caused you," Zidon apologized. "If you allow me, I will return to Mizaim and Jokian."

"What? And go to your imminent death? I will not permit it," Joshua said. "I will go to Jokian's office and resolve this issue. Men, prepare to leave, get your horses, and make sure the camels are ready to go. Keep your swords on your horses during our departure."

"I will come with you," Igal suggested.

"No, put Zidon on the back of your horse. I will do this alone," Joshua instructed, and off he went.

"He is so inflexible," Sethur whispered to Ammiel.

"*Stubborn* is a better word," Ammiel retorted. "It isn't logical that all the decisions are his to make alone. There is wisdom in the counsel of many advisors. Without them, plans fail."[1]

Caleb was standing close enough to hear the whisper. "Shame on you, Ammiel, talking like that about Joshua behind his back. Do you dare to touch God's anointed ones? Do you wish to harm God's prophets?[2] Moses selected Joshua to lead this expedition. Let him lead!"

It took only a few minutes for Joshua to arrive at Jokian's lavish office. He did not wait to be announced and strutted past the two cantankerous guards standing by his doorway. Jokian was sitting behind a large wooden desk that was cluttered with reports and accounting records, chattering intently with a dark-skinned merchant. Joshua threw three pieces of silver on the counter, and all eyes were now looking at him.

"These are pieces of silver, not gold," Jokian remarked. "The price you paid was three pieces of gold; therefore, your tax is three pieces of gold, not silver."

"Consider yourself fortunate," Joshua said. "This is the price you paid the slave broker. The gold you extorted was larceny, and this tax is nothing but robbery. If you want more shekels, then you must take them from us. We are not thieves, and we pay our debts and our taxes, but we do not allow ourselves to be pushed around and manipulated by bullies." And Joshua turned and left the bandit's chamber. His men were waiting on their horses, all with their swords hanging from their belts. Palti, the one they called Wolf, was holding Joshua's horse securely. Joshua straddled his steed, and they noiselessly sauntered down the dusty corridor, aware that at any time Jokian's men could come after them and arrest them. One by one, heads held high, they departed through the Beersheba gate and advanced north toward Hebron, with the young dog that Sethur had fed tagging along behind them. They rode until just before sunset, dismounted, and made camp, preparing for Shabbat.

7

DAY SIX: JUNE 25 / TAMMUZ 6

Shabbat, Day of Rest

Shabbat is the seventh day of the Hebrew week and is a day of rest and abstention from work as commanded by God in the fourth law of the Ten Commandments. This important statute must be observed no matter where you are or what you are doing. The Shabbat is a sign of both God's commemoration of Israel's freedom from slavery in Egypt[1] and His day of rest after His six-day creation.

8

DAY SEVEN: SUNDAY, JUNE 26 / TAMMUZ 7

Palti, Son of Raphu
Drugs, Dreams, and Depression

Shabbat lasted from sundown to sundown. The men decided after Shabbat to get a good rest and wake up very early the next day to get a head start on the roasting sun. It was still dark when they resumed their plodding journey northward. After a few hours of riding, Joshua called for a water break. Sethur's young dog was probably the happiest among them because although he kept up to the convoy, he wasn't used to so much running. He was jumping up and down, doing all kinds of tricks for Sethur, hoping for his second meal of the week.

They dismounted by a small pool of water surrounded by two flourishing tamarisk trees that sucked their moisture from beneath the ground. Joshua had ordered Zidon to sit on the back of Palti's horse, the largest of all the horses, to give Igal's mare a well-deserved respite. The afternoon sun would only become hotter.

Palti noticed his likeness in the still water. He stared for a moment and then moved his hair behind his ears. His broad, flat nasal bridge and widely spaced, bulging eyes did not bother him as much as his poorly formed ears. At least he could hide his ears under his long, shaggy head of hair. He smiled at his reflection. They called him Wolf because of his black hair and matching beard and eyebrows. Nobody ever looked at his ears.

"Are you looking for a fish, Wolf?" Ammiel teased. "While you are fishing, answer me this question. You have only three fish in this pond. Two drown. How many fish do you have left?"

Palti yawned. "Your condescending arrogance becomes quite tedious at times, Ammiel. Waste your slippery logic on Shaphat if you wish, but think harder when you try to deceive me. Only in your world of fantasy can fish drown. In God's real creation, fish cannot drown. If your premise is true, and two fish died, they died of something else. Unless you are even more gullible than I presumed and unable to distinguish between a rodent and a fish?" Palti was intelligent, but not very introspective. He relied on instinct. But he succeeded when others failed because he never gave up.

Palti and his father Raphu were descendants of Benjamin, the youngest of the sons of Israel. Benjamin was the darling of his father, who doted upon him. When the youngest child is born into a large family, the first thing he discovers is that he is surrounded by more capable adults who can do many things he cannot. This makes him ambitious and highly competitive. And Benjamin's trait pumped through Palti's veins as well. He exhibited wolflike qualities both excellent and evil.

Palti had never met a man who talked as much as Zidon. He spoke non-stop when he was riding with Igal, and now that they were resting, Zidon's attention was upon Joshua.

"How far is it to Hebron, Zidon?" Joshua asked.

"My estimate is about a day and a half. We could get there faster, but the camel determines the pace."

"Do you know the layout of the city?"

"It was my hometown before the Hittite war party captured me and forced me into slavery. My family and I walked the streets every day, shopped at the markets, and ate at the taverns."

"So, old man, tell me what happened. How did you end up a slave?"

"I had purchased pottery from a small village close to Hebron, and I was transporting it in a cart pulled by an old mule. Work was flourishing but demanding a lot of my time. I was feeling guilty that I was away so much from my family, so I decided to mix some business with pleasure. We made the trip a bit of a holiday, and my wife packed some meals and brought my seven-year-old daughter along with us. It was a grand day, not too hot, and the sky was blue with only a few white, fluffy clouds. The three of us were laughing and singing when the arrows came. We were laughing because I sing so terribly. It happened very quickly. My wife first, and then my daughter. They came at us on a chariot, one man driving and the other two shooting their arrows."

Joshua winced but listened carefully. The chariots he remembered from Egypt carried only one man. The Hittites, then, had different weapons: three-person chariots.

"The Hittites burned my cart, killed my mule, put me in chains, and then, I suppose, dragged my unconscious body away. I had scraping wounds on back and belly, and cuts on my wrists where they'd tied me with their ropes. I stayed imprisoned in their camp for about two weeks with only water and mouldy bread every second or third day. A group of slave runners passed the Hittite camp on its way to Beersheba, and I was sold to them. The slave runners threw me into a large cage on a cart with three other people."

"How many soldiers did the Hittites have in the main camp?" Joshua asked.

"My guess is two hundred or more," Zidon said. "I saw at least thirty chariots, the same type that attacked my cart, and maybe fifty or sixty horses. Every evening they would gather around their campfire, dance, and tell war stories. Because I speak the Hittite language, I knew what they were saying, but I never let them know it. They would perform their rituals beside a fire pit in the centre of camp. They were communicating with their gods of the underworld. They were calling out to Arinna, their sun goddess, although I heard them cry out to their 'thousand gods.' They have a storm god, a weather god… gods for everything."

Zidon's description fascinated Ammiel, although Palti was practically falling asleep. Religion belonged to the Levites. He was an Israelite. God was his spiritual father, and that was the end of the discussion as far as he was concerned.

Just as they were about to mount and leave, Zidon spotted a plant with ovate leaves and orange berries a little way off from the trees. He got quite excited.

"May the gods be praised, it is the mandrake plant. How lucky we are today," he sang. "Where is our doggie friend?"

"What is a mandrake plant?" asked Palti.

"It is exceptional. Don't you remember the story of Reuben finding the mandrake and giving it to his mother, Leah?[1]" Zidon asked.

Shammua began listening intently. Zidon was talking about his particular tribal leader.

"They call it the 'love plant' or 'love apples,' although it has many other qualities. But we cannot just pull it out, or we will die. Bring the dog and let me get it out of the ground. I must make a furrow around it and expose the lower part of the root. Then we must tie the rope around the exposed root and, on the other end, tie a noose around the dog's neck like this. Now everyone move away. Go upwind!"

Zidon turned to Sethur. "Call the dog! And put your hands over your ears, everyone." Palti snickered to himself, he did not have much to cover as his ears were just flaps of skin.

Sethur called the mongrel, and he came enthusiastically, pulling behind him a long thick root with almost no stem. Just as he arrived at Sethur's feet, the dog fell stone dead.[2]

"Now we can handle this hairy root without fear," Zidon said, picking up the root. "I am sorry about your dog, your eminence, but now we have mandrake. You will see what I mean later."

Palti watched as Sethur bent over, his eyes watering, hoping there was some sign of life left in his little furry friend.

"What kind of man are you?" Sethur shouted at Zidon. "What did this poor mutt ever do to you? He did not deserve to die. Is this how you pay me back for saving your life? You kill a harmless, hungry dog —*my* dog?"

Startled, Zidon tried to defend himself. "Angels do not enter a camp or tent with a dog in it. You are holy men; I just assumed you communicated with angels. I am sorry if my understanding was wrong. Please forgive me. I truly thought I was doing a good thing, getting the mandrake. And I thought no one would miss the dog."

Palti helped Sethur dig a hole, and they carefully put Sethur's friend in. Palti empathized with Sethur. He too wondered how anyone could be so heartless. This poor dog had zero expectations— he did not care if Sethur was skinny, rich, muscular, or famous. All he wanted was to be close to him, to hear Sethur's voice, to have his ear scratched, and perhaps to get a treat. The dog did not care about their mission, the complexities of pagan religion, or the group dynamics of the spies. Perhaps dogs were smarter than people, Palti wondered. That dog had always known what Sethur was saying to it, after all, and the reverse was not true. None of the group understood exactly what it was saying when it barked or yelped. Palti felt terrible. He had not even given the dog a name.

Palti was not sure he liked being in Canaan, and he certainly wasn't sure about Joshua being the leader. How could he allow Zidon to kill Sethur's dog so hard-heartedly? He had spared Sihon, that pig Amorite, yet he'd allowed this harmless animal to die.

Palti got on his horse and pulled up Zidon to the back of his saddle, squirming a bit to make room for the repenting dog killer. Palti noticed Ammiel talking in a low voice to Shaphat. He wondered if the death of the dog was the subject of their murmurings.

"Joshua!" Ammiel said in a stern voice. "We should break up our group into four smaller ones. We could cover ground much more quickly, and we wouldn't attract so much attention."

"I agree with Ammiel," Shaphat grunted. "With the old man and the camels, we are going too slow. Already after five days, we haven't seen much of the land. What kind of report will we deliver?"

"Like I told you before, Ammiel, it is safer if we travel as a group, and we have plenty of time. If we divide up our group, we make ourselves more vulnerable."

"Why does everything have to be done your way?" asked Shaphat. "All the men agree with Ammiel and me. We are thirteen men mounted on warhorses with three camels trailing behind. We are just inviting trouble. Even Hebo agreed."

"There is no logic to your plan, Joshua," Ammiel added. "We want to be clandestine foxes, but we are like elephants tiptoeing on eggshells through the lion's lair."

"Who made this an egalitarian rally?" Joshua said, frowning. "You were all chosen for your talents, but leading the mission was not one of them. This solemn duty is mine. I expect you to do what you do and do it well, but leave the burden of leading this trek to me."

Palti had not seen Joshua so annoyed before. Shaphat and Ammiel were correct, in his mind, but he relied on his instinct, not Ammiel's intellect. Palti understood that whether you were leading or following, you only had control over yourself. It seemed Joshua believed he had a special kind of influence over everyone. But Joshua needed to understand that decisions were the responsibility of the people who acted upon them. He needed to loosen his grip a little bit and listen to Shaphat and Ammiel's point of view. Joshua's stubbornness made no sense to Palti.

As Palti kicked his horse, Zidon bounced forward and grabbed him around the middle. And so they began their gruelling, unpleasant trot.

Just before twilight, after a long and silent ride, they decided to make camp with two warming bonfires.

It wasn't long before the sun dipped behind the hills, and the smattering of daylight shrivelled into darkness, leaving a black sky studded with stars. Palti, like a true wolf, was always hungry. When others looked at the moon, they saw bewitching magic and silvery beauty, or perhaps an immaculate purity laughing at our world of dust. When Palti looked at the full moon, he saw a bright, fresh egg yolk and wanted to howl.

After they finished their meal, they brought out an ampule of red wine and passed it around. Zidon found a clay vessel, cut three small pieces of the mandrake, and dropped them into the container with a cup of wine. He put it over the fire and let it boil.

The men watched him suspiciously.

"Okay, who wants to try?" Zidon asked. "It is very relaxing and will help you sleep. Some believe that you can see the future when you take it."

Ammiel, always the inquiring mind, held up his cup. Shammua and Igal also leaned forward in anticipation. After all the fuss today over the dog, Palti decided he would also try. After all, they were here to investigate the land. Mandrake was, by definition, a fruit or a vegetable that Canaan produced, so why not? Zidon poured the concoction carefully, not spilling a drop.

"Not too much. A couple of sips are all you need," he explained.

The other men declined Zidon's offer, preferring to refill their cups with more red wine. As the night wore on, drowsiness overcame them all, and they fell asleep. Well, nine of them fell asleep. Four of them were dreaming as they had never done before.

Palti's mind was racing fast, and he was sweating intensely. His breathing became constricted and uncontrollable. He became angry, not understanding why. There was screaming and shouting in his head. He thought about the dog that died, and his anger was focused at Zidon for tricking the dog. Then he was furious at Sethur. But as his protruding eyes stared at the stars, his anger slowly subsided. The sky began to change completely. The stars turned bright green, then purple; the moon became blood red. He put his hands in front of his face, but he couldn't see them. He could feel them pressing against his face but saw nothing. He thought he was floating but couldn't see or feel any part of his body. He wanted to rub his eyes but could not find his arms.

Two embers from the campfire shot across the sky. Then two more. The four flashes of light mysteriously changed into animals. There was an ox, and beside him a lion, an eagle, and a wolf. The wolf had wings, and Palti felt its hot breath on his face as he spoke. *Come with me*, the wolf howled. In an instant, they were in a dark cave that led to a rocky cliff. He saw Joshua walking toward the precipice with a cloth wrapped tightly around his eyes. Obediently behind him marched all the tribes of Israel. In a moment, his vision was complete, and Palti fell into a sleep more profound than anything he had ever experienced before. The small wolf had gone, but the smell of his breath was still in Palti's nostrils. Palti's pounding heart assured him that he was still alive, but he felt different. Then he remembered what the wolf had told him, and he shivered in fear and horror, his knees pressed against his chest.

9

DAY EIGHT: MONDAY, JUNE 27 / TAMMUZ 8

The Hills Of Har Yehuda
Geuel, Son of Machi
Fear Only Snakes Wearing Man Skin

It seemed that Geuel had been sleeping for only a few moments when he was woken up by Sethur's grunting and moaning as he exercised not far from where Geuel slept. The horizon was tinged with red, but immediately, the sun popped its head out. It was getting annoying, being woken up every morning like this. Geuel disliked routine.

As the fire smouldered, Geuel thought about the night Joshua told him he had been selected to go on this mission. Geuel's father had been so happy. His father had ambition for him. But Geuel didn't care if he was chosen or not. He believed that if a door did not open freely, whatever was behind that door was not meant for him.

Geuel adjusted his tunic where it pinched his biceps. He was in excellent physical shape, and he didn't have to work hard to maintain his strapping appearance. He took a dry log, smashed it with ease over one of the rocks, and threw the pieces into the fire. The wallop woke everyone who was still sleeping.

"Come on, you lazy lugs! We have things to do, things to see. You will have plenty of time to sleep when you die," he chuckled.

Geuel looked at Palti, who was curled in the fetal position, his small chin tucked over his knees. He had dark bags under his protruding eyes, and Geuel could smell his foul breath even from a distance.

Ammiel, Shammua, and Igal were moving like brain-dead turtles, while Zidon stood behind a far-off tree, relieving himself.

"If everything goes well, we should arrive in Hebron by nightfall," Joshua said.

Geuel decided to go for a short walk, also to relieve himself. Palti scampered after him.

"I had a terrible dream last night," Palti said.

"Probably from that witch's brew you drank," Geuel replied. "You look awful."

"I was taken away by a small wolf with wings. It took me to an enormous black cave on a mountain surrounded by sheer cliffs."

"Wolf, you had a bad dream, nothing more. I believe every event in my life has had a purpose. If I have a setback, and I have had many, I know there is a lesson for me to be learned. I never fail: I either accomplish what I set out to do, or I learn a valuable lesson. Nothing impresses me anymore, except perhaps Shaphat's ability on the battlefield. I wish I could fight the way he does. You should learn from taking that crazy mandrake. Do not do it again. However, your story is amusing, so tell me more if you must, while I groom my horse."

"Don't joke, Geuel. Listen to me. This is serious. In my dream, I saw Joshua leading the entire tribe of Israelites."

"Surprise, surprise. Who else do you think is going to take Moses's position when he dies? Tell me what has made you white like a ghost."

"As he was leading, he was blindfolded, with his hands outstretched like a blind man's. He was walking directly toward the abyss—to certain death."

"It was just a bad dream, Wolf, brought on by the mandrake. It doesn't mean anything," Geuel said, continuing to brush his stallion.

"But in the dream, I saw our banners, and the animals came to life. There was the ox, the eagle, and the lion. The only one was missing was the man. The wolf, who showed me the vision, replaced the man."

"There you go, Wolf. Isn't that just like the devil? It was a drug-induced hallucination. The devil tells you three truths to get credibility and then one lie to deceive you. There is no Wolf banner and never has been."

"Then how do you explain that Igal, Shammua, and Ammiel all had the same dream as I did? They just told me a few moments ago. It has to be an omen."

"Do you want me to interpret the dream, or do you want me to join you in your paranoia? Your nightmare was a fiendish hallucination. God doesn't speak to us through mandrake or wine. He speaks through his prophets, of whom you are not one." With that, Geuel turned around and returned to the rest of the men.

However, although Geuel did not show any emotion to Palti, he was indeed disturbed. If it was an omen, it was one he could live without. He thought it strange that in the seven days they had been travelling, there had been no miracles. He knew God did not perform a miracle unless there was a desperate need, but it was almost like they were totally on their own, without God. And what had they accomplished so far? In life, the disastrous signs or omens always outweighed the auspicious ones.

Enough thinking about this stuff, Geuel scolded himself. *Whatever will be, will be, and when it comes, I will be ready. I am always prepared.*

They rode toward Hebron for about three hours. There was some idle chatter in front between Joshua and Caleb, and a lot of nervous nattering from Palti and his newfound mandrake companions. As they came out of a scrubland of dense trees and bushes, their hearts sank. They saw their friends, the Kenites, drenched in blood, hanging upside down from a group of sprawling saplings.

It was a gruesome sight of naked, disemboweled men. Zidon

vomited immediately. Geuel and the other men got off their horses and slowly circled the brutal massacre. There, amid the other corpses swinging back and forth with the wind, was Hebo's eviscerated body.

Joshua sent Shaphat and Shammua to spread out and check the perimeter. He instructed the others to cut down their friends from the trees. The faces on the Kenites were not bruised or cut, and Geuel surmised that they died slowly, tortured in brutal agony. Shaphat returned with three arrows and presented them to Joshua.

"The Amorites made one of these arrows, but I am not sure about these other two," Joshua said.

Zidon ran over and examined them. "These are Hittite arrows, the same that killed my precious Zelda and my daughter," he sobbed.

"Very strange that the Hittites and Amorites acted together in this atrocity," Joshua said. "I was under the assumption they were sworn enemies."

Geuel lifted Hebo's body with his left arm, cut the rope that bound his legs to the tree branch, and dropped the body on the ground.

"Politics makes strange bedfellows," Ammiel remarked. "This marriage might have come about not out of genuine love, but out of the harsh necessity and reality of survival. Shared interests can bring together brutes with little in common. Sihon knows we are in their land. He also knows we have an army ready to attack, just waiting for the results of our scouting mission. We should have killed him when we had the chance. Hebo would be alive today."

The men cut all the bodies down and began digging graves silently. Palti, looking no better than he did earlier in the morning, kept looking at Geuel with a face that screamed, "I told you so."

Geuel thought it might be another omen. Was this coincidence God's way of remaining anonymous? He would let Ammiel answer that question. It hurt his brain to process thoughts in such a manner.

As the evening came and they made camp, Geuel thought perhaps he saw tears in Joshua's eyes. Joshua was wrestling with his emotions as they all were. What if he truly was leading the Israelites blindly to a precipice? Joshua's tears reminded Geuel of the tears of his father, Machi, the first time he had heard Moses speak. They had been tears of joy as Moses explained that he had come to lead them out of slavery and into a promised land. To Geuel it seemed like almost every month, somebody would declare themselves a prophet and expound their dreams and visions as the direction of God. They would say, "God wants you rich," and all you had to do was follow them. Others would say, "God will heal everyone," and all you had to do was say certain magic words over and over again. He was always torn between questioning the integrity of the self-proclaimed prophet and following the instruction to "touch not God's anointed." He knew that dreams and visions were a legitimate part of the prophet's mantle, but he also knew that false prophets used them as tools to keep their audiences mesmerized. These false prophets knew that nothing captured the attention of a worn-down and beaten people more than angels, heavenly encounters, and God's open gates.

The Israelites in Egypt were desperate for something beyond the reality they were living. Geuel also knew that not everyone God contacted through dreams was a prophet. He recalled King Abimelech's dreams that warned him to leave Abraham and his wife alone.[1] He remembered the dreams of Laban, Jacob's uncle,[2] that warned him not to threaten Jacob in any manner. While God encouraged his prophets and non-prophets to speak His words, He admonished those who told of false visions, because it caused His people to fall into error.

When Moses told of his visions and the simple promise of deliverance from Egypt, Geuel knew this message was from God. Moses didn't promise it would be an easy escape, or that there would be no pain. He simply said God would set them free, and Geuel knew in his heart that these were God's words. In the same way Geuel knew that mandrake, not God, had inspired Palti's dream. It was the snake, the devil, trying to cause problems. He had to tell Joshua what was going on. Joshua would know how to deal with it.

Geuel took a step toward the campfire, and it felt like a hot ember from the fire burned him. Then he saw it. A long, slithering, devil-like mole viper was moving into the taller grass. It was hard to tell its head from its tail because it was moving sideways. Geuel lifted his other foot and crushed its head with his good heel—a solid, direct hit. The snake did not move. For a moment, neither did Geuel. He picked up the snake up and brought it over to the campfire where the men were sitting. Its carcass was dark black with very small eyes and round pupils. Before being flattened, its head had been short and pointy and identical to its tail.

"This has bitten me," he said quietly, holding high the two-cubit long serpent. "What do I do now?"

Gaddi ran over and said urgently, "Lie down, and be as still as you can be. If you do not, you will die." Already starting to feel queasy, Geuel fell to his knees and then plopped down on the ground.

Geuel rubbed his ankle where a pair of puncture marks had started to redden and swell. He had trouble breathing and felt like vomiting. Beads of sweat appeared on his forehead, and he blinked rapidly to see who was around him. Everything was spinning. He gasped for air, but his swollen tongue blocked passage to his lungs. His swollen lips were burning embers; all he wanted was some water to put out the fire. He looked up with his blurred vision and tried to locate Gaddi.

"I need to talk to Joshua. It is important," Geuel whispered hoarsely. "It is about..." And he passed out.

10

DAY NINE: TUESDAY, JUNE 28 / TAMMUZ 9

City of Hebron
Gaddi, Son of Susi
Frightening Moments Resound Like Omens

"Will he live?" Joshua asked. "Did he say why he needed to talk to me?"

"No, he passed out right after he asked for you," Gaddi said. "Whether he lives or not depends on how much poison the snake gave him. It is a deadly snake, the mole viper. However, sometimes they strike and discharge only a small amount of venom. I have seen snakebites that emitted no poison. It simply depends on the snake." Gaddi had seen many bites over the years. "It is in God's hands. We need to keep him immobilized and procure some medicinal herbs that might help him recover."

Gaddi barked out orders for branches so he could put Geuel's leg in a splint. He applied cold water to a clean cloth and wiped Geuel's forehead, trying to keep him cool, calm, and still. He opened Geuel's mouth and forced some water down his throat.

Gaddi, although proficient in battle, was also trained by his father, who had been a healer in Egypt. He knew how to perform minor surgery and was skilled in herbal medicine. His father, Susi, studied as many Egyptian records as he could get his hands on. The Egyptians were more advanced in their medical procedures than any of the neighbouring countries. If someone were seriously hurt or sick, they would come to Susi. Gaddi, like a sponge, slurped up as much knowledge as he could from watching his father. He knew this was probably one of the main reasons Moses had put him on the list to join the mission.

Joshua turned to Zidon. "How far to Hebron from here?"

"About three hours, give or take."

Joshua instructed Palti and Shammua to build a sled, an A-frame that would drag behind the horse. They put Geuel on the travois and headed as quickly as they could toward Hebron.

It was a bit cooler today. Gaddi scratched the itch on his long, curved nose. His face had a rosy hue, and his cheeks, although entirely covered with his thick beard, were jowly. He and his father were members of the tribe of Manasseh. Manasseh was not a son of Jacob—he was, along with Ephraim, a grandson, and their tribe was often referred to as a half-tribe. It was not a derogatory term. Joseph, Manasseh's father, was the favourite son of Jacob. He walked with a strut and always held his head high. His father, Jacob, gave him a richly ornamented robe that always reminded his brothers that Joseph was his golden boy. Jealousy caused his brothers to sell Joseph into Egyptian slavery, but he rose to become the second-most powerful man in Egypt. Gaddi believed that was the reason Joseph's descendants had two tribes, Ephraim and Manasseh. He chuckled as he thought of Geuel teasing him about his name. Geuel belonged to the tribe of Gad, and he always believed that Gaddi was a name that should belong to his tribe, not Manasseh. He hoped Geuel would survive the snakebite.

Gaddi noticed that Hebron perched on several hills and wadis, and ran north to south. Grapevines and fig trees surrounded the tall walls that guarded the city, and flat-roofed stone houses neatly lined the narrow and winding streets. Like in Beersheba, there was a large market as you entered the gates. From the exciting shopping medina,

Gaddi's tender and trustworthy eyes moved to the strange sight of goats perched high in the surrounding trees, munching argan seeds. Hebron was rich in Israeli history. It was here that their forefathers Abraham, Isaac, and Jacob were buried in the Machpelah cave just outside of town.[1] Gaddi hoped their reception would be better than what they had received in Beersheba.

"Quick," Gaddi commanded, getting off his horse. "Get Geuel to the infirmary. I will check the market for the herbs I need. Move him gently, and don't let him move too much."

Joshua ran toward the main building to see if he could find a healer while the rest of the men followed, carrying the sled on their shoulders.

In the bazaar, Gaddi found most of what he was looking for: marigold blossoms, plantain leaves, and mongoose plant. He was amazed that there was also lavender oil, oil of oregano, even scarce echinacea oil. When he finished, Ammiel was waiting to show him where Geuel was convalescing. They had located an infirmary just a few steps away from the public market. Gaddi used the lavender oil to clean and disinfect the wound on Geuel's ankle, which had swollen to almost twice its normal size. He made a paste mixture of the echinacea oil and the mongoose plant, mixed it with water, and poured it into Geuel's mouth. He made a compress of the marigold blossoms and plantain leaves and tied it loosely around the two-hole puncture. All the men were standing in a circle around him.

Geuel began to vomit and shake uncontrollably. His eyes rolled back into his head. He was getting worse.

"Quick," Gaddi ordered. "Put this stick in his mouth. We don't want him to bite off his tongue. And hold him, so he does not fall off this table."

Then, all of sudden, Geuel stopped shaking.

"Did he..." Joshua could not finish the sentence.

"No, he just slipped into a deep unconsciousness. Hopefully we treated him in time, and the snake did not eject his full poison load. The most difficult time will be overnight. He is strong, and the mixture of herbs is in his body now. But only God knows for sure."

Only then did Gaddi notice a beautiful bronzed-skin woman in her early twenties standing behind the men near the closed door. She was tall, and her jet-black hair perfectly matched her dark, wide, antelope eyes.

"This is Donatiya," Joshua said, "the daughter of the master of the house. She has kindly allowed us to use her father's facilities while he is away in Jebus[2] for the week. She is trained somewhat in medical procedures, so perhaps she might be of some help to you."

Donatiya smiled courteously, but her eyes were on Geuel. "We don't get many snakebites here, so it is a learning experience for me to watch you treat this man. You seem very knowledgeable," she whispered in her Hebronic accent. "If you tell me what to do, I can watch him overnight and report to you his progress in the morning." She smiled again.

"There is not much more we can do," Gaddi announced. "We can only try to keep him cool by using wet rags, and make sure that the bandage and herbal compress are kept clean. They will have to be changed a few times before the morning. Are you able to do this?"

"I will stay with him, do not worry. If there is any change, I will send for you." Donatiya gracefully moved to the window to close the shutter. Gaddi could not take his eyes off her.

"Men, go into the market and keep your ears and eyes open," Joshua ordered. "I will expect a full report when I get back. Caleb and I will go to the tomb of Abraham and offer a sacrifice. We need God to intervene and save Geuel."

Hebron's market was much larger than Beersheba's, and a lot more crowded. After some time browsing the kiosks by himself, Gaddi was hungry. There were taverns and eateries grouped in one section of the market. He saw one large establishment with standing room only, and spotted Palti, Shammua, and Igal chatting at a table. Not far from them was a man plucking a lyre—a U-shaped instrument with strings running from the tailpiece on the bottom to the crossbar. Beside him, another man sat, thumping a drum harmoniously to the gyrations of an overweight, underclad female dancer on the stage. The music and the roar of conversation made it hard to hear anything in particular. As Gaddi approached their table, he could see that the men were visibly upset about what had happened with Geuel.

"Brothers," he said, smiling, "we must have faith Geuel will become better. To have faith is to be sure of the things we hope for and to be certain of the things we cannot see. It was by faith that our people won God's approval."

"Save it," Palti interjected. "We need to talk to you."

Palti told Gaddi what the three of them had experienced the night before, emphasizing how real the dream appeared to be. They thought it was one more bad omen because all three of them had an identical vision. Joshua was leading them to a disaster. Palti argued that omen after omen had to be dealt with, and that Joshua was outside God's will. Palti felt they had to do something to correct it.

Just then, four stocky, hairy, tanned soldiers staggered into the tavern. Much to the amusement of the other three, one of them grabbed a goblet of wine from a table. He guzzled it down, spilling much of it down his beard. In fear, some of the patrons got up and left, making room for the rowdy gang. The weapons and tunics they wore made it obvious they were soldiers, but the Israelites could not understand the language they were speaking. Gaddi got up quickly and fetched Zidon to the tavern with him. When they entered, two of the soldiers were dancing with the belly dancer, arms in the air while their comrades clapped out of time with the bass drum.

"Do you recognize these soldiers?" Gaddi asked Zidon.

"Yes." Zidon kept his head down. "Well, I do not recognize the men, but I can tell by their clothing they are Hittites."

The Hittites, bored with the entertainment, sat down together and turned their attention to each other. They talked loudly between belches and swigs of wine, but even Gaddi, who did not understand their language, knew the copious amounts of alcohol were slurring their words. There was loud laughter.

"Avoid eye contact, but try to hear what they are talking about," Gaddi said.

Zidon bent over and pretended to lace up his sandal, listening carefully to every word spoken. He was silent for a few moments. "They are talking about the girl they raped behind the water well yesterday, and how weak her husband was in trying to defend her. They are saying how bad the wine is in Hebron, and that it is not fit to give to their swine."

He suddenly jerked up and bumped his head on the bottom of the table. "Wait. They are talking about a new union, an amalgamation of tribes. They are calling it 'HAJ.' They are saying the Hittites, Amorites, and Jebusites, under the leadership of Sihon, will bring a new era of rule to Canaan, and that this alliance will prevent the Israelite aggression. Gaddi! Everyone knows you are in Canaan! They say that when divided, they were weak, but together, they will be victorious over you." Zidon rubbed the painful bump on the crown of his head. He brought his hand down to see if there was any blood on it.

Palti looked at Gaddi and shook his head. "Another omen, perhaps? How many will it take before we do something? We are doomed, and Joshua is taking us all with him. Why under God's heaven did he spare Sihon?"

The Israelites slipped out of the tavern, and Gaddi headed toward the infirmary to check on Geuel. Donatiya had changed and was wearing a light-blue robe with a white apron tied around her tiny waist. She was wiping Geuel's face gently from a bowl of cold water.

"Any change in our patient?" Gaddi asked.

"Not really. He is talking in his sleep—something about a dead dog, and some nonsense about a cave that leads to a precipice. Nothing coherent." She continued to dab his forehead. "Is he married?" she inquired.

Gaddi smiled. "Yes, he is married—to his sword. No woman has managed to capture this bear's heart."

"He is as large as a bear. Men in our city are not as muscular as he is." She giggled.

"You can go now if you wish. I will sit with him. It is getting dark, and I am sure you have other things to do," Gaddi said.

"No need," Donatiya exclaimed. "It is no trouble. I will watch him through the night. If I must sleep, I will nap on the cot in the corner. Please, trust me to look after your friend."

Gaddi, amazed at her beauty and kindness, agreed and departed for his rooming-house bed across the street. He was tired, and disturbed about his conversation with Palti. He would tell Joshua what they had discovered about the Hittites in the morning. He briefly debated telling Joshua about Palti and his so-called omens. But within minutes, he lost the debate and began dreaming about the beautiful Donatiya.

11

DAY TEN: WEDNESDAY, JUNE 29 / TAMMUZ 10

City of Hebron
Nahbi, Son of Vophsi
There Can Be No Success Without Sacrifice

Sun poured into his dingy, dark room like an overly enthusiastic wine merchant filling an empty vessel for a thirsty customer. The cobwebs in the top corner of the room sparkled. The spider that had spun them scampered away from the sunlight for safety. Nahbi, still half-asleep, reached out to the itch on his back and unknowingly whacked a cockroach off his bed, raising tiny particles of desert dust in the morning light. Nahbi hated dirt and grime, and the cockroach was his alarm clock. He jumped up and finished killing the roach with his sandal before it escaped.

How he hated this land.

Nahbi was different than the rest of the men on this mission. He was slender, lean, and wiry. He loved to run for hours, but there had been no opportunity since they'd left Kadesh-Barnea. The little body hair he had, he kept coiffed and tidy. He liked colourful clothes and constantly nagged his mother to make him new things. He loved the incredible fashion in Egypt. Of course, the Hebrews did not wear the same clothes as the Egyptians, but often Nahbi would sneak off to the palace to watch people going in and out and to admire what they were wearing. He was glad the spies were not wearing their military armour on this mission; it was so ugly. His merchant's tunic was bright red and had a blue belt that fastened it tightly to his body. He made his mother dye it twice to get the correct shade.

Nahbi looked out the window and guessed that it was only a few minutes after sunrise, which gave him about one hour to get ready. They were departing for Jebus today, and they would have to leave Geuel here in Hebron. Nahbi was not happy to leave his comrade; he felt they should all stay and wait for Geuel to recover. Geuel was such a good-looking man and a fine specimen of a soldier. It repulsed him, how that woman Donatiya goggled over him, drooling like a dog over a piece of lamb. Were there not enough men in Hebron to embarrass herself over? Even Gaddi was bumbling around her. What was so unique about her, anyway? She was way too skinny, and if she had breasts, they did not show at all. Her babies would die trying to get her milk.

The roosters were now crowing, and Nahbi entered the courtyard, where Joshua and Caleb were sitting with long faces.

"Good morning. I hope the long faces do not mean something has happened to Geuel," Nahbi observed.

"No, Geuel is improving, but not enough for him to come any further with us," Joshua said.

"So why do you look so gloomy?"

"Caleb and I went to the tomb yesterday afternoon to sacrifice a male goat. As we don't have a Levite priest, we both prayed, asking God for his favour and forgiveness and offering our sacrifice for success in our mission. We need a miracle. However, the sacrifice was not accepted. He told us we initiated our journey at Kadesh-Barnea and that we would be responsible for its success or failure. He said it was our idea to go, and that He does not perform miracles unless there is a reason. He wants us to figure it out on our own, to use our creative ideas. We released the goat and came back, unsuccessful in our attempt."

"This whole mission did not make a lot of sense to me from the start," Nahbi said. "Why in the name of heaven would we need to check the land God was giving us before we got it?"

Caleb's silence said it all.

"So what do we do now? Nahbi pressed. "Do we go back to the Kadesh-Barnea camp?"

"No, we press on. Moses expects a report, and that is what we will give him," said Joshua. "We are on a fact-finding mission. Caleb will stay here and keep an eye of Geuel. The rest of us will go north toward Damascus. Nahbi, go now and get the rest of the men. We will leave within the hour."

Nahbi obeyed reluctantly. The only one who would be happy leaving Geuel and Caleb behind was Zidon because he would then have a horse of his own.

While the sun was still low in the sky, Nahbi got off his mount and passed his reins over to Ammiel. He began to run barefooted alongside the horses. The ground was stable, and there was no mud on the path. He had a lot of things on his mind, and running always cleared them up. He loved to talk to God while running: "You are my defender and protector. You are my God in whom I trust. You will keep me safe from all hidden dangers and all deadly diseases. You will cover me with Your wings, and I will be safe in Your care. Your faithfulness will protect and defend me. I will not fear any dangers at night or sudden attacks during the day. A thousand may fall dead beside me, ten thousand around me, but I will not be harmed. Please, almighty God, do not fail or forsake us on this mission. Protect us and give us success."

After about two hours of riding and running, the sun was directly overhead, and they all stopped to water the horses. Nahbi was soaked in sweat and welcomed the opportunity to get back on his horse. Zidon said they would arrive in Jebus by nightfall if they kept going at this pace. By now, the men had split into two distinct groups: Joshua by himself, and then all the rest of them. Nahbi had heard Palti's nattering about omens. Palti had supporters now in Igal, Shammua, and even Ammiel. Nahbi was surprised to hear about their dreams and was a bit worried himself. Like the others, he did not believe in coincidence, but he did not necessarily believe that coincidence was God acting anonymously.

The tarn reflected perfectly the old olive tree and the junipers growing along its banks. Except for the single croak of an agitated frog, it was so quiet that Nahbi could almost hear the grass growing. He took a few moments to check his reflection in the water and adjusted his head covering, which was always sliding forward. The north wind started to blow gently over the water, cooling Nahbi's clammy face.

"What is that smell?" Nahbi turned to Zidon accusingly. "Zidon, did you break wind?"

"It wasn't me," he said defensively, his face turning red.

The men laughed. "Zidon, confess, and we will forgive you," Sethur said, and even Joshua cracked a smile.

"It was not me," Zidon insisted. "We Canaanites have a saying: 'a fox smells his own hole first.' So it had to be you," he said to Nahbi. The men hooted hysterically.

"Disgusting," Nahbi declared. "Absolutely revolting. Hopefully we can teach you some manners while you are with us." He mounted his horse and gave it a quick kick forward.

As they proceeded in the direction of Jebus, the smell became stronger with each step. Nahbi took some of the loose bindings from his headgear and wrapped it around his nose and mouth, hoping to keep the stench of rotten duck eggs from his nostrils.

And then they froze in the undergrowth of the trees that, thankfully, served as camouflage.

Nahbi rubbed his eyes in disbelief. It had to be an illusion. He was breathing very quickly now, and he could feel his heart thumping in the veins of his temples. The tips of his fingers and toes turned cold, and his pupils dilated to take in as much of the scene as was possible. His muscles tensed, and the hair on his arms bristled. They were far away, but close enough to see these anomalies with their bright red, shoulder-length hair and the extra finger on each hand. They wore animal skins around their loins, and their bodies were without any other covering—except for the splatters of blood and copious neck chains that crackled and crunched as they moved. They were playing some game with what looked like balls. But they were not footballs, Nahbi realized. They were human heads. There were only two things Nahbi thought to do—fight or flee. And he would be insane not to run.

The men dismounted and crawled on their bellies to the top of the bluff, where they could see much more. The disgusting odour was now almost unbearable. Nahbi thought the Amorites they'd fought were giants, but these creatures were one and a half times bigger. Whatever these were, they were not human; they were three times the size of Nahbi. The stench came from the decapitated soldiers that lay in piles everywhere. Nahbi thought he heard the killers speaking, but the noise resembled not words but the buzzing of bees around a nest.

Shaking in fear, Zidon said, "These are the Anakim—the brothers Ahiman, Sheshai, and Talmai—who have terrorized us for years. They live in the caves close to the Dead Sea. They hunt and eat humans. We must flee for our lives. If they see us, we are doomed."

Even Shaphat's face betrayed his fear, and he turned to spit superstitiously. Shaphat believed that to prevent a tragedy from occurring, spitting three times in succession would protect him from any trickery or evil spirits.

"In our tradition, we call them the Rephaim," Ammiel whispered, keeping his voice low. "Before the flood, before Noah's time, they were everywhere, the result of 'fallen angels' having babies with our women.[1] These children were wicked, evil, and violent. The main reason God brought the floodwaters was likely to eliminate them from the face of the earth."

Nahbi wondered why it did not work.

"Look at the size of those melons and grapes beside them," Nahbi commented, trying to focus on something else other than his fear.

"They are not melons," Zidon said, "but pomegranates."

The buzzing became louder, and Nahbi thought he heard sinister laughter as they tossed the amputations back and forth. The men crawled back to their horses and camels and fled as quickly as they could. Nahbi was sure Palti would think this was one more omen.

They arrived in Jebus at sundown. The Kidron Valley, just a short distance from the city, had a plentiful water supply from the Gihon springs, which helped the locals irrigate their crops and provided endless fresh drinking water during the harsh, hot summers. The city was surrounded by massive stone walls to protect it from intruders. Even the giant Rephaim could not scale them, Nahbi thought with relief.

Nahbi slowly recalled his history lessons. Jebus, in the time of Abraham, was called Salem and was ruled by a priest named Melchizedek,[2] a friend of Abraham. When Abraham purchased the cave of Machpelah for the burial of his wife and later himself, Isaac, and Jacob, the Jebusites made him grant them a covenant that his descendants would never take control of Jebus against the will of the Jebusites that occupied the city. They etched the agreement in bronze. The Jebusites, after some time, built two statues of bronze commemorating the contract: two men—one blind, one lame.[3] The blind statue depicted Isaac, Abraham's son.

"So many times I wondered about these bronze sculptures. Do you know their significance?" Zidon whispered in Nahbi's ear.

"The Jebusites have always been jealous and fearful of the Israelites. The statues commemorate the agreement Abraham made with them so very long ago. To understand why they built the figures, you must comprehend a little bit of our history. When Isaac, the son of Abraham, became elderly, he was almost blind. He had two sons with entirely different characters. Jacob was soft and gentle, a graduate of the academies of the local universities, a lover of the teachings of God, and his mother's favourite son. However, Esau, the eldest, was Isaac's favourite. He hated studying, preferred hunting and fishing, and led an unrefined life doing things his way. Isaac considered Esau an ideal specimen of masculinity and was very proud of him. And although Isaac was almost blind, his undaunting love for Esau blinded him even more grievously to Esau's godless behaviour.

"Isaac's wife Rebekah, like all mothers, knew which of her sons had the talents and abilities to be a leader. Isaac was old and dying, and it was customary for him to give his sons his final and irrevocable blessings. Isaac, believing that Esau would carry on Abraham's lineage, told him to hunt some deer and prepare a meal for him, and that he would receive his blessing.

"Excited, Esau took his bow and quiver and went out to the fields to obey his father. But Rebekah had heard everything. She believed the blessing should be given to Jacob, not Esau, because, besides being her favourite, Jacob was wiser and sought God's will in all things. She hastily urged Jacob to follow her orders precisely. Jacob did not dare refuse his mother and fetched two tender kids from the flock. Rebekah prepared the meal precisely as Isaac loved.

"She then dressed Jacob in Esau's festive garments, and to complete the deception, she covered his smooth neck and hands with the skins of the kids. She then put the meal into Jacob's hands and sent him to his father.

"Isaac wondered how his son could return so quickly from his quest, but he attributed it to his exceptional hunting abilities. He ate the meal Jacob brought to him and then put his hands on Jacob's hands and neck (thinking he was Esau) and blessed him with these words: 'And may the Lord give you of the dew of the heavens and the fatness of the earth and an abundance of corn and wine. Nations shall serve you and kingdoms shall bow down to you; you shall be a master over your brothers, and your mother's sons shall bow down to you. Those who curse you shall be cursed, and those who bless you shall be blessed!' The future of the Hebrews now belonged to Jacob, not Esau.

"So the Jebusites, realizing that Jacob was the future of Israel, built the statue depicting Jacob's father with his blindness, reminding all that the covenant made with Abraham was passed down to Jacob."

"Interesting story—but what about the statue of the crippled man? What is the story behind him?"

"The statue of the disabled man depicts Jacob. Much later in life, after a long night of physically wrestling with God, Jacob received his new name, Israel.[4] However, the bodily trauma caused him to hobble for the rest of his life."

"But why would the Jebusites spend the time, money, and effort to build such expensive monuments if they were jealous and fearful of the descendants of Isaac and Jacob? Is it a gesture to honour their memory?" Zidon asked.

Nahbi laughed. "Not at all, old man. They have seen the power of our God. It is a statement of their hope that the covenant made with Abraham will protect them from any future confrontation with our tribes. They knew we would come back eventually."

"So they think that a statue of a cripple and a blind man will protect them?" Zidon asked skeptically.

"Is it so strange a gesture for a nation obsessed with idols?" Nahbi replied.

Nahbi loved these stories and never understood why Isaac loved Esau more than Jacob. Why did so many people feel that being overly masculine and hairy was more desirable than being cultured and educated? Appearances were significant to Nahbi, but they could be deceptive. He remembered his father, Vophsi, teaching him a valuable lesson in Egypt when Nahbi was a small child. Vophsi blindfolded him and brought him into a room where there was singing and warbling of a most melodious bird. When the music stopped, Vophsi took his blindfold off, and Nahbi saw two cages hanging from the roof. In one cage was a beautiful and multicoloured parrot with shiny, bright, blue and red feathers. In the other cage sat a small nightingale with dingy brown feathers, a short beak, and beady little eyes.

"Which of these two birds sang the song you heard?" teased his father.

Nahbi naturally assumed that such a sweet voice could only come from a bird of extraordinary beauty. The small nightingale's homely appearance and the outward splendour of the parrot fooled him. He was wrong about the nightingale, just as Isaac had been wrong to choose Esau over Jacob. Nahbi was glad Jacob stole the blessing from Esau.

Nahbi was surprised at the enormity of the bronze statues as they passed through the gate. If they were placed there to impress visitors, they more than accomplished their purpose.

Little did the spies know how drastically things had changed since Melchizedek was in charge of Salem.

12

DAY ELEVEN: THURSDAY, JUNE 30 / TAMMUZ 11

City Of Hebron
Caleb, Son of Jephunneh
Denial—the Preface to Justification

Back in Hebron, Geuel and Caleb were the only Israelites left. As Geuel was restricted to the infirmary, and it was a beautiful day, Caleb left his drab room and meandered to the cave of Machpelah before visiting his friend. He stopped to watch some farmers who were grafting grapevines. They were taking small, new, budding branches from a bucket of water and binding them with cloth onto large old stumps in the fertile soil. It was a way to improve the vineyard and achieve a high premium of growth. Caleb had not seen this process before, but he found it fascinating that the new vines were a different variety of grape than the old ones growing in the ground. Carefully the skilled farmers cut the bark, re-cut the grafting point, then pressed them together. *We Israelites have a lot to learn from these people if we are going to be successful in this land*, Caleb thought.

He chuckled to himself as he thought about the grafting of the vines. His family roots were not Hebrew but Kenizzite. The Kenizzites were a tribe that, at one time, nomadically hunted through the land of Canaan and eventually ended up in the northern regions of Syria. Being a Kenizzite made Caleb a Gentile, and he did not share a natural bloodline with Abraham, Isaac, or Jacob. Caleb and his father, Jephunneh, were "grafted" onto the old Hebrew vine just as these new vine fruitlings were being grafted onto the old grape stumps. Caleb's family, although initially Gentile, became Hebrews in the fullest sense of the word. In God's eyes, Caleb was no different than any of his tribal brothers, although from time to time he thought he saw tinges of resentment in the eyes of some of the older chieftains. This resentment seemed, at times, to bother his father, but Caleb did not even think about it. The law applied to both the proselyte and the Hebrew-born alike.

But Caleb was troubled that God had not accepted the offering from him and Joshua. He was upset that God had told them it was their responsibility to be successful. How would they succeed in their mission without His help and providence? Caleb was not sure it would work, but he decided to petition Abraham, Isaac, and Jacob to help them. He much respected the forefathers. Their bones were buried here in the cave, and surely they understood the importance of this mission to their nation.

He prayed fervently for their intervention. His comrades were talking about bad omens, and rebellion could be imminent. Disloyalty was foreign to Caleb. The spies were good men, but they were scared and confused because Canaan was so different from the comfortable familiarity of Kadesh-Barnea. They all had their routines and habits, and at Kadesh-Barnea, they could devote as much time as they wanted to spiritual things. There was the tabernacle, and then there were the priests. There were no surprises. Caleb was sure the men had good intentions and were only thinking of the tribes, and it was frightening to face so much uncertainty. However, this was no reason to usurp Joshua's leadership by complaining and grumbling.

It was ironic, Caleb mused. In the sixty-two years Abraham lived in this promised land (and it was *all* promised to him), the only real estate he had ever owned was this burial cave outside Hebron. After him, Isaac, Jacob, and so many other descendants died without redeeming the promise of owning and occupying the land. The Israelites had been strangers and exiles—until now.

Caleb's quiet moment was interrupted by a young voice.

"Are you all right?" a boy asked. Caleb's habit when he prayed was to lie face down with his hands covering his face.

"Yes, I am fine," he said as he rose to his knees. "Just talking to the bones in the tomb." The child reminded him of his son Hur back at camp, and for a moment, he felt a twang of homesickness.

"Huh? You can talk to bones?" the child exclaimed. "Can I talk to the bones as well? Do they talk back?

Caleb smiled as he would to Hur when he asked questions. "The bones are always listening, but it is pretty difficult to hear them answer." He picked up the child. "What is your name, young man?"

"Pagiel... Are you a Hebrew?" he inquired.

"Yes, right down to *my* bones." And he started tickling him, causing Pagiel to burst into hysterical laughter. Caleb lifted him to his shoulders and headed toward the market. "Let us keep that a secret, okay? Just between you and me."

When Caleb arrived at the infirmary, Donatiya was sitting in a chair, caressing Geuel's bite wound with the herbal concoction Gaddi had left her.

"How is my brother doing?" Caleb inquired. "Any changes?"

"He appears to be slowly improving. He opened his eyes earlier and wondered where he was, and who I was. I managed to get some soup into him, so things are looking better," Donatiya said like an angel. "I think the worst is behind him now. We just have to keep the lesion clean and make sure he gets plenty of fluids, so his body can discharge any remaining poison."

Caleb noticed how tenderly she was cleaning around the two puncture holes on his leg, stopping intermittently to wipe his forehead with a cool, damp cloth. He also noticed that Donatiya looked tired, and wondered if she'd gotten any sleep at all the night before. The small dark bags under her eyes suggested she had not. There seemed to be a connection between the two of them. Caleb recognized the look in her eyes when she turned to wipe Geuel's brow one more time—it was the same look his wife, Ephrath, gave Caleb when she bathed him in the privacy of their tent.

Caleb walked out into the courtyard and had just sat down when a lady walked by and said to him, "Are you a Hebrew, one of the men that came with Joshua? My son, Pagiel, said you were a Hebrew."

Caleb was nervous and did not want to jeopardize their mission. "No, I am afraid your son is mistaken. I am a trader from Egypt, and I do not know anyone named Joshua," he said, getting up and moving to the entrance of the courtyard.

Another group of young ladies passed him, and one stopped and said, "I saw you enter the city with Joshua, that good-looking Israelite general. Is he well?" She smiled covetously.

"Lady, I have never met the man. You are mistaken. I am a simple merchant looking to improve my business here in Hebron," Caleb replied.

The women kept walking, clucking as they went, but the one who had asked the question turned for one last glance and smiled before turning the corner. Caleb started briskly walking in the opposite direction and bumped into two of the four Hittite soldiers who had been in the tavern the night before.

"Stranger, I have seen you before. Are you a Hebrew? Do you serve Joshua, the general of the Israelite army?" he demanded.

"Who?" Caleb struggled to use a little of the Hittite language he had learned from Zidon. "No, I have never heard of that man."

"Rubbish," said the other Hittite. "The way you speak gives you away. You are a Hebrew!"

"I am not, I swear—may God punish me if I am not telling the truth. I do not know that man, nor am I a Hebrew." Caleb moved away as quickly as he could without arousing any more suspicion. He should never have told that little boy Pagiel who he was. Just then a rooster crowed, uncharacteristically for the time of day.[1] Caleb found a deserted area by the stone wall, fell on his knees, and wept bitterly. He hated being a spy. He had denied his faith and abandoned his best friend, all for the sake of this crazy mission.

Caleb had skipped lunch and was positively famished, but he did not feel like eating in the crowded tavern. He purchased some flat-bread and cheese from one of the merchant's stalls and headed back to the infirmary, hoping to get some comfort from Donatiya and Geuel. Donatiya certainly had her charms, but Caleb wondered if she was a bit of an ingenue when it came to the real world. Being the oldest of the spies, he had learned that often with a woman, you sacrificed beauty for intelligence and intelligence for beauty. Ephrath, his wife, was not the most outwardly beautiful woman at Kadesh-Barnea, but she was probably the smartest. She often perceived and comprehended things Caleb completely missed. Once, Shammua had wanted him to join a protest against the foreigners camping at the edges of the Israeli camp. Caleb was going to support his brother, but at the last moment Ephrath stopped him. She explained that his aiding Shammua could be perceived as rebellion, and that the subjects of the protests should be decisions for the governors Moses had chosen. Ephrath said he must choose his battles carefully. It did not hurt to lose a few of them as long as Caleb won the ultimate war. Let Shammua go on his own, she said; there was no personal advantage for Caleb to be involved.

When Caleb arrived at the hospice, Geuel was sitting up, and Donatiya was feeding him a bowl of soup.

"Ma sh'lom'cha," Geuel said in greeting as Caleb entered the room with a smile.

"I am great. The real question is, how are you, my brother?" Caleb fired back.

"Apart from the fact that my leg is the size of a cedar tree and has more colour on it that Joseph's multicoloured fleece, not too bad," he said groggily. "God has sent me an angel to nurse me back to health." He looked at Donatiya with drooping eyes, like a puppy dog asking for a scratch on his ear.

She beamed back.

"Our brothers have gone north to Jebus, and they will pick us up on the way back to camp. Your only mission is to get better," Caleb explained.

"With such a beautiful angel looking after me, I hope it is months before they return."

Caleb noticed how delicately Donatiya blushed as she went over to the window and opened the shutters. The cold twilight air wafted into the room, and the medicinal smells of oregano and mongoose found their way out.

The moon was shining brightly as Phineas, Donatiya's father, passed through the Hebron gate on his camel. He had just spent two days with Abdi-Heba, the governor of Jebus, and Sihon, the leader of the Amorites. Sihon had news that the Israelites had sent a delegation of spies into Canaan to gather information for an invasion into their land. He had battled against them, and said these Israelites were skilled. They had destroyed a platoon of his troops. In Sihon's estimation, the only way to repel the impending attack was to forge an alliance between their Jebusite tribe and his Amorites.

First and foremost, Phineas was a healer. He detested violence, he despised the Amorites, and Sihon embodied everything he hated. It was common knowledge that the Amorites had no family values. They were true nomads without a place to call home. Phineas had dedicated his life to healing the sick, but he also had become the head priest of Molech, a position of which he was very proud. He was very influential in Hebron, and Abdi-Heba knew that without Phineas' co-operation, such an alliance could never be entirely successful. But Phineas did not have much choice. If he did not go along with the plan, Abdi-Heba could make things very difficult for the city of Hebron. Phineas was exhausted from the journey and looked forward to seeing Donatiya and relaxing in his home.

As he entered the small doorway to his home, he heard his daughter talking to somebody in the infirmary. When Donatiya heard his footsteps, she ran to him with her arms extended, gave him a loving hug, and kissed him on both cheeks.

"Come, Father. I want you to meet someone," she said, pulling him by his arm. "Father, this is Geuel. He was bitten by a snake just outside of town, and I have been looking after him."

Geuel, half-naked on the gurney, looked up at Phineas and forced a smile.

"He is an Israelite," she said.

13

DAY TWELVE: FRIDAY, JULY 1 / TAMMUZ 12

City of Jebus
Gaddiel, Son of Sodi
Beware Of Canaanites Bearing Gifts

Gaddiel's head hurt as usual. It was morning in Jebus, and he was unusually tired. He had been up four times to urinate in the night, and he could no longer get more than three hours of uninterrupted sleep at a time.

He reached for his wineskin and took a deep drink. The other spies did not know that while they were drinking water, Gaddiel was drinking wine. He did not want them to see, for they would undoubtedly perceive it as a weakness. He simply enjoyed wine and wanted to be left alone with his enjoyment. It did not affect his abilities—he could fight like the best of them, his speech was unfettered, and his balance remained unaffected. Some accused him of a tendency to flush, but he had inherited that from his father Sodi. It had nothing to do with his wine. He took another swig from the wineskin. He was not unnecessarily aggressive. Most of the time, in fact, he was a pretty happy guy. Sometimes his memory got a little foggy, but other than that, nothing gave away his little secret.

The men were sitting at a table, eating their breakfast. Zidon was drawing a map for Joshua in the dirt, and Igal and Palti were sitting together, whispering. Shaphat, as usual, sat by himself. Sethur had found himself another dog and was trying to teach it to retrieve a stick. Ammiel was explaining to Shammua the significance of the two bronze statues of Isaac and Jacob. Just outside of the courtyard, the clamour of merchants getting ready for their customers reminded Gaddiel that he needed to buy more wine. Because of his habit, he had to sneak away when nobody was watching, make his purchase, and secretly fill his wineskins, usually in a dark alley somewhere.

"I want you to go along the wall surrounding the city and look for weaknesses or access points that could be used by our army," Joshua commanded. "We will meet back at this courtyard midday. Shammua and Shaphat, go north; Sethur, Ammiel, take your dog and go south; Nahbi and Gaddi, walk along the east wall. Palti and Gaddiel, take the west side of the wall."

"If it's okay with you, Joshua, I have an old friend I would like to meet. Is it all right if I return by nightfall?" Zidon asked.

"Of course. This is for the report we will give Moses. No need for you to help today," Joshua replied.

Palti and Gaddiel were no more than a block away when Palti started talking about Joshua. Gaddiel wasn't paying any attention to the gossip. But Palti went on and on about omens and his dream.

"The only thing I want is to stop this madness," Palti said. "We need to go back and tell Moses it is a cursed land with nothing to offer our people."

The only thing I want, Gaddiel thought as he took the last swig in his wineskin, *is to get away from Palti and get some more wine.*

"Peace to you, trader," Abdi-Heba greeted Joshua. "I am Abdi-Heba, the governor of this fine city. Let me welcome you wholeheartedly to Jebus. What is your business here?" he asked politely.

"Peace to you also," Joshua responded. "May God bless you and give you health. We are a small group of merchants who have come a long way to explore business opportunities in your beautiful city."

"How far have you come?"

"From near Egypt. We specialize in carpets and pottery, and I can show you some of our wares if you have the time."

"Wonderful news. We are looking for new suppliers, and you are most welcome. How long will you stay?"

"When we complete our business, we will continue our trip north to Shechem. We might finish today if all goes well and God is willing."

"You have come such a long way. I want to invite you to my palace tonight for a specially prepared feast to celebrate the occasion. I will invite some important local merchants as well, who could perhaps help you in your business inquiries. Will you come?"

Joshua was surprised. "Yes, sure, and thank you for your kindness. May God bless you."

Abdi-Heba smiled condescendingly, turned around, and went toward the market, proud of his ability to manipulate people.

The men returned to the courtyard and gave their report to Joshua. Jebus city was on a hill, with an outcrop of rock that dropped away steeply on three sides. Sitting on top of the city, like an eagle in her nest, was a citadel with a belvedere tower. It overlooked its seemingly impenetrable walls and the surrounding fertile farmlands. There were massive gates on Jebus's northern side that would block the path of any enemy and made the city virtually impregnable. In the north end of the city, there was a large, flat slab of rock where local villagers brought their grain at harvest time, thumping and beating it against the rock until each grain separated from the husk. Cavities in the hollowed-out cliff stored the bountiful grain each harvest would bring.

"The city is strategically located. On this steep hill, there would be no problem defending it against an invader's attack," Shaphat reported.

"They have a never-ending water supply, so a blockade would never work," said Shammua.

"I have not seen it before, but it is brilliant," Ammiel said. "The city is in a flanking position."

"What does that mean?" Gaddiel asked.

"It means their soldiers could leave the fortress, skirt their enemy, and attack from behind," Ammiel explained. "The city is very well designed."

"We would have a challenging time taking Jebus," Igal added. "We would expose our troops to attacks from above if we tried to scale the cliffs. We all agree: the city is impregnable."

"You say they have an unlimited water supply, Shammua?" Joshua asked.

"Yes. It runs east, west, north, and south."

"Does water run uphill in Jebus?" Joshua asked.

All the men looked at him, puzzled.

"Water is the essence of all life," Joshua explained. "If we can find their source and learn how they tunnel it uphill to the city, we would find our opportunity."

Gaddiel smiled and reached for his wineskin.

"I have been invited to the palace of the governor for a feast," Joshua continued. "I want you men to mingle and socialize with the citizens of Jebus tonight and see what you can learn from them. How many fighting men do they have? How well trained are they? And what is their armoury like?"

"You are going alone?" Palti asked.

"I am never alone, Palti. God is with me wherever I go."

"Strange that he did not accept nor allow your sacrifice in Hebron, then," Palti said sarcastically, looking at the other men for support. But all eyes avoided contact with his.

Joshua headed toward the governor's palace. He walked uphill near the white chalkstone boulder that someone had chiselled to look like a giant human skull. The locals called the hill Golgotha, which, loosely translated, meant "the place of the skull." Ammiel had told Joshua that according to legend, the actual skull of Adam was buried there on the hill. Joshua wondered if there were any legends as to where the rest of him could be.

The room at the palace, filled with people, music, and laughter, made him feel comfortable. Abdi-Heba beamed with pride when he saw Joshua enter and motioned to him with his arm to come and sit beside him at the front of the room. The table, lavishly adorned with meat and fruit, was also inviting. Joshua, for a moment, smiled and reflected on how God so often prepared a banquet table for him, where all his enemies could see him as an honoured guest.[1] A young lady was standing beside Abdi-Heba with a large vine of grapes, plucking them one at a time and placing them in his mouth. She noticed Joshua's smile and returned it seductively.

"I am happy you decided to accept my invitation to dine with me tonight, Joshua." Abdi-Heba grinned. "I hope it is the start of a long friendship."

"Thank you for the invitation." Joshua smiled back. "You have a wonderful city. We look forward to the possibility of doing business here."

"Yes, and as you no doubt noticed, the city is safe and secure. We are looking to expand our supplier base, and we welcome a mutually beneficial relationship with such fine merchants as yourselves. Please feel free to mingle and meet our local merchants. If you have any questions, or—may the gods forbid—any troubles, please let me know at once."

It was late when Joshua left the festivity. When he returned to his room, he noticed Zidon standing beside his door.

"What are you doing up so late, Zidon?" Is everything okay?" Joshua questioned.

"Master, I have information that I thought you needed to hear as soon as possible. I visited my friend Yaytis today. Well, he is more like a cousin to me, a distant cousin of my mother's, actually."

"Get to the point, Zidon. It is late." Joshua smiled.

"Yes, yes, of course. Yaytis works in the kitchen of Abdi-Heba—

well, actually not in the kitchen, he works as a server, bringing food and wine."

"What do you want to tell me, Zidon?" Joshua said, more curtly.

"It might be nothing, or it could be important. He told me that he was serving Abdi-Heba and his guest on his balcony this morning. His guest was a giant of a man with scars on his face, a big Amorite. He did not remember his name. He thought it very strange that the man did not leave through the door but through the secret panel behind the fireplace. He could hardly get through the opening; the passage leads underground to the outskirts of the city."'

"Good information, Zidon, thank you. "Now, off to bed you go. Get your beauty sleep."

Could it be Sihon? Joshua thought. *What would he be doing in Jebus?*

14

DAY THIRTEEN: JULY 2 / TAMMUZ 13

Shabbat

15

DAY FOURTEEN: SUNDAY, JULY 3 / TAMMUZ 14

The City of Jebus
Joshua, Son of Nun
It Is Not Scrutiny, It Is Mutiny

Joshua had sensed something phony about Abdi-Heba's behaviour during the feast. He could not put his finger on precisely what it was, and at this point, two days later, it did not matter. They would be leaving this morning with all the information they needed. Hopefully, the next time he came to Jebus would be with Moses and their whole army. His biggest concern now was the men, especially Palti. All their talk about omens was craziness. He should never have allowed Zidon a free hand with that mandrake. The men were calling him stubborn and obdurate behind his back. They were blaming him for all the unlucky events that had happed since they had left Kadesh-Barnea. He had to be mentally strong. The indomitable spirit always wins. First, they ignore you; then they discreetly ridicule you. Then they fight you, and then you win. Joshua knew this, for he had been mentored by Moses, the most indomitable spirit-man he had ever known.

Joshua entered the crowded courtyard and immediately noticed that the men were already sitting on the benches. The look on their faces signified something was up. He did not feel like being challenged at such an early hour.

"Good morning, brothers. I trust everyone slept well. Have you all had breakfast already?"

"We need to have a meeting with you, Joshua," Shammua uttered nervously. "All of us."

"Of course. What is on your mind, Shammy?"

Zidon got up and left the courtyard, aware of what was going to be said.

"We are not going any further with you, Joshua," Palti blurted out. "There are too many bad omens. We think we should turn around and go back to Kadesh-Barnea."

Joshua looked each man directly in the eyes to see if there were any dissenters. He wished Caleb were there with him for support.

"So you want to take charge, lead the group, Palti?" he said sternly, as the muscles on his jaws tightened.

"You have not listened to us, Joshua. You want to do things only your way, and we see what happens when you decide things," Ammiel continued. "You let that Amorite live, and he escaped. You insist on us travelling together instead of in smaller, more productive teams. God rejected your sacrifice in Hebron, Geuel was poisoned by that snake, Hebo and the Kenite hunting party were slaughtered, and now we have news that our enemies have allied. Logic says this mission is over."

"We have enough information," Igal piped in. "Joshua, it is time for us to go home. This is not a land in which I want to raise my children. Moses needs to know." He glanced around at the other nodding heads. "And then there were the visions we had, all three of us: Palti, Ammiel, and I. In the absence of your God talking to you, we had dreams. It seems, for whatever reason, that God is speaking to us and not you."

"Do all of you feel this way?" Joshua asked quietly.

They all slowly nodded in unison, including Shaphat.

Joshua took his time, stood up slowly, and shouted, "*Then choke on the disrespect you have shown me today, you mutinous brood of vipers!*" He bent over the table, took his arm, and swept away everything in front of him, knocking plates, cups, and candles to the floor with an ear-splitting boom. When he stood up, spittle had formed at the corners of his mouth and dripped down his beard. His eyes were flaming with anger.

The men's faces were ashen in fear, and they were as quiet as the rats that scurried over to inspect the new food offerings on the floor.

Joshua couldn't get to his horse quickly enough. Things would never be the same; how could they be? Behind him he heard footsteps. Gaddi was calling his name repeatedly. Joshua kept walking, ignored the sounds behind him, kicked his horse into a gallop, and left a dust storm behind him.

Gaddi walked back into the courtyard, covered in dust. "He is gone."

"Good riddance. It isn't what we wanted to happen, but if he wants to go without us, then that is his decision," Palti chirped. "All he had to do was to listen to us and call this crazy expedition off. He took it personally."

"What do we do now?" Sethur probed.

"We cannot return to camp without Joshua," Ammiel added. "I think we should break up into three groups of three men and explore the land our way. Nobody is going to pay any attention to us in such small numbers. Joshua must come back this way eventually, and we will meet him then. We have twenty-eight days to get back to Kadesh-Barnea, and we can see a lot of Canaan in that amount of time. We just need to leave a couple of men here in Jebus to keep an eye out for Joshua's return."

"I will stay," Shammua volunteered, thinking about the prostitutes he had spotted in the tavern the night before.

"Me too," Gaddiel chimed in selfishly. He had found some exciting wine selections and a great wine merchant with whom he had bonded.

"Okay, it is settled. We will have two groups of two men and one group of three," Ammiel decided.

"Where is Zidon?" asked Shaphat.

"He left after Joshua did, probably to follow him since he feels still in his debt," Sethur said. "Crazy old man. Whose horse did he take?"

"He did not take a horse. He took one of the camels," Gaddi said.

Joshua felt he was a patient man, especially for being only twenty-two years old, but he was fuming. He had not asked to lead this mission but accepted the responsibility without question. The men did not say it out loud, but they were questioning his competence. He could see in Palti's wolf-eyed accusations: abuse of power, conflict of interest, and misuse of his position as leader. What did he offer as proof? Omens? Drug-induced dreams? Joshua's show of mercy to an enemy? Joshua's immediate reaction was to let them rot in Jebus, but then he had second thoughts. Maybe he should have tried to explain things, reason with them. Perhaps he could have just asserted himself and crushed the revolt. Perhaps he should go back and try to resolve it—after all, they were all picked by Moses.

No, he decided, *I will go north and try to find them later when I have finished what I started.* He felt betrayed.

Joshua had two fathers: Nun, his biological father, and Moses, his spiritual father. He knew Moses was grooming him to take his place when he died. He had gone up the mountain with Moses to receive the Ten Commandments. Moses had put him charge of all military operations and battles. Moses had taught him as much wisdom and knowledge as he could withstand, and sometimes, Joshua was not sure he wanted any more. He understood that his destiny was unchangeable. But for the moment, his anger surged through his veins, and he tried to put as many cubits as possible between him and Jebus.

Sihon was sitting in his tent, wolfing down a large foreleg of wild boar, when Abdi-Heba's messenger arrived at his camp on his sweltering stallion. A mixture of translucent grease and blood were splattered over Sihon's face. Black flies and gnats fed on the morsels that fell on his beard. Sihon was not sure what bothered him more, the nasty insects or the vexatious Jebusite messenger who stood before him looking like a worm. The messenger had facial features that reminded him of Abdi-Heba. He remembered standing on the balcony with Abdi-Heba the day before, observing Joshua and the Israelites eating their breakfast. The Israelites looked like ordinary traders. Were it not for Sihon, Abdi-Heba would not have seen the danger.

"You see now? The Hebrew pigs will measure your city so they can come later to destroy it," Sihon commented.

"Never!" Abdi-Heba exclaimed naively. "We have a treaty with their respected forefather Abraham. They will not and cannot strike our city unless we agree. The statues bear witness to the covenant he made with us."

"Do you think that these low-life animals would honour a five-hundred-year-old covenant?" Sihon argued. "There is only one way to guarantee the safety of your city, and that is to kill them all before they kill you."

"Where do you think they are going?" Abdi-Heba said nervously as he watched them split up into groups of two.

"It does not matter what they do today. I know they are moving north tomorrow or perhaps the next day, and I will be waiting for them. Abdi-Heba, go to them and welcome them into your city. Attend to their every need, allow them to let down their guard and relax. When they tell you they are merchants looking for new business venues, tell them you, too, are looking to expand your supplier base, and that a mutually beneficial relationship with such fine merchants would be welcome.

"The minute they leave Jebus, send a messenger to my camp on the hill of Gerizim on the outskirts of Shechem. I will prepare a different kind of welcome for them." Sihon grinned and left abruptly.

It was dusk when the messenger arrived at Sihon's camp. He had ridden hard and fast. He grimaced as Sihon looked him over; the Amorite's expression was indeed a frightful thing to witness.

"Abdi-Heba sends his greetings, Sihon, and hopes all is well. The Hebrew leader, Joshua, has just left Jebus. He should pass below Gerizim Mountain just before sundown."

"Wonderful news, Jebusite!" Sihon threw his half-gnawed pig appendage to the dogs sitting at his feet in his marquee, all of them fighting with each other for dominance.

Turning to his soldiers, he commanded, "Assemble the men!"

There were three rows of fighters, eight men in each row. The Jebusite regulars stood in the front, and behind them, at attention, were the Hittites. Behind those were the large Amorites.

"Our gods, Chemosh, Ashtoreth, and Molech, join forces with us today for a particular reason. Our ancestors were fully aware of the chaos and anarchy the Hebrew people, who call themselves Israelites, bring to our land. They were victims of their treachery six hundred years ago. As we stand here on our sacred ground, our enemies pound and threaten at our door, waiting for their spies to find our weaknesses and report back to their army. We will not permit them to do that. Their general, Joshua, will be here shortly, and I do not want you to kill him—that pleasure is reserved for me. You will capture him and bring him to our camp. Now go with the blessing of Chemosh, Ashtoreth, and Molech!"

They scrambled onto their horses and raced down the narrow pathway to the valley at the bottom of Mount Gerizim, the only access to the city of Shechem. They tied up their horses in the scrub bushes, away from the clearing where Joshua would have to pass, and hid quietly behind a group of thick tamarisk trees, ready for their ambush.

The sun was still scorching hot, but it would not be very long before it sank behind the horizon. The only sounds were the honeybees on the lavender and a mother crow barking commands to her fledglings as they flopped and staggered on the ground around Sihon's assassins. The Hittites, skilled with the bow, would firstly fire their arrows as a warning for Joshua to stop. The Amorites would block his flank, making sure he could not retreat. Then the Jebusites would create a wall, fencing Joshua in, and take him prisoner. His capture would be any moment now. They just had to wait.

16

DAY FIFTEEN: MONDAY, JULY 4 / TAMMUZ 15

Near the Town of Gibeah
Heaven Rejoices at the Miracle of Conversion

Zidon was pulling some flatbread apart when his camel bayed loudly outside the window and woke Joshua. Zidon tiptoed over to the fireplace and stirred the aromatic concoction simmering on the fire.

"Ouch," he cried as he pulled his hand away quickly, fanned it in the air, and put his burned finger in his mouth to ease the pain. The pungent bouquet of the liquid filled the small, flat-roofed, mud-brick shack where they had slept overnight. It was only one floor and three rooms: the home of a poor man. There were no other buildings around it, and the courtyard was small. The main room had two beds against each wall, a fire hearth where the food was prepared, and a place where the food was stored. Zidon scooped a goblet into the pot and filled it with the brew.

"Here, master, drink this. It will give you strength," Zidon said as he stood over Joshua's curled-up body.

Joshua, still groggy, rolled over and yawned. "What is it? You did not put that mandrake in it, did you?

Zidon chuckled. "No, this is an exceptional mixture of honey and goat's milk, with some special herbs. It is a drink my grandmother used to make for me when I was little. She used to tell me it was a special nectar of the gods that would bring me immortality. She said that when you drink it, no longer do you have mortal blood flowing through your veins; it changes into what she called *ichor*, giving you strength and energy."

Joshua rolled his eyes then took a sip. "Hmmm. Not bad, old man."

Joshua understood that Zidon was happy when he could please him—probably because Zidon would not be alive if it were not for the Hebrew spies. Sethur had saved him from Jokian's arrow, but it was Joshua who paid the exorbitant amount of gold for his release. So Zidon had been delighted to find Joshua on the road to Shechem the night before. Joshua's horse had trodden in a giant rat hole and maimed herself. When Zidon had found him about five thousand cubits outside of Jebus, Joshua was having a rare temper tantrum, smashing dead branches across an old tamarisk tree, shouting and screaming in anger. He was like an angry fifteen-year-old, venting his fury where nobody could see him. Beside the tree, Joshua had compassionately put his horse out of its misery.

Joshua had been thinking about walking back to Jebus, but Zidon convinced him to come to his brother-in-law's farmhouse, which was not far from there. Joshua was happy to agree; there was just too much tension between him and the other spies. He was feeling low, deserted, and he needed to escape from all the stress and tension. He had to collect his thoughts. And Zidon compassionately listened to his grumblings. Joshua saw in his eyes the kind-heartedness and benevolence a father would show his son. The Canaanites were not that much different from the Israelites. The full moon, glowing in all her immaculate purity, illuminated the trail to Zidon's brother-in-law's property as brightly as Zidon's compassionate heart radiated love and loyalty to Joshua.

Zidon's god was Baal-Jebus, the supreme god of his land. There was a Baal-Beersheba and a Baal-Hebron, but because Zidon grew up close to his brother-in-law, his god was Baal-Jebus. Zidon never knew his biological father; his mother was impregnated when she was only sixteen during one of the rituals she attended at the temple. His mother and grandparents had raised him on their little farm and struggled to make ends meet. According to Zidon, Baal-Jebus gave them light and warmth and sometimes a great harvest. Zidon remembered quite a few summers ago when the fierce heat of a drought destroyed their crops. His young cousin, Hermot, was sacrificed to appease Baal's anger. Zidon clearly remembered the screams and the smell of charred flesh as Hermot was burned alive. The priests called such a sacrifice "passing through the fire,"[1] and it was a regular practice performed to appease Baal and regain his favour. When Zidon's brother-in-law built his home, the home Zidon and Joshua now occupied, he buried Hermot in the foundation of the house to ensure Baal's future blessings upon his family.

Zidon explained that it was on the flat top of the roof where they placed the altar, burned incense, and prayed to their Baal[2] in the evenings.

"I confess that I serve a cruel god. There can be no other way to explain why my daughter and wife were snatched away from me so brutally, and so long before their time. I am sure there was a reason, but I am not smart enough to figure it out."

"I am not sure there is anyone that intelligent," Joshua murmured.

"You see, Joshua, in my mind, there is no such thing as a coincidence. Just because you cannot see a reason for something happening does not mean it just randomly happened. Everything that happens to you is a personal gift from the gods, good and bad. It is what you do with that gift, how you react, that is important. Every event has meaning, but only the person experiencing it can interpret it, give it shape and sense. Perhaps God took my wife and daughter away because there was a better life for them in a different world. They could be spared pain and sickness in this world. Maybe the Hittites chained and sold me into slavery so I could meet and be part of the Hebrew team. That is possible, do you not think, Joshua?"

"Yes, I believe all things are possible," Joshua responded.

"Listen to me. I am doing all the talking as usual. My wife used to complain about it all the time. Tell me more about yourself. You said you come from the tribe of Ephraim—who was the founder of your tribe?" Zidon asked.

"Joseph, Jacob's favourite son."

"Tell me about him, would you? I wish I knew more about my ancestors."

"Joseph had eleven brothers and a sister. His brothers were very jealous of him because he was very close to his father, and they plotted to kill him. They had a hard time bringing themselves to commit the actual act, however, so they sold him to merchants travelling to Egypt and feigned his death by putting animal blood on his tunic. They brought the bloodstained jacket to his father so nobody would go looking for him. In Egypt, the slave traders sold Joseph to the captain of the guard, a man named Potiphar, and he became his servant. When Potiphar's wife tried to seduce Joseph, and he refused, she accused him of rape, and he was thrown into the dungeon to die. But the warden of the prison eventually put him in charge of other prisoners.

"Shortly afterward, two of the pharaoh's close assistants offended the pharaoh and were sent in chains to the same prison as Joseph. While in prison, they both had puzzling dreams, and Joseph managed to interpret their dreams for them. One of the servants would end up executed, he said, while the other would be forgiven and restored to his duties in the pharaoh's palace. This was precisely what happened.

"Two years later, the pharaoh had a dream that none of his advisors could understand. The assistant who had been in prison remembered Joseph's name and told the pharaoh, who sent for him. Joseph carefully listened to the dream. After some time and prayer, Joseph told the pharaoh its meaning: there would be seven years of abundance in Egypt and then seven years of drought, and the pharaoh should store surplus grain for the coming famines.

"The pharaoh was grateful and appointed Joseph as vizier of all of Egypt. Joseph's prediction came true, and even though the famines were terrible, Egypt had plenty of grain in its storehouses. All the surrounding nations came to Egypt to buy grain from Joseph, including his eleven brothers and, eventually, his father."

"What a story." Zidon looked amazed. "Does it have a happy ending?"

"Yes, a delightful ending." Joshua beamed with pride. "The Israelites survived the famine thanks to Joseph's generosity. And then they all went to live happily ever after in Egypt, protected by Joseph's authority."

"So your God is in control during calamities as well as good times?"

"Yes, he directs all events and occurrences."

Zidon looked at Joshua cunningly. "Joshua, do you think there is a reason your men revolted against you? Do you think there is a reason your horse was maimed and you had to destroy him? Do you think I just happened to find you?"

Joshua was speechless. He had an illuminating realization that he had underestimated Zidon. This old man, this pagan, was reminding him that God was all-powerful and ordered all events to his divine purpose.

Joshua smiled an impish smile and took another drink of his ambrosia, which was now getting cold. But when he attempted to stand up, he grabbed the table as pain shot through his leg.

"Are you okay?"

"I must have twisted my ankle when my horse fell yesterday," Joshua said, rubbing his leg.

Zidon bent over and pulled Joshua's tunic up to his knee. "Yes, I can see there is a lot of swelling. You need to take a couple of days and rest it. If you don't, it will only get worse."

"Why are you so kind to me, old man, and why do you stay with me?"

"Firstly, you are my master. You bought and paid for me."

"But I set you free, and you are no longer a slave."

"Secondly, you have shown me kindness and respect. If you permit, I will serve you along your journey and return with you to

Kadesh-Barnea. Do you accept old men into your tribe and faith? I have no home anymore, and the god of my ancestors is cruel and unforgiving. I know nothing of your faith, but I am a fast learner."

"Our God is for everyone, Hebrew and Gentile alike. He would welcome you as a father welcomes his lost son."

"What must I do?"

"Everything you know about spirituality until now will be irrelevant, and in most cases wrong. You must drop the religious beliefs taught to you all your life. If this is too difficult for you to do, then you should not pursue this journey. We have laws, and we have covenants; these are what elevates a person and what lowers him. We humans do not make those determinations—only our God does. These directions are in our holy scrolls, the law of Moses,[3] for our guidance and schooling. But more than all this, it is by faith that we Hebrews win God's approval."

"And what is faith?"

"To have faith is to be sure of things we hope for and to be certain of things we cannot see. It is by faith that we understand God's Word created the world. No one can please God without faith, for whoever comes to God must have faith that He exists, and that he rewards those who seek Him."

"I believe with my heart, Joshua. Please help my unbelief in my head. Rest your leg for a few days, and teach me about your God. I will, in return, draw you a map and show you the best routes north so you can complete your mission—if you take me along so I can assist you. My brother-in-law is out searching for a suitable horse replacement for you, and he will find you something good."

"Let me start by making you supper for all your kindness, Zidon; we Israelites make an extraordinary meal. It goes a long way back into our history. Isaac, the son of Abraham, had two sons, Jacob and Esau. Esau was a great hunter and outdoorsman, and Jacob was a scholar as well as an accomplished chef. One day Esau came back from a hunting trip and was famished. Jacob had just cooked a special stew and was sitting down, meticulously enjoying every mouthful. Esau said, 'Please let me have a swallow of that red stuff you are eating.'

"Jacob thought about it and craftily said, 'Of course, brother, but first sell me your birthright.' As you know, Zidon, our birthright is the sacred position of the first-born, and Esau was the first-born. He was the holder of the inheritance, next in line to carry the family lineage of our patriarch, Abraham. Esau said carelessly, 'Seeing as I am going to die of hunger, what use is the birthright to me anyway?' And before giving him this special stew—which must have smelled delicious, to make Esau so willing—Jacob made him swear an oath.[4] When we Israelites swear a promise, it is to the death; it cannot ever be broken. So Esau sold his birthright, and Jacob fed him his special lentil stew." Jacob smiled. "This special stew is what I would like to make tonight: Jacob's stew. Let us see what your brother-in-law has in his food storage area."

Joshua limped over to the food closet and inspected its contents. He grabbed three carrots, three stalks of celery, and a large onion out of baskets on the bottom shelf. He found jars of spices and selected one half cup of coriander, one clove of garlic, and a bay leaf. Joshua was impressed with how organized he kept his supplies. Rummaging around, he discovered the other spices needed. He took a small scoop of hyssop and two scoops of cumin and put them in a bowl. They were plenty of dry red lentils and pearl barley, so he took two cups of lentils and one quarter cup of barley and put them in a separate bowl on the table. After moving the containers around, he finally found the sumac and put one half scoop in the bowl with the hyssop and cumin. All he needed now was olive oil.

Joshua strained to remember how his mother cooked this dish, which he had watched her do many times. He roughly chopped the cilantro and scrubbed the skin off the carrots, then cut them and the celery into small chunks. He found a medium-sized pot and put it over the fire, adding the olive oil and diced onions. The room began to smell like his mother's tent when he was a child. Once the onions started to turn translucent, Joshua added the garlic, along with the carrot chunks and celery, stirring the ingredients all the time. Finally, when the onions began to caramelize, he quickly added the red lentils and barley to the pot, stirring regularly. He poured in two quarts of water, flavoured the mixture with some chicken broth that Zidon had found, and brought everything to a boil. He moved the pot to the highest position in the hearth, so the mixture would simmer slowly, and added the cilantro, cumin, hyssop, sumac, and bay leaf. He vigorously stirred the contents, put a cover on the pot, and smiled at Zidon, who was staring at him in amazement.

Zidon was not sure what going to happen tomorrow, but tonight they would feast.

17

DAY SIXTEEN: TUESDAY, JULY 5 / TAMMUZ 16

The City of Jebus
Unfettered, Unfeigned Love

It was still dark outside when Simonas pounded loudly on her door. Donatiya was having such a beautiful dream: she and Geuel were running hand in hand through a barley field into a lovely undulating meadow with all the spring flowers in blossom. There was a blanket on the grass, and a feast that someone had prepared for them. The smell of lavender was intoxicating. Geuel gently lifted her and sat down on the blanket, under the shade of a tree loaded with green pistachios. Geuel leaned over, brushed her cheek, looked longingly into her in her eyes, and...

Boom, boom, boom. She started sinking through her cotton bedsheet, down through her wooden bed frame and away from her dream. She desperately reached toward Geuel as she fell, grasping for his hair, his tunic, anything that would keep her there with him. Then *boom, boom, boom* again. She opened her eyes and panicked until she recognized her water vessel on the small table by her bed.

"Donatiya, come quickly," Simonas cried loudly.

She rubbed her eyes, quickly dressed, and grabbed her satchel.

She followed Simonas four blocks to his two-storey, mudstone shack. She passed the primitive ovens and ran up the makeshift stairs behind Simonas. In the room were his five scantily dressed children with their dishevelled sleep hair, all attending to their mother as she screamed at regular intervals.

"Bring me some clean rags and boil some water on the fire. Then all of you go downstairs. You can help your dad prepare his bread loaves for today." She said this with authority but wrapped her command with a kind smile. After a quick examination, she noticed that the baby was in a breech position, upside down. Donatiya had delivered many of the local babies, and she loved doing it, but she knew that a breech baby had little chance of surviving. If the choice were between the baby's life and the mother's, she had to choose the mother. She had to turn the baby around before it could exit, and unless she could unwrap the umbilical cord from its neck, the result would be disastrous. She worked rapidly and meticulously between the contractions.

Donatiya's demeanour was calm and relaxed, and after each contraction, she reassured the mother everything would be all right. The labour continued, and the screaming came faster and louder. Simonas ran upstairs to check what was happening.

"Get out!" Donatiya ordered, her face covered in sweat and her patience dwindling. "Go back downstairs and look after your children. Send one of them to get my father. I might need some help."

There was another contraction and an even louder scream. Donatiya was unable to turn the baby around. "I know you want to push, but don't, not yet," she said in her loudest voice. "It is important. Wait for me to tell you when." Her only option now was to deliver the baby feet first. She grabbed the baby's feet, squeezed them together, and pulled gently—one more contraction.

"Now push hard," Donatiya screamed, louder than her patient. "And again. Push hard, don't stop." The baby was now halfway out. She managed to find the cord and, with her fingers, slipped it away from its neck. "One more time... *push, push, push!*"

The last scream was blood-curdling, enough to wake everyone

within a six-block radius, and then, after the shriek, came the sound of a baby crying, distraught over his new surroundings. Donatiya quickly cut the cord and cleaned the blood and mucus from the tiny boy with a damp cloth.

"Congratulations. You have a strong, healthy son who likes to do things his way," she exclaimed, nestling the baby boy in a swaddling blanket. She looked lovingly into his red, wrinkly face and perfect nose and ears. Something inside her longed to have her very own baby, and she wondered whom her baby would look like more—her, or would it be Geuel?

Simonas and Phineas, both heavy-eyed, were standing in the doorway, beaming with pride, Simonas for his new son and Phineas for his daughter's well-learned abilities.

"I guess you did not need me after all," Phineas said as they went down the stairs and out to the street together. "Come, daughter, let us go home. You need to clean up, as you have a visitor this morning."

"Yes, I must clean myself up, but I am busy most of the morning, Father. Who is your visitor?"

"I have been talking to Yassin, our butcher. His son Danel has expressed interest in you, and I think it would be a good match."

"A good match? He expressed interest, did he? Am I a piece of meat in Yassin's inventory that can be traded or sold?" she said angrily.

"But Donatiya, you are not getting younger, and even I see how you look upon the babies you deliver, wanting your own. It is time to think about these things. I am getting older, and I want to live to see my successor."

"And you think Danel, with his long nose, skinny legs, and goat breath, will produce an heir you can be proud of?" she said haughtily.

"Donatiya, Donatiya, beauty is only skin deep. He comes from a good and wealthy family and is faithful to Chemosh."

"Then you marry him, Father. I will pick the man I will marry, and it will be someone I love."

She stormed off to her small room to wash and change. As she staggered into her room and shut the door, for a second, she could not breathe. She put her hands to her face and broke down sobbing. How could this be? This was not what she expected for her life; it was her worst nightmare. She wanted to tell her father how she felt toward Geuel, but she did not yet know Geuel's feelings. There were moments when she caught him looking at her, and there were times when he brushed against her for no reason. But she had to know for sure before she told her father. She put a cold cloth on her eyes to reduce the swollenness from her crying. She dabbed a small amount of red ochre on her cheeks so she did not look so tired. She brushed her hair three hundred times, as was her habit, put on her white, Egyptian-cotton dress, and went down the hall to the infirmary to see Geuel.

Geuel heard her footsteps, and his heart began to flutter. He had memorized what she sounded like when she walked and knew it was precisely twenty-seven steps from her room to where he lay. He counted the steps when she left, heard the door to her room open, and then counted them again when she came to see him. From his seated position, he quickly scurried under the sheet that covered him and tried to look as helpless as he could.

"Good morning. How is my snake patient this morning?" Donatiya asked, putting on the biggest smile she could.

"Everything hurts today, and I think I need some special attention," Geuel joked.

Donatiya checked his wound, which was healing quite nicely. The swelling on his leg had subsided, and the black-and-blue bruising was almost gone. She cleaned the injury and applied the mixture of herbs with a fresh compress.

"Is something wrong, Donatiya? You are not your usual happy self today."

"No, everything is okay. I was up early delivering a baby, so I might seem a bit tired."

"Are you sure everything went okay? It looks like you were crying."

Donatiya was amazed at how intuitive he was. Should she tell him about the conversation with her father? She forced another smile. "Yes, a baby boy. It was a breech, but both mother and son are healthy."

Geuel reached out and took her hand. She remembered her dream, and she could not help it—she started sobbing again.

"What is it? What is the matter?"

"Father wants me to marry the butcher's son Danel. I hate him, and he is ugly."

"Someone as beautiful as you should be able to choose whom you marry."

"Truly, you think I am beautiful?"

"Your beauty eclipses the bewitching magic of the silvery moonlight." Geuel was a bit embarrassed and wondered where that had come from.

Donatiya blushed but did not take her eyes off the man she loved. "And how many times have you said that to a sobbing woman?"

He leaned forward and gave her a small kiss on her cheek. "If you marry that meat man, I will find one hundred snakes and let their poison replace every drop of blood that I have in my veins." He reached for her hand affectionately and drew her toward him. She felt the cord that was strangling the life out of her slip away from her neck. She wanted to cry as loud as the baby she delivered this morning, only tears of relief this time.

She leaned over him, smiled in trepidation, and returned the kiss, but this time she parted her full lips and pressed them hard onto his, just as her father Phineas walked into the infirmary.

"What in the name of Chemosh is going on here?" he shouted.

Donatiya kept her lips fastened to Geuel's and moved her hands to the back of his head, totally unresponsive to her father's intrusion into her new world.

Phineas grabbed Donatiya and jerked her away.

"Go to your room!" And with his arm shaking in anger, he pointed at Geuel. "And you, get out of my infirmary, and leave my house and my family alone."

Donatiya, sobbing, ran her twenty-seven steps and slammed the door to her room behind her. Phineas followed behind, shaking his head in disbelief.

Geuel found his tunic and his personal belongings, dressed quickly, and slinked out the back door. He would try to talk to Phineas tomorrow when the old man cooled down. Right now, he needed to find Caleb and tell him what had happened. He felt like he had just been run over by a chariot.

18

DAY SEVENTEEN: WEDNESDAY, JULY 6 / TAMMUZ 17

City of Hebron
The Vanquishing Venom of Love

Donatiya had avoided her father almost the whole day before, remaining locked in her room. Phineas, from time to time, would knock on her door and call out to her, but she was more than angry at him. She did not have a right to be angry, Phineas thought; it was he who was incensed. It was bad enough that he'd caught his daughter kissing another man, but it was horrible when he considered who she was kissing. He was an Israelite, a Hebrew. Phineas had made a pact with Abdi-Heba and that scoundrel Sihon to destroy them before they destroyed their culture and people. He was a high priest and spokesman for Chemosh, and his daughter was betraying him. How could he lead his people if he could not lead his family? Abdi-Heba had sent a messenger to him, explaining Sihon's plan of ambush, and Joshua and his men would be dead by now. Soon they would be coming to kill Geuel and his friend Caleb, the only two spies left in Hebron, and now perhaps even his daughter.

Phineas needed to go to his temple and ask Chemosh to help him figure everything out. The temple was the most beautiful building in Hebron, much more elegant than the mayor's palace. Lavishly equipped with small faience objects, rattles, bowls, cat figurines, and ivory clappers, the temple reeked of affluence. There were four nude gold statues of their fertility goddess Ashtoreth, all in different poses, one in each corner of the temple. Precisely in the centre of the shrine, there was a vast, hollow brass statue with the enormous head of a bull and the bulging belly of a man. On his back were gigantic wings. The bull's laughing mouth was wide open, as were his oversized eyes. Inside his stomach was a firebox that could be kindled and kept stoked for hours before any ceremony. So many times in the past, Phineas had officiated the sacrifice, leading a child by the hand, placing them on Chemosh's[1] downward-sloping hands, and then rolling them into the fire. The sacrament's official name was "passing through the fire to Molech."[2]

It was an honour to have your child chosen. During a ceremonial service, the whole area in front of the statue of Chemosh was filled with worshippers clapping their hands and making loud noises of praise with their flutes and drums to engulf the wailing cries of the sacrificed children. How could they expect Chemosh to give so much if they were not willing to provide him with their most precious? Outsiders unfamiliar with their customs and dogmas were often shocked when they heard of the 'passing through the fire' ceremony. But for Phineas and his followers, sacrificing to Chemosh was in no way violent or cruel. Phineas hated the violence and pointless killing for which Sihon and his band of Amorites were famous. Phineas did not kill—he sacrificed for the atonement and favour of his god Chemosh. It was very different.

The strangers that came to the temple enjoyed the unrestricted sexual orgies offered to Chemosh: man with man, woman with woman, multiple partners. That was fine and acceptable, but some struggled to watch a perfect child being offered to Chemosh in exchange for the perfectly created life they had received. It was an unbeliever's logic he did not understand. You could not eat a delicious piece of pie and then throw out what was left because you didn't like it. With Chemosh, it was all or nothing; unless you performed something thoroughly, it was not acceptable. Half-heartedness will not do.

Being the high priest, it was his duty to defend knowledge of Chemosh against opposing religions. He was aware of the Hebrew faith and its many glaring contradictions. They had only one God. How could only one God have the time or interest to be involved in everyone's lives? Impossible—that was why the Canaanites had so many personal gods. They had Chemosh, his father El, Ashtoreth, Baal, and Dagon. More significant, the Israelites looked to the Hebrew God as their heavenly father. This heavenly father told them what to do, but their thoughts and actions were mostly contrary to their God's way.

Phineas's gods had no problem with the Canaanites' earthly nature or desires. In fact, they encouraged them—but demanded payment in exchange for such god-given pleasures. The Canaanites made their plans and then asked their gods to help them. Sometimes they helped, sometimes they did not. The Hebrews would ask their God for a project and then strictly follow His directions. The Canaanites' religion was man-initiated; the Hebrew religion was God-initiated. Phineas had been a healer and high priest for more than forty years, and he had never heard Chemosh or any other god speak to him. Gods didn't talk to people, and they worked alongside you. If he had to wait to hear what Chemosh instructed him to do, he would have been waiting forever. He knew what Chemosh wanted, so he just did it, and hopefully he did not make any mistakes. If he did, there would be a famine, or death, or some other tragedy. If that happened, Phineas would simply pass another child through the fire to Chemosh and win back his favour. Chemosh loved innocent virgins and children. It was a simple formula, and it had worked for years.

As Phineas was walking out of the temple to return home, he

worried about Donatiya's disgrace. Never mind what Sihon and Abdi-Heba would think—what would his parishioners think? His perfect record as high priest would be stained, tarnished to the point where he could lose his prestigious position.

Then it hit him like the sure path of the Amorite arrow. If Donatiya would not listen to him and give up that Israelite, he would arrange for Donatiya to pass through the fire. He would kill two birds with one stone. He would keep her from being with that pig, and at the same time, he would win respect for offering up his only child. He smiled and silently thanked Chemosh for the brilliant idea.

Caleb knocked three times quietly on Donatiya's door.

"Go away, Father," she shouted. "I don't want to talk to you."

"It is Caleb, and I have a message from Geuel."

She quickly unlocked and opened the door. Although her eyes were swollen and puffy, she looked beautiful.

"Geuel sent me, as he was sure your father would not let him into your home. He wants to meet you secretly by the tombs."

Her face turned from a frown to a smile instantaneously, and it lit up the entire room. "Father is at the temple, and I can sneak out right away. Is Geuel feeling all right? Can he walk?"

Now it was Caleb's turn to smile. "Yes, he is fine—limping a little bit and in need of his wooden staff, but he is more concerned about you and your father's anger. Come. Let's go quickly."

As she followed Caleb, she started to panic about the kiss she'd shared with Geuel. It had felt awkward but terrific, which was why she'd kissed him the second time. She hoped that Geuel had liked it. She had never kissed anyone other than her father before. It just happened, and all the strange feelings that raged through her body confused her. She hoped they would share many more kisses in the future, and she was sure she could get better at it. It had all been over so quickly.

Geuel waited nervously on a large stone to see if Caleb had been successful in fetching Donatiya. In the infirmary, when he'd looked into her soft blue eyes, his heart had burned like a house on fire. His invisible tears had stained his cheeks and unsuccessfully attempted to put the fire out in his heart. Her beauty took his breath away. She was a perfect untouched flower in this wilderness of dust, void of any evil and overflowing with kindness and goodness. Her fragrance was more hypnotic than the effects of any mandrake root. What was he to do? He felt like that old tamarisk tree growing beside the cave. How would he be able to give her shade from life's scorching problems?

Caleb had warned him that nothing good could come out of having a relationship with her. They were on a short mission and would return to Kadesh-Barnea in twenty-five days. And Phineas would never, if he lived to be one thousand years old, give his Canaanite daughter to an Israelite in marriage. Caleb understood that the heart did not always listen to the brain, but he was asking Geuel to make the largest sacrifice of his short twenty-six years: if he truly loved Donatiya, he had to cut her loose. For her benefit.

When Donatiya came around the corner with Caleb and saw Geuel, she ran to him and threw her arms around him. Caleb moved away to give them privacy.

"I am so sorry that my father insulted you and threw you out. Please forgive me." Tears flowed afresh from her exquisite eyes.

"It was not your fault, Donatiya; it was mine. I was out of order in giving you that kiss."

"It was not much of a kiss. That is why I gave you another one." She giggled. "I want to come with you when you leave. I will not stay in Hebron any longer. I want to be with you."

"But this is your home, and your father will need your help. You have your culture, and the way you live is so much different than the way we live." Geuel searched for some inner courage and better words to say.

"I do not want to live without you, Geuel. Do you not understand?"

Now Geuel felt real tears rolling down his cheeks.

"If you will take me as your wife," she said, "I will renounce my religion and embrace your God. I love you with all of my heart, Geuel."

The tears he did not realize he possessed were now uncontrollable. Geuel did not know what to say, so he embraced her, put his head on her shoulder, and stroked the back of her head.

19

DAY EIGHTEEN: THURSDAY, JULY 7 / TAMMUZ 18

Kadesh-Barnea
Moses, Son of Amram
The Tabernacle in the Wilderness

It was a hot, dry morning in Kadesh-Barnea, and Moses, as was his habit when the sun began to rise, was walking through camp and observing his tribe's behaviours. It was the first hour,[1] and being the old shepherd he was, he was sensitive to the flock in his keeping. He secretly listened to what they were saying to each other, he checked to make sure everyone had enough food, and he tried to foresee potential problems that might become major issues at a later time. His wife, Zipporah, liked this time of day as well, as it gave her a little extra sleep. She'd reminded him this morning to find his walking stick, as he had misplaced it somewhere the day before. Moses had just passed his eightieth birthday, and although he felt healthy and robust, Zipporah was always worried that he would fall and break what she called his "brittle bones." Instead of arguing with her, Moses, over time, had learned to agree when she made suggestions. As the proverb says, "it is better to live on a corner of a roof than to share a house with a quarrelsome wife."[2]

He had been using the walking stick for about five months now but often misplaced it. She was not a contentious woman by any means, but when she got something in her head, she never let it go.

He had probably left it in the tabernacle after his prayers the night before. He strolled through the tent gate, which was not more than fifty cubits from his tent. The tabernacle was built precisely according to the instruction Moses received from God on the mountain when he received the Ten Commandments. Moses had gathered all the materials from the things the Israelites brought with them from Egypt. There was gold, silver, and bronze that they melted down. Blue, scarlet, and purple fabric, carefully cut and sewn together from clothing and blankets, adorned the walls. Oils, spices, incense, precious stones, and wood that they had brought from their land of slavery[3] left nothing to be wanted. Moses had built the tabernacle in three parts: the courtyard, the Holy Place, and the Most Holy Place (Holy of Holies), which was the home of the ark of the covenant. Some of the sacred objects were placed in the courtyard, which was enclosed by a fence five cubits high, one hundred cubits long, and fifty cubits wide. The people of Israel could not see inside the fenced-in compound unless they were standing at the tabernacle's gate located at the eastern end. Directly across, on the western end, stood the special tent.

As Moses walked through the gate and into the outer court, he noticed that the priests had already prepared the bronze altar for the morning Tamid sacrifice, and the first male lamb was tied to it, kicking and bleating to be set free.[4] Twice a day, the ritual sacrifice occurred, the first at the third hour[5] and the second at the ninth hour.[6]

Animal sacrifices were an essential part of Israeli worship. It was so much different than what the pagans and heathens did. The infidels sacrificed to please and win favour from one or more gods so that crops would grow, the weather would be calm, or sickness would go away. They sacrificed when they needed something, hoping to satisfy their god's hunger enough to get their desires.

The Israelites never performed an animal sacrifice to please God so that He would turn events in their favour. The Israelites sacrificed to purify their flesh, their hearts.[7] Israelite sacrifices took place on a systematic and continual basis because sin occurred continually. But pagan sacrifice—babies, children, and virgins—was nothing short of murder, inspired by unscrupulous priests manipulating their followers to achieve their selfish personal goals. How could a lifeless, man-made idol do anything to help anybody?

There were still a couple of hours before the scheduled communal shacharit or morning prayer service.[8] The Levites were busy cleaning and straightening everything up. As Moses headed toward the tent, he passed the bronze laver, constructed from all the bronze mirrors the women had brought with them from Egypt. As was customary, Moses stopped and washed his hands and feet in the water[9] before going through the door into the Holy Place. As Moses entered, he saw his brother Aaron.

"P-p-peace to you, brother." Moses smiled.

"And to you, Moses."

It was peaceful and serene in the Holy Place, and he could no longer hear the sounds of the priests working outside or the raucous lamb in the courtyard. The soft glow of candlelight bouncing off the menorah, and the golden lampstand on his left side, illuminated the darkness of the tent. The refreshing smell of burning incense welcomed him to this particular room. On the right was the north canvas. Aaron was standing over the Table of Shewbread,[10] fussing with cakes. The table was made of wood but richly overlaid with ornate gold. The dishes, pans, jars, and bowls on top were solid gold and were polished every day. Aaron was putting the twelve loaves in two rows of six, following God's exact instructions in the Torah.[11] Every facet of Israelite life and religion was in their laws.

"Aaron, have you seen my walking cane?"

"No, it is not in here. Did you check the courtyard? You are getting forgetful in your old age, my brother," Aaron teased.

"It is not there either. Zipporah is going to be mad at me if I do not find it. I am going into the Holy of Holies to see if I put it down y-y-yesterday. Speaking of being forgetful, Aaron, are you not forgetting something?" Moses chuckled, looking at the table.

"I have been doing this for almost two years, and I have never..." Aaron stopped mid-sentence and whacked himself in the head. "The blue tablecloth.[12] I forgot the tablecloth." He frowned.

Moses had, when they constructed the tabernacle, erected a thick veil of many-layered cloth between the Holy Place, where Aaron was performing his duties over the table, and the Holy of Holies. Only Moses was allowed by God to enter the Holy of Holies; all others were forbidden, for it was there that God dwelt. God would meet with Moses, and they would talk. Inside this particular room was the ark of the covenant, which contained the Ten Commandments. It was quite large, two and a half cubits long, one and a half cubits wide, and one and a half cubits high, made of wood and overlaid with a sheet of gold on both the inside and outside coverings. Two golden, carved cherubim[13] were fastened to the top and served as handles to remove the lid. The ark was the central focus of the tabernacle, and it was where God met Moses. Aaron's budding staff (the one he used in Egypt to inflict the ten plagues) and some manna (the food that God had provided when the tribes had nothing to eat in the desert) lay on the floor just in front of this particular box. And there beside the manna, amazingly enough, was the walking cane Moses had been looking for.

Moses had become quite worried. For the past sixteen days, every time he came into this room to speak to God, he did not get a response. He knew God was there, he could feel His presence and power, but he received no words or instructions from Him. The last words he'd received from God had come sixteen days ago, when Moses had suggested that they send spies into Canaan. God had responded, "If that is what you want to do, Moses, then do it. You pick out the spies; you make the plan." In hindsight, Moses felt that perhaps he had made a mistake, that they just should have marched into Canaan. God had promised this land to them, and He would undoubtedly give it to them no matter what they encountered. He grabbed his walking cane, put on his best "God is with me" face, and left the tent, angry at himself. Aaron had already left the Holy Place and was in the outer courtyard, meeting and greeting the people who were assembling for morning prayer. Moses did not stop to welcome anyone. He headed straight for the training yard.

From the first day that God had proclaimed His name to Moses at the burning bush,[14] Moses learned progressively more about God and His ways. He came to know the voice of God well during the plagues of Egypt, but more so on the mountain, for forty days, when He gave Moses the Ten Commandments. God revealed His character,[15] and Moses gained considerable insight into His ways.[16] The tabernacle God commanded him to construct was a scaled model of heaven[17] yet to come, so Moses was allowed to see the full pattern of heavenly things.[18] God told Moses that His answer for sin was death but that He was willing to accept the blood of the innocent lamb in place of the guilty. He called it substitutionary atonement. When Adam and Eve were created and then committed the first sin, God had to generate and permit the first death. He took an innocent animal instead of the guilty humans whom he loved, made clothing out of the animal skins, and covered both Adam and Eve.[19] The atonement for the sins of Moses and the Israelites was done through the slaying of the animals on the brazen altar, but this system was not God's full plan. God had told Moses that one day, He would provide a sacrifice to end all sacrifices. He will be known to men as the Messiah, or Christ. He would be the ultimate sacrifice, and there would never be a need for another.

Moses missed Joshua. While he watched the men at their military training, he remembered him fondly. Israel had no greater warrior or closer protégé than his beloved Joshua. If Moses lived longer than Methuselah,[20] there would be no one he trusted more. Moses sometimes fretted about Joshua's age, as he was only twenty-two. It was hard for some of the older men to take his instructions, especially orders they did not like. Joshua had confided in him many times that he found his burden of leadership difficult to the point of overwhelming. Moses smiled. *If he thinks it is difficult now, wait until I die, and the entire responsibility of leading the nation hangs on his neck like an Egyptian millstone.*

He hoped all was going well for the unique band of spies. Moses specifically chose younger men, hoping to avoid any friction over Joshua's leadership. God had told him to select the men, and he did so to the best of his ability.

He could not figure out why God was so silent. How unbearable it was to know the sound of God's voice, to know where He dwelt, and not to hear His voice.

20

DAY NINETEEN: FRIDAY, JULY 8 / TAMMUZ 19

City of Jebus
Monsters, Minions, and Martyrs

It had been five days since Sihon's trap to catch Joshua had been foiled. When his soldiers came back, empty-handed, Sihon immediately killed the small Jebusite messenger Abdi-Heba had sent. When he sent his men secretly to Jebus to question Abdi-Heba about what had happened, Abdi-Heba swore on his mother's grave that Joshua had left as reported.

Not willing to further upset Sihon, however, Abdi-Heba sent some of his best troopers to scour the countryside and see where Joshua had ended up. At a horse market, they captured a man who claimed to be the brother-in-law of the slave Zidon. After some torture, he told them where they could find both Zidon and Joshua. Abdi-Heba's men found the small mudstone shack exactly where the tortured man said it would be, about five thousand cubits northeast of Jebus. They waited for instructions from Abdi-Heba as to what to do next. The orders were to watch and wait.

Finally, someone left the mud hut, and the troops followed him. It was Zidon, on his way to look for his brother-in-law. They captured, shackled, and brought him to Abdi-Heba's prison, then waited for Sihon to arrive to question the prisoner personally.

Sihon was in a foul mood. The alliance was less than fourteen days old, and he was already wondering if making an official agreement with such a stupid tribe was a good idea. They were incompetent idiots. Sihon did not understand what his ancestors saw in humans, apart from the beauty of some of their women, of course. Although Sihon had never met his grandfather, his mother told him the story over and over when he was a child. Shamhazai, his grandfather, was a high-ranking angel and leader of two hundred angels sent from heaven to watch over all the humans. These angels prided themselves on their beauty and intelligence, but watching over humankind had a consequence. Shamhazai argued that God should not have created man, as they were pathetic and full of faults. God responded that had the angels been earthbound and subject to the same challenges man had to face, they would even be worse. Shamhazai did not believe God. He wanted to be tested, so he convinced God to give them earthly bodies.

God was correct, because soon after their transformation, the angels began to lust for human women.[1] Sihon's grandfather led a revolt and defected from heaven to illicitly choose wives for themselves from among the attractive daughters of men. He brought twenty angels with him, and they descended upon the summit of Mount Hermon. These fallen angels, or watchers, as some called them, all made an oath to Sihon's grandfather and rebelled against God, taking human wives. They quickly found what they were looking for, mesmerized women with their charm, and procreated.[2] Their descendants, the Nephilim, lacked many of the good qualities their fathers possessed. Evil was in their genes, and they became savage giants. They plundered and pillaged the earth. Sihon's grandfather, along with his oath-sworn friends, further taught and instructed their children the fighting arts of sorcery and weaponry, including the handling of special knives, shields, and the construction of unique coats of mail. Sihon had forgotten more of his grandfather's formulas and charms than most people learned in their entire life. He still wore the unique makeup around his eyes and could conjure spells and supernatural hexes, but he preferred to rely on his intelligence and size to overcome his opponents. He was a bit smaller than his brother Og but quite a bit more agile. He feared nothing except the prayers of the Hebrews. He knew God existed, and he was aware of His power. But, like his grandfather, he did not want anything to do with Him.

Sihon chuckled to himself. God had sent a flood to destroy all the Nephilim and save Noah, the only God-fearing human on the planet. And yet here Sihon was, the grandson of Shamhazai. The Canaanites explained it by saying the giants made a secret deal with Noah and were towed behind in a separate boat. Others said a couple of Nephilim hid, undetected, amongst the animals for forty days, and one story stated that his ancestors were so tall their heads were still above the water when the floods came.

It is incredible, thought Sihon, *what weak and fearful people will believe.* The truth was that God permitted the righteous Noah and his pure sons to bring their wives on board, and the descendants of the Nephilim were his son's wives, Pandora, Noela, and Noegla. *We will continue to plague and torment humanity until the end of days.*[3] *We come from the spirits and flesh of the Nephilim; we will always live here in this place. We are born from both men and the holy watchers. As for the spirits of heaven, in heaven they will dwell—but the spirits of earth are born on earth, and we shall dwell here forever. We will afflict, oppress, destroy, attack, and do battle with all things of God. We shall work our destruction as we please, and cause as much trouble as we want, and no human will be able to stop us.*

Zidon was curled up in the corner of his cell when Sihon stooped through the jail doorway and walked in. Abdi-Heba's men had laid out on a table his tools of torture, and hot coals burned in the makeshift barrel. The grey smoke escaped through the small cell window. Sihon pulled out his oversized sword, put the tip into the coals, and took what looked like a metal hand-sickle from the table. He started to pick his teeth with it, and it looked like a small toy in his massive hands.

"Get him on his feet," he ordered the guards standing behind him.

Zidon had been beaten thoroughly by his captors and had no strength to stand on his own. His bleeding head drooped onto his chest. The guard grabbed his hair and forced his head up to look at Sihon.

"Tell me about Joshua, old man. Why is he travelling alone, and where are the men who came with him to Jebus? How this interview ends is up to you. I could take out your eyes with my flaming sword and your remove your tongue, releasing you to live a life of suffering, or I could send you quickly and mercifully to Chemosh. The choice is yours."

Zidon, with much effort, raised his head and smiled at the giant. "Woe unto you, Sihon! Woe to your people and your god Chemosh. If your large head had enough brains to fill it, you would remember the mercy Joshua showed you when he spared your life. Instead of wearing your military armour, you should be wearing sackcloth, covering yourself in ashes, and asking the only true God of Israel to forgive you. That will be more tolerable than the day of judgment for you!"

Without moving a muscle on his face, Sihon reached for his flaming sword and, with one mighty swipe, removed Zidon's head from his body. Blood spurted spasmodically to the ceiling of the smutty cell.

Sihon ran his thumb and forefinger alongside the sharp edge of his sword to remove Zidon's blood, and then he put his fingers in his mouth, smiling sinisterly.

"Do you want us to arrest the two Israelites here in Jebus?" Abdi-Hebo offered, still trying to gain Sihon's favour.

"No. My spies tell me one is drinking himself to death and the other spends all his time with harlots. They cannot harm us at the moment. If you want to kill a snake, you must take its head from its body. Joshua is the head of the Hebrew snake. Let the other two flounder and wallow in their addictions. No one is to know what happened here today. Am I making myself clear?"

"Yes," Abdi-Heba said.

"*Am I making myself clear?*" he roared, glaring at them with fire in his eyes, the earth shaking beneath their feet.

"*Yes, sir!*" everyone in the cell echoed in unison, the soldiers raising their arms to their chest with a quick smack.

Joshua was pacing back and forth, wondering what could be taking Zidon so long, when he saw the horsemen approach over the hill, coming toward the mudstone shed. He found his bow, and when they were close enough, fired a warning shot at the feet of the horse of the lead man, which caused the horse to rear up. There were six mounted soldiers, Jebusites, and a mule pulling a cart with a blanket over the top.

"We have your man slave. Surrender, and we will set him free, or we will kill him first, and then you," the captain of the troops called out.

"Where is he? I don't see anyone."

"He is in the cage on the mule cart, and it is your life for his."

Joshua, over the last few days, had become quite attached to Zidon and felt responsible for him, especially now that Zidon had converted and was, in Joshua's mind, vulnerable. Joshua had become like a father to Zidon in his new faith, teaching him the ways of God. Like all babies, Zidon needed encouragement and nourishment to keep growing, and now these pagans had him. There was no choice. Joshua was doing God's work, so surely God would protect him. He had no reason to fear any danger or evil—one thousand men could fall dead beside him, ten thousand around him, but he would not be harmed. Joshua said a silent prayer, opened the door, and walked out. He dropped his bow, untied his sword, and put his hands in the air.

"Release him, and I give myself to you in exchange."

The Jebusites jumped off their mounts and ran toward Joshua with their swords in their hands. They tied Joshua's hands behind his back and brought him to the covered cage.

"I present to you your beloved man slave," the captain laughed, and then he pulled the blanket off the cage, which was empty except for Zidon's bloodied head, his eyes still wide open. The captain clouted Joshua on the head hard with the handle of his sword and knocked him unconscious. They pushed him into the cage and locked the door, leaving poor Zidon's head on the ground beside the mudstone shack for the vultures to feed upon. Then they headed north, toward Shechem and Sihon's camp.

21

DAY TWENTY: JULY 9 / TAMMUZ 20

Shabbat

22

DAY TWENTY-ONE: SUNDAY, JULY 10 / TAMMUZ 21

City of Joppa
Know Thyself—Then You Will Know Your Enemy

Joppa[1] was about one hundred thousand cubits from Jebus. It took Shaphat, Sethur, and Nahbi only a day and a half to get there, with their camel towing behind and setting their pace. When they arrived, the sky above Joppa was an amber red and the ocean deepest blue, crystal clear to the bottom. The triangular line of the sun, small on the horizon and expanding as it neared the coastline, reflected off the sea like fire off a mirror, the colours on the perimeter softening from bright, carroty orange to auburn and beautiful ginger.

The rocky shore slurped up the rays and drank all the light it could. The buildings were bleached white and pristine, with indigo roofs and window frames, and doors set like sapphires in perfect harmony with their buildings. The houses, some like domes and other like temples, gradually meandered from the shoreline and up the hill in different sizes and shapes. The streets were wide and clean, glittering like gold. Down the middle of the road, there was a gurgling brook. It was as clear as crystal, flowing from the largest of all the buildings on top of the hill. On each side of the street, the leaves of fruit trees reflected the sun in all the colours of the rainbow. Joppa was strategically located on the coast in the centre of Canaan, with busy roads that connected the northern regions of Tyre and Sidon to Gaza and Egypt in the south. The natural harbour, located at the bottom of the defendable hill where the walled city stood, was an essential stronghold with valuable access to the Mediterranean Sea. It was impregnable, as many generations of Egyptian marauders had already discovered.

Sethur looked at the hand-carved map of the Canaan coastline in the main square. He could not understand why God had led them from Egypt through the Red Sea, the desert, and all the way to Kadesh-Barnea. From Egypt, they would have only had to follow the coastline, and they could have been here in less than one week, instead of the two years it took them[2] to get to the promised land—if this was, in fact, the promised land. It was confusing to him.

He snickered to himself. He was becoming like Ammiel, questioning everything. He repeated his favourite saying: everything happens for a reason. Maybe God took them the roundabout way because He knew if they saw cities like Joppa, they would turn around and head back to Egypt. It was militarily impressive. Sethur was convinced there was no way their army would be able to conquer it, and he would be sure to tell Moses when he got back.

Sethur found a quiet garden and proceeded with his workout routine. At least he was staying in good physical shape during this expedition. There was not much else good coming out of it. Their personal bags had been stolen as they'd checked into their sleeping quarters in Joppa, and they'd lost everything except the clothes on their backs.

Joppa bustled with back-alley gambling. There were dice tables, rooster fights, and even bare-knuckle fighting. To make some money, Shaphat had decided to participate in a few of the contests. He said it was to earn the prize money, but Sethur believed he did it just because he loved fighting. Whatever Shaphat's motivation, he had started winning right away. Sethur looked at the sun's position in the sky and got excited as he thought of Shaphat's next fight. He had won the last three contests, none of which had lasted very long, and the organizers wanted him to fight their champion. Sethur was going put all the money they had earned from the previous fights in the hands of the bookmakers, betting on Shaphat to win. The odds paid two to one.

Nahbi had just returned from his long run. He hated it when people stared at him while he was running. They did not understand how much enjoyment it brought him. To keep away from the crowds, he ran mostly on trails in the fields outside of town. He did this early in the morning because once the sun moved higher in the sky, it was almost impossible to keep going. Nahbi bathed himself in the bucket of cold water in his room and trimmed his beard. It was against tradition to cut anything from the Hebrew beard, but nobody was watching, and he was far from Kadesh-Barnea. So he moved from uncomely hair to uncomely hair, pruning and edging.

The law of Moses was twofold concerning beards. An Israelite male was forbidden to "round the corners of the head" because the Egyptians cropped their hair short and shaved it to form a circle in order to identify themselves in the worship of their many gods. Neither were the Israelites to "mar the corners"[3] of the beard or alter its shape into an unnatural configuration. But in Nahbi's mind, his beard was a whole lot better when he fixed it nicely. It certainly was not an abnormal configuration after he was done with it. And, for Nahbi, beauty was essential.

Nahbi loved it in Joppa. During his runs along the coast, he often saw giant whales playfully wrestling with their young babies between the white-capped waves that clashed against their massive bodies. Being a coastal city, Joppa boasted many colourful and exotic flowers that came from other countries on the ships at port. Besides the olive trees that highlighted the wilderness, cherry and fig trees grew bountifully. Rose bushes and wild lavender blossomed all along the fences that framed the farmers' fields. Proud, tall sunflowers turned their perfect heads toward the hot Southern sun as if to encourage Nahbi to run faster. Bougainvillea sprouted in bright pink, royal purple, and magenta. Marigolds covered the grounds like a fluffy orange carpet. Gentians sparkled in intense blue, and the forsythia—which he had seen only once, in Egypt—illuminated the cultivated gardens in front of the homes with the brightest yellow you could imagine. Amazing fragrances competed for the air that he rhythmically drew into his lungs. The sensual smell of lavender always overpowered them all. And the women of Joppa dressed in colourful and stylish outfits as if trying to outdo the flora that ornamented his long trail runs.

There was so much beauty, fashion, and art in Joppa that he had thought about just staying and living there. How bad could it be?

Shaphat was forcing himself to sleep longer in the mornings. He would not tell his partners, but he was sore. His muscles ached, and his back was giving him trouble. He needed rest. The fights had been his idea, for he could not think of another way to make some quick cash. And gambling was all around. Shaphat was a risk-taker, and the higher the risk, the greater the gain.

But the men he'd fought up to now were not as experienced as Bucca Drawog, the prizefighter. Bucca Drawog had been fighting for two years and never lost a match. Shaphat was a confident warrior, skilled with a variety of weapons; however, fighters like Bucca focused on hand-to-hand combat and were quite formidable. They said his mother was an Amorite and his father was an ox. When Shaphat had glimpsed him training the day before, he thought the rumour could be true. He was four cubits tall, and his arms were the size of Shaphat's legs. Shaphat guessed that he was a slave forced by his master to earn money, which he was doing quite handily.

Bucca Drawog fought because he had to, for his master, but Shaphat fought because he enjoyed it, and that was the difference. Shaphat knew he had to be careful with this man-beast, who was an experienced bare-knuckle fighter, but Shaphat was a warrior. He planned and anticipated every fight in his mind, moment by moment. He found it relaxing, and it helped him when he was fighting. He did not have to think. He only had to react.

When he got to the pre-arranged location, Sethur and Nahbi were already there. Sethur was arguing loudly with some locals about the betting and odds-against. They were giving him two-to-one odds that he could not beat the ox. Shaphat could see Sethur was relishing the action, probably trying to get it up to two and a half. Nahbi looked bored as usual, more interested in how he looked than what was going on around him. There were bales of hay arranged in a large circle, and someone had raked the ground to clear it of any rocks or sharp objects. There were about forty men gathered around the bundles, and when Bucca stepped into the circle, there was a thundering round of applause. Bucca's size reminded Shaphat of Sihon. But as Shaphat stepped inside the circle, he reminded himself that Bucca was a slave and fought because he had to, not because he wanted to.

The applause turned into boos and jeering, as they were all hoping to see a blood-drenched match. The clean and bearded appearance of Shaphat made Bucca smile a toothless smile. Bucca charged directly at him, trying to grab anything he could, but Shaphat moved quickly to the right, pushed him away, and then positioned himself for another attack. Shaphat knew that the best time to attack was just before your opponent attacked or immediately after. He never initiated an offensive; his defence was his offense.

Bucca threw a short but quick punch that caught Shaphat square on his nose. It was lightning fast and excruciating. Now Bucca had his respect. Shaphat thought his nose might be broken. Successful with the first blow, Bucca tried it again, but just as he moved forward, Shaphat landed a brutal right hook directly to the side of Bucca's temple, which knocked him to his knees. Shaphat smiled and stepped back respectfully to give Bucca a chance to get back up. Now *he* had Bucca's full attention.

As time went on, to the howling pleasure of the spectators, they traded uppercuts, jabs, and many wild swings. Shaphat bobbed and weaved while blood dripped from his forehead into his right eye. Bucca landed a solid punch on Shaphat's chin and knocked him down. He wobbled back up. Bucca smacked him again, and he dropped one more time. The crowd, intoxicated by the flowing blood, was getting raucous. Shaphat was slower to stand up this time. Bucca spun three hundred and sixty degrees and pounded Shaphat on his temple with a spinning back fist. This time, Shaphat crashed toward the dirt floor face first. Bucca raised his arms and grunted in victory, but Shaphat did not stay down. He was pulling himself up onto his shaky legs.

"Stay down, Hebrew!" Bucca growled. "You have lost."

Things were moving very slowly, and Bucca's words echoed as if in a hollow cave, but Shaphat heard clearly what the monster was saying.

"One only loses when one does not get up," Shaphat groaned, "and you will learn today that we Israelites always get up. We *never* give up."

Bucca grabbed Shaphat's beard with both hands and pulled him in a downward motion while smashing his knee quickly into Shaphat's chin. Shaphat slumped and fell, and Bucca raised his arms in triumph one more time. The cheering was deafening. Slowly Shaphat steadied himself with his arms and brought his legs under him, rising for the fifth time. The crowd was now silent as they watched this bleeding, beaten warrior stand up and position his arms once again for battle. Bucca was angry now, but then it happened. As he took another wild swing at Shaphat with his right arm, he left his right side unprotected, and Shaphat mustered all the strength he had left to strike him in his kidneys. Bucca dropped like a giant rock falling from a cliff, wincing in pain. Shaphat seized the opportunity and jumped on him, pounding his head repeatedly—left-right, left-right, left-right—then his elbows. Bucca was not moving at all. Shaphat stopped, stood up unsteadily, and looked down at his opponent.

"It does not matter how many times you knock me down, Bucca.

All people who serve the living God know that it is getting up more times than being knocked down that matters."

The crowd was cheering ecstatically, hailing their new champion. Sethur was quick to find the betting organizers to collect both the prize money and the money he had wagered on his friend.

Nahbi was just trying to clean some of the blood and dirt off of his face. Many of the first-row spectators had the same problem.

23

DAY TWENTY-TWO: MONDAY, JULY 11 / TAMMUZ 22

City of Hebron
A Father's Act of Love

It was a cloudy morning in Hebron, a welcome relief from the roasting sun of the week before. They needed rain desperately, or the crops would wilt and the harvest would be as devastating as it had been two years ago.

It seemed as if the love flowing through Geuel's body now was much stronger than the mole snake's venom. Geuel had patiently listened to Caleb explain the love he had for his wife and the feeling they'd had for each other when the relationship started. Geuel loved Caleb for his attempt at empathy, but Caleb couldn't understand how he felt. It was like a ride on a galloping, wild stallion. Nobody could feel the same way he did. Caleb explained to him that the relationship with Donatiya could not go anywhere. Phineas would never permit it, and neither Joshua nor Moses would sanction it. Even Geuel understood that he had to end it—but how? He melted in her arms like butter on a hot knife. It was beautiful to be together and horrible at the same time. There could be no happy ending. Caleb had tried to convince Geuel to come with him to find Joshua and the men, but Geuel had refused to go.

Geuel had learned from one of the guards that Donatiya had not eaten very much for the past three days. Apparently, she had no appetite. She stayed mainly in her room, and when her father talked to her, she answered with a simple yes or no. With the guard at the front door, she had to feel like a prisoner.

Geuel would stand most of the day and stare blankly at Donatiya's window, hoping for a glimpse of her. He knew she was in there, and he knew she loved him. He went through every possible scenario in his mind: attacking the guard, kicking down the door, rescuing Donatiya, and riding off into the wilderness; knocking on the door, pleading with her father, offering him silver and gold, and receiving his permission to wed Donatiya; waiting until dark, sneaking up to the window, pulling her out, and galloping away to live in the desert together.

But Caleb was correct. There was no solution to his conundrum. So he stood and watched, his heart beating wildly, torturing him with every thump. He had tried to talk to Phineas several times as he left and re-entered his home, but Phineas would not even look at him. At first, his talks with Phineas were soft and pleading. Then they were intense and demanding. Finally, he shouted in desperate anger. But he had to learn to live with his pain.

One day as he looked for Caleb, Geuel passed by the butcher shop. He remembered Donatiya saying her father was going to arrange a marriage with her and the butcher's son. This had to be his shop. Curiosity stopped him and pulled him into the storefront. A young man with a long nose and bushy hair smiled at him from behind the counter and asked, "Can I help you, friend? We have some special prices this week, in celebration of the sacrament this afternoon at the temple."

Geuel stared at him and did not say a word.

"Sir, are you all right? Is there anything I can do to help you?" Danel offered. He looked more closely at Geuel's face. "Wait, I know you. You are that Israelite who has been harassing Donatiya," he hissed. "Get out. You are not welcome here."

Geuel turned around and walked out as quickly as he had entered, continuing to the tombs to find Caleb. Perhaps he could nurse Geuel's broken heart.

Phineas secretly peeked out the window from time to time to see if that Hebrew was still standing across the lane, watching his home. Why wouldn't he go away? When Phineas first told Donatiya there would be a ceremony in the temple tonight, she'd told him she would not go. But afterward, she changed her mind. Phineas was sure that she would secretly solicit Chemosh's help in changing her father's mind about the relationship between her and Geuel. But how could he ever do that? He tightened his jaw and pursed his lips.

The whole city was talking and laughing about this ridiculous incident. He had tried to speak with Donatiya, tried to explain how awkward and disconcerting it was and why it could never work. She'd only said it was not about him; it was about her. She was so naïve. Everything that went on in his family was about him and his ability to lead. If he could not lead his family, how could he lead his parishioners? He loved his daughter, but his duty came first and foremost. Why did she have to be so stubborn? Why could she not listen to reason? Why did the Hebrews have to enter his city of Hebron?

There were so many *whys*, and yet only one *how* to solve all the setbacks. He felt awful about it, but strong men must do difficult things. He had to separate his personal feelings from what had become a necessity. There was no other solution. This way, Chemosh would be happy, his people would be pleased, and Abdi-Heba would be satisfied.

The guard knocked on Phineas's door. Abdi-Heba was asking for an audience.

"Send him in," Phineas said nervously.

Abdi-Heba had arrived last night and was intrigued by Phineas's invitation to the special passing through the fire ceremony that would be celebrated tonight in the temple. Festivity preparations were all around him, and it was difficult not to get caught up in it all. Abdi-Heba loved parties.

"Greetings, Phineas. I trust you are well."

"All is perfect when you serve Chemosh," he muttered.

"Good, good. I bring you news from Jebus. Sihon has captured Joshua, the head of the Israelite snake," he boasted. "We were instrumental in his capture, and Sihon values our participation. It does not hurt to have his appreciation."

"Joshua still lives?" Phineas asked.

"Sihon is like a mountain cat. He plays with his prey before he eats it. You know he eats humans, do you not?" he quipped, revealing his wine-stained teeth.

"That is disgusting. Sihon is such an animal," Phineas replied. "Why does he not just kill Joshua and be done with it all?"

"He probably wants to extract all the information he can, so when the Israelite army marches into Canaan, we will know their weakness and strengths. Phineas, I want to discuss a matter that was disclosed to me in Jebus regarding your daughter."

Phineas looked Abdi-Heba directly into his eyes. It was uncanny how quickly news spread. Already this fat governor was aware of his dilemma.

"And what have you heard?" he drawled.

"Is it true your daughter and the Hebrew pig will marry?"

"What is this camel dung you are spluttering?" Phineas retorted with a red face. "Not in a million years would that ever happen."

"Calm down, Phineas. I did not think so, but I had to ask you. You know, if I had to strip you of your priestly authority, I would do so. What an embarrassment it would be for the high priest of Chemosh to embrace the lustful union of a Hebrew and his daughter. She is blood of your blood and flesh of your flesh. People love to gossip, and I was sure the rumour was not true, but thank you for confirming it. What time is the party at the temple?"

"When the sun is directly overhead. These citizens love to party after the sacrifice, and this will give them most of the afternoon and all evening. Are you settled in your room? Do you need anything?" Phineas said, hoping that all suspicion was now removed.

"No, I am fine. It is good to see you again, and I look forward to the merriment this afternoon. The people on the market streets are very festive. You do a good job here, Phineas. They are lucky to have you."

With that, Abdi-Heba left, and as he passed the guard at the door, Phineas noticed that the Hebrew merchant who had been standing across the street when he entered had now disappeared.

When Phineas arrived with Donatiya at the temple, it was packed with people who were singing, playing their flutes and lyres, and beating their drums. The belly fire of Molech had been burning for a couple of hours. It radiated so much heat that it was hot as soon as they entered the temple. When the crowds saw Phineas, with his regal robes and tall white hat, they cheered and started chanting his name. Phineas raised his arm in appreciation of his subjects' adoration. Donatiya began to walk away, but Phineas grabbed her arm.

"Wait. Today, I want you with me, Donatiya. I want you close to me."

"I do not want to be around you. I need to ask Chemosh some questions."

He squeezed her arm more tightly.

"Stop, Father. That hurts." She winced, but paused when she noticed his ash-white face. "What are you doing? What is going on?"

Phineas motioned to his assistants, and they grabbed her arms and proceeded to tie her hands behind her back. Donatiya was motionless. Her mouth dropped open, and her beautiful eyes were moist with tears. Another assistant stuffed a cloth in her mouth to keep her from making any further sound. He led his daughter to the top of the Molech head with the furnace just below, and embraced her tightly.

"There was no other way, my beautiful daughter. If there were, I would have done it," he whispered in her ear. He secretly drew his ceremonial knife from his robe and quickly pushed it between ribcage and into her heart. He wanted to spare her the pain of the fire. Then he laid her on the downward-sloping arms of Molech, gave her a push, and she rolled three times into the furnace.

The crowd went crazy.

"Today we offer Chemosh the best of the best: my beloved daughter. May he accept our sacrifice and give us all our desires," he thundered in his loudest voice as tears rolled from his grey eyes. The crowd was frenzied with pleasure, applauding and cheering. The drums beat so loudly you could not hear the flutes or lyres anymore. People were dancing and taking off their clothes, chanting praises to Chemosh. Some were kissing each other and engaging in ritual sexual activities. The smell of burning flesh filled the temple. Phineas resisted the urge to vomit.

Geuel could not find Caleb at the tombs and, returning to his room at the boarding house, he was forced to push and shove past the jubilant crowds exiting the temple. He accidentally came face to face with Danel, the butcher's son.

"Are you happy now, Hebrew?"

Geuel had no idea what he was talking about and readied himself for a fight. "What are you talking about, pig-sticker?" he said, fed up with Danel's attitude.

"I should stick you like all the other pigs in my shop. Because of you, Donatiya was the sacrifice. She is dead. She is in the everlasting arms of Chemosh."

Geuel could not believe what he was hearing. Everything seemed to slow around him. Danel was shouting at him, but all Geuel could see were his lips moving. Danel's words crashed into the air like lightning, blinding him for a moment and then, seconds later, deafening him like thunder. He was in a dream over which he had no control, confused by everything his eyes and ears told him were real. Emotion poured like hot oil over his head, down his neck, and into the depths of his stomach. He turned around and staggered with each step he took, looking for his voice, trying to speak, trying to see, trying to hear, trying to make sense of it.

The first time he'd looked into Donatiya's face, he thought he saw the sunrise in her eyes. She was the moon and the stars to his dark and empty world, and now she was gone. The ground beneath him was shaking like his broken, frightened heart. To live without her would be his certain death. He stumbled back to his room, tore off his clothes, and sat in the ashes of the cold fireplace, weeping uncontrollably. He grabbed the black ashes and smeared them on his face, his body, and the top of his head. His tears turned them to mud on his face. He forced himself up, fastened some black goat's-hair sackcloth around his chest and groin, and ran toward the desert barefoot, mired in grief and repentance.

24

DAY TWENTY-THREE: TUESDAY, JULY 12 / TAMMUZ 23

City of Megiddo
All Means Are Sacred When Dictated by Inner Necessity

Tel Megiddo was about two hundred thousand cubits from Jebus, and it took Ammiel and Gaddi the full day to get there. That had been a week ago. Megiddo was situated in the northwestern part of Canaan and surrounded by the fertile and lush Jezreel Valley, also known as Har Magedon.[1] Ammiel had never seen such an abundantly fruitful area in his life. Gaddi and Ammiel had already deduced that it was a critical Canaanite city due to its strategic location along the northern end of what the locals called "the Aruna"—a thirty-one-thousand-cubit valley that connected the coastal plain with the Jezreel Valley. The route was used to surprise enemies and could be accessed by the occupants of Tel Megiddo or by an enemy army trying to conquer the city. From this location, Megiddo controlled the Via Maris (the way of the sea), the leading trade route between Egypt and Mesopotamia.

Ammiel listened with fascination as the local scholars and scribes told of the Egyptian battle of Megiddo about one hundred years prior. He had never heard this story before. The Hittite king of the northern city of Kadesh[2] had advanced his army to take control of Megiddo. Thutmose III, the Egyptian king, mustered then marched with his armies to do battle. A ridge of mountains that jutted out from Mount Carmel stood between Thutmose and Megiddo, and Thutmose had three possible routes before him. The northern route and the southern route went around the mountains, and the third route when straight through. His council of war recommended going around the mountains, but Thutmose accused his generals of cowardice and chose to go over and through the Aruna mountain path, which was only wide enough for his army "horse after horse, man after man."

This history provided useful information, and Ammiel was sure that if Joshua wasn't interested, surely Moses would be. The locals told Ammiel that hundreds of battles had been fought here, in the valley of Armageddon, all in an effort to dominate the route north to Mesopotamia.

Although the Egyptian king had subjugated the city, it prospered, and it was massive. An elaborate palace sat in the northern sector of the city. Ammiel counted four different but equally amazing temples within the walls of Megiddo, which enclosed seven and one half dunams of land. A circular stone altar was the centre of daily activities at the market, where the townsfolk bought and sold their goods. Megiddo offered many different kinds of products, including thin ivory carvings from hippopotamus tusks, more than likely from the Nile River. They displayed intricate likenesses of the pharaoh and some of the gods that the Israelites had seen in Egypt.

The temple that fascinated Ammiel the most was the Great Temple. It was bigger and more elaborate than anything he had seen, rivaling some of the structures he remembered from Egypt. It was ten times the size of what he'd seen in Beersheba and Hebron. There were two large, reddish-brown stables, one on the north side of the city and one in the south, and the courtyard around them was paved with lime. The northern stables housed about three hundred military-trained horses, and the southern stables about one hundred eighty.

Megiddo was a mighty fortress. There were soldiers continually coming and going, and Gaddi and Ammiel would spend hours at their perfect viewpoint, watching them drill in the Armageddon Valley. The soldiers were Hittites, disciplined professional soldiers, which made them both nervous. Only in Egypt had they seen such a display of military power.

To blend in, Gaddi helped in the sanitorium, patching up wounds and supporting the local healers. He didn't talk much but was always listening. Ammiel went every morning to the gathering of the truth-seekers—the "thinkers"—as they espoused their theories and assumptions about life. Most of it seeped into their pagan beliefs. Although Ammiel was not vocal, he loved listening and hearing other ideas, and it certainly did not hurt to make some local friends.

Gaddi was a humanitarian. He believed in helping the sick, the less fortunate, and humanity in general. Ammiel was the pragmatist, always choosing sound logic over useless compassion.

As they watched the Hittites in the valley, Gaddi asked Ammiel casually, "Do you feel the end justifies the means?"

Ammiel smiled; he loved it when he had an opportunity to express his thoughts. "There is nothing more necessary than to appear to be religious, as men will judge you more by the eye than by your hand."

"I do not understand what you mean, and you are not answering my question."

"It is imperative to keep up the appearance of being merciful, faithful, humane, and upright. However, we must always be prepared to act in a manner contrary to the appearance we have created. If that means manipulating the means to accomplish the end, then yes, I think the end justifies the means. That way, everyone will be able to see what you appear to be, and only a very few will know the truth of what you did to achieve the end. Why do you ask, Gaddi?" Ammiel was proud of his answer, although he was not sure it made sense.

"I feel the way we get to our goal is important—maybe even more important than the result. Destiny, or God's will, tells us what we are to the world, but the journey tells *us* who we are. For instance, if my goal in life is to save lives, is it okay for me to cheat, steal, and lie to accomplish that goal?" Gaddi queried sincerely.

"Well, when the time comes for us to march into Canaan as an army, you know we will have to destroy its inhabitants. However, we will establish our land and people. Are we justified? Is that wrong?"

"Ah, a question to answer a question." Gaddi smiled. "My problem with the idea of the 'ends justifying the means' is that you inadvertently put the law into the hands of the oppressor, which in your example would be us. It makes the law subjective. We can rationalize any action if our motivation to attain our goal is strong enough."

"I agree with you. Murder in the law of Moses is debauchery. God is holy, just, and good, and we must reflect on his character. But if God orders the destruction and death of the people, the law is not in our hands; it is simply fulfilling His command. His laws are clear as to what is moral and what is immoral."

"I do not understand it, Ammiel. How can it be moral?"

"This is a difficult question to answer. I do not think any of us, including Moses, fully understands why God would command such a thing, but we must trust Him and recognize that He is indeed holy and just. We must acknowledge that we are incapable of fully understanding God's ways, but we must remember that His ways are always higher than our ways and His thoughts are always higher than our thoughts.[3] We must trust God and have faith in Him even when we do not understand the reasons for his orders. We cannot see the future—only God can. If we trust Him, He will take us safely through life and protect us always."[4]

"It is difficult for me to comprehend. If we go back and tell Moses we should attack, we become the law and will be responsible for many deaths," Gaddi grumbled.

"I disagree. Think of one of your patients. You need to cut him, and blood is spurting everywhere, but to save his life or ease his pain, you must perform the surgery. There is no other option. Someone who does not know your operating procedure would think you are cruel to the poor sick man. But God sees the ending. We do not."

"You have a point, I guess."

"Also, you are assuming that Moses will give the attack order upon our report. Based on what I have seen, there is no way we can win. Have a look at those Hittites with their chariots and soldiers. If we were only fighting this army, we would lose, but now that the Jebusites, Hittites, and Amorites have formed a confederation, it is impossible, to my logical mind, for us to win."

"This city is very well fortified, never mind what we saw at Jebus and Hebron," Gaddi agreed. "If we could, by some miracle, get through Beersheba, Hebron, and Jebus, we would be annihilated here in the valley of Armageddon."

"I do not understand what Joshua was thinking, constantly going north," Ammiel muttered. "He had no plans to come this way. Maybe those dreams of Palti and Igal were true, and Joshua was getting arrogant. Anyway, all has worked out. Joshua will come to his senses and understand that we did the best thing by splitting up. Come, let us go and eat something."

25

DAY TWENTY-FOUR: WEDNESDAY, JULY 13 / TAMMUZ 24

City of Jericho
Walls and Fences Keep New Evil Out, but They Retain the Old Evil Within

Palti and Igal had never before seen a city with such a massive defensive wall. When they arrived, they spent most of the first day just riding around the outside of the thriving city to inspect the magnificent structure. A sizeable earthen rampart surrounded the hill where Jericho stood, with a stone retaining wall along its base. This wall was seven cubits high. On top of it was a mud-brick wall that was three cubits thick and thirteen cubits high. On top of the embankment was yet another mud-brick wall, so from ground level to its highest point, the wall was twenty-four cubits high. No invader could penetrate this bastion of Jericho. All along the fifteen-cubit-thick walls were erected rectangular towers that not only strengthened the structure but gave their occupants an unparalleled view of the surrounding countryside.

The two Israelites could tell that this city was the most prosperous in the land. There were smaller villages nearby that housed several thousand farmers each and no doubt depended upon Jericho's prosperity and security against invaders or marauders. Water was abundant, and the fields were fertile, productive, and lavish with their crops. Once Palti and Igal were inside the city walls, they saw large, well-constructed houses with small gardens that grew vegetables and fruits for personal consumption. In spite of frequent fights and attempts to sack the city, the people of Jericho had invested in their infrastructure, which appeared to be a highly cultured and urbanized trade centre.

"It seems there are a lot of Moabites and Ammonites here in Jericho," Palti noticed.

Igal broke out laughing. "Did you just hear what you said?"

Palti looked puzzled.

"You said there were *a lot* of Moabites and Ammonites."

"Igal, you have to reduce your consumption of mandrake. There is nothing funny at all in what I said."

"Don't you get it? Lot was the nephew of Abraham. Do you remember the story, Palti? God sent two angels disguised as human men to Sodom and Gomorrah, as the stench of those wicked cities burned the nostrils of God. If the angels could find just ten righteous men in either or both cities, He would spare the cities from destruction. It could not be that hard, after all, to find ten good and virtuous men in two vast cities.

"God told Lot to meet the angels at the city gates, and Lot urged them to stay at his house, but before they had gone to bed, men—young and old, from every part of the city—were banging on Lot's door. They wanted Lot to turn over the strangers so they could have their way with them. These were two new, virtuous, unknown men, ready to be accosted. The angels defended themselves and Lot's household by blinding the men so they could not find the door to Lot's home.[1] Lot searched for ten righteous men, but nowhere were they to be found. They were all wicked and immoral.

"In the morning, Lot, along with his wife and two daughters, fled the city behind the angels, and God rained down sulphur and destroyed Sodom and Gomorrah. The angels warned them not to turn back and look, or they would die. Lot and his daughters obeyed, but his wife, who had so many pleasant memories there, turned around for one last look and turned into a pillar of salt.[2] Lot and his daughters fled to the caves along the Dead Sea less than one hour from Jericho. With their mother dead, his daughters were afraid their father would pass away without having a son. They deceived and tricked their father into sleeping with them.[3] This lewd act produced two male children: Moab, the progenitor of the Moabites, and Benammi, the ancestor of the Ammonites."

"So, if Abraham was Lot's uncle, we are related. Correct?" Palti interjected.

"Yes, both tribes are related to us by blood. However, because of their incestuous origins, any contact we have with them brings trouble for us. They hate us, their jealousy blinds them, and they do everything they can to hinder and aggravate our tribes. They also practise the same incestuous acts with their sons and daughters that brought them into this world—all in the name of their god Baal."

"So it is hopeless for them, even though they are related to us?"

"That is untrue. Any foreigner, related or not, can become part of God's people if they turn to Him.[4] He welcomes everyone."

Palti sighed. "Okay, I get it. There are truly a *Lot* of Moabites and Ammonites here in Jericho."

They chuckled as they roamed the streets, looking for an inn for a mid-afternoon drink. They found a small tavern with an empty table and sat down. The tables were close together, and there was a lot of chatter. For a brief moment, all eyes were on the strangers, but Palti and Igal pulled down their headgear and tried to blend in.

"Wolf, something has been bothering me. I have kept it inside since Jebus, but I need to get it off my chest."

"I am listening," Palti said as he motioned for two vessels of wine from the server.

"When we were dealing with Joshua, I think you were too aggressive, almost ambitious, and I don't think you were fair."

"What in the name of Moses are you talking about? Where did that come from?"

"Seriously, Palti, I think—"

Palti stopped him. "Not here. It isn't the place or the time. What is wrong with you?"

"Wrong with *me*? It is you I am concerned about. You have no control over your ambition, and I think you saw Joshua as just another log on the road to hop over."

"I did not see you running to his defence. And if we are clearing the air, I am getting sick and tired of listening to your 'everything is about business and money' garbage. We are supposed to be scouting the landscape, and all I hear is what you would do to make this or that business better, and what the profits could be if you were in control. When will you learn that life is not about silver and gold?"

"Oh, look who is offering life lessons: the intellectual philosopher Palti. Do you think any of our group would agree you know the secrets of life?" Igal snarled. He drank his vessel dry and raised his arm to order two more.

"Would you men mind keeping your voices down?" the man sitting beside them asked politely. "We are trying to have a conversation."

"You might look like a wolf, Palti," Igal continued, "But you could learn a lot from that animal. They are complex, highly intelligent pack animals that hunt together, run together, and protect each other. Wolves are devoted to their families and care for each other. If you insist on being called Wolf, then I declare you a lone wolf. All you care about is yourself and your ambition. You are unfettered by sentiment or a need for companionship. You are driven to forge your selfish and uncompromising path at the expense of others. Like your namesake, Lone Wolf, you perceive all others as competitors, both socially and territorially."

"*Enough!*" Palti stood up and shouted. The entire tavern was silent.

"See, there you go again," Igal continued. "When you cannot win an argument with logic, you resort to violence, hoping if you scream loud enough, everyone will whimper like newborn wolf puppies. You cannot take criticism, and that is your biggest flaw, Palti."

Palti blustered, red in the face, pushed back his bench, and exited through the tiny entrance.

Igal pulled Palti's vessel of wine closer and smiled at the table beside him. He knew how to get under Palti's skin.

Although it was still a couple of hours before sundown when Palti got to his room, he rummaged through his bag, looking to see if there was anything left of the mandrake Zidon had given to him secretly. He was not hungry and did not want to see Igal again today. He would at least have a good sleep tonight, and some incredible dreams. He could hardly wait.

26

DAY TWENTY-FIVE: THURSDAY, JULY 14 / TAMMUZ 25

Desert
Gathering the Team

It took almost two full days of searching to find his friend Geuel, and when Caleb did eventually find him, he hardly recognized him. His face was painted entirely black with ashes, and the black goat's-hair sackcloth he wore was covered in mud and sand, which camouflaged him perfectly in the wilderness. Caleb had to look twice because he wasn't sure the lump he had found was human. It looked like a wild animal. Geuel was sitting under the shade of tamarisk tree with a honeycomb in one hand, and he was swatting the angry bees with his other hand. Bits and pieces of locusts—his diet the last few days—stuck on the honey in his beard. There was a small pond of water, where Caleb led his horse and Geuel's to quench their thirst.

"Greetings, brother. I am so glad I found you," Caleb called out.

Geuel raised his half-human head but did not say a word.

"Geuel, Joshua is in trouble. He has been captured by Sihon," Caleb said. "He needs us now, and you need to snap out of this grief. Your brother and leader is depending on you."

"Joshua? But how? What about the others?"

"They split up. We need to gather the men and get Joshua as soon as we can."

"What do you mean, they split up? Where are they?"

"Shaphat, Sethur, and Nahbi are on the coast in Joppa. Palti and Igal are in Jericho, Ammiel and Gaddi are up at Megiddo, and Gaddiel and Shammua are still in Jebus. I do not know why they separated, but we have to get them all together now and rescue Joshua. I received this news shortly after you left Hebron."

Geuel pulled himself up, using the tree trunk as support. "How many days? When was Joshua was captured?" he said, stumbling toward the pond where the horses were drinking.

"This would be the sixth day."

"*Six days?* Could he still be alive? Geuel jumped into the pond, scrubbing the honey and ashes off his body the best he could.

"If Sihon wanted him dead, he would be dead already. I understand that he has taken him to his camp just outside Shechem."

"So what is the plan, Caleb?"

"You will ride to Jebus and for Gaddiel and Shammua, then continue on to Jericho. Once you have picked up Palti and Igal as well, you will go to Shechem. I will meet you there after I pick up Shaphat, Sethur, and Nahbi. We will come up with a plan once we have all the men together. Now, quick, get cleaned up. I have your weapons and clothing on your horse. There is a bag of bread and olives for you to eat. In the bag, there are some pieces of gold and silver. Get your strength back. We need you. If we all ride hard, we can be in Shechem the day after tomorrow. Now go!"

And with those instructions, Caleb jumped on his horse and galloped away in the direction of Joppa.

Geuel grabbed a handful of sand and scraped it over his face and beard, trying to clean up as well as he could. He removed the heavy sackcloth and sank deep into the water. He repeated the process and wiped his body, arms, and legs with the fine sand until he could once again see the brown colour of his skin. Without drying himself off, he scurried into the clothing Caleb had brought, almost tearing it as it clung to his body. He stuffed the bread into his mouth, jumped on his horse, and trotted off to Jebus. It was only a couple of hours away, and he tried to focus on what Caleb had just old him. All he had thought about for two days was killing Phineas. Now, he had to rescue Joshua. Phineas would have to wait.

Geuel would wrap up his heart tightly from now on and avoid any future entanglements. He would lock it up in a sarcophagus and put it in a place like the cave of Machpelah, where his ancestors slept eternally. There it would endure in a tomb of his selfishness: dark, motionless, and airless. It would never break again. It would be impenetrable and irredeemable, but safe. How much better would it have been if he had never loved Donatiya—never felt the pain of her departure? Love created new problems. He could have avoided those problems by avoiding love. Oh, but how beautiful that love was, however brief. It was the only thing in life worth experiencing; everything else was secondary. Donatiya had made him aware of feelings he never knew he had. When he looked into her eyes, he could see more than if he stood on the highest mountain. He saw spring gardens full of kingly colours, and purpose to the birds flying overhead. And then there was her smell; it was like a fresh field of orchids in full blossom.

He wanted to punish Phineas for what he'd done to his daughter. He wanted to punish Phineas for what he'd done to *him*. He wanted the Israelite army to decimate Hebron—all the temples, all their priests, all their pagan practices. He would vote to attack. He knew deep down that his motivation was selfish, but he did not care. Phineas and his pagan worshippers had taken the most important thing away from him, and he would repay them one-hundredfold.

Geuel's horse passed through the gates of Jebus covered in a dense lather. Geuel gave him to a young boy to cool down and provide with water, then asked where he could find Gaddiel and Shammua. The young boy knew where they were staying, and Geuel tossed him a piece of silver for his help. It was still early in the afternoon when he walked through the door to Gaddiel's room without knocking. Gaddiel was sprawled on his cot, asleep, with a large jug of wine beside his bed.

"This is what you do when your leader has been kidnapped," Geuel barked.

Gaddiel only continued to snore.

"Wake up, you sozzled, useless piece of garbage," Geuel thundered, pushing him with his foot.

"What? Wh-what?" Gaddiel repeated, opening his eyes with great difficulty.

"It is two hours after lunch, and you are already drunk. Gaddiel, what have you become?"

"Oh, it is you, Geuel. I'm glad you are feeling better." And he rolled over onto his face.

Geuel picked up the cot at one end and dumped Gaddiel headfirst onto the floor. "*Get up!* The Canaanites have kidnapped Joshua, and we need to get all the men together. Where is Shammua?"

"He usually is at the woman Rahab's in the afternoon," he said groggily.

"Where can I find this Rahab?" Geuel demanded, by now very angry.

"Toward the end of the street, there is a baker. Her house is right beside his. It is the one with the red curtains on the window."

"Sober up, Gaddiel. I will give you a little time, but when I come back, you'd better be ready. And pour out that poison you are drinking. You won't need it where we are going." He slammed the door and stormed toward the baker's shop like an angry bull.

Rahab's home was where Gaddiel said it would be. Geuel took a deep breath and knocked on the door. A young lady came to the door and smiled.

"I am looking for Shammua. Is he here?" Geuel asked politely.

"Shammua? No, there is nobody here by that— Oh, you mean Shammy. Yes, please enter. Is this the first time you have come here?" She smiled again, this time a little more seductively. "Please sit down. May I offer you a drink? A little wine, perhaps?" Judging by the tone of her voice, she was offering perhaps a little more than the wine.

"Shammua, come down! It is Geuel," he hollered.

Geuel heard some fumbling, a woman's voice whispering, and then some footsteps.

"Geuel, is it you? How are you, my brother? Shammua's head poked out of a room upstairs, smiling sheepishly.

"Without insulting the proprietor of this place, get your clothes on and get down here immediately."

"Come on, Geuel, don't be like that. There are plenty of ladies here—maybe you would want one?"

"Get dressed and get down here—*now!* It is important," Geuel raged in the loudest voice he could muster.

Shammua stumbled down the stairs, looking like a small boy who had stolen a giant honeycomb from his mother's cupboard.

Geuel turned to the young lady and asked if he could have a private conversation with his friend. She pulled a sour face and went upstairs, giving the two men some privacy.

"Sihon has kidnapped Joshua. Caleb has gone to Joppa and Megiddo for some of the others. We will go to Jericho, pick up Palti and Igal, and meet them at Shechem. Then we must rescue Joshua."

Shammua immediately came to his senses, finished dressing, and followed Geuel back to fetch Gaddiel.

"How do we know he is still alive?" asked Shammua.

"We do not know. We can only hope. Get your stuff together, and let's go. Have you paid your rooming charges and horse fees?"

"We are both paid up until next week."

"Let us ride. And you can explain to me why you split up on the way to Jericho. As to the state I found you both in, I will leave that to God to judge."

On the way to Jericho, Shammua and Gaddiel awkwardly explained what had happened—that Joshua had grown angry at the meeting and left in a huff. That the men decided to continue the mission but in smaller teams, and that Shammua and Gaddiel had remained in Jebus to wait for Joshua to come back after his trip up north. They did not use the word *mutiny*, but Geuel figured it out quickly enough. He was so disgusted with them that he did not bother to explain what had happened in Hebron. They rode through the night, stopping only a couple of times to rest the horses, and arrived in Jericho very early in the morning. The horses were exhausted. It was necessary to trade them for three fresh mounts in order to get to Shechem the same day. Geuel found the stable manager doing his chores and negotiated fresh horses for an excessive amount of silver. The manager knew exactly where Palti and Igal were staying and gave them directions, hardly able to contain his excitement to count his silver until after they left.

27

DAY TWENTY-SIX: FRIDAY, JULY 15 / TAMMUZ 26

City of Shechem
All Seems to Be Lost

Palti was comatose on his cot when Shammua, Gaddiel, and Geuel entered his room. He was not sure if it was real or a mandrake dream—the line between the two had become very thin over the last few days. He rolled over, thinking if he ignored the hallucination, it would go away. But he heard urgent voices that seemed to come from the other end of a tunnel, and he felt a searing pain in his chest. *What appears to be does not exist, and what does exist does not appear to be reality.*

"Palti... Wolf, wake up!"

Palti jumped out of the cot, terrified, shrieking between short breaths. "No, No, No."

Geuel grabbed him by both shoulders and held him firmly against the wall. "Everything is okay, Palti. Calm down, relax, take a deep breath."

Palti's frightened eyes darted among the faces of the intruders, still not awake or aware of who was in his room. Sweat beaded on his forehead and began to drip down his face.

Shammua reached over to the table and held up what remained of the small mandrake plant.

Palti's drug-deprived brain screamed instructions, and animal instincts replaced his subjective thoughts. Geuel slapped him hard on the face.

"Palti, come to your senses," Geuel barked. He grabbed the mandrake from Shammua's hand, threw it on the floor, and stomped on it like the viper that had bitten him, squishing it flat. "Joshua is in trouble. Sihon has captured him. We need the team to unite and rescue him."

That sobered up Palti immediately. "Joshua is in trouble?" he mumbled.

"Yes. Quickly, get dressed. We will all go to Shechem and meet the rest of the men. Where is Igal?"

"He goes to the market early, so you will probably find him there. He has a deal with a couple of merchants."

"What do you mean, a deal?"

"All I know is he has some partners with stalls there. He does not tell me much."

"Gaddiel, help Palti get ready, and meet us in one hour behind the stables. You still have your horses, correct?"

"Yes," said Palti. "I am surprised that you found us. We have been incognito."

"You think too highly of yourselves, Palti. The first person we asked knew where we could find you. Come with me, Shammua. Let's get Igal."

There was already a hubbub of activity when Geuel arrived at the marketplace. Men carried pots and blankets, and a woman was sweeping the dirt floors. There was laughter, loud voices blaring instructions, and the sounds of hammers banging. In the middle of it all was Igal, lecturing a group of six men. Igal did not recognize Geuel and Shammua at first, but then, with a big grin, he greeted them warmly.

"Shalom, my brothers. Come to do some shopping, I see."

"Shopping?" Geuel fumed. "When did our mission become shopping and leisure?"

"I was joking, my brother, and I am glad to see you have survived. That nurse has done her magic, I see."

"That so-called nurse is dead, and Joshua will be following her soon if we don't rescue him."

"What are you talking about?" Igal said, now serious.

"Joshua is Sihon's prisoner. He needs our help before it is too late. What in heaven are you up to here?"

"I made a deal with these local merchants. There were six booths all selling the same type of merchandise, and their customers would go from booth to booth and barter for the best price on the same articles. For a small percentage of what they sell, I divide up the products, so each booth does not conflict with the others. Each booth now specializes in certain items, thereby eliminating duplication, and customers cannot play vendors against each other to get the price down. Margins and profits are up, and sales have not dropped whatsoever," Igal said proudly.

"You idiot," Geuel declared. "Do you think we can yoke ourselves with unbelievers? What do righteousness and wickedness have in common? What fellowship can light have with darkness? Your relationship with God will eventually be damaged and compromised. But you are smart enough to figure this out on your own. Leave this place now, gather your things, and knock this Jericho dust off your feet. We are all going to Shechem to free Joshua."

Meanwhile, in Joppa, Caleb was having a hard time finding the men. He had walked up and down the streets, asking people if they knew of their whereabouts, without any positive results. He turned down a dirty lane and saw a group of men shouting and cheering, and curiously approached them to see what was going on. There in the middle of the crowd was the bleeding face of Shaphat, who was fighting another man. Standing high on a box was Sethur, arguing and pointing at different men, shaking his head no then nodding as if to say yes. Shaphat was the first to recognize Caleb and, with great determination, he knocked out his opponent with one mighty blow. Sethur lifted his arms in victory, laughing and gathering the shekels and silver pieces the men were handing to him. The crowd began to disperse.

"What is going on here?" Caleb asked Shaphat.

"We are prizefighting, Caleb. It's good to see you, my brother," he said between two fat lips.

Sethur finally saw Caleb and came running over with a bag full of coins. "Brother Caleb, we are blessed to see you. How is Geuel?"

Caleb was speechless but did not want to lecture them. He would save it for later. "Joshua is in serious trouble. Sihon the Amorite has captured him and taken him to his camp close to Shechem. Where is Nahbi? We must leave at once."

"After his morning run, Nahbi usually visits his friends along the beach. He does not like the 'atmosphere' here at the fights," Sethur replied sarcastically.

"Sethur, go find Nahbi and meet us at your horses in one hour. Shaphat, clean yourself up and get all of your things. We must go to Megiddo and find Ammiel and Gaddi. Joshua's life is at stake. We must be in Shechem by Shabbat."

Three hours after Caleb had entered Joppa, the four riders, Nahbi included, were trotting quickly toward Megiddo. They spotted two men from afar.

"It could be trouble," Caleb said. "They look like soldiers. Let us ride side by side to show them our strength."

As they got closer, they recognized Ammiel and Gaddi and kicked their horses into a full gallop to meet them.

"Shalom, brothers," Ammiel called out. "What a surprise to meet you here. What are you doing?"

"We were coming to find you. We need to assemble the men. Sihon has captured Joshua. Why did you leave Megiddo?"

"The city is impregnable. We could find no weakness or vulnerability, so we returned to find all of you," Gaddi said. "We saw a huge movement of troops marching north, probably to Mount Hermon. The Hittites were armed to the teeth. We counted three hundred chariots and more than ten thousand infantry troops. They had more horses than we could count."

"Let us turn our horses around and get to Shechem, then," Caleb replied. "Hopefully, Geuel has found the other men. May God give us speed and keep Joshua safe."

They entered Shechem late at night, found a stable for their horses, and searched for a rooming house. It was Shabbat, but they would have to exercise its special provision. When an individual's life was in danger, the faithful were permitted to violate the strict rules of Shabbat and do everything they could to save that life. And that was what they were going to do: save Joshua's life. They were not desecrating the holy day; they were consecrating it.

28

DAY TWENTY-SEVEN: SATURDAY, JULY 16 / TAMMUZ 27

Shabbat

Caleb looked at the men in front of him and wanted to cry. Who could believe that in just twenty-seven days, they would end up like this? Gaddiel's hands were shaking in his abstinence from wine. Palti was not much better; he had become dependent on mandrake. Igal was making deals and partnering up with the Canaanites. Shaphat was fighting for prize money. Sethur was gambling not only on Shaphat but on four other fighters as well. Nahbi had more boyfriends than he had fingers. Shammua slept with anything that wore jewellery and makeup. Ammiel and Gaddi, the most intelligent of the group, already felt defeated, observing the military muscle and impenetrable walls of the cities they had visited. Then there was poor, broken-hearted Geuel.

Caleb, overwrought with anxiety, had turned and tossed all night. Sleep was a stranger while Joshua was captive. It was now up to Caleb to lead these men, and how different they were now than when they had left Kadesh-Barnea. The room stank with body odour and sweat. The men were arguing with each other about who knew what. It was at this point that Caleb stood up and spoke.

"Brothers, as I am the oldest in this group, I wish to address you all. Firstly, let me tell you how disappointed I am in you. To allow Joshua to ride off on his own is deplorable."

"Caleb, you don't understand," started Palti. "You were not there—"

"*Quiet.* I am talking," he commanded. "Secondly, we are Israelites, men who were chosen by God to be His children. We must fear the Lord and serve Him with genuineness and truth. The living God told us to put away the gods our fathers had served beyond the river and in Egypt. Every square cubit of success we have had as a nation has been God's gift to us. What we are inside is what we are outside. We are not hypocrites. We are to serve our God in sincerity and truth. Our God is a God of truth. We must worship Him not just on the outside, but with what we have inside. We must put away the gods our fathers served."

"Why the lecture, Caleb? We are all circumcised and obey the laws of Moses, or at least try to obey them," Ammiel interrupted.

"If it is disagreeable in your sight to serve the Lord in sincerity and truth, choose for yourself today whom you will serve: the pagan gods your fathers served or the gods of the Canaanites, in whose land you are now standing. You can choose to follow the bad examples of your ancestors, perhaps even your parents, and make the same mistakes they made by being loyal to the things they served. You can choose to follow the seductive teachings of Baal and the temple worship of Chemosh, but my point is *you must choose for yourselves.* Do not do something just because your mother or father did it. They could be wrong. Do not take the values of the street vendors, the gamblers, or the mandrake users because they seem intriguing. Think for yourself. Choose for yourself."

"Caleb, what are you talking about? Did you find idols in our possession? None of us would break Moses's law," Gaddi said. "If you found idols with someone, tell us who, so we may stone him."

"There are no wooden or bronze statues in your possession, Gaddi, but what has become the most important thing in your life? What comes before your God in priority?" He looked at Gaddiel and

Palti. "Is there an idol for wine or mandrake, which you both serve so fervently?" He looked at Shaphat. "Does fighting come before your devotion to God? What is your real love, Shaphat?" He walked over to Sethur. "How about the gambling idol? Is there such a thing? Shammua, are women your gods? If so, you will be a very busy man."

There was some chuckling.

"There is nothing funny in what I am saying. Does lusting for gold and silver compromise your God-given values, Igal?" Caleb sighed. "As for my family and me, we will serve the living God. The choices you have made are between you and your maker. I will not comment any more on this subject. We are all grown men and should know right from wrong."

The room was quiet, and no one was looking Caleb in the eyes.

"But because of your treasonous act—*yes*, your mutiny—we must desecrate Shabbat, the day we should be resting and feeling joy, and invent a plan to find and rescue our beloved leader and commander, Joshua. I have received information that Sihon's camp is not far from here on Mount Gerizim. There are two mountains, as you saw riding into the city. Mount Gerizim forms the southern side of the valley. There are only two ways up or down this mountain: an easy way and a challenging way. Sihon will have situated his troops all along the easy route, and he won't expect an attack from the steep side. There is very little shrubbery, and the route is treacherous. We will need ropes and spikes, and we will need to depend on each other to mount the precipice. I cannot think of any other way, since to charge them head-on would be suicide. We will come at them from behind, rescue Joshua, and hopefully ride away. Are there any questions?"

"Maybe we need a diversion—something to focus their attention on the accessible route?" said Ammiel.

"Good idea, but no, I thought of that. Sihon knows we celebrate Shabbat, and he will not be expecting anything to happen today. Plus, we need all the men we have to free Joshua. We will leave the ropes up and descend them quickly once we have Joshua. Our horses will be waiting."

"If God is with us on this mission, why is he so silent? Why are we having so many difficulties?" asked Ammiel.

"Ammiel, God works in ways that we cannot fully understand. You, of all the men here, should know that. If we did not have problems and everything went smoothly, we would not need to rely on His help. Maybe we grow with our faith in Him. I don't know. Our nation's history, and my personal life, taught me lessons. His power is made perfect in our weakness. When we are weak, we lean on him more for strength. There is a purpose for everything that happens, and He is working on everything for our good."

"So tell us, Caleb—where has God been for these twenty-seven days? Why has Joshua been captured? Why did He not accept the sacrifice you and Joshua offered Him in Hebron? Why has He not given us miracles to help in this venture Moses sent us on?"

"I do not know, Ammiel," Caleb said. He turned around, banged his shin on the edge of the table, and winced in pain. "I do not know," he repeated, rubbing his leg.

And in truth, Caleb wondered how things could be any worse. The fortified cities possessed walls too steep to scale. Giants feasted on humans. The armies of the Hittite nation, the Jebusites, and Amorites had allied with one purpose: to decimate the Israelites. The men had abandoned their spiritual walk, and Joshua, if not dead, was in deep trouble.

Then Caleb remembered standing beside Joshua in the tent of Moses when Moses said, "God has allowed me to select one leader from each of the tribes—except for the Levites, of course—and to send them as spies into the land of Canaan." He did not say God *told* him to send them on the mission; he said God had *allowed* him to send the spies. Could this be the reason they had not seen God's hand, leading and protecting them? Was this just an idea initiated by Moses?

God had not forsaken them. He would never abandon his people. But Caleb wondered how long He would wait before He came to their rescue. He prayed it would be quick.

They arrived at the base of Mount Gerizim and tied up their

horses in some nearby bushes. The mountain was high, but the most challenging part, the sheer face, was only a small part close to the top. They began their ascent, and the way became steeper and steeper. They all stopped for a quick drink of water and stripped to the waist in the heat, fastening their swords tightly around their middles. It was now necessary to use wooden spikes and ropes. The men tied themselves together, and Geuel went first. Shaphat followed, and Gaddiel and Shammua were next.

The rocks felt jagged and sharp against Geuel's flesh, but he did not notice the pain—the exhilaration pumping through his veins numbed everything. He had to keep his mind clear. He could not think about Donatiya. As they scaled the face higher and higher, step by unsure step, he could hear the men below him breathing heavily. He would look for an opening in the rock and pound the acacia spike as deep as he could into the crevice. He hoped with all his heart that it would hold not only him but the men coming after him. He reached out to the next ledge with his left arm then moved his right arm beside it. A snake slithered quickly over his right arm. Startled, and remembering that mole snake in the desert, he lost his grip with one arm. Dirt and pebbles fell into his face as he wobbled back and forth on his left arm, trying to get his right arm back in place.

"Are you okay up there?" Shaphat called out from below.

"Yes. I just lost my balance for a moment. Still feeling the effects of eating nothing but honey and locusts for two days," Geuel joked. But sweat saturated his brow. He did not feel like looking down. Although he was not afraid of heights, he was scared of not succeeding. He saw the snake sidewinding along the ledge, trying to escape the mountain climbers. It was not much further to the top; he had to keep going. His muscles were screaming for a rest. Each time he pulled himself to the next spike, he exhaled with relief.

Finally, with one last heave, he reached the top ledge, dragged himself slowly along, spun around on his stomach, and pulled on the ropes to help Shaphat. The top ledge was just a bare rock face with burnt brown lichen between the cracks. There was no shrubbery to hide them, but plenty on the other side where the mountain descended. Geuel's bleeding elbows and knees rubbed against the rocks. His hands were numb from pulling on the ropes. He looked at his arm to see if the snake had bitten him, but there were no punctures. For a split second, Geuel again thought about Donatiya and the happiness he had felt when he was with her. Was there a more significant pain than a beautiful memory of joy during unbearable grief? He felt an urge to simply jump over the ledge and plunge to his death —but then he remembered Joshua, who needed his help.

Once they had all scrambled over the precipice, the spies crawled on their hands and knees to the cover of the bushes, from where they could see the black tents and the campfire burning. Without making any sounds, they stood up and took their swords out of the scabbards. They scoured the camp, looking unsuccessfully for any sign of Joshua. Caleb gave a hand signal, and they spread out in a semicircle and started to close in. Quickly and quietly, Shaphat grabbed one guard, placed a hand over his mouth, and slit his throat. They remained unnoticed. Shammua, with one carefully placed thrust, slew another guard in silence, and then another dropped. Soon there were four executed Jebusites, but there were at least another fifteen in camp, some Amorites and some Hittites. The element of surprise was over, and they were now the centre of attention. The soldiers came running and roaring at them, swords drawn. But they were no contest for the Israelites, and soon only one Hittite was left battling with Nahbi. Nahbi swept his legs out from under him with one leg, dropped him on his back, and raised his sword for the final kill.

"Wait," Caleb commanded.

Nahbi obeyed, holding the sword against the lower part of the guard's throat.

"Where is your prisoner Joshua? What have you done with him?"

With blood spewing from his nose and mouth, the Hittite soldier started to laugh.

"All this is for revenge of Joshua?" He laughed harder. "He was in that cell over there for two days. Then Sihon took him to Mount Hermon. He is not here, you Hebrew swine. But I can tell you we showed him real Canaanite hospitality. We beat him within an inch of death. Sihon would not permit him to die and decided to take him to the mountain of his ancestors. He cried louder than a baby, Hebrew, asking for his mother to help." The guard giggled fiendishly.

Caleb nodded, and Nahbi pushed his sword with two hands through the guard's windpipe and into the ground underneath him.

"Are we all okay? No wounds?" Caleb asked, looking around.

"Thanks be to God, we are all okay," Gaddi responded. "What do we do now, if Joshua is not here?"

"We go to Mount Hermon. Let us go down the ropes, just in case there are more soldiers down the access trail. No need to kill anyone else on our Shabbat. We have a long trip ahead of us."

29

DAY TWENTY-EIGHT: SUNDAY, JULY 17 / TAMMUZ 28

Mount Hermon
Joshua—the Man of Sorrows

Joshua had been Sihon's prisoner for nine days. He had spent two days at Sihon's camp on Mount Gerizim before being thrown into a mule-drawn cage and transported for two days along bumpy roads to what looked like the headquarters of the new confederation of Jebusites, Hittites, and Amorites at Mount Hermon.[1] There were thousands of soldiers here, all under different banners. For nine days, Joshua had been beaten and tortured. They had shoved slivers of bamboo under his fingernails, burned the bottom of his feet with hot irons, plucked his beard one hair at a time, and almost drowned him in barrels of water. He had eaten small scraps of dry, mouldy bread only twice since his capture, and he was always hungry. They forced him to defecate and urinate in his four-by-four-by- four-cubit cage, and he had to push his excretions out between the wooden bars to make a place where he could lie down.

At night the guards took turns banging the bars with their swords and calling his name to keep him awake, until his desire to sleep was more powerful than even his desire to eat. The previous night was the only night they'd left him alone since his capture. He'd slept at least seven hours. Perhaps they were getting bored with him. He would see Sihon from time to time when he came to gloat and taunt him. Sihon's brother Og had come from Bashan to join him at camp, and the two of them, at night in drunken stupors, would have a contest that involved urinating on Joshua from a distance. Og was much, much bigger than Sihon, but by their faces, one could tell the family resemblance.

Joshua's heart felt like it was rotting. He wondered if there was any pain more significant than what he was experiencing. He just wanted everything to be over. His twisted nerves tried screaming instructions to his brain, but his animal instincts had replaced his subjective thoughts. He wanted only to run, to hide, and—if they would let him—to fight. Everything good he had learned over the years had evaporated into the thin air of Mount Hermon. The imaginary scorpions of time ran up and down his body when he closed his eyes, consuming his youth and any beauty he might have had at one time. His ideals, once fruitful and prolific, were now a clouded, and distant memory. He reluctantly embraced the two new, ghoulish friends—hurt and pain—that would not leave him alone. He wanted them to go away, to befriend someone else, but they insisted on frolicking with him. The only visitor Joshua really wanted was death. Death was like the wind in his face—he could feel him all around but was unable to take his hand. He wanted to go gently.

The guard opened the door to his cell for the first time in nine days.

"Follow me," he ordered sharply.

Joshua was disoriented, and thought he was hallucinating again. He did not move.

"*Come*," The guard commanded again, grabbing Joshua's arm and dragging him out of his tiny world.

Joshua managed to stand on his wobbly legs. The guard was behind him now and shoved him forward. The thrust propelled him to the ground, but his knees and arms kept him from hitting the dirt face first.

"Get up!" the guard shouted.

Joshua mustered all his strength and pushed himself upright again. He put his left foot forward, then his right, and then repeated the process. The guard, impatient with his speed, rammed him once more. This time Joshua quickly moved his legs under his torso and kept his upright position.

The guard escorted him to the entrance of a tent containing a long table with rocks of different sizes placed on it. Sihon sat on a stool at the end of the table.

"Hello, Joshua. How do you say it in your language—*Shalom*?" Sihon quipped. "You must be very hungry. Are you hungry? We have heard that when you do not have food, your God provides you with something called manna. I was not sure what size the manna is, so as you can see on the table, I have offered you a variety. Call upon your God now to change the rocks into manna, so you can eat. If you do not eat something, you will die."

Joshua shook his head. "We Israelites do not depend upon bread alone to sustain us, but on everything our God says."

"It is as I thought," Sihon said calmly. "Rumours and lies, all of it. How could your God allow your suffering and hunger? You cannot magically change these stones into food because nobody can do that. Neither can your God. It is impossible. But let me show you what I can do for you".

Sihon opened the flap of the tent. The guard pushed Joshua inside.

"Please come in. Seeing your God will not help you," he said, smiling courteously, "I have prepared a table for you, and a bath that you so desperately need."

Two maidens were working diligently beside a large barrel, pouring hot water from a kettle drum that had been heated over the fire. Beside the bath were a chair and table with fresh fruit, cheese, meat, bread, and a vessel of wine.

"I want to start our relationship over from the start, Joshua. You are a strong man and a courageous man. You spared my life, and now I will spare yours. I admire your courage. Please eat, drink, and clean yourself up, and later on we will have a little talk." With that, Sihon snapped his fingers, and the ladies left the tent. Sihon pulled the chair out from under the table and gestured for Joshua to sit. Joshua ran to the table and stuffed whatever he could grab into his face. One hand had the bread; the other hand had the meat. Some of the food was getting into his mouth, but most of it he was pressing against his face and dropping onto the table.

Sihon giggled. "See? We are alike in some ways. This is the way I eat every night. The maidens will wait outside the tent for you. When you are ready to call them in, they will put ointment and bandages on your feet." He turned and left Joshua in the tent.

Joshua ate so quickly that he vomited up most of the food he had forced down his throat. It was delicious in his mouth, but his stomach had shrunk from not eating for so many days, and he had swallowed too much for it to handle all at once. After some time, however, he started to feel better. He scrubbed himself clean in the tub, taking sips of the wine. It did not take long for him to start feeling heady as the alcohol flowed through his body. He had sores on his backside that were very tender in the hot water, but he relished these comforts as he never had before. After he dried himself off, he called for the maidens, who came immediately, giggling and whispering to themselves. After they had treated his feet with a white ointment, they wrapped them tightly with clean bandages. Joshua pointed to his backside and asked them if they could use a little lotion there as well, and they both giggled again and went to work. The maidens were caressing his back, and one reached sensuously forward to the front of Joshua's body, still giggling.

Joshua jumped up in shock. "No, no—do not do that."

"But sir, we were told to take care of your every need. Do you not need a woman?" she asked bashfully.

"No, I do not want a woman. You have done a fine job, thank you. You may go now."

"But Sihon will be angry with us. Please, sir, let me be obedient to his orders."

"No, please go now," Joshua insisted, red-faced.

They grabbed Joshua's clothing and left the tent, and Joshua fell asleep within minutes. He dreamed that someone was staring at him, woke up with a fright, and found himself looking directly into the battle-scarred face of Sihon.

"The ladies washed and dried your clothes. Put them on," Sihon commanded as he looked at his long fingernails. "We are going for a ride. Did you sleep well, my friend?"

Joshua was silent.

"There is plenty of time to sleep when you are dead, but you will lose your value to me then. If I wanted you dead, you would already be dead. Do you understand that?"

Joshua nodded as he slipped into his freshly washed clothing, wondering what Sihon was conniving. Outside the tent were two horses and four other mounted soldiers. Joshua was still showing signs of weakness when he walked, as his feet were still very sore. Sihon helped him get on his horse and then jumped on his.

"Follow me," he shouted, kicking his horse into a gallop. Joshua's horse automatically followed behind Sihon's, and they rode a trail that led up the mountain.

Mount Hermon was the highest mountain in the region, and it captured a lot of the precipitation that the dryer regions of Canaan craved. Random faults broke the limestone on the mountain. Snow covered its three peaks, and as it melted, it fed springs and brooks down the rock channels and pores and eventually became the Jordan River. The valley was fertile with vineyards, and pine, oak, and poplar trees grew everywhere. Mount Hermon could be seen from a great distance. It marked the northern limits of the Israelites' promised land,[2] but Sihon called the mountain Senir and believed that his ancestors, the watcher class of fallen angels, had been here when they vowed to take wives from among the daughters of men. It was a holy place for Sihon and his brother Og, so it was fitting that the entire HAJ alliance would meet here to discuss their strategy concerning the upcoming battles with the Israelites now camped at Kadesh-Barnea.

At a clearing by a precipice, Sihon got off his horse and motioned for Joshua to dismount. It was a perfect afternoon, with not a cloud in the sky. Sihon walked to the edge of the sheer cliff, and Joshua stumbled obediently behind, taking three steps to Sihon's one.

Sihon was delighted when he heard that Joshua had been captured and was on his way to him. He now had the head of the snake—or did he? Sihon was different than the Anakim, his six-toed, six-fingered, slow-thinking cousins. Not all battles were won by brawn alone. Only intelligence and insight won wars. Was it possible to persuade Joshua to work for him? If he could do that, then he could easily obliterate the Israelite army camped on his doorstep. Joshua was just a human, and humans were weak. He would make Joshua even more vulnerable if he starved him for a while. Sihon smiled. His grandfather would be proud.

"What do you see?" Sihon asked.

"Everything. It seems I can see forever," Joshua responded.

"Over there is the Sea of Galilee, one hundred and fifty thousand cubits away." Turning to his left, he pointed. "And over there, the city of Damascus." Turning again, this time to the right, he said, "That is the city of Dan. All of this farmland is the richest and most fertile in the world."

"It is quite the sight," Joshua stated.

"Do you see all the troops and military camps? The chariots and the horses?

"I see," Joshua replied.

"Count them if you want. With the Jebusites and the Hittites, we are more than one million men."

"Impressive," Joshua said, unimpressed.

"What do you not see?" Sihon pressed.

"Sihon, stop beating around the bush," Joshua sighed. "What is it that you want?"

"You do not see Hittites fighting Jebusites, and you do not see Amorites killing Hittites. We are united because we have a common enemy. We are a new people, and we call ourselves the HAJ."

They stared at the enormous armies in front of them.

"Joshua, your God has forsaken you. He did not feed you; however, I did. He did not release you from the cage—I did. Your men declared mutiny on your leadership, so they have already deserted you. I am going to give you an opportunity that you cannot refuse."

"Let me guess. If I bow down and worship you, you will give me all these lands?" Joshua snickered.

"Well, these lands are mine to give if I so choose. All these inhabitants pay me some monetary tribute, but no, that is not the opportunity I am offering. Joshua, I admire your courage, and I want to make you an offer. But before I do, I want you to consider your options carefully. You are a smart man, and you will make the right choice. You can either throw yourself off this ledge with my help, and call out to your God to save you, or you can become one of us. I will make you my commander, and you will report only to me. I need information and somebody inside the Israelite army, somebody I can count on."

"You are asking me to give up my God?"

"Not at all. We Canaanites have many gods, and if you choose to worship yours, you are free to do so however you please. We are considerate and respectful of everyone's personal beliefs. We believe in diversity and tolerance, but we will not lie down, and we will not be dominated by a nation that has no tolerance."

Joshua thought about his options for a moment. He looked at the monster before him, and his respect grew.

"Let me understand what you are saying. I continue leading the Israelites, and I continue serving my God, but I report to you. When you finally destroy the Israelite army, you compensate me with land and status. Am I correct?

"See, I knew you were bright, Joshua. Yes, that is my offer. Or you can spread your arms like an eagle, and I will throw you down this mountain right now," Sihon barked.

"It is an exciting proposition, Sihon. I need to think this out very carefully. You must give me two days for my answer. I have seen qualities in you today that I never imagined existed. You are wise and crafty. However, I must search my soul for the correct response. Is that acceptable to you?"

"Certainly, my friend. Of course, you must consider how many lives will be saved or destroyed by your decision." Sihon smiled. "You may have your two days."

They got on their horses and rode back to camp. When Joshua got to his tent, he fell prostrate on his cot and prayed until he fell asleep.

30

DAY TWENTY-NINE: MONDAY, JULY 18 / TAMMUZ 29

City of Hazor
Digging Down Deep

Mount Hermon had been visible since the day before, but as hard as they were riding, it seemed they were making little progress. Its snow-capped peaks taunted them. Hazor, just seventy-five thousand cubits away from Mount Hermon, was the largest of all the cities the spies had seen in Canaan. It was located just north of Lake Galilee and was the gateway to Mesopotamia. There were people everywhere: citizens, merchants coming into the city, and soldiers leaving to go north toward Mount Hermon. The spies rode, unnoticed, through the city gates. The palaces and temples, about one hundred dunam in size, were in the upper town, and massive walls protected them. The lower city, quite a bit larger at seven hundred dunam and protected by a massive rampart, was where most of the citizens lived in their mudstone houses. Hazor maintained commercial ties with Babylon and Syria and brought in large quantities of tin for its flourishing bronze industry.

The spies were exhausted from their travel, so they checked their horses into the stable and went to find suitable lodging. Caleb was concerned about the men, who were divided into two distinct camps that argued continually about the viability of invading Canaan. Shaphat, who was always willing to fight someone, was eager for the invasion. Shammua, who felt guilty about being caught soliciting harlots, agreed. Palti and Gaddiel, who had not, perhaps, completely stopped using their artificial confidence builders, disagreed. They felt the cities were too fortified for the army to conquer. Both Igal and Sethur saw business opportunities and money to be made in this new land, and encouraged the assault. Win or lose, they knew life would be lucrative here.

Gaddi and Ammiel were continually arguing about the need to kill so many people. Gaddi felt that the price to pay for a victory was too high. Ammiel's position was that the strong survive, while the weak do not. All Geuel could think about was avenging Donatiya, and after he did that, he did not care what happened.

Caleb could think of nothing beyond saving his friend Joshua. In fact, the only thing that united them at the moment was their respect for Joshua and their shared desire to avenge his capture. They found a small tavern in the upper city, ordered some bread, cheese, and yogurt, and swilled it down with wine.

As they were arguing back and forth, a group of six men came into the tavern and sat down two benches away from them. It was obvious they too were travellers, as they were dressed entirely in black and kept to themselves. Thinking there might be an opportunity to gain some information, Ammiel started up a conversation.

"It is a great city, do you not think? Hazor is the largest city we have seen."

"Yes," one of the men answered. "We have never seen a city this size."

"From where have you come, traveller?"

"My name is Pirati, and we are from the area of Hor in the south, near the Negev Desert."

"Such a long way to come. What brings you to Hazor?" Ammiel asked.

"We are village people, small farmers and keepers of goats, and they call us Perizzites. Walls protect none of our villages; everything is open. We have heard that a foreign army waits to invade our beloved countryside, and a confederation of tribes has come together to defend our land. They call themselves the HAJ. We will attempt to join this alliance, and although we do not have silver and gold, will contribute human resources—all of our young and fighting men—if the confederation will protect our villages."

Caleb looked at his men.

"Ah, yes, we know what you are talking about," Ammiel said, thinking quickly. "We thought of doing this same thing. We met yesterday with Sihon, the leader of this great union."

The six men now showed sincere excitement, while the other Israelites looked confused.

"Tell us about it. Where are you from?" Pirati asked.

"We are from the south coast, and they call us Hivites. We came to join their alliance as well, but, alas, they turned us down. They said they had enough volunteers, but if we wished to contribute gold and silver, it would be well used."

"They rejected your services? Quite unbelievable," Pirati declared.

"Yes. In fact, we were lucky to get away. After we told them we did not have any silver or gold to offer, they grew furious, and we had to run away to save our lives," Ammiel said. "Fortunately, we escaped, and it was just barely."

Pirati and his friends, frightened, started grumbling back and forth to each other.

"Well, thanks be to Baal we met you—you have perhaps saved our lives. If they rejected *you*, who look like warriors, what would they say to us? We will return to our villages and tell the people that we tried but they turned us down."

"Let us buy you men a few vessels of wine, at least," Ammiel added.

"We have enough to buy *you* some wine, for you have done us a great service." And Pirati lifted his arm to summon the server to refill all the vessels.

"Tell us all about the Perizzites. We would love to know more about you," Ammiel pleaded.

Two hours later, the Perizzites left the tavern, found their horses, and left Hazor for the south as quickly as they could.

Caleb was smiling. "Well done, Ammiel. Where do you come up with this stuff? At least there is one less tribe in the confederation now."

"Yes, but the Perizzites will go to Mount Hermon tomorrow as planned," Ammiel added slyly.

"What do you mean? They will be halfway home tomorrow with their tails tucked between their legs," Igal interjected.

"Nahbi, you are the fashion expert. Take Igal, our astute businessman, to the market, and have eleven black goat-hair costumes sewn together, just like the ones the Perizzites were wearing. Get the matching headgear as well. I loved the way they looked. We will want to look exactly like the men who sat here a few moments ago. Can you do that? Do you have enough shekels?"

"I thought they looked horrible—like poor villagers, dressed in nothing but black," Nahbi responded. "If you think we need new outfits, I have some great ideas."

"No. Do exactly as I have told you. Spend some of that money you won backing your prizefighter. We need these black outfits tonight at the very latest, so pay extra to have them made quickly! Oh, and Nahbi? Have them make one extra outfit for a giant, a five-cubit man. Pay what you must for the rush job," Ammiel said, grinning mischievously.

Back on Mount Hermon, Sihon learned that his camp on Mount Gerizim had been attacked, and fifteen of his soldiers had died.

"Damn those Israelites. I thought they had split up and were enjoying the comforts of Canaan," he said to his brother Og. "They are like the smell of the back end of a camel: it just does not go away. Og, I put you in charge. Keep everything going. Tomorrow those idiot farmers, the Perizzites, are coming. They have asked to join the HAJ army, and have pledged their young men to our troops. Please treat them nicely, and do not eat them for lunch. We are going to need as many men as we can muster to destroy these worms. These Perizzite villagers are exposed to minimal opportunities for growth, education, culture, or entertainment. They have developed a minimal vision of life. Tell them we will protect their communities, towns, and homes —we want their young men to fight for us."

"Understood, brother," Og replied. "What about your prisoner, Joshua?"

"Leave him. He has nowhere to go. Trust him, but verify everything he says and does." Sihon smiled once again. "I made him an offer he cannot refuse."

Sihon and eight other horsemen headed south. As they were cantering leisurely toward Shechem, they saw from a distance a group of riders coming in their direction, arranged head to tail in a snail-pace procession and dressed in entirely in black. Sihon recognized from their attire that it was the Perizzite delegation. He was in no mood for pleasantries and certainly did not want to explain anything to small-minded villagers. So he kicked his horse into a gallop and sped past them with his entourage, leaving the poor travellers, who had pulled aside to let them pass on the narrow trail, in a cloud of dust.

He was pleasantly surprised by the size of the Perizzites riding their horses. These would make a great addition to his army. Og could handle them for the time being while he focused on those pesky Israelites who'd invaded his Gerizim camp. According to the report he'd received, they had climbed up the impossible face of the mountain flanking his encampment. He had to admit, these Hebrew pigs were imaginative and resourceful. He would find them and finish them, like he should have done when they were in Hebron.

Sihon was sure Joshua would agree to his proposition. After all, Joshua was a man like any other, with the same desire for power, position, and riches. What human in his right mind would turn down such a lucrative offer? In the years that he had walked the earth, he could not think of anyone so stupid as to make the wrong choice when there were only two options. Sihon laughed proudly to himself. *Let us see... On this hand, you die, and on the other hand, you get all the gold you could dream of, an army of one million men at your beck and command, and a great land so rich and fertile that it grows pomegranates the size of watermelons.* What would anyone choose?

Caleb and the men, in between coughing and sputtering, dusted off their new garments.

"That was Sihon. What are we waiting for? Let us go and kill the pagan," Shaphat fumed.

"Relax. Keep your temper under control," Caleb commanded. "We have a plan, and we will stick to it. It is a good thing Sihon will not be at the camp, for he knows what our faces look like."

"But there were only eight of them! We could put them in their grave and continue our mission to find Joshua," Shaphat complained.

"It is too close to their camp. They would find out quickly, and it would destroy our plan. The best plans fail when we fail to keep to the plan. Shaphat, think about your fighting strategy. You are up against an opponent twice your size. Your strategy is to keep a distance and pummel him with leg kicks and jabs. He wants to get you in close and get all his weight on you, giving him the advantage. If you get angry and succumb to his grappling, your chance of victory is a lot less than if you stand your ground and keep your distance. You make a plan and stick with it if you want to win."

"There are times when you have to modify and change your strategy. Believe me—if anyone knows that, it's me."

"Only when you must, Shaphat, and at the moment, there is no need to change our fight plan. We will stick to our scheme, and that is to find Joshua and set him free. The dust Sihon showered on our clothing is nothing to the dust that will cover his grave one day."

31

DAY THIRTY: TUESDAY, JULY 19 / AV 1

Mount Hermon
The Sting

Og was happy Sihon had left. He hated taking orders from anybody, especially his younger, smaller brother. He should be in charge of this confederation, not Sihon. After all, it was he who was King of Bashan. He ruled over sixty cities, all fortified with high walls, gates, and bars to lock the gates.[1] And that was just the walled cities. Many villages, almost too many to count, were also part of his empire.

He knew the Hebrews better than anyone. It was he who had gone to Abraham[2] so long ago and informed him that his nephew, Lot, had been captured after the kings of Babylonia—Ellasar, Elam, and Goiim—had sacked the cities of Sodom and Gomorrah. Of course, he had wanted Abraham to go to battle. He'd wanted him to perish, as Og had been hopelessly in love with Sarah, Abraham's beautiful wife. But as usual, Abraham's God prevailed, driving out the invading armies and rescuing Lot. But although Og had hoped for a different outcome, it all worked out okay: Abraham had rewarded Og with wealth beyond his dreams for informing him about his nephew's capture. Og even begrudgingly became circumcised[3] to put to rest any suspicion the Hebrews might have about him. As a result, they left him alone, and he could do whatever he wanted.

For all intents and purposes, Og had lied when he'd confessed his commitment to their God. But why would the grandson of Shamhazai bend his knee to any mortal or god? Was he not a god among these puny humans? They sang songs about him in Bashan. They played music on their lyres and flutes, on their drums and cymbals, extolling his power and abilities. The God of the Hebrews might have sent his grandfather and comrades in chains to tartarus,[4] the underworld below hades, but He left the mighty Og here on earth to reign.

Og had just finished having a quick nap, and he was hungry. He had to have his bed specially made when he arrived at the camp, for it was nine cubits long and four cubits wide. Sihon and Og were not like the barbaric Anakim who had six fingers and six toes and lived in the caves that bordered the Dead Sea. Og thought of himself and his brother as more genetically evolved. They were Rephaim: smart and cunning as well as mammoth. There were advantages and disadvantages to being so large. Og loved the fear he saw in people's eyes when they saw him for the first time. History had taught Og that when it came to the driving instincts, fear had no rival. Fear has a way of bending people, and Og always used it to his advantage. Nobody could match his strength—he could pick up a full-grown horse and throw it to the ground without much effort. One night, during a drunken stupor, he'd put twelve men on a long-broken tree trunk, squatted underneath it, and with his shoulders firmly against the bottom, stood up on his two legs, much to the laughter and cheering of his brother.

Unfortunately, he bumped his head on everything, and there was not an entrance he did not have to duck to enter. His leather shoes never lasted more than three weeks, and his clothes often ripped when he stretched too far. Small, delicate things, like brushes or ropes, were difficult for him to hold. He loved women, but they were petrified of his attentions. When he got angry with them for whatever reason, he would strike them and unintentionally maim or kill them instantly. He had, however, learned to live with the negatives. They were nothing to the advantages, especially the fear he generated.

His attendants brought in his midday snack, which comprised two whole ox livers, one kidney, three steaks from the shoulder of a sheep, and a complete pig's head. Along with it, there were twelve eggs, a huge pile of goat cheese, two plates of mushrooms, fifteen carrots, and three cauliflowers. On the dessert plates, there was a mountain of figs, six apples, half a bucket of yogurt, and—his absolute favourite—an uncooked human heart. Og ate five times a day. It was one of his greatest pleasures, and he never let the day's worries or concerns interfere with his routine.

But just as he was sitting down to enjoy the moment, one of the guards called out and asked permission to enter his tent.

"What do you want?" he roared in anger. "Can it not wait? I am dining."

"The Perizzite delegation is here, Your Highness," the guard sputtered nervously from outside. "They asked for Sihon."

"Tell them I am busy. When I finish, I will call the idiots," he said, his mouth stuffed with goat meat. "Show them around the camp. Amuse them until I am ready for them."

"Yes sir." The reply came quickly, and Og heard the guard's footsteps withdraw.

The Israelite spies were grouped on the outskirts of the camp, waiting for the guard to return and grant them permission to enter.

"Remember, men: let me do the talking, stick close together, and always keep your hand on your sword," Caleb instructed.

Ammiel showed no emotion, but inwardly he fumed at Caleb's words and wondered who had made him king. Caleb was not even a real Hebrew by blood. However, it was best to keep his mouth shut. Caleb's was Joshua's friend, end of story. But Ammiel was getting sick and tired of being subordinate to everyone.

"Do you have the extra outfit?" Caleb asked.

"Got it," Nahbi whispered. "It is in this bag."

The smiling guard approached on his own, and it was apparent by his size that he was either a Jebusite or Hittite.

"Sihon is not in camp. However, Og, his brother and ruler of Bashan, will see you when he is free. In the meantime, let me show you around."

With the amount of horse and foot traffic, the men had to be careful where they stepped, taking giant steps over the pungent horse dung. There were rows and rows of black, makeshift tents, their occupants sitting outside them, tending small campfires and sipping hot beverages. The piquant smell of pig meat permeated the air and competed with the scents of leather and animal hides. In the gorge below the camp, the sound of soldiers marching and barking orders to each other was relentless. Caleb estimated a force of at least fifty thousand. It was not hard to locate the Amorites because of their size. The Jebusites and Hittites were harder to identify. He assumed the Jebusites made up the infantry, while the cavalry, with their large chariots, looked more like hardened Hittite legionnaires.

Caleb struggled to find words that would impress his Hittite escorts. "I thought the HAJ army was larger than what I see in down in that valley."

"What you see there is just one of our twenty military corps. There are five specialist divisions. Is has taken some time for us to blend the fighting styles from each tribe. We are more than one million men now unified under Sihon."

"Wow, quite impressive." Caleb continued to flatter. "It is a remarkable sight to see three different nationalities working together so closely."

"Yes, three different societies, but one people. We are all proud Canaanites."

"Well," Caleb echoed, "we are here to make it four societies. We are eager to join forces and stop the impending threat of the army that is camping at Kadesh-Barnea."

"You are welcome, my brothers." Their guide smiled affectionately.

They came upon a group of about fifteen men dressed in white gowns and tall hats that were walking around a large campfire. They were chanting and throwing something from a bucket toward their feet, then picking it up again and repeating the process.

"What are they doing?' Ammiel asked, knowing he was disobeying Caleb's direct orders.

"Those are the finest and holiest priests and enchanters in all of Canaan. They are throwing bones to see what Chemosh wants from us today."

Geuel immediately thought of Donatiya. He gripped his sword handle tightly and examined the priests to see if Phineas was among them. But Caleb saw Phineas first and squeezed Geuel's shoulder tightly, urging him without words to exercise self-control. Then, as the priests danced in circles, the ritually blood-smeared face of Phineas emerged, his eyes closed, his head stooped, his voice warbling deep baritone incantations.

"We have an extraordinary guest at our camp," the guard boasted. "The high general of the Israelite army—he goes by the name of Joshua—has secretly joined our cause."

All the men stopped and looked at Caleb.

"I suppose I should not speak too quickly," their guide explained. "Sihon has made him an offer he cannot refuse, and his answer is due tomorrow. He is one tough son of a harlot, and will be a great addition to our forces."

"That is wonderful news," Caleb said. "Where is this gift from God?"

"He is not far from here. I will take you to his tent. Follow me this way, if you please."

They hardly recognized Joshua, sitting alone by his campfire. His tattered beard looked almost completely torn out, his face was black and blue with bruises, and his clothing hung from his emaciated body. He was not wearing his sword or his sandals, and blood- and pus-soaked bandages covered his feet.

"Brothers," their guide said, "I must take your leave. It is my turn for training, and the rules are stringent here. I will send my colleague to continue your camp tour as soon as I get to the training field."

"We will wait here for him," Caleb offered.

As soon as he left, the men sauntered over to Joshua, hoping not to attract any attention.

Caleb beamed. "Joshua, it is us, your brothers."

Joshua looked up and rubbed his eyes in disbelief. "Caleb? Is it you?"

"Yes. We are going to get you out of here. I see your bandaged feet —are you strong enough to walk?"

"Yes, my feet are much better than they were. How are we going to do this?" Joshua whispered. "What is your plan?"

"Are you strong enough to carry a man on your shoulders?" Caleb was smiling ear to ear now. "The plan is for you to put Nahbi, the lightest of us all, on your shoulders. We will dress you in this black tunic, which will come down to the bottom of your ankles. There are enough giant Amorites around that nobody will notice a tall Perizzite. You will just have to take off your bandages and wear Nahbi's sandals, as that will be all that anyone will see of you. We were eleven men coming into camp and will be eleven when we leave. Hurry now, Joshua. Go into your tent with Nahbi and put on this black tunic."

When Joshua came out of the tent with Nahbi on his shoulders, the replacement guard was just approaching them.

"Greetings, Perizzites. I am Yolos. Kerret sent me from the training field to continue your tour, but there is no need," he said with his Hittite accent. "Og has finished his business and is ready to see you now. Follow me."

"The pleasure is all ours, Yolos. Nevertheless, before we meet with the mighty Og, we wish to go back to our horses to fetch the wonderful gifts that we brought from our land."

"No need. I can send someone to get them for you. When Og summons you, you are smart to run. He hates to wait."

"But it would not be the same if someone else brought our gifts. We wish to see Og's eyes shine when he sees what we brought. We wish to do it ourselves. Would you kindly grant us this small favour, my friend?" Caleb said cordially.

"Okay, but let us hurry. Come this way, it is a shorter way to the paddocks."

As they stepped forward, Joshua stumbled and almost fell. Nahbi instinctively squeezed his legs around Joshua's head.

"Are you all right?" Yolos said to Nahbi, now the tallest Perizzite

"He had a little too much to drink last night," Caleb explained. "We were celebrating our visit to camp, and he has been staggering all day."

"I know that feeling," Yolos laughed, looking at Nahbi's face. "Here. They say the best thing for a wobbly leg is a little more medicine." He handed Nahbi a vessel from inside his tunic. Nahbi did not know what to do, so he graciously took the container and swilled a lengthy slurp.

"You are right, Yolos. I feel better already," Nahbi spluttered with a smile.

Joshua staggered between the men, looking down at his feet. Each step he took was excruciatingly painful, and it was everything he could do not to fall. Shammua walked behind him, leading him right and left with a small push of his hand. Joshua could hear the horses neighing and snorting, so they had to be close. He put one foot in front of the other, then did it again, methodically. Still, he stumbled and fell.

Yolos laughed again—until he noticed that Nahbi was in fact two people. But before he could reach for his sword, Shaphat silenced him forever.

The four men watching the horses in the paddock came running over to see what the commotion was all about. Geuel, Igal, Gaddiel, and Shammua killed them quickly. They found their horses, took an extra one for Joshua, helped him up, and sped away. They prayed they had enough of a head start to escape. Nobody turned around to check. They leaned forward and galloped as fast as they could.

32

DAY THIRTY-ONE: WEDNESDAY, JULY 20 / AV 2

Jezreel Valley
Beauty Is In The Eye Of The Beholder

The Israelite spies fled until the darkness made it impossible to go any further. They found a cave in which to sleep for a few hours, relieved that their rescue of Joshua had been successful, but there was no time for jubilation. Og would be coming after them soon. Nightfall gave them some respite, but as soon as the sun began to rise, they would have to be vigilant and move as far away as possible from Mount Hermon.

When Sethur wandered out of the cave to relieve himself at the next dawn, he saw the horde of riders speeding toward them. Instantly, Joshua and his men jumped on their horses, leaned forward, gave them a hard kick, and bolted away. Their choice was to fight or flee, and there were too many of the enemy, so the decision was simple: run today and live to fight another day. Joshua's body was still very sore from the torture he had endured, and it took all his strength to keep his body low on his mount. The thirty-five pagan predators racing toward them were sitting high on their horses. They broke their two-by-two formation and spread out to form a web, whipping their horses with their leather reins.

Racing ahead, Joshua saw the labyrinth of small green saplings, the boulders, and the thick fallen oak tree that ended the trail. On the other side of this barricade, he could see a very steep incline covered in loose sand, rocks, and muck. Caleb was the first to jump the barrier, barely clearing it with the back legs of his mare. Joshua and the rest of the men were right behind. Joshua's upper body bolted forward as the front legs of his horse hit the rocks on the incline first, and for a moment, his horse stumbled. Then her hinds came down with a thump and a thud. They were riding downhill at a forty-five-degree angle, and the horses could at any moment go forward flipping over their heads. In pain, Joshua tightly shut his eyes and gripped the mane tightly. His horse's eyes were wide with fear, and her nostrils snorted and flared with every step. Joshua was lightheaded and unstable, and he knew he had to trust his horse because he had no sense of balance whatsoever. He started gagging spasmodically and resisted the urge to vomit.

"Lean back as far as you can and squeeze with your knees," Caleb blurted out, wiping the mud from his face and hoping someone would hear him. "Get your backs against your horse's rear end, and just let your horses be the horses they are."

The upper half of the men's bodies thrashed up and down in jerks and spasms. The branches of the saplings growing on the incline smacked the horses' forelegs and chests and whacked the men's legs with the pain of an executioner's whip. Joshua held his breath and prayed that his mare found her footing.

Og's men pulled their horses to a full stop at the top of the hill, just before the fallen oak tree. They watched with a military respect as their eleven intruders and one captive escaped. They could never ride like that, and certainly not down a precipice as steep as the one before them. They dismounted and began shooting arrows in their direction, but Joshua and his entourage were now out of range. They would have to go around to where the mountain was a little more friendly in its decline, and that would take at least half a day. The

Canaanites were sure the Israelites would be heading for the Jordan River toward the east.

The spies were now in the verdant Jezreel Valley, a couple of hours from Armageddon. They had to decide which way to go. There was an easy route along the Jezreel to the Jordan River and then south toward Jericho. Or they could go up to Megiddo, through the treacherous Aruna pass to Yehem, and along the Philistine plains back to Beersheba. Og and his men would assume they would take the quickest and easiest route. Very few travellers made it through the Aruna pass. But Ammiel and Gaddi had travelled it once already, and they knew the way.

The Hebrews headed toward Megiddo.

Back at the main camp of the HAJ confederation, the captain in charge of Og's squad walked hesitatingly into Og's tent, knowing full well how upset his commander was going to be. He approached Og, who was sitting on his oversized throne, fell to one knee, and bowed his head. His eyes were squeezed shut, and his heart was pounding faster than a hummingbird's wings. .

"Give me the news. Are the Hebrew pigs dead?" Og hissed wondering why the captain's tunic was sopping wet with sweat. Og became aware that the captain was having trouble breathing and was wobbling on his one knee.

The captain's breathing was difficult, and he felt dizzy. "No, Your Highness. They escaped down a sheer cliff, and my men had to go a different route to get around the precipice. But I am sure we will capture them soon. The only route they can take is through the Jezreel Valley, heading east. We will get ahead and ambush them," he said, his mouth dryer than the Negev Desert in the middle of summer.

Og's stomach cramped and made him want to retch. Then his face began to twitch. The headache that had started when he heard that the prisoners got away was now like a hot sword searing the right side of the Og's brain.

"You let them escape?" Og's voice was unrecognizable. He clenched and unclenched his fists, feeling the muscles in his forearm tighten and then relax. He was so sick of the incompetence that humans demonstrated consistently.

"Y-y-yes, sir," the captain stuttered. "We almost had them, but they did things with their horses that we have never seen before."

There was a pregnant silence. The captain took a deep breath, held it for a few seconds, then exhaled slowly. He'd delivered the worst part of the news, and he was still alive.

"I am truly sorry, sir," he repeated. "What are your orders now?"

Og turned around calmly and picked up his heavy sword in both hands. "You are sorry, you say?" Og repeated quietly. "Sorry is something you say to your wife for the hurt you caused. Then you kiss and say you will try harder next time. There will be no next time—it is me who is sorry for making you a captain."

And, with cat-like speed, Og removed the submissive head of his kneeling minion with one blow. Og's blood-curdling shriek made everyone within earshot shiver.

The spacious flat of the Jezreel Valley was beautiful this time of year. Surrounding it were Mount Carmel and the Gilboa mountain range one side, and Mount Tabor, Mount Moreh, and the Nazareth ridge on the other. These highlands were nothing compared to Mount Hermon, but they all fed into the River Kishon, which in turn forced its way into the Jezreel Valley. It was a well-known passage for travellers going south to Egypt or north to Mesopotamia. It was known as the valley of Armageddon. The alluvial soil that made up this fertile valley eventually crossed into Lower Galilee, making it one of the most important agricultural regions in all of Canaan. Joshua smiled as he took in the bountiful wheat and barley growing wild, their stalks gently blowing in the wind. He was sure anything, with care, could blossom and grow here. It was indeed the land of milk and honey promised to his ancestors. The baby-blue sky was littered with soft white clouds floating toward the east.

Different shades of green permeated the landscape. Dabs of emerald, olive and fern shone in the sun, and where the dark shadows of the clouds touched the terrain, the vegetation became dark teal. The air was ripe with the pleasant, dewy petrichor of a post-rain evening. The rainy season had come and gone, but the swampy muck on the lower part of the narrow trail was the harsh consequence of the surrounding mountains draining into one area. The mud was deep and bottomless. Joshua and his men rode single file, their horses nose to tail.

In the distance, a group of about thirty people ambled toward them on foot. As they came closer, it became obvious they were a colony of lepers. Their hair was messy and uncombed, their clothes tattered. The man leading them started ringing his bell and calling out, "Unclean, Unclean." As they got closer, the Israelites recognized the swollen lumps on their skin and the scabs on their arms and legs. The laws of Moses contained stringent instructions about approaching lepers. Among the sixty-one defilements of the ancient Jewish laws, leprosy was second only to death in seriousness.

Fortunately, there was no wind blowing—if there were, they could not get any closer than one hundred cubits. The disease was considered so revolting that a leper wasn't allowed to come within four cubits of any other human, including his family.[1] It was an uncontrollable disease that could remain in the body, latent, anywhere between five and twenty years, even if there were no initial outward symptoms.

The strong, good-looking man leading the lepers called out, "Greetings, travellers. Have you some alms for the poor, maybe some dry morsels of bread that you could spare?"

"What is your name, leper? Joshua responded.

"I am Orus, leader of these pathetic wretches."

"Orus, we feel your pain. With pleasure, we will give you some food and some silver if you would only let us pass. We are forbidden to be any closer to you than four cubits, and as this path is so narrow, we will defile our laws unless you move over and give us our space."

"Consider yourselves fortunate to feel pain, traveller. Many of us have lost that ability. You want us to go into the quagmire so you can ride past us? Death may be a better state than the one we are presently living, but death by drowning in mud is not what we will do today. You are on horses. Surely it is up to you to move over?"

"As you wish," Joshua responded, moving his horse toward the edge of the trail.

"Before you try, kind traveller, please let me inform you that we saw, not far from here, what appeared to be a horse head, or at least its ears, sticking out from the mud. The bog almost swallowed him whole. But perhaps I can offer another solution. About one hour behind us is an elevated mound; we could all walk back and try there? You need not worry about me, because the disease has not infected me. My wife is in this group. I have chosen to be with her and her disease. Being in this world without her would be much more painful. So we can walk together?"

The men obediently dismounted. They walked their horses behind the collection of lepers, who were now walking back in the direction they had come. Orus explained to Joshua how devastated he had been when his wife started showing symptoms. At first, light-coloured skin patches appeared on her arms and chest, but they became redder and redder each day. Her sense of touch dissipated to almost nothing, and when Orus held her hand, she could not tell. She would complain of numbness one day, then the next day, she would jump out of her skin because it felt like needles. She started losing weight, and then her hair started falling out in patches. She began blinking more and complained about her eyesight. Eventually, the skin patches became larger and scaly, and it was apparent that she was infected.

The high priest had declared Orus and his wife lepers and forced them to move out of the city. Orus, though he was losing weight and sympathizing with his wife's symptoms, did not show any other characteristics of the disease. He visited the dubious priest, who, after examining him and not seeing any outward signs of the disease, put him through a seven-day ritual. On the first day of the formality, outside the city, the priest took cedar wood, a crimson cloth, and a live bird and dipped them into a vessel containing water and the blood of a second bird. He then sprinkled this mixture seven times on Orus and set the live bird free. He washed Orus's clothes, shaved off all Orus's body hair, and put him into a tub of water to bathe. Then he took Orus by his hand back into the city but forbade him to enter his home. Orus had to sleep in the stables with all the sheep and goats for six more days. On the seventh day, the priest made him shave his face and head one more time, launder his clothing, and bathe again. On the eighth day, the priest brought him to the temple with offerings, oil, and a live sheep. He lacerated the sheep, daubed Orus's right earlobe, thumb, and big toe with the blood, and declared him healed. He admonished Orus to stay away from his wife. Orus tried to stay away, leaving fresh food at her cave daily, but he loved her more than his own life and soon joined her in her cave—much to the chagrin of the priest.

As expected, he was ostracized along with his wife and forbidden to enter the city. Meanwhile, Papis, the governor of Megiddo, had a dream that if he banished all the lepers and other impure people from around his city, he would see his gods in all their glory. So Papis issued an edict banishing lepers from all regions surrounding the city, pushing them east toward the Judean Desert. That was the reason they were on the trail.

"Are you married?" Orus asked Joshua.

"No," Joshua responded, quite enjoying the company of his newfound friend, "not yet. The truth is I have not met the right person."

Orus laughed. "When you do, it is incredible. There is nothing more wonderful than sharing your life. Would you like to meet Hurriya, my wife?"

"I would consider it an honour."

Orus ran ahead and pulled a woman toward Joshua. She would not come willingly, and Orus had to talk sternly to her. Soon he was pulling her again toward Joshua, smiling from ear to ear though careful to keep her the minimum of four cubits away.

"Joshua, I would like to introduce you to Hurriya, my beloved wife. Hurriya, this is Joshua, leader of this band of Israelites."

Joshua looked at the woman beside Orus, and his heart overflowed with pity. She had no fingers on her hands, and her nose and one of her ears were missing. Her teeth and pink gums showed where, at one time, her upper lip must have been, and her face glittered with a red scaly substance. Joshua had to dig deep into his imagination, but if her soft green eyes were any indication, she might have been a beauty at one time. Through tears she forced a smile, which only showed more unhealthy teeth.

"It is a pleasure to meet you, sir," she sighed.

Perhaps she was wondering about Joshua's thoughts. She might have been surprised to learn that he was wishing for someone to love him as Orus loved her.

When they arrived at the clearing, the men walked their horses away from the path, rummaged through their provisions, and gave what they could spare to Orus, along with a bag of silver for them to purchase provisions when they could. Once the lepers passed them to continue their journey east, the spies jumped on their horses and cantered west toward Megiddo and Mount Carmel.

Mount Carmel was a 12,500-cubit-tall range of hills that ran from the Mediterranean Sea and sloped gradually toward the southwest. It formed steep ridges up to eight hundred cubits high on its northwestern face. Just as the Jezreel Valley formed a natural passageway, Mount Carmel formed a natural barrier that had a significant impact on migrations and invasions.

The Israelites started their ascent where the Kishon River flowed into the Jezreel. The land was changing and was now covered with odoriferous plants and flowers. There were hyacinths with their bright crimson, purple, and pink blossoms; yellow jonquils with blood-red centres; tazettas; and white, black-centred anemones, all growing like weeds. Olive and laurel trees stood tall, like rebellious giants worshipping the rays of the scorching sun. The rainy season had carpeted the ground with a green blanket of meadow and pasture that crept up the mountain. Along the bank of the Kishon, thick, overgrown bushes housed many different species of small birds, all cheerfully chirping up to the aquamarine sky. It was a pleasant reprieve for the travellers before they had to face the treacherous Aruna pass.

33

DAY THIRTY-TWO: THURSDAY, JULY 21 / AV 3

Aruna Pass
The Canaanite Evangelist

Ammiel and Gaddi knew that the problematic pass, as you climbed higher, became very narrow and scaled very high altitudes. Deeply furrowed ridges permeated the dangerous, rocky ravines. The Aruna pass began only five thousand cubits from Megiddo, but it was used mainly by sheepherders, as well as criminals on the run. It was a great place to hide, for the mountain formation, a mixture of limestone and flint, was characterized many hidden grottos and caves. As the spies began their ascent, Joshua turned around and cringed at the sight of Mount Hermon, with its snow-capped peaks, in the distance. It housed memories he could never forget.

For the Canaanites, any high knoll, hill, or mountain was a holy place, and Mount Carmel was no exception. The Hebrews came upon an assembly of clerics and congregants sitting in an flat, natural amphitheatre carved into the meadow, beside what looked like an old Abrahamic stone altar.

"Let us go and see what is going on," Ammiel suggested.

"We should keep going," Joshua insisted. "We do not know where Og's soldiers are."

"But look, Joshua," Igal said. "They have a table of food and fresh fruit for their adherents. Our food supply is low, especially after we helped Orus and his people. We can pretend we are interested and feed our bellies at the same time."

"Are you scared of the Canaanite gods, Joshua?" Palti asked facetiously.

"Okay, you have one hour. Eat your hearts out, and then we leave," Joshua commanded. "I would not mind checking out that altar," he added. "It looks familiar."

The men dismounted, tied up their horses, and sat down, listening to the self-proclaimed oracle. He was expounding the virtues of Melgart, Baal Sūr, a tutelary god of the Phoenician city of Tyre. Tyre was not far from Mount Carmel on the coast. Ammiel, unsurprisingly, knew all about it.

"If you follow me and my teachings," said the oracle, "do not look behind you at the life you used to live or the things you might have to give up. If you do, the serpent of hades will crash through the forest and thickets of Mount Carmel and destroy your life and the lives of your loved ones. The serpent will move as a black tempest, with claps of thunder and flashes of lightning."

With that proclamation, he took out his ceremonial knife and appeared to slice his arm. Blood dripped from his forearm. "However, if you follow me and the worship of Melgart, you will have prosperity beyond your wildest dreams. You will never get sick, and will have a protector unlike your world has ever seen." He held up his arm, wiped it with a white cloth, and presented it to the crowd. The blood had stopped—there was no sign that the flesh had ever been cut.

"How did he do that?" Sethur whispered to Ammiel in amazement.

"He has a bladder of blood hidden under his sleeve," Ammiel mused. "When he pretended to cut his arm, he punctured the bag, and the blood came pouring out. I have seen this 'miracle' done before."

After inspecting the ancient stone altar, Joshua found Caleb standing with the men and listening intently to the priest.

"Caleb, I have not thanked you for rescuing me from Sihon's camp. It was brave and unexpected," Joshua said.

"You are my friend, and the leader of these rebellious comrades. However, in order to mobilize them, I had to make them a promise. Unfortunately, I have to ask you to make the same promise," Caleb responded.

"Anything. I would not be here if Sihon had his way with me. He wanted me to be his spy, to turn on our people, or he was going to throw me off the top of Mount Hermon. What do I need to promise?"

"You cannot tell Moses the men rebelled and refused to follow you."

"But it was mutiny, Caleb."

"It was a promise I had to make to get the men together and rescue you. I gave them my word that you would agree."

"Then I will agree, and I will forgive them. This secret will stay in Canaan. But how can I ever forget what they did?"

The oracle had finished his homily. He stood in front of the table of food, shaking hands and embracing his congregation as they partook of the refreshments. His condescending face had to hurt, smiling so widely and so often. But it was the smile of a man confident that his words were those of Baal Sūr—and confident that his coffers were growing by the minute.

Joshua hobbled behind Caleb at the back of the line of food seekers.

"Welcome, weary travellers, to the 'Arms of Armageddon' outreach. We are a group of dedicated believers espousing the heavenly virtues of our god, Melgart. Our temple is in the heart of Megiddo. Are you staying for the sacrifice tonight?"

"Thank you for your hospitality, kind sir, but no. We are going through the Aruna pass to Yehem on the other side of Mount Carmel," Joshua answered.

"You are going through the pass? Be careful. It is laden with treacherous cliffs and precipices, crags and scarps. The hidden caverns are home to some of the most dangerous criminals in Canaan. For sure, you will need the protection of Melgart, my children."

"We are seasoned travellers—merchants, actually. We thank you for your advice, but I am sure if we are careful, we will survive."

"But a little insurance never hurt," the oracle insisted. "For a few pieces of silver as an offering to Melgart, I will pray that the 'king of the cities' will protect you. It is simple logic. Would you not rather please Melgart and have his protection than die falling from the cliffs of Aruna pass? Or find out that Melgart is genuinely god rather than be killed by the murderers hiding in those caves?" The oracle smiled cunningly, his mouth full of shiny teeth.

"Your offer is kind, but we will decline. The God we serve is jealous, and we will live as long as He wishes us to live. The length of our lives is predetermined beforehand. For those who trust in our God, the months and years we shall live are protected by his constant love for us. When the time comes for us to die, it will be the perfect and right time. We will gladly pay for any food that we consume, but we do not need your prayers or your god's protection."

"It is as I said: you are welcome to share our refreshments, but you can drop your offerings in the basket at the end of the table to pay for what you have consumed. If you ever happen to be in Megiddo, please come and visit us at the 'Arms of Armageddon' temple, just for a chat. I need to correct your theology. God does not love his worshippers—he demands their devotion, and the penalties are horrific if you do not do as he orders. I hope you do not have to learn that the hard way." He smiled again and quickly turned to the next people in line, shaking their hands warmly and starting his spiel all over again.

After the men had their fill of food, they jumped on their horses and continued up the ever-increasing incline of Mount Carmel. Oak and pine trees now replaced the olive and laurel trees, and although the landscape was still green, the trail was littered with stones and pebbles, making it more difficult for the horses to walk comfortably. The men sat quietly, balanced on the middle of their mounts, as their surefooted horses continued up the challenging terrain.

As they forged ahead, they spotted several ravens circling in the distance, probably feeding off a dead carcass. All they could hear was the Kishon brook babbling down the rocky mountainside. The headwind cooled the horses' muscles as they climbed higher and higher. Along the trail were clusters of overturned rocks, evidence of badgers looking for their supper.

Gaddiel saw it a second or two before Joshua did. He could have reached out and touched its snout, and he could see that the huge black bear had three cubs behind it. Gaddiel froze in his saddle, but his horse reared, and Gaddiel, full of wine as usual, fell backward onto the ground while his horse bolted away. The bear went for Gaddiel's right thigh immediately.

Joshua and Caleb could not believe their eyes. They had never seen such an animal before. The bear started to throw Gaddiel around, but Gaddiel fought the bear with his bleeding hands and ripped himself free from the mother's jaws. He rolled down the slope, over a steep embankment, and into some rocks and bushes. The bear, still protecting its young, started to charge the other riders, rearing up on its hind legs and roaring. The men backed up their frightened, bucking horses.

"Gaddiel, are you okay? Joshua called out.

"Yes. I cannot move my leg, and there is a lot of blood, but I am alive," he bellowed back.

The bear heard Gaddiel's yelling and charged down the slope. It was amazing how fast it could run up and down the hills. The bear closed its jaws on Gaddiel but instead of biting, shook him back and forth like a dog shakes a dirty rag. It bit and pulled away, nipping him again and then pulling away. Gaddiel tried to throw himself away from the bear again, but his timing was terrible. He fell another fifteen cubits before landing face up. The bear got right back on top of him, and Gaddiel instinctively grabbed it by its throat with both hands. The bear was just one huge muscle mass, and so powerful that Gaddiel knew he could not control it. He removed one hand and searched the ground blindly for a rock, keeping the other hand tightly on the bear's neck.

Gaddiel felt a tooth sink into the bottom of his neck, and the crunch of what he thought was his skull, just as Shaphat and Caleb drove their swords into the back of the bear's neck. The bear immediately let go of Gaddiel and reared up on its hind legs, roaring in pain. It took a wild swipe at Shaphat and knocked him head over heels. Igal and Sethur then plunged their swords into its belly, and it took its last breath, dropping to the ground just beside Gaddiel.

"Gaddi, see what you can do for Gaddiel," Joshua commanded. "Shaphat, are you okay?"

"I am fine. She knocked me down, but it looks like her claws missed me."

"Gaddiel, can you move?" Joshua spluttered. "What in God's creation was that animal?"

"It was a bear," Ammiel answered. "Igal and I saw a few of them when we came through the pass last week, but when they heard us on the trail, they hurried away. My guess is this female felt her cubs were in danger when we came upon them by surprise."

"I have never seen a bear before, but I now understand the proverb, 'It is safer to meet a bear robbed of her cubs than to confront a fool caught in foolishness.'[1] The wrath of the she-bear was incredible," said Joshua. "Where are the baby bears now?"

"They scampered away, probably to their cave. They were older cubs, one and a half years old by their size, so they will likely survive on their own."

"Palti, Nahbi, cut up the she-bear. We can use the meat as we travel. Gaddi, will Gaddiel be able to ride?"

"Why do you not ask him yourself? It must be all the wine in his system, but apart from the wound on his thigh and the bite on his neck, he seems to be okay. The punctures missed all the important blood vessels." Gaddi smiled. "He is one lucky Hebrew."

"Can someone pass me my water bladder?" Gaddiel pleaded. Gaddi passed him some water. "No. My water bladder, please."

Shammua found it where Gaddiel had dropped it on the trail.

Sethur, meanwhile, had chased down Gaddiel's horse and brought it back to the others. The horses were calm now that the threat of the bear was gone.

"Are you sure you are okay to ride, Gaddiel?" Joshua repeated.

"Yes, let us go. It will be dark soon. I just want to get out of this God-forsaken land."

The men helped Gaddiel onto his horse, and they continued on their way.

"Joshua," called Palti, "you know that proverb about the she-bear? The last part of it stung me like a hornet: to meet some fool with an idiotic project is worse than meeting a bear protecting her cubs. This folly we are on, this mission, is pure foolishness."

"Why do you say that, Wolf?" Joshua said.

"It was not born of God; it was Moses's idea."

"Moses was acting on behalf of the tribes. He asked God about it, and God said if Moses wanted to send spies, he could go ahead," Joshua responded.

"That is my point, Joshua. Our best ideas, our greatest plans, end up in a disaster if it is not God who ordered them. It may have seemed like a *good* idea to Moses, but it was not a *God* idea. Just look at what we have been through. Where has God been? We have not seen any miracles or interventions. Everything good that has happened has been our doing. As terrible and dangerous as our encounter was with the bear, it is better than to meet a foolish man on the trail of his folly."

"Why do you think the proverb says that, Palti?" asked Joshua.

"Allow me to answer," interjected Ammiel, always looking for exciting and contentious arguments. "The rage of the she-bear is short-lived, and her power is circumscribed within a narrow limit. Our encounter lasted only a few moments. We have more to fear from our foolish brothers than from all the beasts of the forest, for the devastating consequences of one man's folly can last a lifetime."

34

DAY THIRTY-THREE: FRIDAY, JULY 22 / AV 4

Near Elron
Troubled Souls

The men had found a deserted cave. The stars in the sky were non-existent tonight because the gloomy clouds covered them like a blanket of ash and soot. The moon was fighting with all of its strength, but it was badly losing the battle, and its embarrassed face was nowhere to be found. But as dark and groggy as the atmosphere was outside the cave, it could not rival the haunting darkness the men's troubled souls were facing. Eventually, they fell asleep one by one, and the morning came with a heavy and depressing drizzle of rain.

As was the routine, Sethur was doing his exercises, and the men had started a campfire to cook some of the bear meat they had brought with them. They could not, of course, hang the bear meat for a few days as was proper, but they cut and scrubbed off what fat they could and cut it into twelve large steaks. It was delicious, like small venison or wild boar.

For the past thirty-three days, Joshua had endured the hardest job on Earth: leading an unruly group of spies specially selected by

Moses. God described the Israelites as a "stiff-necked" people, and the spies were precisely that. Although they were committed to serving their God, their shared idealism and independence were only one side of a double-edged sword. The other edge was each man's complete, stubborn belief that he was correct and would change the world to his way of thinking. These Hebrews were very difficult to unify and almost impossible to lead. *Sihon thinks it is difficult to lead a coalition of one million people made up of three different nationalities,* Joshua thought ruefully. *It would be far easier to be the ruler of a million Canaanites than the leader of these eleven Jews, who all think they are kings.*

"Brothers," Joshua began, "let us talk about this mission Moses sent us on. We have been travelling for thirty-three days now. We have only one grave responsibility. The report we give will be the basis of Moses's decision to invade or not. If this is indeed just a human-made mission, then we have to turn it into something God can use. What words will you give Moses when we return? We still have seven days to think about everything, but at this moment, where do we all stand?"

"Attack," Shaphat said. "These Canaanites do not frighten me at all."

"Stay in the desert," Nahbi said. "Now we see how bad this land is, with its strongly fortified cities, unshakable walls, people united under a new confederation, and armies of more than one million professional soldiers. Yes, the land is fertile and productive, but the Canaanites are not going to give it up easily or quickly. Why would God want us to see this and then attack anyway?"

"Are you scared, Nahbi? Perhaps the necessary fight might muss up your hair?" Shaphat laughed.

"Why are you like that, Shaphat?" said Nahbi. "We are trying to have an intelligent discussion, and you resort to insulting your brother."

"Sometimes I am not sure if you are my brother or my sister," Shaphat snapped back, laughing hard. "Although it could be bad luck to take an early vote, I vote to attack." He kissed his sword three times.

Nahbi was livid that Shaphat would question his masculinity, especially in front of everyone. He pretended it did not bother him, but he was deeply embarrassed. He made up his mind that whatever Shaphat voted, he would propose the opposite. If Shaphat was in favour of attacking Canaan, Nahbi would quietly vote against.

"Stay in the desert," Palti countered. "This is not a land for us. We rescued you, Joshua, at great peril to our own lives. It was us who saved you, not God. If this mission was God-ordained, then where has He been all this time? We have been cheated, robbed, kidnapped, chased, bitten by a snake, and even mauled by a bear. Even our dreams warn us that this is an impossible mission. I will vote to stay in Kadesh-Barnea and never enter Canaan."

"To be fair, Palti, the hallucinogenic mandrake caused those dreams," Caleb snarled. "It was not God."

"If we are indeed following God's will, He will make it work out for the good of our people despite our efforts and our actions," Joshua continued. "You saved me from Sihon and my imminent death at his hand, but it was God's hand that guided you to do it."

"We must stay out!" Gaddiel hiccupped. "The true test of a task is if it brings you closer to God. Is there something noble, right, or praiseworthy that comes from doing it? How can we imagine that this mission is born of God? Let us be honest: our hearts have turned cold to the things of God because of this mission. Where is God, why no miracles, why all the troubles and tribulations? This journey is not a God idea. And if God is not in it," Gaddiel pronounced, "then I am not in it either."

"I will drink to that," Shammua said in mockery. "Listen to the man who walks righteously, hand in hand with God, as he stumbles to the tavern. Brilliant intentions and plans often end in disaster or a wineskin, correct, Gaddiel? I vote to attack. This land contains nothing but deprived and decrepit people."

Gaddiel tried to jump up and smack Shammua, but his leg caused him to stumble and fall. Gaddi came over quickly to help him up and look at the wound again.

"Attack," Igal offered. "Lots of business opportunities and prosperity for us to seize."

"Retreat," Sethur said. "The cities are too strong, and the armies are too big."

"Stay out," Gaddi agreed. "You can make excuses and justifications all day, and your method and your procedure can even sound reasonable, but it does not alter the fact that your idea is simply that —*your* idea. Not God's. God did not tell us to come into this land and inspect it. Moses did. The imminent deaths of the innocent are not worth what we would gain."

"Stay out," Ammiel said. "The distractions, armies, and depravity would decimate our tribes. It is truly a stupid idea to move our people here."

"Attack," Caleb said proudly, glaring at Ammiel.

"What say you, Geuel?" Joshua asked softly.

"I do not know what I will say. All I want to do is kill Phineas. I need time to think about everything."

"Geuel is correct. Brothers, think long and hard during these next few days on our way back to Kadesh-Barnea," Joshua said. "Try to be objective and put the future of our tribes first. I will not try to influence you, but talk amongst yourselves. It is undoubtedly the most critical question you will ever answer in your lives.

"There seems to be a lot of questions about God's involvement in this mission," he continued. "Let us stop all the bickering. Our orders were to embark on this mission and report back on what we found. The decision was not ours to make. Remember, at the very beginning of time, the Lord our God placed Adam in the Garden of Eden to work and watch over it. The Lord said to the man and woman, 'You are free to eat from any tree of the garden, but you are not to eat from the tree of the knowledge of good and evil, for on that day you eat from it, you will certainly die.'[1] God's desire was for Adam and Eve *not* to eat from the tree—only one tree. God gave them freedom to choose from any of the many other trees in the garden. Any day, any afternoon, any month, they could select any tree to eat from except the forbidden one. God enjoyed watching them and was equally pleased if they chose an orange, an avocado, or an apple. They were free to eat from any tree.

"It is not for us to criticize Moses's decision to send us here. God permitted Moses to choose and send us, just as He permitted Adam and Eve to eat from any other tree in the garden."

Ammiel considered the men's words very carefully. He had Gaddi, Sethur, Gaddiel, and Palti in his "no" camp. He had to get Igal, Shammua, and Shaphat to recognize his objective thinking. There was no sense in talking to Joshua and Caleb—they were and always would be in the "yes" camp, and there was nothing he could do about that. Reasoning and logic were potent tools, however, and Ammiel was a master at them. He would also work on Geuel. Geuel was an emotional wreck at the moment, but Ammiel would find something to get Geuel on his side. Everyone had a weakness, after all. The challenge was to find it and then exploit it.

"Shammua, I want to talk to you about your vote to attack. I get it. We have seen how depraved the Canaanites are." Ammiel started his formidable reasoning. "However, we have all done things we are not proud of. Do you want to destroy these people for your sins? Will you feel better? I know you find God's ways strange at times, and so do I. I also know you are a good friend of Joshua. Apart from Caleb, you are probably the closest. But it is folly to assume something is good because people you like and respect agree it is good. Joshua believes it would be a good idea to attack, but just because he feels that way does not mean it is the right thing to do. You cannot accept an argument blindly. It is our responsibility to analyze the repercussions that will follow and make our own decisions."

"Did you not see Moses give Joshua his blessing when we left camp, Ammiel? It was to him and him alone. Who am I to argue with this divine authority?" Shammua responded. "I have learned my place in the order of things."

"By that remark, I am assuming you are referring to what we all did in Jebus with Joshua. I know Joshua, at the time, saw it as a sudden flash of disrespect. But all of us, myself included, saw it differently. We had to take charge, formulate a strategic plan to bring us back to God's order, execute it tactically, and face any risks with a sense of justice and purpose. We were not wrong—Joshua was. We are not minions. We are Israelites, all gifted by God. Shammua, we tried to save this venture. Unfortunately, Joshua's capture was a result of the risk we took. I feel his pain, and I do have pity for what he went through, but it was Joshua's choice to leave us, not ours. Your place in the order of things is much higher than you think."

Ammiel jumped off his horse and walked alongside Shammua, holding his reins tightly in his hands. He reached out and stroked Shammua's mare's sweating neck. He studied Shammua's expression and smiled tenderly. "You are Shammua, a descendant of Reuben, the first-born of Jacob. Your opinion is important. Please do not be impulsive and agree to attack because your leader thinks it is the right thing to do. At Kadesh-Barnea, we live a supernatural existence. We get manna from the heavens, water flows from rocks, clouds of glory lead the way through the desert. At night, a pillar of fire gives us light so we can see where we are going. Do you want to give that up for what we have seen these thirty-three days? I do not. From morning to night, we have cried out for a sign that God was with us, but we did not find any signs. I have a crushing and unsettling feeling that God has disappeared from our midst. I cannot wait to get back to camp, where I know he dwells. Our people, our leaders, can be mistaken, confused, deceived, and irrational. This does not change because there are more than two or three who believe the opposite of what we know is right. It is truly the foolishness worse than meeting that she-bear. If you do not express your original ideas, if you do not listen to your inner being, you will betray not only yourself but all those who depend on you. You will have betrayed Moses and our tribes by failing to stand up for your ideas. You must take ownership and responsibility for your own life and future. Nobody has as much power over our present and future as you do right now."

Shaphat, now listening carefully to Ammiel's words, interjected. "What makes you think you are right, and we are wrong?"

"Shaphat, the issue is not who is right or wrong. The issue is what is best for our people," Ammiel insisted. "A gazelle trapped in a bush is much better than two running along an open meadow. We know God is with us at our camp. His miracles and provisions happen daily. If this land is so fantastic, then where has God been hiding? And *why* has He been hiding? I know you, Shaphat. You hold honour as one of your highest attributes. But what honour is there in becoming farmers and sheepherders? Do you really want to shovel dung and pull weeds for the rest of your days? This is what we would all become if we take this land. Tell me you wish this for your family and our tribes. Can you be jealous of those living on these lands when we have so much more at our camp now? I will take the trapped gazelle over the gazelles in the meadow any day."

Caleb made a mental note that Ammiel, Gaddi, Sethur, and Gaddiel were cynical about coming into Canaan. He nervously watched Ammiel's animated conversation as he was rode beside Shaphat and Shammua. Although he was sure there was no fear in Shaphat or even Shammua, they had already demonstrated their criticism of Joshua's leadership. Ammiel would talk to them tonight when they made camp. He would feed their murmuring and complaining to get them to change their minds.

Inevitably, the men felt some remorse after seeing what had happened to Joshua. Caleb would use the next seven days to coax the others over to his and Joshua's side. But he could not match Ammiel's ability to put forth a persuasive argument. Caleb and Joshua were similar in many ways but substantially different in how they perceived their relationship with God. Joshua believed that his faith would give birth to good deeds—that he was righteous by his faith alone. Joshua believed God would work through him to achieve His purpose without much effort of his own. Caleb, on the other hand, believed that while his good deeds were evidence of his faith, he must do righteous and virtuous deeds to justify his position in God's kingdom. He considered himself righteous by what he did, and not by faith alone. Without good deeds, where was the evidence of faith?

They meandered south. As usual, Joshua and Caleb led the unusual procession of opinionated ombudsmen. They were only seven days' riding from Kadesh-Barnea.

35

DAY THIRTY-FOUR: JULY 23 / AV 5

Shabbat

36

DAY THIRTY-FIVE: SUNDAY, JULY 24 / AV 6

City of Gath
The Darkness of Unbelief

At daybreak, the men continued their journey back to the main camp. Igal took a refreshing swig of water from his animal-skin bladder, gargled, and then spit it out. Although he knew it would be no easy matter, he was looking forward to the prospects and opportunities that would come when they occupied this territory. The Canaanites, in his opinion, were not the smartest people, and with his business acumen, he could manipulate and dominate trade in their cities. Gaddi accused him of being selfish and argued that the collateral damage would not be worth the price of occupation. Something deep down twanged when he listened to Gaddi's compassionate arguments. Igal was human, after all, and an Israelite just like Gaddi. It was sad, but in Igal's mind it was unavoidable. The reward would be well worth it. Joshua and Caleb were in favour of advancing the army, and though their reasoning was different than his, it benefited him greatly. Would it be the best for the tribes? It all depended on how you looked at it.

As the sun reached its highest point in the sky, the men arrived at the outskirts of the Philistine city of Gath. It was massive, the largest city the men had encountered so far: over fifteen hundred dunams in size with a population of about ten thousand people. The huge stone boulders that made up the walls and gates were much stronger than the traditional sun-dried mud bricks they'd seen in Jebus and Hebron. The outside fortified walls, six cubits thick and eighteen cubits high, were made of rocks so big that even a team of oxen couldn't drag them. But it did not take long for the men to figure out how the stones were put into the wall. There were dozens of men the size of Og among the citizens walking along the streets. They were not as big as the Anakim they'd seen outside Hebron, and their hands showed five fingers instead of six, but they were still a fearsome sight.

"Let us keep going south," Joshua commanded. "I have had enough of these Rephaim. They are everywhere."

"You see, Joshua," Palti piped in. "This land has a copious number of giants. How could we ever succeed in a campaign against them? They alone would be enough to stop us, but when you put them into castles and garrisoned cities like Jericho, Megiddo, and now this Philistine city of Gath, we would be insane to attempt to overthrow them."

"I know your position, Palti," Joshua groaned. "But, for some reason, you constantly forget the power of God. It is not me or Moses who is leading us—it is God. You see yourself as a teeny-weeny grasshopper about to be squashed by the big bad giants. But to God, we are all like grasshoppers—some bigger than others, perhaps, but grasshoppers all the same.[1] How do you know how we appear to the Rephaim? Maybe God made us look like gigantic angels. You fail to appreciate all that He has done for us in the two years since we left Egypt. Would you rather return to the land of slavery?"

"I think our life there was not as bad as the life we would have here," Palti blustered. "We are neither militarily nor mentally able to take this land from these people."

"Let us get to the omphalos of all this and be honest, Palti. You are just scared," Igal jeered.

"Perhaps you not do not see the threat of danger, Igal. Fear has plenty of value from a survival standpoint. It keeps us alive. I have this nagging feeling that this land brings nothing but pain and harm. I think we all should have a little fear. It will keep us rational so we can be aware of the real dangers that lurk here."

"The real danger is your unbelief, Palti," Caleb quipped.

"And you, the non-Jew Hebrew, will teach me about my ancestor's beliefs?" Palti ranted. "What a joke that is."

"Palti, guard your tongue," Igal growled.

"No. I have had it, Igal. When we see more of the Rephaim, Joshua tells us to get out of here, and that is acceptable to everyone. But when I say the Rephaim are everywhere, you and Caleb attack my faith. What a great way to win an argument. Admit it: this is the most useless, hopeless, and ineffectual assignment in the history of our nation. It is not fear, Igal, to admit a mistake. It takes great courage. You should try it sometime."

Igal jumped off his horse, drew his sword, and pointed it directly at Palti.

"Come, Wolf. I will show you what courage is, you snivelling little pup." Igal waved his sword back and forth like a puff adder ready to strike.

"Now we see the true Igal, the businessman," Palti mocked. "When he cannot win an argument, he resorts to another type of business, which he knows nothing about—his sword. Do not think all of us are stupid. We know the only reason you want our army to attack Canaan is for the profit you think you might realize. You think of no one but yourself, Igal."

"I think you had a little too much mandrake for breakfast, Palti. You are hallucinating yet again if you think my sword will not remove your head for your insolence," Igal said.

"Enough!" Joshua said sternly. "Get back on your horses, both of you, and keep your mouths shut. I am sick and tired of your anger and insubordination. If God runs the world—and we know that He does—then everything that happens to us, good or bad, is the will of God. Whatever happens is for your good."

"Okay, our wonderful leader, explain this to me," Palti said. "Just ahead of us are two trails, one to the right and one to the left. Who knows what is on each trail? If we choose the wrong one, we could all die. Explain to me the difference between our free will and predestination."

"And so it is in life," Joshua conjectured, as he took a bite from a juicy apple. "Each new choice we make creates new circumstances for us to figure out. Because God carefully attends to every detail in our lives, there are no accidents. We choose which way to go, and then He directs our steps. As we respond to the circumstances, even those beyond our control, God is always guiding and governing the details. We are not in control of everything—God is. Does this mean the outcome of our day is inevitable and my choices irrelevant? Of course not. God holds all of us accountable to make wise choices and to respond to circumstances in the right way.

"Catch!" Joshua tossed the apple he had started to eat to Palti. "Go stand against that tree over there and put this apple on your head."

"Why w-w-would I do that?" Palti stuttered.

"You want me to explain the difference between free will and predestination, correct?"

"Yes, but a simple explanation would do just fine." Palti scrunched his small forehead and frowned, trying to disguise his fear.

All the men jumped off their horses to watch. With Palti, anything could happen, and they smelled blood.

Palti slinked over to the tree; if he had a tail, it would be between his legs. He turned around, leaned back, and with his canid jowls faced Joshua.

"Now, I want you to lift your right leg," Joshua commanded.

"Okay." Palti did what he was asked and stood tall, but the apple fell off. "How is this?"

"Good. You have exercised your free will." Joshua smirked. "Now lift your left leg."

"Of course, standing on my right leg, I cannot do what you ask," Palti said. "What is the purpose of this charade?"

"That, my brother, is predestination. Try as you may, you will never lift your second leg. There are events in your life you cannot ever change. They are predetermined." Joshua pointed his bow and arrow directly at Palti. "Now, Palti, pick up the apple and put it back on your head."

Palti trembling, did as he was commanded and closed his eyes..

Joshua took a deep breath and pointed the arrow at the apple. "We have choices in life, just as I have a choice now to shoot the apple on your head. Do I do it or do I not?"

"Please do not, Joshua!" Palti opened his eyes as wide as he could while the other spies roared at the entertainment.

Joshua lowered his bow, turned his back to Palti, and studied the smiling faces of the men. " Just as copper and tin are melted together to form your bronze weapons, our free will and God's predestination, when pounded together on the anvil of our souls, create harmony and cannot be separated. When we understand this truth," Joshua continued, "we will experience good outcomes—maybe not always in our eyes, but most certainly in God's eyes. We must trust that He is working out His plan through our choices and circumstances. Whether we make detailed plans or resort to casting lots, all is under God's control."

Without any warning, Joshua spun around and fired the arrow directly into the apple that was wobbling on Palti's head. It was a perfect shot. Palti, gasping, crumpled to his knees, leaving the apple welded to the tree where his head had been only moments before.

"The sharp arrow of truth always finds its mark, usually when you least expect it," Joshua said stoically.

Palti, gathering his composure, stood up. There were numerous well-used goat trails on either side of the apple-infused tamarisk tree.

"So tell me Joshua," Sethur asked, "if we approach this trail and walk down it, but I stop and go back to the other path, does that thwart God's predestined plan?"

"Not at all. God would have known that you would stop and reverse. There is no 'thwarting' God's plans. The Canaanites attribute everything to fate and believe that whatever is must be. We Israelites believe that whatever God ordains must be, but that God's wisdom never ordains anything without a purpose. Everything in this world, for us, is working toward a great ending. We Hebrews believe in the hidden potential to escape our fate. We look to the unknown and unnoticed—to the divinely provided thing that we can use to change the outcome."

"So God knows exactly what we will report to Moses, and what will happen based on that report?" Sethur continued.

"He does."

"Then what is the purpose of it all?"

"It is difficult to understand sometimes, I admit. But remember the story of Jacob's son Joseph. God allowed his brothers to kidnap him and sell him as a slave, and then they lied for years about what had happened to him. That was a terrible thing, and God was displeased, but the wickedness of Joseph's brothers worked toward a greater good. Joseph ended up in Egypt, where he became a prime minister. He used his position to sustain a country during a seven-year famine, until even his own family came to him for help. If Joseph had not been in Egypt before the famine started, millions of people, including our tribes, would have died.[2] Sometimes it is only when you look back at your footsteps years later that you can understand the reasoning for our calamities and troubles. Perhaps the only reason for this mission was to assist in the conversion of our friend Zidon before his death. There is more joy in heaven over one sinner who repents than ninety-nine righteous persons who need no repentance. God sees things differently than we do, and His priorities are different. The purpose of it all, Sethur, is to walk and talk with God, which is His original purpose in creating us. A lot of things have got in the way since creation, but our purpose has not changed."

Joshua got back on his horse and kicked it into a trot, moving to the front of the procession.

"You see, Gaddi?" Sethur whispered to keep Ammiel from hearing. "This is why I am voting in favour of conquering the land of Canaan. There are only two types of people: those who love God and those who hate him."

"That is not exactly true, Sethur. Some people are indifferent to Him or do not have strong feelings either way. Many people are somewhere between loving and hating Him. A lot of weak and confused people follow Chemosh or some other god, even if their intention to find God is sincere. It is possible to be sincerely wrong in our beliefs. There is no doubt that there are evil manipulators and false prophets who prey on the weak and common people, but that does not make their victims all haters of God. Canaan is a palimpsest, encompassing layers of evil and good people, sinners and innocents. That is why I am voting not to attack. Apart from the casualties we would incur, there would be too many others, in between hatred and love of God, who would die. All life is precious and worth protecting, do you not think? I know you understand this. When the dog died digging up the mandrake, you were visibly shaken."

"It is true what you say. However, my vote is still to attack... at least for now."

37

DAY THIRTY-SIX: MONDAY, JULY 25 / AV 7

Eschol Valley
Facta, Non Verba

Caleb had a restless night. He woke up in the morning and knew he had to do something drastic. He waited until Joshua rode into the Eschol Valley to do his morning reconnaissance, then gathered Shaphat, Shammua, Igal, and Sethur and laid out his plan.

"Men, we have only a few days before we return to Kadesh-Barnea and give our report to Moses. Joshua has had a tough time these days and needs our support. We all know that the only decision is for our people to invade and occupy Canaan—to take our promised land by force. Unfortunately, four of our brethren feel differently, and that has caused a division in our ranks. That schism will only grow and will ultimately cause discord and disharmony among our tribes. Joshua would never approve of this, but I have come up with a plan that I feel is the only way. We will give our dissenting brethren a choice this morning: either they agree with us and advise Moses to attack, or we will take their lives here on the Philistine plain. It is for the good of our nation."

"Are you crazy, Caleb?" Shaphat blurted. "They are our brothers."

"They will not choose death. They will choose to live, but this way we will make them promise to agree with us," Caleb insisted. "And once a Hebrew makes a promise, he cannot go back on it."

"You saw Palti yesterday," Igal said. "He was ready to rip my head off."

"Yes, but that was when only you opposed him, not the five of us," Caleb said. "It is our duty to our tribes to save as many human lives as possible. So we will make a tough decision. If necessary, we will sacrifice our four brothers so that our tribes—two and a half million people—may live in the land God has promised us. It is only common sense. Would we sacrifice four to save our nation? We must maximize the sanctity and future of our society. We must prove ourselves worthy of the blood our ancestors shed to get us here, and the milk that our mothers fed us."

"But Caleb, who says our nation will perish if we do not attack?" asked Shammua.

"I need you to remember God took us out of Egypt, and it was not easy. The pharaoh did everything he could to keep us there, but God caused ten supernatural plagues to persuade him to let us go. Then God divided the sea for us, so we could walk to the land He promised us. As the Egyptians chased us, He caused the sea to fall upon them and drown them all in revenge. When we did not have food, He provided us with manna from heaven until our bellies were full. When we were dying from thirst, He made water come from the barren rocks so we could drink until we had enough. When it was cold in the desert night, He led us with a pillar of fire. When it was too hot in the scorching desert, He led us with a pillar of smoke that shielded us from the burning sun. If God were to command us to make ladders and scale the heavens, we should obey Him. We cannot let these four brothers cause discord and doubt, for it is God who leads us. Although they call their reasoning logical and rational, they are simply doubting their true leader, and the fear that always follows doubt has paralyzed them from doing what they know is right."

"Why all the loud voices?" Gaddi said as he approached with

Palti, Gaddiel, and Ammiel by his side. "Are you having second thoughts about your vote?" he chuckled.

Caleb drew his sword and pointed it directly at Ammiel's throat. "We want you to make a solemn promise that when we get to camp, you will vote to attack. If you do not, I will take your life, or you will take mine," Caleb announced.

"Caleb, put your sword away. This is not how we settle disputes amongst our brethren," Gaddi insisted. "What is wrong with you?"

Caleb moved his sword quickly to Gaddi's abdomen. "I am serious. Listen to me carefully." Shaphat, Shammua, Igal, and Sethur drew their swords hesitantly and stood behind Caleb in solidarity.

"What in the name of tartarus is going on?" Palti roared, drawing his own sword.

"If we keep the laws between 'man and God' and between 'man and man,' everything will go fine for us in Canaan. No other nation will be able to touch us. We will have material prosperity, and we will live to change all of Canaan. However, if we don't keep the Torah, if we break our end of the bargain, if we are rebellious and selfish, then this land will vomit us out, our enemies will attack, and we will suffer and fail. The solution to our problems has nothing to do with the external threats we have seen. The giants, the tall walls around the fortified cities, the confederation of enemies—these are nothing to the power of God. What we have seen with our eyes are not reasons to retreat from the land God has promised us, but symptoms of a deeper problem that can affect us only if we do not keep our bargain with God. If God is with us, who can stand against us? And I am willing," Caleb finished, "to take your lives or to die today, protecting what is right. Give us your word that you will agree to advance into Canaan, and you give Moses and Joshua your support. You all have witnessed God destroying the most powerful nation on earth, the Egyptians. Will He not also give us victory over the Canaanites?"

"And you are willing to take our lives if we do not agree with you?" Ammiel said, astonished.

"Or you can take mine," said Caleb.

"We will make you a deal," Ammiel lied. "Put your sword away, and we will advise Moses neither to attack or not to attack. We will simply tell him what we saw and let him make the decision. Will you agree to that? It is not right, an Israelite fighting and spilling the blood of another Israelite." Ammiel was determined not be coerced by this Gentile-cum-Israelite.

"I made you a promise that I would not tell Moses of your mutiny, and I promised that I would get Joshua to agree. Do you solemnly promise you will vote to advance into Canaan?" Caleb said, relieved there would be no bloodshed.

Having no other choice other than to fight, the men all nodded in the affirmative.

"May God have His perfect way," Gaddi confirmed.

"But if you ever pull your sword and point it at me again," Palti whispered in Caleb's ear, "I will remove the hand that holds it."

Joshua rode back from scouting the Eschol Valley with a smile. "Come, I found a farm with some grape-mounds we can take with us to show Moses. There are pomegranates and figs as well. It is not far. You are not going to believe the size of the grapes."

As the men approached the valley, the rich and fertile land reminded them of the valley of Armageddon. The grass grew wild everywhere, littered with yellow dandelions, and the smell of clover permeated the air. Two brooks ran down the sides of the hills, gushing and babbling along the river rocks to a melody of their own making. Birds chased butterflies, and the abundant honeybees searched for the brightest blossoms to pollinate.

Ammiel thought about bringing up the confrontation with Caleb to Joshua, but he did not want to spoil the moment. He had not seen Joshua smile in quite a few days.

There was a small orchard attended by a husband, his wife, and their two children, whose mud-brick house nestled close to one of the prattling creeks.

"Good afternoon, kind farmer," Joshua said in greeting. "It is a fine day to be working with your crops."

"And a good day to you, travellers. Yes, it is a beautiful day. I would offer you some refreshments, but we are a poor family and have only enough for ourselves. I am sorry we have nothing to spare. However, the brook offers all the water you can drink and carry."

"We would like to purchase some fruit from you—grapes, figs, and pomegranates. Would you sell us some?"

"With pleasure. Please take what you need. Your donation would be very much appreciated."

"I have not seen grapes that size before—they are the size of a man's fist!" Joshua snickered.

"Well, we have seen the size of the creatures that eat these grapes, so it should be no surprise," Palti added sarcastically.

"We would need to purchase a cart to pull the fruit that we choose. Have you another wagon?" Joshua asked.

"No, sir, only this one. However, I can build another in the next few days. I will sell you this one, and perhaps you will need a mule to pull it as well? I happen to have four strong mules," the farmer said.

"Thank you for your kindness. We will take the mule and the cart, loaded with fruit. Shaphat," said Joshua, "go with Shammua and take an entire vine, root included, and load it onto the cart. Gaddi, you and Ammiel can gather a few baskets of figs and pomegranates. Caleb, have a good look around and see if there is anything else we should load onto the cart. Igal, you can settle our debt with this kind farmer and his family. What is your name, farmer?"

"I am Kaboul, and this is my beautiful wife, Pigat."

"And your boys, what names have they?"

"Aqhat and Yassib," Kaboul said proudly.

"What is wrong with the older boy?" Joshua inquired.

"Oh, yes. Aqhat is blind. We do not notice it anymore." Kaboul smiled. "He lost his eyesight a few years ago when he got red spots all over his body. It broke our hearts at the time, but he lived through his disease, and we enjoy every precious moment with him. He is quite talented, and while I don't expect you will understand, we are blind to his blindness now." Kaboul called out, "Aqhat, come here. I want you to meet someone. Fifteen steps. There is a large rock on your left side."

Aqhat grabbed his staff and walked with assurance over to Joshua and Kabul.

"Hello, young man," Joshua bellowed.

"Good day, sir. You need not raise your voice. I am only blind—my hearing works as good as anyone's," he said with a childish smile.

Joshua, amused by Aqhat's quick wit, smiled back, even though he knew it would go unnoticed. "Aqhat is an interesting name," he continued in a quieter voice. "Can you tell me what it means?"

"I, of course, played no part in naming myself, kind traveller, but I do love it. A long time ago, we had a terrible drought in Canaan. There was a king sage named Danel who ruled over the land. He had no son and prayed to god many times to remove such a curse. Finally, God granted him a fine son, whom Danel named Aqhat. As he was a powerful king, Danel summoned extremely talented artisans from around the kingdom to make a special longbow as a gift for his son's sixteenth birthday. One of the craftsmen, Kothar, was especially talented and had been commissioned in the past by the beautiful young goddess Anath. The only thing that surpassed her beauty was her vigour and ferocity in battle. Even though the bow and nothing to do with Anath, she was jealous. She was outraged that a mortal would receive it and not her. Anath made Aqhat numerous tempting offers for the bow, but Aqhat rejected them all."

"Let me guess what happened next," Joshua mused. "Aqhat used the bow to kill Anath. Am I correct?"

"No, quite the contrary. Anath killed Aqhat, for mortals do not kill gods. I am fortunate I only lost my eyesight. Anath was kind to me to let me live."

"Perhaps it was not Anath who took your eyesight, Aqhat. It sounds like the disease of the red spots had something to do with your loss."

"Perhaps you are correct. However, the red spots came from somewhere, did they not? My honour is that I was the recipient of something from the gods. They considered my life important enough to be involved in. And what is your name?" Aqhat asked.

"I am called Yeshua or Yehoshua[1] in our language and Joshua in your language. It means salvation or deliverance."

Joshua glanced over at Shaphat and Shammua. They were transporting only one bunch of grapes, but it was so heavy that they had to carry a thick pole on their shoulders with the bunch of grapes carefully strapped in the middle. The pole threatened to break with each step, bending and bowing as they sauntered toward the cart.

"Aqhat, you are a fine young man, and I pray that the true God blesses you and your family with all things good. I know many people who have eyes but cannot see beauty. They have ears, but they do not listen to the truth. They have hearts but cannot find compassion. You have lost your eyesight, but you see the good in things more clearly than most. I will remember our conversation. We must go now. Thank you, Kaboul, for your kindness, and may God protect you."

38

DAY THIRTY-SEVEN: TUESDAY, JULY 26 / AV 8

City of Gerar
The Screaming Sounds of Silence

They were travelling much more slowly now with the mule pulling the wheeled cart heavily laden with fruit. The horses were strolling in a line but resolute in their return to Kadesh-Barnea. Ammiel was thinking about the family of the young blind Aqhat and the promise Caleb had forced the spies to make at Eschol Valley. Would Aqhat's family be caught in the crosshairs of the violence that would inevitably occur when the Israelite army came to occupy Canaan? Ammiel had given his word to Caleb, and a man was only as good as his word. In the beginning, the Word was all things, and the Word was with God, and the Word was God. God used words to create the heavens and the earth. Ammiel's word was a binding contract in God's court of law. It was one thing to break your word to an unbeliever, and they had certainly lied and deceived many Canaanites to accomplish their mission. But when it came to a brother, an Israelite's word spoke volumes about his integrity. Ammiel wondered: should giving his word supersede his convictions and conscience?

His thoughts went over and over the question. Of course, there was no arguing with a sword pointed at one's neck. Caleb's frustration had overwhelmed his sense of his perspective, and Ammiel had learned that it was always better to bend a little than to break—to lose a battle or two but win the war. If he had to feign submission to impose his will, then so be it. Compromise never felt good, but if he could make Caleb feel understood, respected, and honoured, Ammiel would keep him off balance. When the time came to stand in front of Moses, he would not relinquish anything.

Ammiel started to prepare what to say to Moses. The trick was not so much what he said, but how he said it. Ammiel knew his rhetoric would create a desirable climate. He thought maybe he would start with a rhyming riddle for Moses to figure out.

What does a man love more than life?
What does he hate more than death or mortal strife?
What does a satisfied man desire?
What do the poor have, and the rich require?
What does the miser spend, and the spendthrift save?
And each man carry to his grave?

Ammiel smiled. The only answer to all these questions was an overwhelming *nothing*.

He thought of the bear that they had encountered a few days before. If the scenario had been different, and they had seen her with her cubs from a distance, the best strategy would have been to stand still and do nothing. If they had run, she would have charged at them, and they would not have survived her attack. Doing nothing was sometimes the best strategy. One could fight or flee, but one could also freeze. It was a natural form of defence. Ammiel would keep his word to Caleb and give Moses his assessment of Canaan, but he would twist everything around so Moses would decide to do nothing. What was *not* in Canaan was more critical that what was there. Sure, the land was fertile, the crops abundant, the rivers and mountains beautiful. However, there was no real piety, no true worship or reverence of God. There was no peace, contentment, or happiness that Ammiel had seen. There were no miracles, signs, or wonders like what they as a nation had witnessed almost daily since leaving Egypt.

The men stopped to rest on a hill not far from the city of Gerar. The heat was blistering. The horses, mule, and men all needed water. Caleb looked at the city and recalled the story of Abraham and Isaac. Both had lived here many years ago, and both had a similar story. Abraham loved his wife Sarah dearly and was scared that the Philistines living in Gerar would kill him and steal his wife. So he convinced Sarah to tell everyone that she was his sister. But Sarah was so beautiful that King Abimelech fell in love with her. God intervened before Abimelech could touch Sarah, directing Abimelech to leave her alone because she belonged to Abraham. Abimelech, in fear of God, gave Abraham gifts of livestock and servants by way of apology.[1]

Similarly, Isaac, Abraham's son, moved to the productive area of Gerar to avoid a famine in the land. Like his father, he told everyone his wife Rebekah was his sister in order to keep husband murderers away. But Isaac made such a fortune in Gerar that the king sent him away, banning him from the land of the Philistines.[2]

Caleb wondered if his own son, Hur, would be like him. He hoped that Hur would perceive the world in all its nuanced complexity and not reduce it to a simplistic either/or proposition as, it seemed, his brothers on this mission had done. Why could not the men love themselves and trust their God-given instincts? When they made themselves less than they were, they diminished the One in whose image they were created. As long as they saw themselves merely as grasshoppers against the giants in life, they set themselves up for failure. If they wanted to create anything new and to enter this beautiful land, or any promised land, then they had no choice but to leap, like those grasshoppers, into the unknown—to believe in themselves and to trust in God's faith in them as His people.

When it came to pursuing their walk with God, finding a deeper purpose in life, or even mastering a skill, taking some action was always better than doing nothing. Caleb was proud of himself for doing something about the impasse the spies faced. Drawing his sword and threatening the men was probably not the best solution, but at least he had done something. The men had made him an unbreakable promise—and surely a good outcome excused any wrongs to attain it. He had to do something ugly to achieve something beautiful, and he could live with that ugliness.

Caleb wrestled with the idea of telling Joshua what he'd done. He was not sure Joshua would approve of his methods. Joshua was content to let things unfold naturally.

"How are our provisions, Caleb?" Joshua asked. "We will be in Kadesh-Barnea in a couple of days. Do we need anything from Gerar?"

"I think we should be fine, Joshua. With all the fruit, there is no need for anything extra," Caleb responded.

"Good news, then." Joshua paused. "Caleb, I am worried about Geuel. Have you noticed how sad he is?"

"Yes. Even more concerning is that since Hebron, he has lost a lot of weight and sleeps in excess. He seems to have lost interest in this mission, and whenever I talk to him, his speech is slow and his mind seems to be somewhere else. He has difficulty making simple decisions. I thought with a little time, he might snap out of it, but his love for Donatiya seems to be an all-consuming fire. I hope once we get back to camp, and our lives become normal again, his heart will heal." Caleb took a deep breath. "Joshua, I must tell you something. I am not sure you will approve, but I think you need to know. Two days ago in the Eschol Valley, when you left, I—"

"Joshua, Caleb!" Ammiel hollered, sprinting up to the two of them and breathing hard. "Joshua, come quickly—it is Geuel."

Geuel was silently sitting on a log, bent over his hand and oblivious to anything around him. His fingers were dripping in blood as he clutched his treasure. The other men were standing in a circle around him.

"Geuel, my brother, what have you found?" Joshua asked. "What are you holding so tightly that your hand bleeds so profusely?"

"My ear." Geuel turned his head, showing Joshua the primitive surgery he had performed on his mutilated earlobe.

Joshua's heart flooded with compassion. "You cut off your ear, Geuel? But why would you do that?"

"I cannot bear the pain of hearing her voice anymore. I want you to give me permission to go back to Hebron and deliver this ear to Phineas. I will make him eat it before I take his life. I can be there and back in less than a day."

"Geuel, my loving brother. I am truly sorry for your pain, but removing your ear and killing Phineas will not lessen the ache in your heart. Only time can do that. Besides, perhaps you forget, but Phineas is with Og at Mount Hermon. He is not at Hebron." He turned to Gaddi and, without words, instructed him to start the cleaning process. "I understand your desire for revenge, Geuel. Donatiya was a victim, innocent and pure. And revenge, at times, can be a good thing. But like all good things, it comes with consequences. Revenge leads to retaliation, and eventually, instead of bringing satisfaction, it can ruin you. Just like your love for Donatiya, hate is powerful and very difficult to control. God said, 'Vengeance belongs to me—I will repay. In time their foot will slip, for their day of disaster is near, and their doom is coming quickly.'"[3]

"God also says, 'An eye for an eye, a tooth for a tooth, hand for hand, foot for foot,'"[4] Geuel replied. "Phineas took Donatiya's life. Therefore, his life should be forfeit."

"And I am sure it will be, Geuel, but you must let God avenge this atrocity. Let God do his job, and you do yours. It can happen at any time and in any circumstance, and it so often happens when we least expect it. It is God's promise, and we must be good servants and await our master. Even if He becomes delayed, we will not lose faith. He will do what He has promised to do."

"But I cannot think of anything else, Joshua. I am a broken man. All the talk about what to tell Moses means nothing to me. I want my woman back, and her murderer brought to justice," he sobbed.

Joshua wrapped his arms gently around Geuel, pressed his cheek against his blood-coated face, and kissed his forehead. "God will hasten His word to perform it.[5] Do not fear, my hurting brother. Leave the vengeance to Him. God's timing, like all His ways, is perfect. He is never early; neither is He ever late. He is in complete control of everything and everyone," he said, his heart breaking as Geuel sobbed like a baby. "There has never been an event in our history as a nation that has ever put a wrinkle in the timing of God's eternal plans, which He designed before the foundation of the world."[6]

Joshua and Caleb walked together back to their horses.

"You were about to tell me something, Caleb," Joshua said. "Something about when we entered Eschol Valley?"

"Do you truly believe God is in control of everything? I mean absolutely everything?" Caleb said suddenly.

"He would not be God if He were not in control, would he, Caleb?"

"But we can help God achieve His purpose, correct?" Caleb continued.

"Do you think God needs us to help him, Caleb?" He chuckled. "I don't. He sees the beginning and the end of all things. He knows the outcome of everything.[7] God wants us to work with him in companionship and co-operation, but He does not need anyone's help. I believe that God disdains the poor, imperfect assistance of men in the performance of that work. Attempting to complete what God begins betrays our pride and ultimately offends God.

"Caleb, God's gifts are either free, without ropes attached, or they are not gifts at all but earned rewards.[8] To think we can bring anything to our lives, no matter how good or pious it seems, is to deny the true nature of God. Our morality, and the deeds that emanate from our flesh, are as filthy rags compared to God's righteousness. Both adversity and good come from the mouth of the Most High."[9]

"But do you not think, if we perform deeds of righteousness, that God will give us forgiveness and a great reward?" Caleb argued with trepidation, worried about how he had strong-armed his fellow spies. "I am sure that it is only by good works—and, of course, the will of

God—that we can be forgiven our sins and gain access to the world to come. Those whose good deeds are plentiful will be successful. But those whose good deeds are few and far between will lose their souls, and in hell will they abide."

"I think that the performance of good deeds of righteousness is a result of God empowering and working through us. We cannot earn, nor do we deserve, God's pleasure by anything we do—we do good deeds because He works through us. It is impossible to *earn* His love. It is a wonderful gift." Joshua smiled.

"It is so frustrating for me, Joshua. I do not understand what I do. It seems although I know what is right, I do the opposite, the things I hate. Goodness does not live in me," Caleb rambled.

"This is the battle that lives within us all," Joshua replied. "We must serve God and His laws with all of our hearts and minds, beseeching him for his support and assistance because our human nature serves only the law of sin. Now do you understand why God does not need our help? What were you going to tell me before Ammiel called us to Geuel?"

Caleb picked up a rock and hurled it as far as he could. He sighed deeply and turned around to look Joshua square in the face. "Nothing too important, my friend. I just wanted you to know that in private discussions with all the men, the vote now is one-hundred-percent affirmative. We all agree to that we should go forward and enter Canaan." He said this with a sheepish smile, still not entirely sure he had done the correct thing. But at least it was something.

39

DAY THIRTY-EIGHT: WEDNESDAY, JULY 27 / AV 9

Kadesh-Barnea
Homeward Bound

The men, now only six hours from Kadesh-Barnea, were a completely different group than when they'd left thirty-nine days before. Joshua's cuts and bruises, along with Gaddiel's bandages, were persuasive evidence of the experience they'd had and a sharp contrast to the ripe fruit they carried in the mule-driven cart. Contention and animosity had replaced the patriotism and partisanship they'd felt when they started their journey. Disarray had replaced their unity. Anger and jealousy hid behind their ragged eyes. The familiar rocks jutting out of the dune embankments, which had cautioned them almost forty days ago, now seemed like cheering spectators encouraging them to push across the finish line just a few hundred cubits ahead.

Joshua stroked his tattered beard, glad that it had started growing out again. He was happy when Caleb assured him that all the men were in favour of advancing the Israelites into Canaan. Moses had charged them with a list of particular things to investigate on their journey. He'd said, "Go up there into the Negev and on to the hill country and see what kind of country it is. Are the people who dwell therein strong or weak, few or many? Is the country in which they dwell good or bad? Are the towns they live in open or fortified? Is the soil rich or poor? Is it wooded or not?"[1] Joshua wished Moses had phrased it differently, leaving the questions open-ended and saying instead, "When you return, tell us what you saw. How did you experience this new place? How fertile was the land? How were the people there?" This would have allowed each man to develop their own story to tell Moses.

Instead each man was faced with a dualistic yes or no vote, and each man thought he was right. It was one man's opinion against another's. *I guess it does not matter now*, Joshua thought, *since Caleb said we all agree*. He knew that the few disastrous events of this mission would outweigh the auspicious ones in some of the men's minds: the deaths of Zidon and Donatiya, Joshua's capture and torment by Sihon, Geuel's broken heart, the mutiny of his friends. It was hard sometimes to accept that God was in charge of the circumstances no matter what. *These events occurred to teach us something or to make us better people. Just as the heavens are higher than the earth, so are God's ways higher than our ways and His thoughts higher than our thoughts. Because God is omniscient, He knows what He will accomplish through us. He knows what we will do in any circumstances. His plans for us will never fail. They will never be flawed by missing information or some unknown detail. This mission has been full of tragedy and suffering, but even these things were part of God's plan. It is true: it was not God's plan to send us to spy out the land of Canaan—that came from Moses. But God permitted it for reasons beyond our understanding.*

It was also hard for Joshua to understand why God did not intervene. He scolded himself. *What treachery I am thinking? I would not do what Moses did, and I would not do what God did... God, forgive me.* Joshua knew that constantly querying why something happened, and looking back longingly at the days before, brought failure. God was much more interested in forming character than shaping circumstance.

It was so easy to forget the everyday miracles of God, from the minute Joshua woke up and felt his heart beating inside his chest until he closed eyes at night. The sun rose on the horizon every day without fail, giving warmth and light not only for him but for all the flora, without which they could not get the food they needed to grow, reproduce, and survive. The night sky sparkled with the galaxy's brightest stars. The bewitching moon hung in the sky in all her immaculate purity, laughing at the hubris of man. The newborn baby left the womb and arrived into her mother's arms, so innocent, perfect, and beautiful. Love existed between humans like Geuel and Donatiya. All these things were just as powerful as God parting the Red Sea and destroying the most powerful civilization in the world.

Joshua could hear a drum beating steadily in the distance. He remembered momentarily the drumbeats and pagan rituals on Mount Hermon. These drums, however, were announcing to the tribes at Kadesh-Barnea that visitors approached. His heart beat double-time with each thump of the big bass drum. He glanced back to see smiles on all his worn-out men.

The temptation to kick their horses into a trot was strong, but the horses were exhausted, and they had a bulky cart being pulled by a now-depleted mule. So they slowly sauntered toward the tents and the crowds that were forming to greet them.

The last seven hundred cubits seemed like an eternity. Men, women, and children from all the tribes were lined up on both sides of the riders, chanting *Joshua, Joshua, Joshua*, clapping their hands and cheering as the men approached the camp. The spies, smiling respectfully, nodded to the left and right, clapping their right fists on their chests with a thud.

Joshua turned to the men. "Go to your tents, bathe and eat, and catch up on some of the sleep you have missed. Do not discuss with anyone what you have seen or done. Save it for our meeting with Moses. Not a word to anyone—that includes your girlfriends, your wives, your fathers, your mothers, even the Levite priests. What I ask is very important. I will let you know when we will meet with Moses and give him our report. Now go, and we will see you all again very soon. Gaddiel, go with Geuel to the healing tent and have the physicians look at your bandages and wounds."

The sight of the tents and the pleasant, familiar smell of simple meat cooking over campfires decompressed Joshua's aching body and mind. They were finally home. Amidst the cheering, Joshua could hear the crows warning the young children, who were chasing them with long sticks, to stay away. Amused dogs joined the impromptu game, racing behind the children and barking. He watched Caleb leap off his horse and run toward Ephrath and Hur. Joshua felt a tear roll down his mud-caked cheek as they hugged and passionately kissed each other. He was not sure if the tear was happiness for Caleb or sadness that there was no one like that to greet him.

Then Joshua spotted Moses. Joshua had forgotten how handsome and tall he was, his snowy white hair and beard blowing in the cool breeze. His muscular frame repudiated the fact that he was almost eighty-three years old. Standing beside his beautiful black wife Zipporah and his two sons, Gershom and Eliezer, one would not think him a day more than forty. He secretly wished Moses would make one of his sons his successor because the burden of leading Israel was more than Joshua could bear. Meritocracy—the belief that leaders should be chosen for their abilities and not because of birth or wealth—had always been the chosen form of succession for the Hebrews. Joshua knew Moses loved both his sons, but as painful and disappointing as the decision was for him, he did not feel that they should lead Israel. Joshua honestly did not see himself as Moses did, but his love and respect for Moses were enough to earn his consent to the decision.

As Joshua got off his horse, Moses left his family and ran toward him with his arms wide open. He gave Joshua an enthusiastic bear hug and kissed him on each cheek. "Barukh ha-ba, my son," Moses stuttered, smiling warmly.

"Barukh ha-nimza," Joshua answered politely, looking directly into his dark eyes.

"You look horrible. You have lost weight—and what happened to your beard?" Moses asked.

Joshua smiled. "It is a long but interesting story to tell, sir."

"I am sure it is. Go to your father's tent and get some rest. Eat, drink, and clean yourself up. We will meet at d-d-daybreak tomorrow, after the first sacrifice in the tabernacle. Bring all the spies with you, and you can tell me the stories. Judging by the incredible fruit on the cart you have brought back, it would seem this land is even better than I imagined. As much as I am curious to know what you saw, I can wait one more night to hear all about it. The good news is you are back. Zipporah will instruct the servants to prepare a lavish celebration, and we will celebrate your safe return tomorrow night. Can you do that, Zipporah?"

"Immediately and with pleasure, my husband," she responded, and ran toward the scullery tents.

Moses took a ring from his hand and slipped it onto Joshua's middle finger. "I am so happy you have returned safely, my son. Take this ring as a symbol of my joy. It was g-g-given to me when I was in the Midian, before I was called to go to Egypt. We will bring all the fatted calves we have in camp and feast as we have never done before, giving thanks to God for protecting you all during your mission and delivering you back to your people. You have made me a happy man."

Behind them, fourteen-year-old Gershom suddenly burst out crying. "Father, that ring was my grandfather Jethro's ring. Why would you give it to Joshua? I thought one day you would reward me or Eliezer with it. Have we not always done what you have asked of us? Have we not been good sons? You have never given us even a young goat to celebrate with our friends. But now Joshua, who you call your son, returns after forty days and is given our inheritance. Do you love Joshua more than your own blood?"

Moses shook his head, his eyes showing disappointment. "Do not worry, my son. You will inherit much when I die, all my material possessions. Your brother Joshua risked his life so that our nation might prosper and flourish. The ring I have given to Joshua represents my authority. Even more, it is circular and has no beginning or no end, like the love I have for him. When I die, Joshua will assume my mantle as leader of the nation of Israel."

"He is not your son, and he is certainly not our brother. He is the son of Nun," Gershom huffed.

"Herein lies one of the many r-r-reasons why Joshua will inherit my mantle, Gershom, and not you or Eliezer. I will always love you as my sons, but self-seeking individuals who care only for themselves become engulfed in jealousy. For where envy and self-seeking exist, confusion and every evil thing can also exist. Your jealousy keeps you from being rational. Rejoice and celebrate with me that Joshua has returned, and let us all give thanks to God."

"It is okay, Moses. I understand how your sons must feel," Joshua said, and he turned to Gershom with the ring in his hand. "Please, Gershom, forgive me and take your father's ring."

Gershom angrily turned his back on Moses and Joshua and marched away with his brother, leaving the ring in Joshua's hand.

Moses smiled and put the ring back on Joshua's finger. "Your humble reaction to Gershom's harsh words only confirms that you are as much my beloved son as they are. I am sorry you had to hear all this. I will see you tomorrow after morning sacrifice." And Moses sallied behind his hotheaded sons.

40

DAY THIRTY-NINE: THURSDAY, JULY 29 / AV 10

Kadesh-Barnea
The Day of the Vote

Moses sat quietly on his elevated seat, which overlooked his tribal council of seventy elders. They were nervously chattering in anticipation. They all had groomed themselves specifically for this critical meeting, and most of them wore loose, white ceremonial garments. Perfumed air filled the tent, and all the candles burned brightly. There was a pulsating rhythm of chants from the Levite priests as their deep voices resonated with final prayers. Moses stood up, raised his arm, and clenched his fist. The room was silent.

"Members of the council and my faithful Sanhedrin, I have summoned you all here today to listen to the report of the twelve spies' mission through Canaan. We thank God that they have come back to us safely. As you are all aware, we stand at the crossroads—or better said, the threshold—of the land God promised to Abraham. God rescued us from our captivity in Egypt and has miraculously led us through deserts, seas, and the wilderness. I wanted to take you immediately into Canaan, but you came to me and said, 'Let us send men ahead of us to spy out the land, so they can tell us the best route to take and what kind of cities are there.' It seemed like a good thing to do, so I selected twelve men, one from each tribe. Sitting beside me are those twelve brave men. I will ask each of them firstly if we should assemble our army and enter Canaan, yes or no. If they wish to add anything or explain how they came to their decision, they may do so. As you entered the tent, you saw the fruit they brought back with them: grapes larger than pomegranates, pomegranates larger than melons, and figs sweeter than a bee's honey. Let us start with Caleb, from the tribe of Judea."

Caleb rose to his feet and cleared his throat. "My beloved people, my vote is a resounding yes! The Lord, our God, is bringing us to a fertile land—a land that has rivers and springs and underground streams gushing out into the valleys and hills; a land that produces wheat and barley, grapes, figs, pomegranates, olives, and honey. There we will never go hungry or ever be in need. Its rocks have iron in them, and from its hills, we can mine copper. You will have all you want to eat, and you will give thanks to the Lord your God for the fertile land He has given you."

Caleb, knowing that the other men would say pretty much the same thing, did not want to oversell the idea, so he quickly sat down to the applause and excitement of the Sanhedrin.

"Thank you, Caleb. Now we will hear from Ammiel, from the tribe of Dan," Moses announced.

"My fellow Israelites, descendants of Abraham, Isaac, and Jacob, my vote is an emphatic no! While Caleb tells the truth, and it is a rich, ripe, and fertile land producing grapes the size of which we have never seen before, it is also a land of giants, fortified cities, and pagan cults. There are Anakim three times the size of an Israelite, with six fingers and six toes. We are but small grasshoppers to them. They drink the blood of humans and play games with the decapitated heads of their victims. There are children of the Nephilim and Rephaim, demonically possessed with a single purpose to destroy all things godly. These demon forces have formed an evil alliance of the different tribes in Canaan. The Hittites, Jebusites, and Amorites have sworn to fight—no, to decimate—the Hebrew people. Their cities are fortified with walls as you have never seen before, and they would be impossible to conquer. Their exceptionally well-trained armies even have three-person chariots, better chariots than we saw in Egypt, which would wreak terrible havoc on our army. It is my opinion that this is a war we cannot win."

The room was so quiet you could hear a tent peg drop. Caleb stared at Ammiel in disbelief—Ammiel had broken his promise.

"Well, l-let us hear from the others." Moses stuttered a bit. "Igal, son of Joseph, from the tribe of Issachar, what say you?"

Igal got up slowly and looked at his audience. "I say no." And he quickly sat down.

"Sethur, from the tribe of Asher, what is your vote?" Moses continued.

"There is too much pain, too much death, in the land of Canaan. I vote no!"

"Palti, son of Raphu, from the tribe of Benjamin, please stand and give us your vote," Moses commanded.

"My vote is a forceful no! Canaan is a haunted land. There are drugs, which I almost became addicted to, and the demonic dreams terrified us. We asked for God's help but could not find God anywhere. It is not a place I would want my family or loved ones to live. God is not in this forsaken land."

"Gaddiel, son of Sodi, from the tribe of Zebulun... how do you vote?"

Gaddiel limped to his feet, his leg and neck still in bandages. "If God were with us, who could stand against us? But everyone and everything stood against us, including wild bears, and I have the scars and wounds to prove it. I vote absolutely no. We are much better off here, in the presence of our living God."

"Thank you. Please sit down, Gaddiel. Shammua, from the tribe of Reuben, please stand and give us your vote," Moses continued to stutter.

"Honourable brothers, I stand here with no visible wound, but if you were all to look closer, you would see I contracted an awful disease in that cursed land. I have blisters and sores on my body that will not go away, and I vigorously vote no! Let us stay here and worship our God. I, for one, do not want to become a lowly farmer fighting disease and sickness at every turn."

"Shaphat, your vote, please," Moses commanded.

"You all know me well. I am not afraid to fight—quite the opposite, in fact. I am not scared of the armies or the people there. What frightens me the most is the corruption and sin that are so blatant and pervasive. Sadly, I too vote no to protect our people. We are safe here; God communicates with us. We did not see our God in this land of Canaan. There has to be a better place for us to live."

Shaphat sat down slowly and glanced at Caleb's ashen face.

"Nahbi, son of Vophsi from the tribe of Naphtali, may we have your vote, please?"

"Most venerable elders, without a doubt, there is beauty in this land, especially along the coast. Joppa, for instance, had flowers I had never seen before. The Jezreel Valley was especially fertile, but it led to Megiddo, a city we would never be able to conquer, and we would lose so many men in the attempt. I vote no from my conscience. I do not think it is the land for us."

"Geuel, from the tribe of Gad, please stand up and address the council," Moses instructed.

"I have seen the most brutal act of violence possible: a religious man sacrificing his virgin daughter by throwing her into a fire to appease his friends and a pagan god. The people that live there are without conscience; they are without souls. My vote is also an emphatic no. We are much better people than those who live there, and they would eventually corrupt us." He found his seat again.

"Gaddi, son of Susi from the tribe of Manasseh, please stand and give us your vote."

"My decision to vote no is for reasons much different than those my brothers have offered. In this land, there are horrible people, and yes, there are giants and many hateful people. However, the first casualty in any war is the heart. It becomes like stone. Many innocent, deceived people are doing the best they can with whatever they have in Canaan. These are the people I fear will die as collateral damage if we attack: the men, women, and children who are not part of the incestuous corruption and degradation that we saw. Honest people are working hard in their fields, women are caring for their families, children are growing up. The cost of the invasion would be much too great. We Israelites are better than that. We stop and care for the hurting children and widows, and we heal the sick. There is no winning side in this war we contemplate."

"Thank you, Gaddi, for your insight. I was hoping for better news than what I have heard so far. We have ten noes and only one yes. Now I call upon the commander and leader of this group of spies to give us his report. Joshua, son of Nun, from the tribe of Ephraim, please address the council."

Joshua unhurriedly stood up and glanced at Caleb, who was shocked at what he had just heard from his companions. When their eyes met, Caleb shrugged and gazed at the dirt floor.

"Honourable elders and fellow brothers, I did not volunteer to be a spy on this mission. Our beloved leader Moses chose me. Before I was chosen and given this task, I was ready to lead our army into Canaan and face whatever would be there—not in hubris or blind confidence, but because this is the promised land given to us by our living God. I did not have to see what was there to determine whether or not I wanted to go. It did not matter to me what we might find in Canaan. If God said it was to be our land, then who could argue with Him? However, I was chosen, along with these brothers who sit with me in front of you. We were to find out what the people were like, to check out their cities and fortifications, to verify that the land is fertile and productive. You have seen the cart of fruit we brought back, and the soil is indeed incredibly rich and fertile. There are, certainly, obstacles to overcome, but with God, all things are possible. It is true that some giants and armies will want to prevent us from occupying the land, but when God arises, all his enemies will be scattered. Did not God just two years ago destroy the most powerful nation on earth, the Egyptians, just to set us free from slavery and bondage? Did *we* do anything to make that happen? Not really. The issue is not what is in Canaan; the problem is what is in our hearts as a nation.

"We know if we keep the laws between man and God, everything will be okay. Who will be able to touch us? We serve a living God, and the Canaanites serve dictators and tyrants. They pray to lifeless stone statues and wooden gods that have no power to do anything. We will find prosperity in the land of Canaan, and we will change the landscape if we keep our bargain with God, obeying his laws and precepts. If we break His commandments, if we break the Torah, then the land will vomit us out, we will suffer, and we will be defeated even by small children throwing stones at us. I do not see any external threats to keep us from going in and occupying Canaan. The only danger that will keep us away from God's promise is our lack of faith in what God can do for us if we trust Him. I vote an overwhelming yes to the question. And we should attack not tomorrow, not next week or next month, but *now*. We can miss this opportunity by obsessing over how to execute it. The Egyptians could not stop us, the blistering heat of the desert could not stop us, the Red Sea could not stop us, the Amalekites at Rephidim could not stop us, hunger and thirst could not stop us. Who in this tent thinks the Canaanites could? If God is for us, who then can be against us? Could they be that foolish to stand against the Creator of all things? Listening to what has been spoken here today, I am not angry at my brothers. They told you what they saw and what they feared, and they were sincere. But I am telling you it is not what is in Canaan that we should fear. It is what is in your hearts."

Joshua sat down, and the men could hear his knees crack as the pregnant silence of the tent gave birth to the final words of Moses.

"This meeting is adjourned. As tomorrow is Friday, I will give everything prayerful consideration and inform you of my decision when I have made it on Shabbat," Moses announced.

The Sanhedrin, the council of seventy elders, exited the tent single file, murmuring to each other and shaking and nodding their heads.

"You broke your word to me," Caleb screamed at Ammiel. "You

made me a promise and then broke it like a common pagan." His eyes were bursting with flames of fire, and the ground practically shook with his anger.

"It is better to break a promise to you than a promise to God, Caleb. Besides, you forced us to a promise with a sword to our necks," Ammiel responded calmly. "That was the reason the other men sided with my logic. Anyone crazed enough to take a sword to his brothers must have an ulterior motive. I do not know what it is—that is between you and your conscience—but my conscience is clean."

Ammiel and the other spies slunk out of the tent behind the Sanhedrin, leaving Joshua, Caleb, and Moses looking at each other with befuddlement.

"What just happened here?" Moses asked Joshua.

"You wanted a report, and that is what you got," Joshua replied.

"I did not want a report; the tribes wanted a report. I simply thought it was not a bad idea."

Moses grabbed the end of the table, picked it up, and flipped it over. It just missed landing on Joshua. Goblets and hot wax splattered on the canvas wall. Moses looked like he had just sacrificed a goat, so saturated in red wine was his white tunic.

"I made a mistake by allowing it, didn't I? It was my foolish pride. God gave His word and promised to provide new land in which we could live and prosper. Our people, in fear, grumbled and complained about what they could not see and wanted me to send spies to check everything out. I talked to God about it, and He would not tell me what to do, hoping I would choose obedience, ignore their complaining and fear, and embrace His promise. I felt I had to take charge. It was my desire for control that caused this to happen. I see it now: my pride snared me, and instead of trusting God's promise of provision, I created a plan to send twelve spies. It was not God's plan, it was all mine. How could I deceive myself so badly to think for one second that the land prepared for us could be anything other than amazing? I am horrified at my foolishness, as much as I am at the rebellious, seditious nature of our nation."

Joshua looked at him sympathetically. "The men's desire not to enter is primarily fuelled by their desire to prolong our supernatural existence here at Kadesh-Barnea. Their mistake is not trusting in God enough to see that we would be able to conquer, settle, and prosper in Canaan. You heard them repeatedly say, "We are not able." Their doubt caused them to question our resources, and their self-assurance is negligible. They see themselves as tiny grasshoppers about to be squished by big bad giants. They are just afraid, Moses. Fear always follows doubt and self-deprecation, and that fear paralyzes us all."

"What bothered me the most about their reports is that they all started with positive statements about the land overflowing with milk and honey. But they quickly replaced these with negative descriptions of the fortified cities and the overpowering people who live there.[1] They began with flattery and ended with what I would define as unbelief. How could you and Caleb observe the same land and the same occupants and interpret everything so differently?" Moses remarked. "Their negative attitude and narrow perspective saw only failure and defeat, yet you and Caleb saw possibility and potential success."

"What will you do, Moses?" Caleb asked.

"I will seek God's face and ask Him."

"But we must march into Canaan, Moses, and we must go now," Joshua pleaded. "You know that is what we must do, correct?"

"I must talk to God and ask Him to forgive me for my pride, and our people for their unbelief," Moses repeated. "I made a horrible decision to send you on this mission. I must seek God's wisdom, and when I know what it is God would have us do, I will announce his decision after Shabbat."

41

DAY FORTY: FRIDAY, JULY 30 / AV 11

Canaanite Battle Plan

Sihon had never been more disappointed in his brother Og than he was at this moment. Og had been foolishly tricked into letting Joshua and his companions escape. Sihon thought of sending Og back to Bashan, but the message it would dispatch to his troops would be one of defeat, and he had to keep up their morale. He even thought of lying to everyone, announcing that they had found the Hebrew spies and killed them all. But later, if they saw Joshua alive while fighting in battle, they would think he was some special type of god that had risen from the dead.

There was nobody more pusillanimous than Sihon. He purposely exaggerated all potential dangers and calamities in his mind and was in a constant state of agitation. His only objective now was to destroy the Hebrew army. Once he had accomplished this, any remaining problems would be easily solved. If he could not lure the Israelites to fight in Canaan, he would attack their camp at Kadesh-Barnea.

He was continually developing his progressive strategy. He knew the Israelite tactics of using troops in battle, and they were famous and effective. However, a solid long-term plan was much better than individual tactics, and this was what he needed to win the war. He would give the Israelites a false sense of security. It was of paramount importance that he exploit the Israelite sense of superiority. In their delirium of hubris, their ineptitude and poor judgments would cause them to suffer defeat. The morale of all his troops—Hittites, Jebusites, and Amorites—would have to be at its highest. Sihon knew from experience that one did not elicit bravery by giving speeches in the heat of battle; veteran soldiers thirsting for blood scarcely listened, and rookie recruits overwhelmed by their fear quickly forgot. Everything was in the actual preparation for battle. You had to crush both false and accurate reports of your adversary's strength and keep alive the troop's indomitable spirit.

Sihon looked around the tent at the sullen faces of his commanders, who were sitting and arguing around the war table. The table was covered with half-empty goblets, maps strewn in disorderly piles, and blood-covered bones that the priests had hurled. The smell of their soiled tunics permeated the air, overpowering the rank smell of garlic and alcohol on their breath. How Sihon hated human incompetence. But he needed to get past his disgust and speak directly to the soul of his commanders. The smallest word of praise from him was treasured unto death by his men, and the slightest rebuke could reduce these hardened soldiers to tears. They all feared his rages. They did not fear the Hebrew God, Chemosh, or the devil, but they trembled like children at Sihon's anger.

"What do our soldiers fight for?" Sihon snarled above their voices.

"For the land of their ancestors: Canaan," one said.

"For Chemosh, Baal, and their other gods—for their freedom to worship as they see fit," said another.

"They are poverty-stricken, hungry misfortunates who are unable to do much more than fight," Sihon countered. "They are mercenaries—soldiers doing it for the money and perhaps, if they survive, fame. From this moment forward, double all salaries for our fighting men. Foot soldiers, officers, mounted troops, archers, chariot drivers, all men. I want titles, medals, and awards presented to those who show courage and bravery weekly, and report back to me with the results."

"Do you realize how much gold you are giving away with this gift?" Og snarled.

Sihon did not answer his brother. "I want two thousand men dispatched to each of the cities of Beersheba, Hebron, Jebus, Jericho, Joppa, and Shechem. They will occupy the cities, take control, then wait for the invaders to come."

"Only two thousand men in each city?" Og whined again, shaking his head. "What good are two thousand men against an army of six hundred and fifty thousand?"

"Og, you will sit quietly, or you can leave the tent," Sihon bellowed. "Do you understand me?" He turned back toward the others. "As the invading Israelite army approaches the first city, more than likely Beersheba, I want you to burn it to the ground. I want you to burn all the food storerooms and granaries, but bring with you all the sheep, goats, and cattle you can. We can use them to feed our armies. Kill the rest and burn them. The men will go north from Beersheba to Hebron, passing through farms and villages. I want you to burn those crops to the ground as well, leaving nothing that their army or people can eat or use. Once the Israelites give chase and come to Hebron, you will do the same. Burn it to the ground, so there is nothing left. If any of the locals resist my command, kill them as well. We will lure these venomous Hebrews into the valley of Armageddon, where my well-paid, grateful soldiers, charioteers and horseback riders will be waiting for them. It will be the battle to end all battles."

The smiles on the faces of the men in the room shone brighter than the flickering candles.

"Ingenious. By the time they get to Shechem, we will have twelve thousand men, a huge herd of animals for food, and a starving enemy," one commander commented.

"I am not worried about the twelve thousand men," said Sihon. "If we lose them, so be it. The strategy is to get the Israelites into the valley of Armageddon. I will have troops hidden on all three mountains: Carmel, Tabor, and Gilboa. As they enter the Jezreel Valley going toward Megiddo, we will surround them and finally annihilate these disgusting people."

"Truly, they are disgusting," another commander agreed. "However, they are also numerous. Their numbers will work to our advantage because it will take time for them to travel from city to city. That will give our tiny troop contingency time to escape." He beamed as if the whole plan were his idea.

"And what if they do not attack? What if they decide just to stay at our border?" asked Og, intrigued by his brother's plan.

"Then we will attack them there, in full force," Sihon replied. "But the advantage is always for the surprise and counterattack. I want them to come into Canaan, and why would they not? There is so much more here than in the dust bowl they occupy now. Their spies have seen our bountiful crops, our freshwater rivers and brooks, our fertile landscape. I do not think they would be so stupid as to pass on such an opportunity. If you want to catch a rat, you need two things: a delicious-smelling piece of cheese and a trap that will kill him when he comes to eat it. We will set up headquarters at Megiddo, but I want messengers coming to me every day, advising me of their movements and our progress. It is imperative that you start your destruction only when you see the Israelites coming to the city you are occupying. If they do not come, the city stays the way it was before we got there. Does everyone understand my orders?"

"Yes, sir," they all sang in unison. "Long live Sihon."

"Good. Now make it happen." Turning to his assistant, he ordered, "Send me that priest from Hebron—what was his name?"

"Do you mean Phineas, Your Highness?" his assistant asked.

"Phineas, Pineas, Tineas... Whatever his name is, send him to me. I need him to ask Chemosh about something."

"Something has happened to him, sir. There was a strange occurrence both in his mind and his body. He became raving mad after that Hebrew Joshua disappeared from our camp. He was foaming at the mouth and thrashing around, and we bound him so he would not hurt himself or others. We hoped he would recover, but unfortunately, he did not. Not knowing what to do, we turned him loose in the woods. He wanted to be among the wild beasts. He, in his delusion, thought he was one. We put out bread, meat, and wine for him to eat and drink, but he refused, choosing instead to eat grass and tree bark. He tore off his clothes and now lies all night in the forest, mooing like a wounded ox. I am afraid there is no hope for him."

Sihon snickered to himself. He knew Phineas was as dumb as an ox, and now he was living like one.

42

DAY FORTY-ONE: SATURDAY, JULY 31 / AV 12

Shabbat
Vote Results

As Moses lay face down in the Holy of Holies, interceding with God, Ammiel and Sethur, in vindictive spite, started spreading a false report as to what they had seen in the land of Canaan. They shared many details about the fortified cities, naming them one by one, describing the high walls and armies that occupied them, and exaggerating the strength of their armaments. They told wild stories of the giants they saw and fabricated events of the most gruesome nature. They lied about the productivity of the land, telling people they barely had enough food to feed themselves, and warned whoever would listen that this was horrible land. The rumours spread like wildfire, and the people started to cry out loud in distress. They complained about Moses and his leadership. They told each other it would have been better to die in Egypt or even here in the wilderness than to go into this horrifying land. The groups grew larger and more worried, reporting to Moses that their wives and children would be captured and eaten by these giants. Like a consuming wildfire, the complaining reached a point where the entire camp decided that they wanted to choose another leader and go back to Egypt. In their minds, it had to be better than what waited for them in Canaan.

Joshua and Caleb called loudly to Moses to come out from the Holy of Holies. And when Moses came out of the tabernacle, his face glowing, he found both Joshua and Caleb with torn clothing, fearing for their lives.

Joshua was standing high upon a rock, pleading with the throngs of people. "What you heard is not true. The land we explored is an excellent place, and if the Lord is pleased with us, He will take us there and give us that rich and fertile land. Do not rebel against God, and do not be afraid of the people who live there. We will conquer them easily. The Lord is with us and has already defeated the gods that protect them, so do not be afraid, and do not believe the lies that you have you have heard!"

The riotous hordes began to gather rocks and encouraged one another to throw them at Moses, Joshua, and Caleb. But just as the first rock was thrown, a dazzling radiance appeared over the tabernacle tent. It was so powerful the people had to shield their eyes against it.

Moses kissed Joshua's hand and helped him down from the rock. Moses then took his place as a brilliant light shone over his head, and he spoke with a booming voice to the people. "How much longer will you reject your God? How much longer will you refuse to trust Him, who has performed so many miracles among you? God has warned me he will destroy all of you and make me a father of a different nation much stronger and more powerful than you are! I cried out to him and begged Him not to kill you all, and I pleaded for His mercy, asking Him to show His great love and to forgive your sin and constant rebellion.

"Our God, who is slow to anger and full of forgiveness, will indeed forgive you as I asked Him to do, but as surely as He lives, and as surely as His presence fills the earth, He promises that none of you here today will live to enter the land of Canaan, the land of His promise. You have all seen the incredible light of His presence. You have also seen the miracles He performed in Egypt and the wilderness. Unfortunately, you have tested His patience to the limit. Over and over again, you have refused to obey Him. None of you will *ever* enter the land that He promised to your ancestors. None of you who have rejected Him today by believing these false reports will ever enter it. Only Joshua and Caleb, His faithful servants who have remained loyal to Him, will be allowed to enter.

"Because of your wickedness and complaining, we as a nation will be sent back into the hot desert, back into the unforgiving wilderness. God swears as surely as He lives that none of you over the age of twenty will enter that land. You will all die in the desert except for Joshua and Caleb. You said your children would be captured and killed in Canaan; however, because you have complained against Him, it is you who will die, and I will bring your children, who are too young to know right from wrong, into the land you have rejected. Your children will wander painfully with you in the desert for forty years, suffering for your unfaithfulness, until the last one of you present here today dies. Forty years you will wander without purpose, in circles—one year for every day the spies that you chose explored the land. And you will know what it means to have God against you.[1] Thus has God spoken."

When Moses had finished, the Israelites mourned bitterly. Early the next morning, they regretted what they had done and apologized profusely. They initiated another plan to invade the nearby hill country in Canaan and told Moses they were now ready to enter the land that God had given them. They were genuinely sorry for their attitude and were fearful of Moses's prophecy, for his predictions always came to pass.

Moses rebuked them sharply. "If you are truly sorry for your actions, then why will you disobey the Lord now? You will not succeed with your plan. The Lord has told you we must go back to the wilderness. You had your chance, and the door of opportunity to Canaan has closed. If you go now to do battle, your enemies will defeat you. The Canaanites will prevail because He is not with you.

You will all die in battle because you refused to follow Him when you had the chance."

But once again, the people did not listen to the words of Moses and gathered a large contingency of ten thousand soldiers.

"Surely God will forgive our ignorance and pride, and we will do now what we should have done in the beginning," they cried. "If you do not come with us, we will go on our own, take the land that has been promised us, and God will forgive us. It should be easy. Joshua and Caleb said to invade the hill country first and then proceed north."

"It is true that God has forgiven you. If He had not, you would all be dead by now. This is the eleventh time since we left Egypt that God has pardoned our nation. However, His instructions now are to go back into the wilderness. Your children and your grandchildren will inherit the land. You will not," Moses commanded sternly.

Again, thinking they knew better, they rode off without Moses, Joshua, or Caleb, and as Moses predicted, they were slaughtered. Only a few men managed to escape, and they returned to camp that evening to tell the story. They cried out to the Lord for help during the battle, but He paid them no attention.

And so it was. The nation of Israel packed up their camp and went back into the desert, on the road toward the Gulf of Aqaba. They sojourned as nomads for forty years until the last of the adults died from plague and disease. Along with Ammiel, Palti, Gaddiel, Gaddi, Geuel, Nahbi, Shaphat, Shammua, Igal, and Sethur, six-hundred thirty thousand men died in the desert. It was a tragic setback in Jewish history.

43

FORTY YEARS LATER: SUNDAY, DECEMBER 7 / KISLEV 17, 1401 BCE

Death Of Moses

There is a time for everything and a season for every activity under the heavens—there is a time to be born and a time to die. Just as the battle-scarred alpha wolf meanders away from his pack when he knows it is his time, so Moses, now one hundred twenty years old, rose very early one morning and painfully climbed up Mount Pisgah in solitude.

As was his recent habit, he spoke his thoughts out loud in a quiet but rich baritone. It was amazing. When he talked to himself, he never stuttered.

"Everything in between our birth and our death is our legacy. It is now my time to die. My long life abounded with defining moments. Like everyone in life, when I faced a new crisis, resistance was my typical response. With each predicament I found myself in, a choice always emerged with it: to resist or to accept, to respond in fear or faith, to say yes or no. Now, as I make this final transition from life to death, regret and remorse permeate my soul. I failed miserably at times."

He stopped his ascent for a moment, wiped his brow, and took a long drink of water from the leather bladder he carried over his shoulder. Tears dribbled down his weather-worn cheeks.

"Alas, my punishment is more than I can bear. God called me His friend, and yet I failed him. God chose me to lead my people, yet I alone ruined them. God gave me a task and empowered me to accomplish it, accompanied by signs and wonders. But my faith, when I needed it most, faltered. I heard, but I did not listen I let the fearful, wavering voices of my people silence the sure, still voice of God. I will never be allowed to cross the Jordan River. I will never smell the flowers, nor will my feet feel the fertile silt that I can see so clearly on my way to the peak of Mount Pisgah. I have spent the last forty-two years of my life earnestly pursuing what I see now as an empty dream."

Moses dropped his walking staff, fell to his knees, and buried his face remorsefully in his hands. Blood oozed from his right knee onto the jagged rock. "I made a lot of critical choices, and I see upon reflection that some were amiss. My banishment from the promised land is the price I must pay for my crime."

He reached for his cane and pushed himself back onto his feet, continuing his climb with a slight limp.

"My labour was the work of heaven. The overwhelming responsibility of being God's spokesman was frightening. I knew if I made the smallest error by omitting, augmenting, or compromising God's directives, I had the potential to destroy our entire world. God's love brought me forgiveness, but his justice for my crimes demanded payment. He has forbidden me to enter the land of milk and honey. There is always a consequence for disobeying God's instructions. A cut or a wound will heal with time, but the scar forever remains. The scar tells the story of your survival but is a constant reminder of the crime committed."

He took the last few steps to the top of the mountain with short, raspy breaths. "That was forty long and dry years ago. Today, standing on the peak of Mount Pisgah and surveying the beauty and vastness of this promised land that we Israelites are about to enter, I am sickened. My tongue cleaves to the roof of my mouth, and my guilt, more abysmal than the floodwaters of Noah's time, deluges my soul. I was their leader and their liberator. I brought this group of slaves to freedom. I turned a fractious collection of individuals into a nation. It was I who mediated with God, performed signs and wonders, and gave the people their laws. I fought with them when they sinned, and I fought God for them, praying for their forgiveness. It was my heart that broke when they repeatedly failed to live up to God's expectations. Now and forever, I am banished from entering the promised land. My punishment is severe but just."

He snatched his walking stick and threw it as hard as he could over the precipice. Moses watched it twirl, bounce, and rebound down the serrated surface of the cliff's face, which seemed to take an eternity.

"What was my crime? I was proudly admiring my spiritual beauty. I fell unwittingly into this devil's trap like an unsuspecting rabbit sticks his head through the patient hunter's twine loop. My pride destroyed my hopes and aspirations. My ego has been my nemesis. It led me to my present ruination and exile, and it leads me now to my death."

Moses sluggishly lay down, shut his eyes, and folded his arms around his chest. And then, on that windy mountaintop, Moses died. The next day, the Lord buried him in a valley nearby,[1] a short distance away from the promised land of Canaan.

The children of Israel wept for Moses for thirty days. As with all mourning, the days of weeping came to an end,[2] but the grief never ended. The loss of this great leader would always be painful, and the world would never be the same again.

Just before morning prayer, Joshua meandered through the camp at Acacia toward the training area. Diligent women were already preparing the morning meal for their families and stoking their campfires before the morning sacrifice. When he approached the training arena, fifty young men were practising their combat skills. The clamour of the soldier's swords and shields in the training arena was always soothing to Joshua's soul. In the middle of the platoons, barking instructions, was his friend Caleb with his son Hur.

"Good morning. Is everything going well?" Joshua asked in a raised voice.

Everyone stopped their fighting out of respect for Joshua's presence. There were no older men anymore; they had all died in the wilderness, according to the prophecies of Moses. Joshua and Caleb were now the most aged warriors.

"Everything is perfect, commander," Hur replied.

Hur reminded Joshua so much of the younger Caleb forty years before. He was loyal, muscular, and perhaps even a little better looking. Caleb had told him that his grandson, Uri, the youngest son of Hur, had fallen in love and would marry the woman Azubah if Joshua would give his blessing. Joshua willingly blessed the union but warned that the wedding celebration would have to wait. There were more pressing issues for the tribes to deal with.

Joshua, now sixty-two years old, had never married. He'd had plenty of opportunities and wished to abide by Hebrew traditions and have a family, but whenever he got emotionally close to a woman, he would find things he did not like about her. The memory of Orus and his unselfish love for Hurriya, his disease-laden wife, always made him step back and reassess his potential relationship. Orus loved Hurriya in spite of her ugliness and deformities. So Joshua was willing to wait for the right person. There must be someone that he could feel love for, like Orus did for Hurriya.

Joshua made his way through the camp and stood on the bank of the Jordan River. He bent over, cupped his hands, and took a long drink of the cold, fresh water. Joshua splashed some water on his face and arms. The Jordan River originated from the base of Mount Hermon and flowed all the way into the Dead Sea. Whenever Joshua looked upon it, it dredged up painful memories of his suffering at Sihon's fortress. He took off his sandals and washed the bottoms of his scarred, red-and-purple feet. *Everything that happens in this world happens at the time God chooses. He sets the time for birth and the time for death.* God had been chosen Joshua to be Moses's successor as leader of the nation of Israel. Joshua was shocked to discover that some of the dissenters actually believed he had killed Moses. Such blasphemy. He had loved Moses more than anyone. He stared with his steely eyes at the walled city of Jericho on the other side of the narrow, shallow Jordan River.

Joshua knew that God also set the time for war,[3] and he understood the time had finally come to take the land God had promised them. Their forty-year punishment had turned Caleb's beard white, turned the nation of Israel to repentance, and turned Joshua's insecurities into determination and confidence.

Joshua had a plan: he would send spies. This time, there would be no vote.

AFTERWORD

Reflecting and meditating on the mournful silhouette of the elderly Moses, standing by himself on Mount Pisgah as he looked back at his life, I decided to write this novel. For we will all one day stand at the end of our lives and reflect.

We will remember the choices that shaped us into who we are. I confess that I have at one time or another lived within the skin of each of the ten rebellious spies. I identify with their characteristics, emotions, fears, and obsessions better than anyone. I have been that hardworking businessman that Igal embodied, always looking for an angle or opportunity; Palti, the superstitious, determined wolf relying on his instincts to overcome his obstacles; Shaphat, the risk-taker, always ready for a fight and eager to draw first blood; Ammiel, with his logical mind, questioning everything and anything; Sethur, who believed that dreams were more reliable than facts; Shammua, who wanted to be the best in everything he did and always sought validation and approval; Gaddi, the kind humanitarian and true philanthropist; and Gaddiel, seeking diversions and obsessing over wine. I have been seethingly vain and narcissistic as was Nahbi, and many times as lovelorn as Geuel blinded by my emotions.

Moses was unquestionably the greatest prophet who ever lived, a miracle-working leader chosen by God to take the Israelites out of Egypt. He also transcribed the first five books of the Old Testament, the Torah, which contains the laws that the nation must follow. But Moses had defects, as all of us do. God's instructions and promises, whether we are aware of them or not, are true and unchanging.

In the words of John Piper, "Nothing, absolutely nothing, befalls those who 'love God and are called according to his purpose' but what is for our deepest and highest good. Therefore, the mercy and the sovereignty of God are the twin pillars of my life. They are the hope of my future, the energy of my service, the centre of my theology, the bond of my marriage, the best medicine in all my sickness, the remedy of all my discouragements. And when I come to die (whether sooner or later), these two truths will stand by my bed and with infinitely strong and infinitely tender hands lift me up to God."

NOTES

1. Friday, June 17 / Sivan 29, 1439 BCE

1. An object which functions as a flag but differs in appearance, consisting staff with an emblem at the top. Keil, *Commentary on the Old Testament*, 1:66. John MacArthur, Revelation 1-11: *The MacArthur New Testament Commentary* (Chicago, IL: Moody Press, 1999. Rev. 4:8; J. A. Seiss, *The Apocalypse: Lectures on the Book of Revelation* (Grand Rapids, MI: Zondervan Publishing House, 1966), 106.
2. "Now go! I will help you speak, and I will tell you what to say" (Ex. 4:12-13).
3. "But you came to me and said ... Let's send men ahead of us to spy out the land" (Deut.1:22-23).
4. Judg. 20:16.
5. Num. 1:40.
6. Num.13:16.
7. 1387 BC.
8. The twelve months of the Hebrew calendar correspond to the period from about mid-February to about mid-March.

2. Day One: Monday, June 20 / Tammuz 1

1. "Make two trumpets of silver; make them of hammered work. They shall serve you to summon the congregation" (Num.10:1-2).
2. The full military service comprised six hundred three thousand, five hundred fifty men, twenty years old (Num 1:46).
3. Israel fought with Amalek (Ex. 17:8-16).
4. Based on Sefer HaSichot 5749, vol. 2, pp. 536–540.
5. Joshua was Moses' "faithful servant...never budging from his tent" (Ex. 33:11).
6. "I (Moses) selected twelve men" (Deut. 1:22-23).
7. Jacob was later renamed Israel.
8. Gen. 15:18-21.
9. Judg. 1:16.
10. Ex.18:1-7, Num. 10:29-33.

3. Day Two: Tuesday, June 21 / Tammuz 2

1. Gen. 34:1-29.
2. 2 Kings 23:10.

4. Day Three: Wednesday, June 22 / Tammuz 3

1. Num. 18:2-4; 6.
2. Gen. 49:16-17.
3. Num. 10:25.

5. Day Four: Thursday, June 23 / Tammuz 4

1. Gen. 9:18.
2. Gen. 9:25-27
3. Gen. 21:25-30.
4. Gen. 26:25.
5. Gen. 21:33.

6. Day Five: Friday, June 24 / Tammuz 5

1. Prov. 15:22.
2. Pss. 105:15.

7. Day Six: June 25 / Tammuz 6

1. Deut. 5:15, Ex. 20:8–11.

8. Day Seven: Sunday, June 26 / Tammuz 7

1. Gen. 30:14–16.
2. Josephus (circa 37–100 AD).

9. Day Eight: Monday, June 27 / Tammuz 8

1. Gen. 20:3.
2. Also named Israel.

10. Day Nine: Tuesday, June 28 / Tammuz 9

1. Gen. 23:1–20, 25:9, 49:29–32, 50:12–13.
2. Present-day Jerusalem.

11. Day Ten: Wednesday, June 29 / Tammuz 10

1. Gen. 6:1–2.
2. Gen. 14:18–20.
3. 2 Sam. 5:6.
4. Gen. 32:24–32.

12. Day Eleven: Thursday, June 30 / Tammuz 11

1. Allusion to Matt. 26:69–74.

13. Day Twelve: Friday, July 1 / Tammuz 12

1. Pss. 23:5.

16. Day Fifteen: Monday, July 4 / Tammuz 15

1. 2 Kings 16:3, 21:6.
2. Jer. 32:29.
3. Josh. 8:31–32.
4. Gen. 25:29–34.

18. Day Seventeen: Wednesday, July 6 / Tammuz 17

1. Chemosh and Molech were the same. Judg. 11:24 has been thought by some to be proof of this, since it speaks of Chemosh as the god of the Cananites while Molech is elsewhere their god (compare 1 Kings 11:7, 33).
2. Lev. 18:21.

19. Day Eighteen: Thursday, July 7 / Tammuz 18

1. Hebrew daytime hours began with dawn and ended with sundown, varying with each season of the year.
2. Prov. 25:24.
3. Ex. 12:33–36.
4. Lev. 1:7, 6:1–6 / 8–13.
5. Between 9:00 and 10:00 a.m.
6. Between 3:00 and 4:00 p.m.
7. Heb. 9:13–14.
8. Acts 2:15.
9. Ex. 30:17–21.

10. Ex. 25:29.
11. Lev. 24:5–9.
12. Num. 4:7.
13. Winged angelic beings.
14. Ex. 3:14.
15. Ex. 34:4–7.
16. Pss. 103:7.
17. Heb. 9:23.
18. Heb. 8:5.
19. Gen. 3:21.
20. Methuselah lived to be 969 years old.

20. Day Nineteen: Friday, July 8 / Tammuz 19

1. Gen. 6:2.
2. 1 Enoch 56.
3. 1 Enoch 15:8–11.

22. Day Twenty-One: Sunday, July 10 / Tammuz 21

1. Present day Jaffa/Tel-Aviv.
2. Ex. 13:17–18.
3. Lev. 19:27.

24. Day Twenty-Three: Tuesday, July 12 / Tammuz 23

1. Armageddon.
2. A different city than Kadesh-Barnea.
3. Isa. 55:9, Rom. 11:33–36.
4. Prov. 3:5–6.

25. Day Twenty-Four: Wednesday, July 13 / Tammuz 24

1. Gen. 19:4–5.
2. Gen. 19:26.
3. Gen. 19:30–38.
4. Ruth 1–4.

29. Day Twenty-Eight: Sunday, July 17 / Tammuz 28

1. Known today as Jabal el-Shaiykh.
2. Josh. 11:17.

31. Day Thirty: Tuesday, July 19 / Av 1

1. Gen. 3:4–5.
2. Gen. 14:13.
3. Zohar 3:184a.
4. 2 Peter 2:4.

32. Day Thirty-One: Wednesday, July 20 / Av 2

1. Midrash of Vyikra Rabba 16:3.

33. Day Thirty-Two: Thursday, July 21 / Av 3

1. Prov. 17:12.

34. Day Thirty-Three: Friday, July 22 / Av 4

1. Gen. 2:15–17.

36. Day Thirty-Five: Sunday, July 24 / Av 6

1. Isa. 40:22.
2. Gen. 50:15–21.

37. Day Thirty-Six: Monday, July 25 / Av 7

1. The name *Joshua* comes from the same root Hebrew name as *Jesus* and is interchanged in the Bible (Neh. 8:17).

38. Day Thirty-Seven: Tuesday, July 26 / Av 8

1. Gen. 20:1–16.
2. Gen. 26:1–33.
3. Deut. 32:35.

4. Ex. 21:24.
5. Jer. 1:12.
6. Pss. 18:30.
7. Isa. 46:10.
8. Paraphrasing of Abraham Booth.
9. Lam. 3:38.

39. Day Thirty-Eight: Wednesday, July 27 / Av 9

1. Num. 13:17–20.

40. Day Thirty-Nine: Thursday, July 29 / Av 10

1. Num. 13:27–29.

42. Day Forty-One: Saturday, July 31 / Av 12

1. Num. 14:1–38.

43. Forty Years Later: Sunday, December 7 / Kislev 17, 1401 BCE

1. Deut. 34:5–7.
2. Deut. 34:8.
3. Eccl. 3:1–8.

PRAISE FOR THE TWELVE SPIES OF MOSES

"In *The 12 Spies of Moses*, Bruce Hampson has done a masterful job on taking the biblical narrative and writing a plausible account of how the 12 spies' mission may have unfolded. The 12 Spies of Moses is creative, imaginative, humorous, and thoroughly entertaining, as he grapples with the underlying question was the 12 spies mission God's idea or Moses'."

— Rev. Wes Mills, President, Apostolic Church of Pentecost of Canada, Calgary Alberta

"Bruce Hampson's novel *The Twelve Spies of Moses* is an action-packed adventure story from the cover to the last chapter. Historically set in 1350 BCE, it deals with one of the greatest mysteries in the Bible; why did the Israelites have to go back to the desert wilderness for another forty years after their escape from tyrannical Egypt? The story involves a great many religious insights, but you don't have to be religious to enjoy this book; it is a fictional narrative based on hard to research facts from hundreds of sources, including the best of them all——THE BIBLE. From Moses to Joshua, the Spies and their Enemies, Bruce brings all of the characters to life and somehow manages to not only to get inside of their lives but also their souls in this great adventure. He also reveals to the reader a lot about the conflicts and emotional experiences of the time. So many of them will certainly resonate with us all in this Modern day. It was a pleasure to read."

— Brian Hodge, businessman, and entrepreneur, Toronto, Ontario

"In his novel, *The Twelve Spies Of Moses*, author, Bruce Hampson in the true genre of "Biblical/Historical Fiction", brings to life the Biblical narrative of the twelve spies who were commissioned by

Moses to enter the land promised to them by God and to investigate its inhabitants, prior to leading the nation of Israel in to take possession. Hampson imbues the spies with personality and character (where the Biblical account is silent), and animates their interaction with each other and with those whom they confronted and with whom they battled with graphic, descriptive language that causes them to leap from the pages of his novel and into the imagination and mind of the reader. The encounters, both those recorded in Scripture, and those that the author creates, evoke strong identification with the reader. One feels like you are alongside the players as each paragraph pulsates with passion and pathos, and each chapter emanates a rhythmic movement from one battle to another. Bruce has brilliantly moved beyond the scope of the Scriptural account to present an imaginative account of what the experience might have been like for the 12 spies in the Old Testament book of Joshua. The author further speculates that it may not have been merely Moses's disobedience and rebellion against the direct command of God to "speak to the Rock" (to bring water for the thirsty tribes of Israel), when he twice smote the Rock with his rod, but his arrogance and pride in going ahead of God and commissioning the spies on their mission without God's direct command, that resulted in his being forbidden to enter the land. Moses is personified throughout the narrative, and, delivers a final soliloquy in the closing pages. Readers who avow a strict allegiance to the Biblical account, and to adding nothing thereto, will have to put aside their orthodox interpretation and read the book as it is intended—as a novel to derive the full impact of its message. While Hampson is theologically qualified to offer commentary on the typology and metaphors of the Biblical story, and to apply their metaphorical application to a life of faith, he refrains from doing so in the interest of crafting a story that distills the Biblical principle of obedience and surrender to the will and commands of God as the only guaranteed safe passage to the Land of Promise. I greatly enjoyed the manuscript and couldn't put it down once I opened its pages. I heartily recommend it, both as a fascinating work of fiction and as a novel that reveals powerful principles for life."

— Dr. Donald M. Carmont M.A., Ph.D., C.M.C., author, speaker, Surrey, British Columbia.

"The *Twelve Spies of Moses* is a masterpiece of mixing Biblical truths and sanctified fiction to teach us facts of every day living. We are challenged with decision making. There are daily choices that we all must make. Will we choose to do our own thing and suffer the consequences or will we live by faith in God and His ways?

Bruce has captured a very unique way of presenting truth and engaging the reader to make the right choices. This book will challenge you and hold you spellbound from cover to cover. Well done Bruce Hampson!

-Rev. Ed Bradley, pastor, teacher and missionary, Mapleridge, B.C.

"Reading '**The Twelve Spies of Moses**' was an epiphany for me. Having been raised during the 1960's in a religious household, I fell away from my roots. I distinctly remember seeing a stage presentation of 'Jesus Christ Superstar' in the early 1970's. I was taken aback by how human the characters seemed - from Jesus, right through to Judas. Although I did not revert to the religion of my youth, the experience did allow me the latitude to see myself as spiritual, if not religious. ***The Twelve Spies of Moses***, has much the same appeal. The characters are human, multi-faceted, imperfect, and entirely relatable. I could imagine myself as just about any of them.

As a teacher, I know the importance of 'taking iconic personalities off the shelf', as it were. When we read biographies of great people, we long to connect to some piece of them. It allows one to move beyond the mystique in order to better understand the context and the issue(s). This book does that. Loyalty, trust, love, hate, bravery, cowardice - it's all there. A great read, regardless of your ideology."

- Roger Ford, retired teacher. Port Coquitlam, B.C.

ABOUT THE AUTHOR

Jewish roots, a background of a Christian minister, and extensive knowledge of the Bible sparked the author's interest in the story of twelve spies and their forty-day exploration mission to Canaan that had affected Moses' decision on proceeding to the Promised Land and extended Israelites' migration by another forty years.

While some of the events and many characters are based on historical figures and incidents, this novel is a work of fiction.

Bruce Hampson and his family live in Vancouver, Canada.

https://brucehampson.com

https://facebook.com/bookasthebirdsfly

ALSO BY BRUCE R.HAMPSON

"Little minds are interested in the extraordinary, great minds in the commonplace."
Elbert Hubbard

The lie is that we are all born extraordinary. The truth is most of us are all just born average. The knowledge and acceptance of our own mundane existence does not mean we would never achieve anything – on the contrary, that is exactly where we start. In order to become great at something, we must humbly acknowledge we are not already great, that we can do better. There is no progress, no development without movement. It is vital to keep trying to do different things, and by the process of eliminating our non-talents, there is always a chance we would discover what we are better at. The process takes time, risk and work, but seeking to become extraordinary, we cannot settle on who we think or what other people say we are. Throughout my life I have been told numerous times I would fail, I was no good, I would never achieve anything significant. Was it my ego that would drive me to prove everyone wrong? Maybe. Did I fall and stumble so many times that I had lost count? Absolutely. But my hunger for more, for higher and better always pushed me to get up, to keep moving. Do I pretend I have reached the extraordinary? Not at all. But every hat I have worn in life, every experience I dared to undertake, has enriched me and made a part of who I am.

In writing this common-place novel, the first person I thought of pleasing was myself. Not entirely a memoir, not entirely a fictional story, it incorporates real historical facts and characters, that have been meticulously researched, and my ancestors' account. However, more often than not I let my imagination flow.

As Pablo Picasso said, "we all know that Art is not truth. Art is a lie which makes us realize the truth, at least the truth that is given to us to understand". Most of us connect with art, because with a little bit of imagination we can find ourselves in it. It is my hope that you can find yourself somewhere in this story, where truth and fantasy, facts and dreams, intertwine till the lines are blurred. What makes a person an artist is not what they have, but what they do with what they have. It has very little to do with skill. Being an artist is a matter of sensibility, how you relate to the world. Facts come from the outside and are subject to interpretation. The truth comes from the inside. Truth is not defined by the top three results in our Google search. It is debateable, and I attempt to demonstrate just that, brush stroke by brush stroke, throughout this story.

Picasso would understand.

This is not a story about a human being; this is a story about a human becoming.

Made in the USA
Thornton, CO
05/30/23 11:56:42

a960f191-9975-4676-971c-9cd94f5ab21bR01